THE PRICE OF PEACE

THE SEVEN ISLES
BOOK ONE

A.R. KNIGHT

CHAPTER I

LAST BIRTHDAY

The Guardian of the Isles, Protector of the Aegis, Hero to the People, requested the strawberry tart. Waited for it. The blistering kitchens scalloped in the mountainside treated her addition to their evening dinner onslaught at first with disdain then, with Ami's gentle clarification as to the tart's intended, with reverence.

At least she waited in twilight. A cold black iron rail her stalwart companion on the overlook serving as the front entrance to those few who braved the food factories above Noctia's busiest, only city. The brush-pocked slope fell away below her, curling out towards the ocean. Along the way, rock and plant ceded to sculpted stone and lantern light. Every home, every building sloping their stone dew-catching roofs towards rain barrels.

Ami ran her hands along her arms, tracing the orange filament on the tunic's sleeves. Almost the same shade as the hot forges back home, the ones she worked in, laughing, not all that long ago.

Noctia's waters held sails, each one telling its own

story. To the left stuck up the sloped triangles from Kance, cutters built for beauty and speed. They could wrestle the slightest breeze and burst over the waves. Next, a rare broad leaf from Vis's western coast, its amber sides oiled and curled, keeping the Kance ships separate from the jagged Rana knives.

Last, as ever in the largest berths, were the thick-masted Foti galleons. Cargo moving on and off, swarthy curses and sea talk rising all the way up here.

"Guardian," came a hallowed voice behind Ami, and she turned to see a woven basket held out towards her. Face bowed, wrapped in culinary's slight gray shift, the server looked like a supplicant. "Your request is ready."

"Then hand it to me," Ami replied, fighting off a sharper word when the server didn't move. "I'm not your lord."

"Please," the server said.

Ami looked past the pathetic form as she took the basket, found the chef watching them. Hunting for a reason to knock the server around. She gave the man, covered in a day's grease and splatter, the slightest glare.

He gave her a broad grin in return while the server scampered for the safety of his next delivery.

No matter how long she lived here, Ami would never embrace Noctia's customs. And, she suspected, the chef would never stop needling her with the same.

The walk from the kitchens to her destination grew less and less civilized with every step. Noctia's forms and functions dissipated as Ami scaled the mountainside, boots crunching on fresh gravel. A necessity given yesterday's rain, the pebbles spread to keep hapless, distracted visitors from slipping off the slope side. To her right, a single tied rope separated Ami from a long fall. Every so often a Foti-crafted post rose from the rock, a torch burning near Ami's eye level to light the way.

The minimal measures meant, at dusk, few braved the perilous pathway. The way back would be deserted. If Ami decided to return that evening at all.

Twenty minutes from the kitchen—Ami had timed the walk—the path stopped, turning hard left into the mountain itself. No cavern greeted Ami, but instead a filigreed purple-and-black smear. Noctia's straight edge abhorrence made Ami feel almost queasy up close: the arches and swirls in the gateway defying any easy focal point. Someone, when Ami first came here so long ago, had delivered some exhausting speech as to why Noctia did this. The late hour hid the reasoning in her memory.

Holding the basket in her left hand, Ami turned her attention instead to the pair scrambling up at her approach.

Playing cards scattered around a low burning fire at the gateway's entry, the heat a welcome touch as the ascent cooled things enough for Ami to tug her cloak a bit tighter. A meal's remnants, two bowls, a soup pot, sat near twin stone benches. Their former occupants now faced Ami, the picture of Noctia's nonchalance.

"Guardian," said the first, standing taller than Ami, though his youth made the stance shaky. His voulge wobbled in the gravel, the curved spear's end catching the firelight like some jittery insect. "We weren't expecting you?"

The second one, older but no more sure of himself, kept both hands on his own voulge to keep it steady. Behind them, joining their food on the ground, lay two chakrams, the sharp discs doing no good in the dust.

"Who were you expecting?" Ami replied, keeping her left hand free at her side.

"Nobody, honest," the youth said. "It's late."

"I noticed. Stand aside."

The two parted, their loose purple-and-black mail clanking at the motion. Ill-fitted. Scraps thrown up for appearances. It'd been like this last time too, near the end.

The tunnel through wasn't far, but Ami took her time. For one, the level ground marked a break from the uphill climb and the cave gave her cover from the wind. Mostly, though, she reserved the minutes for the carvings.

Faces and years etched into the sloping cinnamon-colored walls. Done in detail, the heads emerged from the stone into sharp relief, showing the people who had done so much for so many. By now, Ami knew them all, and she repeated each name as she went, though the faces covered both sides. In a few more, so she'd heard, they'd begin doubling up, adding another row below the old ones.

If things lasted that long, anyway.

Claiming a patch at the right side's end, haloed in Ami's torch's glow, was the one face she really knew. Somehow, they'd managed to capture the kindness in Catya's hard features. Determination mingling with the exhaustion already setting in, even though the sculpting came a month into her . . . what, would you call it a reign?

Ami sniffed, stuck the torch in the holder at the exit. She'd pick it up again on the return. More efficient than lining the whole tunnel with the things.

She wouldn't need the light for this last stretch.

The cave ended in a steep bowl, the rock sweeping away beneath her into a cozy crater. Steps, complete with another rope handrail, marched down towards the crater's center. Above, Sichi, the pink moon, took its place in a cloudless sky. Lucky. Not even Ami was cynical enough to deny the wonder the moon's light made of the crater's bed.

Lelune, purple six-petaled plants growing near the ground, stretched and bloomed in Sichi's glow. The crater wore a violet carpet, glimmering across the bowl until the steeper sides made a sloppy edge. Dart bugs feasted on the miracle, blue lines appearing for instants as they went from one blossom to another.

If she didn't have a tart to deliver, Ami would've stayed up there for an hour just watching. Maybe she would still, after dessert. After Catya.

Her left hand, freed from its torch duties, found its way to the hilt at Ami's waist. Just touching the wrapped metal helped, as it always had. Stability, defense, death, all in Ami's control.

Thus buttressed, she took the steps down at a near skip, her cloth boots scuffing each step before sliding on to the next. No gravel here, and the stolid stone spoke to her as it always did. A hard language to learn, an easy one to use.

The crater's center held a domed cap, a loose mushroom cloak. This being Noctia, the dome matched the blooming flowers, with black metal lacing the Kance-crafted canvas. The metal ran down off the dome's edges into the rock, both keeping the cloth secure and serving as a funnel to any visitors.

A single entry, single file, with a single guard stationed outside.

Unlike the buffoons on the ridge, this one, a Ward, stood in full regalia. Voulge stamped on the stone, chakrams looped on her back, and the small circle shield tied tight to the woman's right wrist. Ami found no fear in the face looking at her, straight in the shadow cast by the flowers.

No torches out here. Not tonight.

"Guardian," the Ward said. "You're late."

"The kitchens were busy," Ami replied, then tilted her head. "Your friends at the guardhouse said I wasn't expected?"

"They don't listen," the Ward said. "A problem to be corrected." She tilted the voulge towards the weapon on Ami's waist. "Remove it."

"You're new?"

The Ward blinked. Definitely new, then. Might as well cut her a break.

"I'm Catya's Guardian," Ami said. "She's got nothing to fear from me."

"All the same—"

"I'm not taking this off." Ami kept it measured, raised the tart's basket. "It's getting late. Move."

Every new Ward meant another power struggle. Every time, now, went faster than the last. None had forced Ami's chosen from her hip, and this one wouldn't be the first.

The Ward came to the same conclusion, stepping aside and waving Ami through. Ami gave her a nod as she went past. Enough politeness to ensure a smooth encounter the next time.

The inside had a miserable air. Always did, save the very first time Ami's eyes graced the Wound. Then, she'd been awed by legend made real. Now, her stomach curled and a familiar frown found her face.

In the crater's exact center sat a pit wide enough to swallow Ami whole. A perfect circle, one with a bottom nobody could see. Torches dropped inside would vanish into unknowable depths. Noctia histories claimed some brave, doomed souls had tried to climb down, only to have their ropes pulled up, the explorers never seen again.

Sitting in a cushioned chair overlooking the Wound, as

she had been without ceasing for the last eleven years, was Catya.

"Throne treating you well?" Ami asked.

A bad joke, and one Catya met with a slow sigh. Or maybe it was the wind, free to whistle inside through the dome's loose metal fence.

Ami felt more stares on her as she went in, two other Wards watching from the dome's far sides. These two held to the same high vigilance, their arms at ready.

Not, Ami suspected, because of her.

"I have a surprise," Ami said, grabbing the small side table, dragging it over near Catya, the pit, and her chair. "Know what day it is?"

Catya looked Ami's way at that, a slow turn, wispy white hair blowing across her face. Was there a smile in there, or was Ami imagining things?

Ami opened the basket, took out the tart and the two Foti heaters. She cracked each one, the thin sticks melding minerals and steaming for several magic minutes. Ami rested the tart on top, then glanced back into the basket for utensils.

Only one set, but that wasn't the problem—on the road, Ami, Catya, and the others shared everything—what had Ami's hand hesitating was a covered cup. On top sat a small note scribbled on thin Tamas paper.

"She'll eat this. Enjoy the tart."

Ami felt a hand on her own, saw the weathered skin, the rough nails, the weak grip. She followed Catya's arm up to her shawled shoulder, to the broad necklace. Bronzed and mottled, the band held seven small stones, each one dim.

So faint now. So fast.

Catya put up a genuine smile as she drank the cup, a thin version of the tart's filling. Ami, after reconciling with herself that the tart shouldn't go to waste, scarfed the dessert with just enough skill to keep the strawberry from blobbing all over her.

In between bites, Ami talked. She ran over Noctia's gossip, visitors of note, the ongoing conflict between Whent and Rana. Catya listened, said nothing.

She hadn't spoken in a while. That happened to every Aegis, or so Ami had been told. What they didn't say was how close to the end the silence meant. A year? Several?

Or less?

As she finished the tart, Ami slowed her stories. Catya's loose smile fell to a concentrated frown, her friend's eyes falling to the pit.

The Dark Below. That's what Noctia called it, whatever lay down there. The name seemed to whisper as Ami thought it, a harsh sound, a blade scraped against the rock. Ami leaned towards the pit, looking down into its yawning black, her left hand reaching out and gripping Catya's.

The sound came again. Not a wind's whisper this time, no. With it came footsteps, the Wards moving closer. One set aside their voulge to take up a chakram. Ami kept hold of Catya's hand.

The scrabbling grew louder, closer, and more frantic. Something yelped, hissed, gurgled. Catya drew in a sharp breath, and the golden stone on her necklace flared ever so slightly.

The sounds ceased. No whimpers, no dying cry.

The Wards relaxed. Ami sat back on her heels.

"You've still got it," Ami said. "Happy birthday, Catya."

Her friend, the Aegis, protector of the Seven Isles,

turned her withered face towards Ami. A question lit Catya's eyes.

"Thirty," Ami answered. "Still a youngster."

Not a soul in the room thought Catya would see thirty-one.

CHAPTER 2

SWING AND A HIT

Three paces out and the branch held firm. On the fourth, the golden brown wood trembled. Wax held his arms out, had his feet heel-to-toe, and waited for the rustling wind to quiet. Not that Vis ever truly stopped talking: if it wasn't the wind, then the birds and beasts would fill the air with their chatter.

And, if not them, Wax and his friends.

A whoop came up and over to Wax's right, a bubbling delight as Sawi dove past him, riding a vine down from the canopy. The vine tightened, swinging Sawi up before Wax's branch. She released, her body stretching through the gap between the vine and her target.

"Thief," Wax called after her, breaking off his careful walk for a two step jump into the open air.

Vis spread below him, a dense pack flush with greens, yellow, blues and reds. Needles and nettles. Leaves and loam.

Wax didn't spare a glance for it, instead keeping his view locked on the giant frond ahead and below. Sawi had already landed, disappeared into a slide down the long leaf, its sides cupping up like a tube cut in half.

Letting the landing take his legs out from under him, Wax lay back on the frond, slapping his hands to his sides to pick up speed. He lifted his head, watched Sawi hit the frond's upturned end and sail into space.

A chance.

Wax, feeling the frond's every vein against his bare back, scalloped through the end and followed Sawi into the air, his bigger body giving him enough height to backflip, to reach upwards and snag a loose line Sawi didn't reach.

Spindly and weak, the vine tore out with Wax's pull, but the resistance gave more curve to Wax's flight, let him reach a thicker, winding tree trunk. Gnarled and twisted, the trunk lit up like a target as Wax let the faltering vine go. Tight leather shoes helped his feet grip the bark as Wax landed, swung around, and found a branch to run down.

Sawi, going by her voice, was somewhere below and to his left. Going by her words, she thought she had the race won.

Always cocky, that one.

A bird, its black feathers belying a glistening red under-coat, startled at Wax's arrival, squawking outrage as Wax blitzed by, dodging the creature's egg-filled nest. The branch narrowed before him, ending in a slight twin prong.

No obvious next move.

Up ahead lay the finish, a blossoming sana flower. Its white-edged, pink pedals stuck out flat, letting the blue-gold middle reach for the sun. Those same pedals forced away encroaching trees, giving the sana its own place in the canopy.

And giving Wax an idea.

As his foot hit the last, thin spot on his branch, Wax swept his right hand to his waist, snatching off the coiled, oiled rope from its belt-like wrap. Wax found himself in the air, a weightless moment with loose leaves above, crowded jungle below, and he threw the rope ahead.

A narrow tree waited, the rope catching on the speckled white bark and holding fast. Wax's free-fall turned into a swing, though he had to throw his body aside to keep from caking himself against the tree's trunk. Instead, taking only a few leaves to the face, a scratch to the shoulder, Wax soared past the tree and into the sana's space. As he flew, Wax pushed up on the rope, telling the clinging stickers on its end to let loose. The rope obeyed, sliding free and trailing after Wax as he shot towards the sana.

The beautiful flower claimed its domain with more than petals: the stalk climbing to the canopy had a rippled body, hard plates giving way here and there to jutting thorns. More than one Vis native had found himself impaled at the end of a run like this.

Not that Wax would ever have that problem.

Floating free, Wax struck the sana towards the stalk's center, right above the jagged, tooth-like thorns. His feet found purchase on the rough surface, his left hand gripping the stalk while his right wound the rope into position.

Wax couldn't hear Sawi anymore. Just that angry bird.

The climb went quick, Wax's fingers finding gaps in the sana's defenses. His boots nestled into slight ridges, marks made by creatures with claws. Sweat ran free, droplets running over Wax's sloping orange-and-azure ink. His hair, at least, wasn't a problem: cut short yesterday to be ready for the ceremony, his bangs no longer threatened to stab Wax's own eyes. Not once did he feel his arms burn, his legs call out for a break.

Why would they? This was life, this was everything on Vis.

Getting atop the sana was a bit tricky. The flower's stalk ended in a bulb, the spherical sides curling up and away from Wax. He studied, taking his left hand to peel some sana bark free and stick it in his mouth. Chewed, the tangy sweetness hitting as Wax's saliva broke the stiff stuff down. Sticky, too.

Wax fished the bark out, rubbed it on his hands. Tested planting palms on the sana's side, felt the suction. Not enough to hold him for long, but in a rapid climb?

He'd get points for originality, anyway.

Wax minced a couple more bark bits in his mouth, gave his hands a good coating, whooped once—a wordless challenge to nature—and jumped. Hooking his legs as best he could around the upturning outside, Wax scrambled, placing his sticky hands one after another. The juice sloughed off with every slap, every tearaway.

The white pink petal waited, shining like a dawn cloud above. Wax made a lunge, his hands coming loose, his legs not quite managing a hold. His left fingers stretched, found the petal's edge. Held.

And dropped.

Sawi's arm swung down, her hand latching onto Wax's wrist as he started to tumble. Laying flat on the petal, Sawi pulled, bringing Wax up enough for him to get a grip.

"Nice save," Wax said, sprawling out on the petal along with Sawi, both looking up towards the glaring sun. No clouds today. "Would've had it though."

"Would you?" Sawi said, not bothering to look his way. "Your rope's coiled."

"I'm fast enough."

"Then next time I'll let you fall."

Wax smiled. Beneath him, the sana felt both firm and buttery. Comfy enough to get ideas, but Sawi was sitting up already, heading towards the sana's middle. Her sun-bleached hair wrapped around the flower perennially found resting among the locks, the small discs in her ears matching Wax's in the youth's dark green color. For now, anyway. She unwound the pouch from her tanned woven stalk shorts, opening the small bag and filling it with blue and gold tendrils.

"Not going to relax a minute?" Wax asked, following her lead. The pouch tied into the knee-length weaving, making it easy to carry along on tree-jumping journeys like this one. "It's beautiful up here."

"If I said yes, we'd be up here an hour." Sawi grinned. "If you'd been faster, maybe we'd have the time."

"You should've warned me, I would've tried harder."

"A warning? Where's the fun in that?"

They poked and played, the spoken-word sortie that always ended these adventures. Back home, they'd catch every eye roll their friends and families had to give. Up here? A private, special game.

"See that?" Sawi said as they rewound their pouches, sitting on a different petal and looking out towards the northern sea.

"Looks like a Foti ship," Wax said, shielding the sun with his hand and guessing at the squared sail, the black-wood deck rising high over the waves. "Second one this week."

"Almost the end of summer," Sawi mused. "Bet they want to get one more run up north."

Wax shrugged. "So long as they keep bringing those candies, I don't care."

Sawi laughed. They dangled their legs over the distant drop. Their fingers found each other, and they watched the ship cut its slow way over the waves towards the inlet marking their home.

Vis spread out around them, rippling hills covered with color. Hawks and vultures swooped at their eye level, while distant hoots and hollers marked creatures making conversation. A lingering brilliance, something Wax took in with a deep breath and a happy sigh.

"Think Pan's wondering where we've gone?" Wax said.

"He's nose-deep in the dirt," Sawi replied. "Should we go rescue him?"

True, the afternoon was getting on. While Vis was plenty magical at night, that magic was best experienced somewhere safer than up here. Like, say, back home. With a warm meal and a seaside bath.

"Guess so."

THE RICH BLACK earth parted without resistance, thick grains rolling off Pan's fingers. He lifted what remained to his nose, took a slow sniff. Read what the scents told him.

The day had been good already, it was about to get even better.

In the distance Sawi or Wax called out, their happy cries burnishing Pan's mood. Golden sun shafts danced on the forest floor, leaves giant and small rustled, and Pan's loaded satchels rested on his legs as he squatted, reaching for his next target.

Beneath a fallen log, coated over with moss, lay the true treasure: morels, big and fluffy, perfect for any meal. Wax and Sawi could spend all the time they liked jumping up in the branches, Pan would get the better reception for his work down below.

Not to mention the shade, the option to walk barefoot and feel the ground beneath his toes?

He slung off a satchel, let it rest on some moldering leaves next to him while Pan went to work. Cutting the morels loose came easier with the Foti knife, a simple gray blade, wrapped at his waist. Every cut tore another beige mushroom free, every toss added to the harvest.

The find was so good Pan didn't even hear the change around him. Animal voices flying up and dying fast to silence. A crackle on the forest floor behind him. The soft breath as something new approached.

Pan did hear the sputtering hiss just fine. He spun, falling from his squat to land butt-first in the dirt, knife held out in some feeble threat. Morels spilled from the overturned satchel.

A hanoko, sandy yellow fur, dark lines between the gold, and slobbering from its twin forked tongues, snarled as someone else ruined its ambush. The furred, six-pawed beast stood on its hind legs, its tall vantage giving it four swipes at the rigid bamboo pole swatting it. Pan's eyes followed the pole to its wielder, though he should've guessed.

Covered in blue and gold ink, Bliss knocked the claws aside before poking the hanoko in the chest. Not a killing blow, not even a wounding one, just a warning. The hanoko, green eyes at about the narrowest slits Pan had ever seen, gave another nasty, spitting hiss—a shower Bliss would likely want to wash off—and fled, twin tails whipping through the brush.

Bliss tracked the creature's flight for a few seconds

while Pan reloaded his satchel. Hanokos could come back, play their prey into thinking they'd won only to strike from somewhere new. This one, though?

"Think you gave it a good scare," Pan said. "It won't attack again."

Bliss sent him a frown, one hand leaving the pole to flicker through a language few knew, save Wax, his family, and a few friends.

'You can't know that.'

"Nope," Pan replied, "but I can guess. Nothing wants a whack from your pole unless it's desperate, and there's too many easier things to eat around here."

'Like you?'

"Apparently." Pan stood, shouldered up his satchels. "I'm grateful, but what are you doing here?"

'Brother asked me to keep an eye on you because he was going to be busy.'

Pan narrowed his eyes at the girl, tried to pick out a tell from her straight expression.

"You're getting better. I don't know if you're lying or not."

Bliss's face brightened, her hand flashed faster, too fast for Pan to follow and she had to repeat the gestures.

'Really? I've been practicing!'

Pan laughed, "Then practice holding it to the end next time. Doesn't do any good if you give up the lie halfway through." Pan nodded past her, through the woods back towards home. "C'mon, the bags are full and I'm hungry."

Bliss looked past him now, but in the opposite direction. Pan matched her look, saw no sign of Wax and Sawi.

"Don't worry about them," Pan said. "My guess, they'll get back home without ever touching the ground."

'They're going alone a lot.' Bliss signed, but she matched Pan's walk.

"Because they both know what's coming."

'Is it really that big of a deal? Sawi's not leaving, right?'

"Change is change," Pan replied. "Right now, things are good. Tomorrow? Who can say?"

CHAPTER 3
A CITY LOFTED

Traders said Wax's home was the most beautiful spot in the world. Nestled into a bay with soaring, tree-coated hills on all sides, Kitaye used its scenery. Oiled docks jutted out into turquoise waters, small waves lapping up onto a soft white sand beach. Walkways crossed the dunes, leading up to thatched, frond-covered workshops, markets, restaurants and anything else a person might want. Ladders, both rope and wood, dangled down from the huge trees, leading curious eyes to search skyward and find a whole second city nestled in the branches above.

Wax's family, along with all the Kitaye natives, lived among the leaves. Safe from predators, both natural and human. Though Wax hadn't seen a raid from Kance or Rana in his life, stories told of incoming pillagers landing to find empty shells and raining arrows.

A time or two of that and the invaders had found easier targets.

"Like you," Wax said, shimmying down a peeling palm tree to land next to Pan and Bliss. Sawi had gone ahead, the late afternoon pulling her to obligations Wax refused to think about.

"Like me what?" Pan asked, not stopping his walk, loaded satchels swaying as he went over sticks, mashed leaves, and hiked through muddy patches.

"Bliss said you were about to be a hanoko's dinner," Wax said, scampering ahead of Pan and throwing up his hands as if they were claws. "Too deep in your own head again?"

Pan shot Bliss a look declaring the feisty girl a traitor, she just grinned back. So Pan held up his prizes instead.

"It was a good spot," Pan said, then noticed Wax's missing pouch. "Sawi take yours again?"

"I gave it to her as a gift," Wax replied, walking backward. He danced as he moved, feeling the contours on his bare feet—the climbing shoes came off once Wax hit the forest floor—and dodging sticks, stones without looking. "Trying to be nice, you know?"

Bliss spun her fingers. Pan laughed, "Definitely lost the race."

The banter beat back and forth as the trio neared Kitaye, the distance measured more by cooking spices filling the air than meters walked. By the time they hit the city's outskirts, all three could hear their own stomachs rumbling, a sound not even the hollow bamboo flutes and coconut drums could drown out.

The thick trees made the city's appearance an instant thing, a step or two from isolated wander to crowded bustle. Wax hesitated at the last step, still buried in ferns and buzzing insects, while Pan and Bliss kept right on going. It'd be hours, now, till he could leave the city again for the jungle's trance, hours that couldn't pass quick enough.

'Coming?' Bliss asked, glancing back his way. Her bamboo staff didn't look so ridiculous on her back anymore. When had she grown so? 'Or are you scared?'

"Scared?" Wax snorted, stepped on through. "Scared of what?"

'How much cooler I am than you.' Bliss stood straighter, stretched, showed off the new tattoo on her upper right arm.

"When did that happen?" Wax grabbed his sister's arm, took a closer look. "You're too young."

An off-center circle covered her shoulder blade, with thorns pointing inward along the edge. A sana flower sat in the middle, its purple petals the only color in the otherwise black ink.

'It's not about age,' Bliss signed, pulling her arm away. 'Skill matters.'

Wax tried to see Bliss, hit by descending sunlight along her right side, as the defender that tattoo said she was. Wax didn't have one on his shoulder, most of the city didn't. A badge like that put you on the front lines if Kitaye or its people needed you. Some disaster, like a fire, or a predator, or someone lost in the woods.

For all that, Wax couldn't see it. Bliss still looked as she always had, a goofy girl with a strong swing. And yet, he caught a different slant to her look back his way, something he did recognize.

A slant any older sibling would know.

"Hey, that's cool," Wax said. "Congrats, little flower. Proud of you."

For once, Bliss didn't flinch at her old nickname.

'Jealous?'

"Not at all. While you're watching Pan gather mushrooms, I'll be swinging up top. You can have the ink. I'll keep the trees."

Pan didn't hear the slight, the man long gone towards the city's market. He'd pawn off all those mushrooms for a better dinner, breakfast, and maybe some other trinket. With nothing of their own to trade, Wax and Bliss didn't bother going towards the shoreline shops, instead heading straight to the cook fires.

Kitaye spread around the entire inlet, neighborhoods separated by groves. In those groves, on the forest floor, cleared out areas worked as places for meals, for games, and gatherings. From sun up till sun down Wax could find a snack here, could find people he'd known from his first breath waiting to ask him what he'd seen that day, what he'd found out there.

Ask his dad, and Wax's elder would describe when Kitaye used to empty itself out, everyone dashing into the forest or alighting on the massive cupped leaf boats to go fishing in the sea. At the day's close the city would come alive with the returns, everyone sharing in the plenty, a nightly communal feast.

Wax could see pieces of that past now, as he and Bliss went by deeper workshops, gardens, storage thatches to their own clearing. Gatherers from his neighborhood dropped their findings onto a vast table in the center, where others would come, take what they needed and return to their smoldering fires to roast the prizes for dinner. The meals smelled good, the table overflowing with fruits, coconuts, strung up fish, peppers and more. A good day.

"A sad picture," grumbled Wax's father as his children caught up to him at the table. The bent-backed man sifted through spindly purple-pink dragon fruit, shuffling a few into his satchel. "You're lucky you don't know the past."

"Hello to you too, dad," Wax said, his father glancing at him in response, hunting for Wax's pouch and not finding it. "Gave it to Sawi today. As a gift."

"You lost the race again," His dad huffed, shook his head. "You can't keep making that bet if you never win, Tywinax."

Wax frowned at his dad's shadow, his formal name. The man doubled up his son in girth, a progression aligned with his swap from jungle runs to culinary captain. New ink painted over the old, completed loops on his father's back with yellow flourishes marking the change in profession. Wax's own marks remained open, waiting for his future to arrive.

"Don't act like you didn't do the same thing," Wax countered, slipping a reach in to nab a sweet pepper.

"Yes, but I won."

Bliss had the biggest grin on her face when Wax turned around, pepper prize in hand.

'Laugh now,' Wax signed back. 'He'll be on you next.'

'For what?' Bliss shot back. 'I'm perfect, remember?'

'Till he sees that marker, you mean.'

Bliss narrowed her eyes, but she didn't adjust her staff. When they'd entered the cooking circle, Bliss had shifted the shoulder strap holding the bamboo stick in place to cover the fresh ink. Someone would tell their father eventually, but not yet.

And, no matter how much he might want to, that someone would not be Wax.

"Go get your mother," their father said, a big woven bowl now laden in his huge hands. "She won't want to miss the meal."

Wax and Bliss didn't need to ask where their mother was. With the Foti ship coming in, she, along with Kitaye's other traders, would be at the water's edge looking for a deal.

If the cooking circles split by neighborhood, the seaside market split by skill. If you knew something well enough to sell it, you earned a spot along the shoreline. Whenever new ships came by, and more came almost every day, Kitaye's charmers flocked to their spots to hawk Vis's treasures.

Sprawling away to both right and left from Wax's central entry, the market followed the inlet around its swoop. Tall signposts with waving painted flags sectioned off various wares, with foods and plants to the right and crafted goods on the left. Every booth, thatched wood and fronds all, held a display counter and wall racks. Each, too, had a master and apprentices.

Wax's mother ran a mushroom spot on the right, a narrow booth between more popular mango and pineapple slingers. Pan had beaten his friends there, already unloading the morels from his satchel when Wax and Bliss walked up to the front.

Wax's mother, freshly repainted this morning in orange patterns signaling her rank—master—and role—trader— held a scrawny Foti's attention. The wiry, thistle-bearded man turned over a puffball in his hands, whistling at the size.

"She'll carry crated," Wax's mom said as her son drifted closer. Bliss moved past him to help Pan, leaving her staff stuck in the sand like a pole. "We have several more, if you'd care to bundle up?"

The Foti nodded, "I'll take'em if you got'em." He looked up, seemed to notice Pan for the first time. "You have any shrives in there?"

Wax glanced at Pan. No way he'd found any of those

today. Pan would've been gloating the whole way back if he had.

"No luck," Pan replied. "Didn't go deep enough."

"Tomorrow, will you?" The Foti asked. "Have a bad need for one. Or as many as you can get."

"It's not a quick journey to go that deep," Wax's mother said, throwing up a sad smile. "We'd need to prepare, and there's no party—"

"I can pay well," the Foti man interrupted. "Enough to make it worth your while." Wax's mother sighed as the Foti man bowled her over with his words, "I'm saying I've got better things. Real Foti gear that'd change your lives. Nobody will give you what I've got for your bananas, for your baskets. Get me those shrives, though, and you'll have it."

"Have what?" Wax asked.

The Foti man gave Wax a nasty grin, reached over his shoulder and pulled at the weapon sheathed behind his back. Everyone on Vis knew what a sword was, everyone knew the things weren't necessary. No hunter needed a sword when spears, bows and arrows were around.

Weapons of war, so Wax's father said, served only to bring war to the ones wielding them.

But it was hard to deny the perfect silver cut on the sapphire-blue metal as the Foti man drew the blade, as it caught the sunset and held the fire.

"Bring me three shrives and the blade's yours," the Foti said. "Bring me five and I'll give you the knife that goes with it."

"The knife?" Wax wrinkled his nose. "Why a knife?"

Quicker than Wax could grab a leaf, the Foti flipped a hand to his waist, drew out a smaller blue-shaded blade the length of his forearm. Holding the larger sword in front, the

Foti man stabbed forward with the smaller blade, right towards Wax's stomach.

"Block with one, gut'em with the other. Quick way to end a fight," the Foti man kept up his grin. "From what I've seen, this pair would make you king of the isle."

"Five shrives?" Wax said, ignoring his mother's frown, Pan's and Bliss's confused stares. "Two days?"

"Two days." The Foti replaced his weapons, spat in a palm and held it out towards Wax. "Deal."

Wax matched the spit, slapped his palm against the offered one. The Foti chuckled, took the packed puffballs from Wax's mother, and fished in his shoulder bag. Pulled out a fresh cast iron pan and set it on the counter.

"As we agreed," the Foti man said.

"As we agreed," Wax's mother replied, though her charm had fled, leaving nothing but ice in its wake.

"Two twilights, friend," the Foti man said, giving Wax a nod and venturing off back towards his ship.

Wax watched the man walk for a few strides back towards the inlet's center, where the main docks sat. The only ones that could hold a ship the size of this one, those docks bustled now as trading flew into full swing.

Wax's mother wouldn't be the only one late to dinner tonight.

CHAPTER 4

BROTHERS

If days in Kitaye buzzed, then the nights sang. Wax dangled his legs off his family's treehouse and watched pink moonlit waves visible through hanging branches, rope platforms and the like. Sichi shone bright tonight. In his right hand, Wax spun a reed through his knuckles, back and forth. Normally, about this time, he'd be meeting Sawi for a dash along the beach, maybe a snack up in the canopy somewhere. Normally . . .

"Well look who's still here," said a muscle-bound, grittier version of Wax, though Quik would likely say Wax was the scrawnier, goofier copy of himself. Red armbands and a crimson feather taken off some kill marked Quik's role. A woven chain hung from his neck, its end a wooden disc carved with the hunter's clawed sigil. "When's the last time you spent a night at home, brother?"

"Don't remember."

Quik slid his legs off the platform, let them drape. The brother had a couple years on Wax, and it showed in the completed red and black circles on Quik's arms. A couple scars, too, from hunts gone awry.

"I'd say that's a sign you're gone too much, but I know you won't take it that way," Quik said.

"How would I take it?"

"That I'm trying to tie you down to this family. Responsibility and all those words you treat like curses."

"Thought that was your job? The family?"

Quik glanced down at his hands. No reed spinning there, just fingers flat on thighs. They both wore thin weaves for sleeping, no decorations, no tools. No planned adventures.

"You saw what Bliss did?" Quik asked.

"Following your lead." Wax avoided looking Quik's way. The trees were more pleasant scenery than his brother's judging stare. "She's good with that staff."

"She is. Kitaye's lucky to have her." Quik took a deep breath, always a sign he was going to embark on some speech. "We'd be lucky to have you too, if you'd take it seriously."

"Meaning?"

"Mom told me about your deal with that Foti. You're going after shrives? Just two days?"

"I'm fast enough to get there." Wax shrugged. "He's offering a real sword, Quik. I saw it."

Quik snorted, "The only thing you'd do with a blade is cut yourself."

"Or cut the next hanoko that makes a move on Pan." Wax pointed out beyond the trees, where the Foti's ship marked its shadow. "You see how big they're getting? How many new things are on every one that comes here? We're offering the same stuff. Nothing changes for us."

"You're saying?"

"I'm saying dad and mom talk about how we used to

get raided until we built the tree houses. Foti, Kance, Rana. They're growing stronger, we're staying the same."

Quik smiled, drawing Wax's look. His brother's face held laughter, light mockery.

"And your single sword will change all that?" Quik asked.

"It'll be a start. It'll convince the city to—"

"This is about Sawi, isn't it?"

Wax blinked. "What?"

"She's getting marked soon, and you won't be for another year at least. So what's poor Wax going to do to measure up?"

"That's not—" Wax stopped, sighed. "What do you even know about it? You've never had anyone. You spend all your time with the hunters."

"I know," Quik said, apparently giving up the fight before it even started. "But I'm going to get on this one."

The admission answered why Quik was out here in the first place. He and Wax didn't exactly do the heart-to-heart thing. Probably because they both kept their days busy, kept themselves apart.

Nonetheless, the idea of Quik jumping on some Foti ship and sailing away had Wax laughing.

"How're you going to do that?" Wax said, Quik's calm face stealing away some mirth. His brother seemed serious. Ridiculous. "Are you buying passage with your looks? With those claws?"

"I'm strong, enthusiastic, and they won't have to pay me much," Quik replied. "That's all it takes."

"But why? Why leave?"

"The same reason you head into the jungle every day. Adventure. A chance to find something new."

"Or someone?"

Quik's smile grew, "It's a big world out there, Wax. Just might be someone on the other isles I'm looking for."

"Can't fight that, then," Wax put a hand on his brother's shoulder. "When does she sail?"

"Thanks to your shrive gambit, a few days at least. Maybe longer." Quik's smile faded. "Rumor is there's Kance clippers running around. Their second queen wants to make a name for herself."

"With piracy?"

"With plunder." Quik stood up. "If you're really making that run, you'd better knock yourself out fast. Any later than dawn and you're not getting back in time."

"Always taking care of me."

"Hey, you get yourself hurt, I might have to come take care of you."

"Please." Wax picked himself up. "Bliss is going to be the one running this show when you're gone."

Quik didn't deny it, and both brothers left the edge to go back inside the three room tree house, hammocks and mosquito netting draping down from the corners. Music, dancing, the occasional hoot and holler from both human and hornbill set Wax to dreaming fast.

WAKING CAME FASTER, came with the same cries. The party for some in Kitaye never stopped, and Wax rolled from his dried rope hammock wondering how those poor people could miss a day for the night.

Bliss and Quik shared their room, the larger of the two, along with the family's living essentials. Two rain barrels swapped places as they filled up, a scoop from one with his wood cup giving Wax a refresher. Next came a mango, some dried jerky from two boxes along the tree house's sole counter. Various weaves and gear hung over each of their hammocks, and Wax grabbed his rope, his thicker shirt and shorts for the day.

He'd swing faster with lighter clothes, but the shrives weren't in safe territory. Better something that could turn a claw or deflect a thorn.

After filling a water skin, tucking more fruit and jerky into a large shoulder-strapped satchel, Wax dipped outside and jumped on the rope ladder heading down. He left his feet off the rungs, letting his hands control the descent all the way down.

Kitaye's all-night revelers mixed now with other early risers. Hunters, gatherers, traders found their friends and made for the cooking circles. A few, like Wax, took off towards the forest. None, though, made for the western edge, the more difficult terrain and, after a long ways, the deep fens and caves where shrives could be found.

The comfortably chill air melded into an ankle-deep fog as Wax went towards Kitaye's outskirts, leaving the inlet behind. The route to the shrive's location wasn't exactly a road, but he'd traversed it before, albeit over several days and with many more people for a city-wide mission.

A fun thing, those, when all Kitaye would pull together and select a group of novices, of experienced adults to go together and find true adventure. A staple five, seven years ago, they'd all but vanished now thanks to the same Foti types offering Wax this deal.

Unlike this one, most traders from the other isles didn't want anything special. Fruits, weaves, herbs and crafted tools made the hay for Kitaye, so why risk larger, longer journeys?

From what Wax heard, too, Mottilan, the isle's only other city, on Vis's eastern coast, had adopted the same posture. Most of the island was left alone to do as nature wanted, its secrets kept undiscovered. At least, until Wax decided to go looking for them.

"Actually doing it, huh?" Pan called, snapping Wax from his explorer daydream. His friend, for once carrying his own rope with his mushroom satchels, leaned against a tree to Wax's right. "Bliss thought you would."

"What are you doing here?"

"What's it look like?" Pan replied, holding up two satchels. Like Wax, he had on a thick emerald weave. Climbing shoes already on. "You want to get shrives, so do I."

Wax eyed the rope around Pan's waist, "You're not fast enough."

"Don't tell him he's not fast," Sawi said, pulling Wax's bewildered eyes back towards town to see his girlfriend walking up. Next to her, climbing rope also around her waist and looking real smug about it, was Bliss. "We help each other and we'll get there and back in time and okay, easy."

For a hot moment Wax wanted to protest, and he spread his arms out to that effect, but before a single word left his mouth, Wax read the expressions. Pan, Sawi, and Bliss all bore grins that wouldn't brook denials. They had the right gear, satchels and water skins filled and ready. The day was young and perfect for adventure.

'Dare you to say it might be dangerous,' Bliss signed.

Wax shook his head, smiled. "Didn't plan on being a babysitter today, but fine. You all want to go get some shrives, let's do it."

· · ·

THE CLIMB STARTED a few groves past Kitaye's end. The tree, marked with a red-dyed rope around its base, stretched from ground to canopy. Steps carved into the massive trunk made the scaling easy, Wax taking the lead. The shoes held their grip on the wood, his hands had more trouble with the morning dew, but that's why Wax went first: his big fingers swept off the wet, cleared the way for the others. Sawi went last, ready to grab a rope if the owner fell.

Just below the highest leaves, Wax stopped at a major branch heading west. This high options abounded but swinging with speed meant picking a course that'd keep momentum. Drops along giant fronds or flowers would give him velocity, while vines loosed at the right moment would send Wax rocketing upward to regain the lost altitude. Instinct would get him the rest of the way.

"First stop," Wax said, the other three waiting mid-climb behind him, "is Ying's Roost. Everyone know the way?"

"Been there a hundred times," Pan said.

"Better than you," Sawi added.

A look down caught a nod from Bliss. All right, then. Time to jump.

Wax picked his route before taking a step. He left his rope wrapped around his waist, double-checked his mango-filled satchel and water skin were tied tight and snug against his back. All good.

One step, then a burst forward, each foot placed right ahead of the last. The branch didn't wobble until Wax hit its narrowing end, a long fall beneath him. With a stride's length left on the branch, Wax planted his right foot and leapt.

Wind hit his face, the wet air swam through his weave, but Wax's hands found the white-flowering vine looping low through the open air. His hands slid along the green spine, scattering petals as the snake loosened its canopy hold. Loosened, but didn't lose.

The vine caught and Wax swung forward, the way ahead blocked by giant split-leaf fronds. The massive ferns filled the gaps between the trees, providing good cover to hunters below and sweet slides for swingers above. As Wax swung up, he let the vine go, releasing his legs into space. He flew almost sideways, the vine he'd been holding swooping back for Pan to grab.

Wax hit the frond on his back, bouncing off the leaf's right side to stick in the center stalk. Lurching forward as he slid, Wax stood from a backslide into a leaning fall. Bunching his legs, Wax jumped as the stalk went near vertical, conserving his momentum and leaping over the fern's dipping center.

Hitting the frond across at a run, Wax fell forward, scrabbling up with his shoes, his hands, trying to keep as much speed as he could. One bad slip here and Wax would slide all the way back down. Not fatal, but it'd slow the trip.

And Sawi would never let him live it down.

The fern had strength in its great emerald leaves, though, and they held Wax's pulling, kicking form till he neared the frond's tip. Another vine waited, this one already loosed and dangling from some past swinger.

Risking a glance, Wax caught Pan's form sliding down the first frond. Behind him, way back, Bliss took her running leap onto the vine. Sawi climbed onto the branch behind her.

Wax gave the day's first whoop, his voice ringing through the jungle.

How could Quik want to leave this?

CHAPTER 5
SHRⲘM HUNTING

They took breaks when necessity demanded it, like when Pan missed a jump and wound up on the wrong fern, or when Wax took the wrong angle and scattered several birds enjoying their own mid-morning snack. The foursome picked out perches to settle, munched a mango or a banana, then went back to it. Grumbles about sore muscles replaced whoops as the hours passed, but they flew.

Gathering parties on Vis moved quick, but their quartet put Kitaye's larger efforts to shame. No carts, no heavy satchels weighing Wax and his friends down meant they could stick to the air, could tap dance along thin branches or loop under a sana thorn to keep up the speed.

The fen emerged as the day dipped into afternoon. First came the heavier air, the thicker smell and insect clouds. Sweeping through the jungle meant swallowing bugs as a matter of course, but Wax found himself coughing after every swaying vine. Found, too, those vines harder to come by as the fen brought the canopy lower, the larger trees and their strong limbs fading for long grasses and lanky shrubs.

At Wax's wave, they dropped from the bark-coated heights to the soft floor. Climbing shoes went into pouches, bare calloused feet offering better traction in the muddy ground.

The fen, too, signaled its territory with different music. Bird calls gave way to frogs croaking, to the ripples of larger, worse creatures sliding about the muck. And the buzzing bugs.

'This place is the worst,' Bliss signed. 'You want to know why I'm not joining your sect?' Bliss turned to Sawi. 'Because gatherers have to come to these places all the time.'

"The price we have to pay for freedom," Sawi shrugged. She bent down, scooped some cool mud from the ground and spread it on her arms. "Lather up, people."

If speed meant the occasional bug in the mouth, standing still in a place like the fen would mean a month without sleep, body aflame from mosquitos and worse having their way. A little mud on the right places, though, and Wax could walk out of here a bath away from feeling fine.

"Looking good," Pan said once they'd all made themselves into mud monsters. "Shall we?"

Shrives tended to make their homes beneath rotting, fallen trees on the fen's edges. Slimy water mingling with fresh, juicy tree trunk produced the miraculous fungi. Blue and white, with a nighttime glow, the shrives worked medicinal wonders. They also, as Wax understood it, wouldn't take anywhere else. The other isles could take a mango, steal a banana and give growing a go, but not a shrive.

They were Vis's treasure, and Vis's alone.

Bliss took point now, swapping the swinging rope for

her bamboo staff and leading the way with its blunt end. She swished it through the waters when they had to cross, used it to clear brush from their rock-and-log bridges.

Circling the fen's border brought them alongside mangroves, the white-barked and soft-leaved thickets adding their own special odor to the air, a pungent, nose-wrinkling life. Birds hidden among the branches watched as they passed. Pan, here and there, would snap another mushroom, or a reedy plant, and stuff it into his satchel.

"You're here for shrives," Pan said when Wax asked the point. "I'm here for everything else."

Wax dropped back next to Sawi, though the thin routes Bliss found meant he walked a step ahead or behind more than beside. She looked like she always did away from the city: at peace.

"You're not?" Sawi replied, throwing a smile at the marsh around them. "Isn't all this beautiful?"

"Give me the canopy any day."

"You've got to appreciate where you are, Wax," Sawi said. "Especially if this is what you want to do. Kitaye doesn't always want sana strands."

"Getting serious on me, Sawi?" Wax poked her in the shoulder, his finger sliding off the mud.

"Only when you need me to be."

Pan's whistle drew their attention ahead, where their rock-and-log path ran out. Not into the fen's swirling waters, but the rising, mossy stones marking Vis's western edge. The mountain—really several, a chain jutting up like a wall keeping the jungle from the vast ocean beyond—spiked from the swamp as if planted like some vast stone seed. The foothills lay to the north, here the mountain stood alone.

"So we're moving fast," Wax said. They all stood on a

soft thicket, formed when a tree had fallen over who knew how long ago. "Do we know where we are?"

"I didn't whistle because I was lost," Pan said. "Your sister noticed something."

Bliss, taking her cue, pointed her bamboo staff towards the mountain. It took Wax a moment to follow the staff's end past the obvious outcroppings and overgrown nooks to a shadowed patch, one marked by a broken stump.

"The thicket's source, unless I miss my guess," Sawi said.

"So what?" Wax added, looking at the ground to make sure he hadn't missed something. Just rotting leaves and branches, already being claimed by the fen's fungi. "No shrives here."

"Not the stump, you morons," Pan said. "What's behind it?"

Wax shrugged, felt Bliss tug on his arm. She was already signing when he looked.

'—obviously not talking about the stump. There's a cave!'

Wax felt a shiver at the word, let his eyes float up that way again. Sure enough, now that he looked for it, the mountain did seem to curl in right behind that stump. Even if he didn't quite buy Bliss's optimism, the possibility warranted a look.

Sure, shrives could be found under mossy logs if you were lucky. But in a good cave? One not cleaned out?

They could find enough to get more than a sword and a knife.

"We could have the Foti giving us everything they've got," Wax muttered. "Let's go!"

'Not even a thank you?' Bliss signed as Wax took off his rope. 'For my amazing eyes?'

"Everyone in Kitaye will thank you when we're done," Wax replied.

"It's been so long since anyone's found a new cave," Pan added. Wax threw his rope up, felt it bite. "And with traders in the village?"

"Pretty lucky," Sawi said.

"Not luck," Wax called as he climbed up, hit the stump after a minute. "All talent! Bliss, you're amazing. There's a cave up here for sure!"

Leaving the muddy marsh for dusty rock felt, if nothing else, easier on the ankles. Wax had his shoes back on—the cave offered a sharp, irregular floor—as he went beyond the half-circle opening. The arching entry looked so perfect Wax stared at it while the others climbed up, trying to figure out what might've made such a smooth ceiling with a scrabbly floor.

Nothing he knew of, anyway.

Sawi took a couple torches off her back, the short sticks and palm oil-soaked wraps meant for any nighttime travel now coming in handy. Sawi kept one, Bliss took the other. Using jagged flint, Sawi struck her torch alight.

Bliss kept hers back, signing that they only needed one at the moment. Best keep the second in reserve.

"How deep you think this cave's going to be?" Wax laughed. "I give it a few minutes walk, if that."

'Then we get the torch for tonight,' Bliss replied.

"Speaking of," Pan said, "let's go, Wax. I don't want to lose daylight before we leave the fen."

Fair point. Nasty critters liked the night, and slipping off into the swamp without good sight risked a swift drowning.

Sawi took the lead, striding off with Wax beside her. Bliss and Pan followed, the line going single file as the cave narrowed. The rock walls weren't pure: plants stretched towards the sun near the entrance, while further back mosses and animal remnants made their marks. Nothing valuable, nothing dangerous.

But the cave kept going.

"Sloping down," Sawi muttered after they'd past Wax's five minute prediction. "How much farther do you want to go?"

The cave spread not far beyond Wax's shoulders, a stifling setup that, nonetheless, kept to its smooth ceiling, rough ground plan. Somewhere along the walk a small stream joined them, trickling along half-hidden beneath the rock to their right. Could be, on rainier days, the little trickle overran its banks and played over their path.

"Pan?" Wax asked. "You're better at keeping time. Should we bail?"

"Not yet," Pan said, his eyes dark in Sawi's torch light, but eager. "Can't you smell it? There's something good up ahead."

Wax sniffed. He'd found the cave air a dusty sort of thin, as if it didn't get shuffled around much. Now that Pan pointed it out though, a familiar loam lingered beneath. A mushroom's addition.

Sawi took Pan's enthusiasm and kept going, their reward appearing only a few more minutes down the sloping stretch.

The cave broadened out, a shallow sweeping rightward, as if they'd walked into a clam's bottom shell. The stream joined the turn, pooling in the room's middle, and with it came Pan's delight.

Shrives, easily fifteen or more, crowded with other mosses and mushrooms along the pool's edges. The reason wasn't hard to find, confirming Wax's earlier thought: the stream, when flush, carried sticks, plants, dirt down here where the stuff clumped up. Moist, devoid of predators and other natural problems, the fungi had a perfect home.

"Now this is worth it," Pan said, stepping past Wax and Sawi to look closer. "These are primes, guys. They're untouched. We'll clean out the Foti with these."

Wax shared his buddy's grin, "Told you." Threw his sister a shoulder pat. "Great eyes, Bliss."

She nodded, folded her arms and watched, smiling, as Pan started stuffing his satchels. Sawi to Wax's left, held her torch higher and made her way around the pool's edge towards the room's back.

"It keeps going," Sawi said, pointing with the torch towards another, still-descending way forward. "Want to explore?"

Pan hummed, "After we gather these? Think we got what we came for. I vote we get out of here, start back."

"But we'll never come here again," Sawi said, looking right at Wax.

Together. That's what Sawi meant. Upon return to Kitaye they'd be roped into their roles, Sawi especially, and journeys like this, with the four of them, wouldn't be possible. Escaping for an afternoon around the city was one thing, a multi-day escapade across the isle . . .

"Pan, holler when you're about done with the shrives and we'll turn around," Wax said. "Bliss, you watch his back, since we all know he won't do it."

Pan didn't object, Bliss only shrugged. Sawi's smile grew.

The slope grew steeper after the shrive room, the stream joining the walk and forcing careful steps. The walls glistened now, strange stones growing from the floor and ceiling. Drips and burbles echoed. A different symphony than what Wax knew, and both he and Sawi kept quiet as they shuffled, just listening. Embracing nature.

Sawi stopped at one point, angling the torch down and left. A small purple-blue cluster twinkled in the firelight. Glowing.

"What do you think that is?" Sawi whispered.

"No idea," Wax replied, reaching and opening his pouch. "Think I should take it?"

"Pan might have a clue," Sawi agreed.

Wax reached, peeled the mossy plant off the rock. Warm and soft to the touch, the purple-blue skin rubbed off on his fingers as he tossed the prize in the pouch.

"Look," Wax said, wiggling his glowing hand.

"Guess if the torch goes out, we have other options," Sawi said.

Another few minutes brought the pair to a larger room, this one easily triple or more the size of the shrive chamber. The water, in Sawi's torchlight, glimmered a deep blue. Clear and clean.

"Hey," Wax said. "I could use a bath?"

"You definitely could," Sawi replied, matching his mischievous grin. She set the torch down on the rock. Touched the water, whistled. "Warmer than I thought."

"Perfect." Wax took off his satchel, stuck a leg in. Like the sea on a hot summer day. "Joining me?"

"Thought you'd never ask," Sawi replied, and she hopped in, disappearing into the deep.

Wax slid in the rest of the way, found himself kicking his feet as no bottom waited for him. On the third kick he felt something brush his leg, his stomach, and Sawi popped up before him, eyes sparkling. Her arms wrapped around Wax's neck.

"Not quite like a sana at sunset," Sawi whispered. "But it'll do."

CHAPTER 6

VISITORS

The nuzzle knocked Svarde off his thin bed onto the cabin's clean, blond wood floor. Not exactly a pleasant wake-up, but that's how Kivi liked it. Better, anyway, than a lick.

Svarde, rubbing his right temple, rolled onto his back and looked up at the ferrite. Kivi's head, a snouted, slate-and-silver rounded stone, poked over the mattress and snorted. The sound, like someone throwing a rock against a wall, dispelled Svarde's remaining sleep in a snap.

"What're you smelling?" Svarde asked, sitting up. His long, sun-bleached hair matted against his neck, back. Cool enough in the cabin, but Kivi always made the bed a sauna.

A sauna. There was something Vis could use. Whole island probably didn't have one. Only plants, swamps, bugs and . . . Svarde shook away the grumbles as he stood up, saw the early afternoon glow out the cabin's netted windows.

The mountainside ran away beneath Svarde's house, a steep descent down to a flat beach and a glittering ocean. A long walk, one now doable with steps and a cleared path the whole way. Not that anyone would use it.

Except him, anyway.

Kivi stretched off the mattress, her four speckled black granite paws carrying her like an uncoiling spring to the floor near Svarde. She snorted again, flicked her bright orange tongue to the east. As she did, Kivi's tongue nipped her lips, throwing sparks.

Svarde frowned. Kivi didn't get agitated much these days. Only when a hanoko or some other stupid creature came close by, and all the beasts around here knew to leave Svarde alone by now.

Maybe something new needed to be taught a lesson.

Kivi led the way along the mountainside, curling along a path originally tight but since, thanks to time and effort, widened out by Svarde and his rock-chewing friend. Clad, for the first time in days, in more than his skivvies, Svarde walked with a gilded hand crossbow ready to fire. A satchel, Vis-woven and bleached by sunlight, hung on his shoulder, beneath his orange-and-gray cloak. Enough food and water in there to last a week: Kivi tended to pull Svarde into long chases, and the hunter had learned to prepare.

That preparation, too, shown in the twin axes looped at his back. He'd sharpened them last night, watching the stars. They were ready for blood.

"If we're lucky," Svarde whispered, "you'll taste some today."

He tried not to think what it meant that he spoke to his weapons, that he'd last had a conversation with a real person . . .

Kivi snorted again, stopping and arching her rippling stone-scale back. As long as Svarde was tall, Kivi's form shifted, rocky plates sliding around and readying up for a leap.

"Hold on," Svarde said, crouching and slow-stepping next to Kivi.

The path here dropped hard, relying on some well-hewn rocks to end at an outcropping. A cave, one Svarde had dallied with a few times before ditching, waited there. And, of course, a way down to the fen. Not his favorite destination: the bug bites earned in an hour spent there would follow him for a week.

A way down, though, could be used to go up. From above, the footprints stood out on the cave's dusty, weedy opening. Several people had climbed to the entrance and, by the look of things, gone inside.

"That has you nervous, Kivi?" Svarde asked the ferrite.

Kivi waggled her head, three emerald eyes gleaming at Svarde. Not the humans, then.

"Well," Svarde said, easing back a few steps and taking the satchel off his back, "that cave ends in a pool. We'll see soon enough who's taking a look." Svarde opened the satchel, pulled out some well-cured meat from their last hunt. A rain water-filled skin. "In the meantime, I'll be having that lunch you robbed from me."

But, when Svarde offered a piece to Kivi, the ferrite refused, its stare never leaving the cave's mouth.

CHAPTER 7
FIEND

He's been calling our names for a few minutes now," Sawi said as she and Wax laid on the pool's edge, torch helping to dry them and their weaves. "How long before Pan sends your sister to investigate?"

"They're not that dumb," Wax stretched. Felt the rock scratch. Not the most comfortable spot to relax, but swimmers couldn't be choosers. "Though I'm not sure how much more my back can take."

A few more minutes watching Sawi in the firelight would be a treat, sure, yet the day would be ticking towards sunset. Any chance of getting back to Kitaye had already fled, meaning they'd need to find a good tree to sleep in.

Preferably one well away from the fen and its endless insects.

"Ready?" Wax asked, standing up.

"No," Sawi said, and Wax stopped, frowned her way. She had a different tone as Sawi watched the pool. "This is it? The last one of these we'll have?"

"You don't know that. We could always sneak away."

Wax pulled on his weave as Sawi, sighing, did the same. "Maybe I'll join the gatherers too, then we'll go together."

"You're already marked otherwise," Sawi said, touching Wax's shoulder, the notched half-circle there promising a future among the hunters.

"We'll have the city then. Wild nights, beautiful days," Wax tried.

Sawi picked up the torch. "Maybe."

Pan shouted again, this time edging the calling with more than a little irritation. Ending it with a threat about leaving the two behind.

"We're heading your way!" Wax called back as Sawi took the first step, torch held out ahead.

It was her second step that made the pair pause. This deep in the cave, the only sounds beyond their voices came from the stream's drips. Not even a breeze whistled. So when a low rumble began behind them both Wax and Sawi turned, curious. In the pool's center, the water looking black at the torchlight's end, ripples grew. Bubbles, at first small but burbling larger, appeared in the center.

"What do you think that is?" Wax asked, turning to face it square. His hand went to his rope, instinct without reason.

"You think something was in there the whole time?" Sawi asked, holding the torch back towards the pool.

The rumbling grew, the low bass gaining flavor, less the rhythms of moving earth and more a growl's living tenor. Sawi backed up a step and Wax matched her.

There were rules about hunting in the jungle, starting with never letting yourself get cornered. Any creature could be dangerous in tight spaces, best to keep things open, give yourself options.

The cave didn't offer many, save one:

Run.

Sawi and Wax slipped, scrabbled, pounded their way back up the cave. In between breaths, Wax shouted ahead, told Pan and Bliss to get themselves going. Behind, the creature left the pool with wet slaps, the spitting, growling sound following every lunging smack forward.

The gross noises, the sudden appearance dashed memories by as Wax followed Sawi's silhouette. When he'd been a small kid, there'd been talk about monsters like these. Kitaye had buttoned up for months, only allowing armed and wary groups to go out searching for goods. Few ships came then, and Wax remembered day after day spent on the beach with the city's hunters watching the children every minute.

And he remembered, just like this, when a fiend—that's what they were called, fiends—sloughed free from the waves. Wax had a stick, had been playing with Sawi and some others in the sand. The fiend barreled onto the shore, roaring and biting its several, shark-like heads. Wax remembered its rage, its scaled, blasted body already wounded from something, and then someone's hands picked him up, carried him off as Kitaye's hunters, whooping challenges, ran the other way.

There weren't any hunters here. Nobody to carry Wax away either. All he had was instinct, speed, and Sawi leading the way. They splashed into the clam room, a swift look enough to confirm Pan had completed his shrive harvest. The two were gone. Good. Sawi went right, picking her way around the water's edge, torch held high. Wax followed, trying not to slip.

The fiend didn't care to be careful.

The growl reached a triumphant pitch, a golden spittle spray flying into the room before the creature followed it.

Propelled by slippery fins, the thing, looking like a soaked, maned hanoko, blew up through the passage and landed in the dirty water. The splash drenched Wax in cool water, pushed him against the room's wall. Sawi's torch tumbled from her hand as she fell forward, the water catching her as she reached the room's far side. Hitting the wet rock, the torch sizzled, shadows and smoke playing out across the room.

"Get up!" Wax called, wiping his eyes and making another step.

Three or four more strides and he'd be free. Sawi made it to her knees, reached for the torch. Her hand snared the handle when the fiend surged from the pool, blowing the water forward in an angry wave. The crest ran over Sawi, soaked the torch and killed its glow. The gnarling growl filled the room, echoing.

Wax froze. He couldn't see a step in front, couldn't tell where to go. His legs shivered, the rocks were slippery. The fiend was right next to Sawi, and Wax couldn't do a . . .

His hand moved as fast as his mind, his left snapping into his pouch and yanking free the glowing moss. Wax's right ripped the rope from his waist.

Sawi swore, yelped. The fiend smacked rock.

Wax threw the fungus, watched it soar and strike the fiend's back, a roiling, slimy ocean blue mane. The creature reared up at the slap, didn't turn around, its back fins continuing to push the monster forward.

"Hey!" Wax yelled. "I'm still here!"

The fiend didn't seem to care what he said, but the creature sure noticed when Wax's rope latched its grapples into its fur. Hissing hot, the fiend spun, its fins cracking against the cave. With the glowing fungus on the thing's back, Wax found his view plunged into shadow again.

"Run Sawi!" Wax called, hearing the fiend shuffle into the water. He pulled on the rope, the grapples coming loose.

Not much of a weapon, that. Sawi, too, didn't reply. Maybe she'd made it away.

The water churned on his left, the burbles coming closer. To stay meant to die, so Wax risked it, took a quick step forward and then another. He wobbled, but kept his momentum, went for a third, almost to the far landing and a fast sprint to salvation.

The fiend swept a fin under Wax's planted foot, wiping Wax out and sending him crashing into the pool. The filmy liquid stuck to him, Wax's hands and feet kicked and hit things that might've been sticks, might've been leaves, or might've been the fiend's fins.

The creature figured out its bearings fast, sliding to where Wax fell and planting a fin on the man's chest. Wax's lungs imploded, air rushing out at the weight crushing him to the floor. Water ran over his mouth, his eyes. Filled his nose, but Wax couldn't cough, couldn't do anything save choke as the fiend's leonine golden eyes, the only things visible in the dark, leaned in close.

For all his jumping, all his wild swings through the jungle, not once had Wax felt death come close. There were thrills, brushes with danger, but nothing real. Nothing that'd stick beyond a campfire story.

His mind locked on those two eyes, his muscles twitching and failing, spots in his vision turning the fiend's golden glare into four, eight, twelve shifting circles. Everything else faded, every feeling. Until, at last, those dancing, pretty lights vanished too.

CHAPTER 8

AXE AND STONE

The fiend had its prize. Svarde and Kivi could tell that much. The ferrite's slits glowed orange, the beast releasing its too-high body heat and giving the monster a good look. Helping, too, was an odd purple splotch on the fiend's back end, currently off to Svarde's right.

"Go get it, girl," Svarde said, and Kivi snorted.

The hunter raised his crossbow, fired a quarrel. The bolt struck the fiend right where its face met the water, the barest instant before Kivi charged into the fiend's side. Though the creature must've been more than triple Kivi's size, not much matched a ferrite's density. Kivi splashed into the fiend's middle, rolling the monster, now sporting a bolt from its forehead, onto its back.

"Fins?" Svarde muttered, reloading as he walked forward.

Fiends had a way of surprising you. Coming up with all sorts of ways to break natural conventions, as if a mad god sat in some secret hole mixing-and-matching the worst ideas.

52

Not that it mattered: Svarde had killed plenty before, and he'd take this one too.

He raised the crossbow as the fiend swatted at Kivi with its fins, gnashed at the ferrite with its jaws. The fins bounced off, steam gushing where water found Kivi's vents. The teeth?

The fiend had been roaring and hissing, but when its fangs bit Kivi's hide and broke off, those guttural noises turned into pained yelps. The fiend flailed harder, throwing its head back into the pool. Svarde sighted where the thing would rise again as Kivi raked with her rock claws.

And a damn man's head rose from the water, spluttering and coughing. Must've been the fourth the idiots outside were yelling about.

"Get away," Svarde shouted. The kid splashed toward Svarde's voice with weak strokes. Not fast enough. "Keep going!"

Svarde dropped the crossbow, dashing forward with just enough precision to keep his footing. He reached out, gloved arm catching a scratched, soaking hand and pulled the young man free. Without another word, Svarde threw his rescue behind him, heard the man hit the rock floor and start retching.

Alive. That would be enough.

While Svarde played hero, the fiend found some energy. Realizing its fins wouldn't do much to Kivi, the fiend swapped to rolling, turning over Kivi. The ferrite's weight worked against it, Svarde's friend falling off the fiend to splash into the pool. By the time Svarde turned back to the fight, Kivi was sputtering herself, buried beneath the fiend's bulk.

"Get off her, you moldy rag," Svarde said, marching into the shallow pool as he drew his axes.

The water chilled up to his thighs. The fight's splashing had Svarde blinking as he neared the purple glow—Kivi's orange steamed out beneath the water and the fiend's sloppy mane. The dark only mattered if your target was hard to hit, and a fiend this size was an easy mark.

Svarde went for the frenzy, aiming to draw the fiend's attention more than try for a straight kill. He swung the axes fast and light, cutting through the mane and drawing long, red lines along the creature's body. The fiend responded like Svarde wanted, turning its golden eyes at him and roaring with its busted maw.

"There you are, you big ugly," Svarde said.

Face to face, nowhere to run. A quick kill either way.

A fin whipped Svarde's way, meeting an axe instead. The left-handed blow cut the offending limb clean away, giving Svarde a window to step in and silence the fiend's awful sounds with a fatal finale.

As the monster fell limp, Kivi squirmed out from its bulk. The ferrite snorted, dragged itself to the pool's side and shook, steam flying out and the welcome orange glow returning. Svarde retrieved his axe from the fiend's head, took a closer look at what he'd slain.

The signs stood out: the mane, so clotted in motion, had black-and-burned splotches. The fiend's skin carried more grievous wounds along its belly and back, ones not delivered by Svarde's swings or Kivi's claws. He glanced back towards the man he'd saved, found him sitting up and looking back. Thin, wearing a Vis weave.

Not a fighter.

Svarde ran his fingers along the fiend's skin, feeling how thin and loose it felt. Breaking down. The slow disintegration dooming any fiend who tried to breach the surface while the Aegis still lived.

"She's not dead yet, then," Svarde said to Kivi.

But for a fiend to make it this far, to still be this strong . . . she must be close.

"Who are you?" asked the man, now on his feet, though his hands were on his knees.

While thinking up an answer, Svarde felt something brush his left leg. He reached down, pulled up a Vis rope. Clever things, though Svarde himself would never use them. Such thin strands to trust with your whole weight, soaring through those trees.

"Doesn't matter who I am," Svarde replied, holding up the rope. "This yours?"

The man gave his name on the walk back, the two following Kivi up through the cavern's twists and turns. Tywinax, though everyone called him Wax.

He waited for Svarde to give his own name in reply, as if it was to be an equal exchange.

"Why were you here?" Svarde asked instead.

Wax frowned, then focused on getting his footwork right. Nimble enough, like every Vis. Svarde reached out, grabbed Wax's weave and stopped him cold. Kivi sensed the move, spun 'round with her emerald eyes.

"I asked you a question," Svarde said. "Answer it."

Wax gave Svarde a straight look. Not filled with fear, but an exhausted wariness. A look Svarde himself had seen so many times when—

"Shrives," Wax said, shrugging himself free from Svarde's loose grab. "They're hard to find, but that pool had a bunch."

"That's it? Shrives?"

"What else would we be looking for?" Wax asked, that straight stare looking confused now.

Me, Svarde wanted to say, but shook his head instead.

Who knew if anyone looked for him anymore, if anyone cared. Then again, he'd abandoned the only one he cared about, so why wouldn't the world return the favor?

"You okay?" Wax asked. "Appreciate the save from whatever that was, but you're looking a little lost."

Svarde pushed Wax around towards the exit. "Keep moving. Always a chance there's another."

At that possibility, Wax finally took Svarde's point and ran.

CHAPTER 9

CLIFF NIGHTS

She'd held her torch in one hand, feeling the heat clash with the cave's cool air, and her bamboo staff in the other. Bliss watched as Pan gathered the shrives, sighed with him when Pan finished and neither Sawi nor Wax were to be found. The two had a habit of vanishing, with a reason neither Pan nor Bliss felt like talking about.

At least the passing time gave Pan an excuse to cut playtime short, his shouts down the cavern at least getting Wax's reply. Bliss had been ready to tease her brother at his return, that fun ruined when Wax's next yell echoed on up.

Run, and run fast.

They both hesitated, Bliss tightening her grip on the staff. The cave wasn't a great fighting place for her, seeing as its tight corridors meant she'd be stuck stabbing straight ahead. No wide sweeps, acrobatic jumping strikes.

"Your brother's goofy, but he's not stupid," Pan said, moving past Bliss. "Let's go."

'What if they need help?'

"Then they'd ask for it."

They'd cleared the cave, found the hunter and his strange pet watching. The man had asked who they were, what they were doing, but Pan cut the man off. Said they had two friends in the cave who were in trouble.

The hunter, though, paid more attention to the rising snorts from his pet. The rocky beast eventually made its own move, scrambling down the mountainside and dashing into the cave without a second glance for Pan, Bliss, and the shrive-loaded satchels. The hunter, flipping a curse Bliss had never heard before, followed.

For too many minutes Pan and Bliss stood on the overlook, the sun fading towards dusk. Sawi emerged, crying, her right leg bleeding where something had bashed her against the rock. Pan went into nurse mode right away, breaking out the bandages, the poultices he always carried on these wanders.

Bliss listened as Sawi described the thing, but she kept her eyes on the cave. Her torch still burned. She could, she wanted to run in. Her brother might die, would . . .

Wax stumbled out. Purple bruises coated his chest, visible through the weave. Scratches littered his arms and legs, though they didn't have Sawi's depth or deadly purpose. The cave's walls, floor, the most likely culprits.

Bliss dropped her staff, wrapped her brother in a hug, and for the first time in her life felt him leaning on her. Wax sagged, his lungs almost wheezing. Bliss steadied her legs, wrapped her arms around Wax and held him, held him like their mother might if they'd had a bad dream, if they felt sick.

On the whole, an alien experience.

"You have a camp?" The hunter, emerging behind with his pet, asked nobody in particular.

"We were going to head back," Pan answered, finishing's Sawi's dressing.

"To Kitaye?" The hunter was the snorting one now. "Not tonight, surely."

"Not anymore," Wax said, separating from Bliss, putting himself between the hunter and his friends.

A dumb move. Wax wasn't in a state to fight a fly, much less a hulking man like that. Bliss caught the axes, both back in their sheathes. The hunter held a crossbow in his hand, idle at his waist but loaded. Ready. The rock monster hunched, steam escaping from cracks in its stone scales, near the hunter's legs.

Bliss figured she could get to the hunter's hand with her staff in less than a second, whack the crossbow aside. That might buy time for Wax and the others to run—the rock monster couldn't be that quick, could it?—which would leave Bliss alone, but one could sacrifice herself so three could live.

Vis asked that of his people from time to time.

"Then come with me," the hunter said, nodding towards his right shoulder. "My place isn't far, and there's room enough on the floor for you. We can tend those wounds and talk about what happened."

Wax didn't have a ready reply. Sawi had her hands on her wounded leg, her eyes near-closed. Not listening, or not caring. Pan held a frown, but he wasn't the type to make a call like this.

Bliss poked Wax with her staff, getting him to turn around. The hunter watched, bushy eyebrow raised.

'He saved you?' Bliss asked.

'Saved me and Sawi both,' Wax signed back. 'And you two. That thing was fast.'

'You trust him, then?'

'If he wanted us dead, he could've stayed away.' Wax glanced back at the hunter. "We're exhausted, hurt. If you'll take us in, we'd be grateful."

That was how Bliss's chats with Wax tended to go. A few signs back and forth and her brother would find the obvious conclusion. No matter how strange the hunter might be, he hadn't tried to kill them yet, and Vis at night had plenty of things that would.

Along the mountainside path to his cabin, Svarde introduced himself to the group, spun a story that rang, to Bliss, as maybe half true. Svarde spoke of himself as a tired fighter looking to retire and live out his days in peace, but unless Bliss couldn't tell age worth a damn, Svarde would have a whole lot of years to spend alone.

Wax and Pan took turns telling their tale in return while Bliss walked with Sawi. Svarde's ferrite—what a name— kept the absolute back, snorting and shuffling along the well-trod rocks. Bliss gave Sawi her staff for the walk, her friend needing the support as she limped along.

Bliss tried to get some details from her, but Sawi kept her mouth shut. That, more than anything, made Bliss curious. Sawi wouldn't hesitate to go flying off into the deepest jungle, wouldn't balk at the thorniest climb. She'd scared off hanokos before. But here she was, stumbling, shaking, and breathing quick even though any danger had long since passed.

What had been back there in that cave?

Svarde's cabin swapped the mood. The thing looked like a box with a sideways triangle stacked on top. It pressed up against the mountain, mashing awkwardly against the rocks. Not at all like the treehouses back in Kitaye, the ones mingling with the trees, leaves, and branches like close friends.

Seeing the cabin flipped Bliss into a smile, a stifled laugh. Wax, Pan, and even Sawi snuck glances at each other as Svarde went into a loud description of how he'd built the place, the effort put into dragging the wood up here and beating it into submission.

"Looks nice," Pan managed when Svarde paused.

"Where are you from?" Wax asked. Svarde didn't look much like someone from Vis, but the bigger tell than his body was how he'd built this thing. Nobody from the isle would've strung up a home this way. At least, not anybody paying attention.

"Foti, as much as that matters," Svarde said, leading up the last steps to the cabin's sole door. "Been a long time since I've set foot on that blasted place."

Reaching the cabin smoothed out the conversation, the foursome settling in at Svarde's direction. Early Fall warmth meant Svarde's blankets could be spread across the floor, making beds for the group. They split their fruits, tossed in some of Svarde's salted fish, and devoured.

Wax and Pan tried to probe Svarde for more details about who he was, what he wanted, where he came from, but the hunter clammed up as soon as they were inside. As if being in his own space reminded him that these four Vis wanderers might not be forever friends, that they might be going home and telling others what they found here.

Bliss never let her staff leave her side. Svarde hung up his axes, his crossbow, while Kivi curled near the door, emerald eyes watching. Svarde was human, as vulnerable as any to a good whack on the head. But Kivi?

Bliss studied the creature while she ate a mango. Where were the weaknesses? The slits where the steam burst from every now and then?

That led her eyes to the axes. Sharp, thin enough to get in one of those cracks, perhaps.

That was the plan, then. Knock out Svarde, hope Kivi wasn't fast enough to get her before Bliss could snag an axe and deliver a hopefully mortal slash.

"Bliss," Wax's voice yanked her out of the daydream. "We're going to stay here tonight, okay?"

'Sure,' she signed. Didn't seem to be other options: Sawi looked half asleep already, laying down on the fur blanket. Pan's eyes drooped as he leaned against the back wall, a shrive satchel in each hand. 'You feeling better?'

Wax glanced down at his bruises, the scratches now salved with aloes.

"Danced with death and made it out alive," Wax said. "Hard to feel better than that." He glanced at Svarde, who'd left his bed and seemed to be stuffing a pipe. 'I know you. Don't stay up all night. We'll have a long walk tomorrow.'

'Of course, brother.'

'Wake me up if you get worried.'

Bliss smiled, nodded towards her staff. 'You'll know.'

She gave Svarde two minutes before she followed him outside. The other three were asleep already, the sun long since dropping into darkness. Kivi's emeralds were shut too, the creature rumbling snores through the cabin.

Svarde sat on the cabin's seaward overhang, a stride-wide ledge lingering over space. He had his pipe near a striking stone, and a few quick flicks with the flint had it smoking. Bliss watched from the cabin's front corner, staff in hand.

Not that she was a spy, but trusting an armed and deadly stranger wasn't something you did and survived. At least, that's not what the Kitaye hunters told her when she'd started running with them. A secret habit, one her brothers wouldn't like.

But then, when she saved their dumb selves, they'd come around.

"You going to stay there all night?" Svarde asked, not turning to look at her, his face lit by the pipe's glow.

Bliss shrugged, looked out to the left, watched the stars. A cloudless night. Little wind. Surf sounds rose up from far below, a gentle cushion.

"Noticed you don't talk much," Svarde continued. "Not scared, are you?"

Bliss flashed him a glare. Judged the steps around to the ledge and took them. Refused to look down, instead keeping near the cabin's wall until she came within slugging distance of Svarde.

He looked at her, a searching evaluation Bliss recognized because she did it so much herself. He wanted to find her weaknesses, her strengths, her fears and whether she had a fighter's spirit.

So she snatched the pipe from his hand and put the end to her lips, took a draw. Felt the harsh weed climb down her throat and smite her lungs with a mint heat. She held the pipe back, coughed, hacked, as Svarde chuckled.

"I get it," Svarde said, pulling his water skin out and handing it over. "You've got to prove yourself to the stranger. I see you. I see your staff."

The water was about the best thing she'd ever drank there in that moment. Some in Kitaye used traded-for pipes from Foti, most rolled their own if they bothered. Bliss did neither, didn't plan on it. Why spoil nature's own scent with a burning weed?

"Not the answer you were looking for?" Svarde asked. His grin fell away. "Your bamboo stick won't do a damn thing against what was in that cave. You want to protect your brother in there, you'll need something better."

As if Svarde knew what she could do with the staff. Just because it wasn't iron like those axes didn't mean it couldn't be just as deadly.

"That thing's a fiend," Svarde said. "Heard of them before?"

Of course she had. Everyone knew what fiends were, how they shouldn't be seen unless . . .

"You're getting it now." Svarde nodded. "If there's a fiend up here, then the Aegis is breaking."

And if the Aegis, the shield on Noctia, was getting weaker, then fiends could be anywhere. Bliss looked east, as if she could bend her view around the mountain, over the jungle all the way to Kitaye.

"Everything's at risk," Svarde said. "What we don't know is whether this is the first. You've not heard of any others?"

Bliss shook her head. Tried to think back. The last Renewal, the call for a new Aegis, hadn't been more than a decade ago. This ought to be far too soon—

"Then it might be early," Svarde said. "We can warn them. Get ahead. Make sure the isles have their defenses ready."

We?

"I came here to get away," Svarde grinned, "but, truth be told, solitude isn't all it's made up to be. Felt good to swing those axes today." He looked her way. "What do you say, Bliss? Mind if Kivi and I join you on your return journey?"

CHAPTER 10
THE RETURN

Three days slow walking brought them back to Kitaye. Injured, Wax didn't try to suggest the faster swinging, bounding leaps they'd used before. Sawi's limp and Svarde's general glares towards the tall trees ruled out the idea. Instead they hiked, first on swampy ground and then on soft forest floor. Pan, Wax, and Bliss played caretaker, finding water and food for the group in turns.

Svarde, for all his mysteriousness, kept his survival skills to himself. He brooded over fires, puffed on his pipe, took roaming wanders, and sharpened his axes till they gleamed. Nobody managed to get much out of the man, a silence Wax attributed to going and living on a cliff for who knew how many years.

Kivi, neat though the ferrite was, didn't exactly hold conversations either.

Sawi spent the traveling days in a muted haze. She shrugged off Wax's attempted affections: hugs and invitations to climb up at camp to see the sunset from the sky.

Instead she'd roll out a blanket borrowed from Svarde and collapse.

On the last night, when Wax started making another overture to climb to the canopy, Svarde, without looking his way from the campfire, told Wax to leave her be.

When Wax asked what gave Svarde permission to say that, the man only said to look at Sawi.

"Everyone handles death differently," Svarde finished, before whistling to Kivi and setting off on one of his walks.

Another oddity. Before this trip, Wax always felt the jungle was his second home. He'd curl up on some branch and feel as safe sleeping as if he were back home on his own hammock. Now, with Svarde stalking about and Bliss, often, shadowing him, Wax found the nights fitful, stressed.

Kitaye, thankfully, marked the end of all that.

As they hit the outskirts, Svarde asked the group to stop, to circle up.

"Tell everyone what happened," Svarde said first. "They'll ask, and you have to be clear. A fiend attacked you. Use that word, and only that word."

"You think people will believe us?" Pan asked. "It's too soon."

Svarde pointed at Sawi, then Wax. "You still have your wounds. Show them. Make your families and friends understand. Anyone leaving the city now should go in a group, and be armed."

"Don't know who you think we are," Wax said, "but nobody's going to care what we say."

"That's on them," Svarde replied. "You can only show people the truth. They have to believe it."

'What is he going to do?' Bliss signed to Wax, who repeated the question.

Svarde glanced at Kivi, resting at his right knee. "You said a Foti ship's in town? I plan on catching a ride. Kitaye isn't the only place that should know fiends are coming."

Sawi broke for home, as did Bliss, leaving Wax, Pan, and Svarde heading towards the docks. A hot afternoon wore on, the walk covering Wax in sweat despite the forest shade. Early cooking spices swept in over the sea breeze, a tantalizing prospect after days burned on berries, plants, and the odd critter pegged by Svarde's crossbow.

Kitaye's crowds spared their stares for Kivi, the ferrite getting pestering attention from kids and concerned mutters from parents. Svarde himself looked enough like the Foti visiting, though the twin axes sparked a few called offers to trade.

The man didn't say a single word to any.

Wax found himself watching Svarde more than his own footsteps. Being silent and focused in the jungle was one thing: never knew where a nasty plant or predator waited, but Kitaye was a peaceful place. Svarde could've relaxed, could've taken a hand off his crossbow and said hello. Instead, Svarde looked lost in long ago memories.

"Someday we'll be able to do that," Wax said to Pan as they neared the beach, the trading stalls.

"What, look like we had too many mushrooms?"

"No, he's got stories, Pan," Wax replied. "He's lived! Done things we can't even dream about."

"Stuff that had him living alone on a rock," Pan tilted his head towards Svarde. "You want that for yourself, go get it buddy. Svarde said he's leaving, bet you can go back and claim his cabin for yourself."

"You're just scared."

"Scared of what? We're not doing anything."

"That's my point!"

Wax missed the chance to buff up his argument as the trio hit the dock leading to the Foti ship. The three days in port hadn't changed it much, except now the crates onboard had Vis goods instead of Foti equipment. The ship itself buzzed, the sailors readying the boat for a departure, Wax overheard, coming the next morning.

"Just in time," the Foti man said, striding down his boat's big ramp to the dock. "Saw you coming and said, there's proof Vis knows how to make a good man."

Wax glanced a question at Pan, a good man? Svarde loomed behind them, fishing for his pipe while Kivi sniffed the calm water off the dock's side.

"A good man sticks to his deals," the Foti explained. "Guessing those are the shrives right there? Had to convince my crew to wait for you." The man's eyes sparkled as Pan opened the first satchel, revealing the silver-blue fungi. "Now there's a beautiful sight."

"Wasn't easy to get either," Wax said. Never give up anything in a negotiation, so his mother said, and take what you can. "A fiend attacked us while we were grabbing them."

The Foti's smile died, the hand reaching for the bartered blade halting in its tracks.

"What's that word you used?" The Foti asked, voice dropping to a near whisper.

"A fiend," Svarde repeated, cutting Wax off. "Not some jungle cat or a plant. A fiend. You know what that means."

The Foti looked up at Svarde, his face firming up. An acceptable answer provided. "You were there?"

"He was," Wax said, trying to stand a little taller. Pan just looked back and forth. "Without him, we might've died."

"Might've died," the Foti folded his arms, metal bracers

gleaming in the orange-purple twilight. He focused on Svarde. "You're not from Vis, are you, friend?"

"Been here long enough," Svarde replied. He held his pipe over one of the dock's torches, caught a light, brought it back. "It came from the Dark Below. I'm certain."

The Foti flicked his eyes at Wax, "He's certain, is he. Everyone catches a creature and calls it a fiend these days, as if the whole world's fishing for a crisis. You saw this thing?"

Wax ran a finger over his chest where, through the weave, his bruises made their show.

"Gave me this. I've never seen something like it before." Wax pointed at the sword. "We brought the shrives as promised."

"You'll get your reward," the Foti ran his hand through his scraggly beard, tied at its bottom with a simple knot. "Seeing a fiend changes things, is all. Changes a lot, if it's true."

Svarde stepped up onto the ramp, moving Wax aside by his sheer bulk. Reaching into his ragged shirt, Svarde pulled out a palm-sized circled linked to a tarnished bronze chain around his neck. The man had worn the amulet every moment Wax saw him, but Svarde had never pulled it out till now.

The shadows made it hard to see the amulet's detail, but the seven circles were clear enough. Each held its own design inside, and all had curling lines linking them to the largest of the seven in the amulet's center.

Behind Wax, Pan stifled a gasp, falling into a cough. The Foti's reaction matched it, the man freezing up, then going slack, arms drooping to his sides and his shoulders slumping.

"Believe me now?" Svarde asked.

"Didn't want to," the Foti man replied. He unclipped the sword, handed it to Wax. Took out the little knife and flipped it Wax's way too, wearing the same faraway look Svarde had sported the whole way through town. "What're you doing here then?"

"Looking for a ride," Svarde said.

The Foti nodded, straightened, as if being returned to normal business was an invigorating switch.

"Noctia?" The Foti asked.

"The Crowned City," Svarde agreed.

"Easy enough," the Foti waved for Pan to hand over the shrives. "Can sell these there just the same as on Kance. We're sailing tomorrow?"

"At dawn," Svarde said. "No later."

"You'll be spoiling my crew's last night with that order."

"They'll be risking their lives otherwise," Svarde said. "Unless you're geared up to fight fiends on this boat?"

The Foti's look went to the sword he'd just handed to Wax, then the man shook his head.

"Peacetime for us. Carry more cargo without the cannons."

"Then your decision's made."

Wax felt Pan tugging on his weave. He backed up a couple steps while Svarde and the Foti fell into other conversation, both heading up the ramp towards the ship's deck. Kivi gave Wax and Pan a friendly snort, then followed Svarde.

"I was listening," Wax said, holding the sheathed blade in one hand, the knife in the other. "What'd you pull me away for?"

"You don't want to be in that, Wax," Pan said, gulping. "What they're talking about, that's not for us."

"Not for us?"

Pan hefted the other shrive satchel, "Not for me, anyway. I'm going to get rid of these, have a nice meal." Wax shrugged, looked back at the Foti boat, and Pan grabbed his shoulder, twisted him back. "Sawi's ceremony is tomorrow. Shouldn't you be helping her?"

Yeah, Wax should be, but there was still time. This, whatever this was, would be gone soon. He'd tasted the wider world, and who knew when he'd get seconds?

"Do you even know what that amulet was?" Pan asked, tone drop-shifting from friendly warning to angry urgency.

"I would if you hadn't pulled me away."

"It's a Guardian's amulet, Wax. Not just any medal. You saw the seven circles? The only ones who get those are the ones who make it to the end."

"The end?"

"The ones with the Aegis." Pan looked with Wax, watching Svarde on the boat as he spoke, now to a whole slew of Foti sailors. "He's not that old either. I bet he was there, right there at the last Renewal."

Wax threw a skeptical, squinted-eye glance at Pan, "How would you know any of this?"

"Because my grandfather was a Guardian, a couple times ago," Pan said. "His Renewal didn't make it far. Gave up, I think, but grampa talked about these. How he wanted one."

"So Svarde's a Guardian? Who cares?"

"Wax, I don't know what'd make a Guardian like that go live alone, but it can't be anything good. What he's been talking about, fiends and all, they'll kill people," Pan said. "That's not me, that's not us. You got your sword."

Wax held up the sheathed sapphire blade. It seemed a

little plain now, next to what he'd just seen. Who cared about a sword if he couldn't do anything with it?

"Can I have the knife?" Pan asked.

"What?"

"I harvested the shrives and carried them most of the way," Pan said. "Really, I should be the one getting the goods, not you."

"My idea, my blade," Wax bit back, but grinned. "Sure, you can have the knife."

Pan tied the small knife to his belt, put a hand on Wax's shoulder. "C'mon. This isn't our problem."

No matter how much Wax wanted it to be.

CHAPTER II

RITUAL

Bliss made it through a coconut, fish, and seaweed combo before her dinner in the cooking circle was interrupted. Sitting at her family's chosen cookfire, signing with Quik and her father, Bliss had only just set down the wood fork and spoon before several shadows fell across the bright flames.

The trio, two women and a man, wore gray-black weaves climbing from their ankles up to their necks. Unlike the one Bliss sported, these weaves skipped the gaps, showed no skin and had finger-thick cords. Over their heads, cloth wraps looped their necks, ready to be lifted should a face covering be needed. They were uniforms that demanded respect, ones Bliss hadn't seen since her childhood.

"You're back," Quik said, quiet, his own half-eaten dish forgotten.

The woman in the middle pointed at Bliss without saying a word. Bliss looked at her father, who nodded.

"If the Lira want you, you go," he said, though the

sudden lines around his eyes, the tightness in his arms told Bliss this wasn't going to be good.

When Quik rose to follow, the male Lira put a strong hand on Quik's shoulder and forced him back to the log he'd been sitting on.

"But Bliss doesn't talk," Quik protested. "You won't know her signing?"

If Quik's argument made an impression, the three Lira didn't show it. Again, the middle woman flicked to Bliss with her hand. This time, they started walking. This time, Bliss followed.

If the return with Svarde drew attention, walking with the Lira drew the studied opposite. The black-clad trio led Bliss in silence, and everywhere they stepped, from the cooking circle through Kitaye's tree-covered, dirt streets people took a single glance then turned away.

Were they hiding, like Bliss ought to have done? Was Bliss being led to some torment she didn't know, that others wouldn't want to remember?

She scoured her memory during the walk, Kitaye's normal nighttime beauty fading to a blue as anxiety lightninged her nerves. Not once had her parents mentioned the Lira, save in passing during old tales. Hidden warriors, excused from the normal bounds of Kitaye's laws, its society. Shadowy protectors, coming and going at invisible whims.

Who they were, how they were summoned, Bliss didn't know, couldn't guess.

She reached for her staff, hoping holding its firm fibers would bring some comfort, but her back missed its weight: she'd left it at the cookfire. Bliss had her weave, her hands, and nothing else.

The Lira didn't look back the entire walk. Either they

heard Bliss's bare feet padding after them or they assumed, correctly, that nobody would be foolish enough to flee.

Their path led Bliss away from the city. Kitaye's torches and conversation dwindled to darkness and the jungle's nighttime noises. Insects, no longer scared by smoke, came to investigate. Ferns and branches, some with thorns, encroached. Bliss threw away the wonder, focused on getting her feet planted, swinging her legs and hips around minor dangers.

Wherever she was being led, Bliss figured it wouldn't look good to arrive scratched up and bruised.

At some point—without the sky, without bearings beyond dim trees and sana stalks, time tracking was an impossibility—the Lira stopped. A small clearing, enough to hold their foursome and no more. Noctia lelunes bordered the circle, catching the moon's light and opening into a vibrant crimson. The flowers weren't natural to Vis. Someone had brought them here, planted this with purpose.

The lead Lira, the woman who'd beckoned Bliss over, unslung her rope from her waist. With a quick snap, she launched the rope up towards the branches above. To Bliss, looking that way showed nothing more than a shadowy snarl. The Lira's rope, though, found something. With a tug, coupled with snapping sounds, like twigs meeting their splits, the rope fell back to the dirt.

Following it not a second later came a thick rope ladder. Double-tied, with real rungs. Not the slapdash knotted climbers too many Kitaye houses used, but a real ladder. The lead Lira and the man jumped up the rungs quick, their hands and feet alighting, barely, on each wood cylinder before flipping up to the next.

The last Lira touched Bliss's shoulder, pointed to the

ladder. Bliss swallowed, looked up. But what choice did she have, really? Even if she ran now, Bliss would have a hard time making it back to Kitaye. And the Lira would follow, might not be so nice the next time around.

She'd chatted with Wax often enough about adventure. She'd been training with the hunters, trying to make that her sure destination. That meant bravery, courage, a willingness to confront the unknown.

Well, here was her chance.

The rungs were cool to the touch, the ladder swayed as she climbed. Her bare feet scooped with every footfall, the arch wrapping around the rung as her hands gripped the next. Below, the Lira started up after her and they scaled in silence, the ladder moving along with them.

Bliss emerged into a treetop cluster. Vines, massaged into tight patterns, brought thick branches together into a natural platform. Overhead loose leaves provided the slightest separation from the sky. Were it not for the curving, carved walls around, Bliss assumed she could've seen the ocean.

Instead, she saw Lira.

A quick count suggested more than twenty. They arrayed around the larger-than-it-looked space, low lit with blue-and-purple mosses. At least, that's what Bliss thought the stuff was, the clumps stuck in the treehouse's darker corners. On the walls, too, hung canvas cloth with words written in red dyes.

Bliss moved away from the ladder as the last Lira reached the top, her eyes roving, scanning the walls. The Lira themselves didn't seem to pay her much attention, and she couldn't read much in their dark weaves. The wall hangings offered more: names, years, locations all across Vis.

The ladder snapped up, clicking into place, and with it the tenor changed. The quiet conversations ended, the Lira turning almost as one to look at Bliss. One, the woman from before, came from the crowd and handed Bliss a scribbling cloth, a wood board, and a charcoal pencil. That last instrument held Bliss's attention: only the Foti bothered bringing those here, and the only reason anyone would use it over dye-and-stick would be precision.

"You saw a fiend?" the Lira asked.

Bliss shook her head. Used the pencil at their silent stares.

'My brother saw it. I did not.'

The black fuzzy scribble would've been hard to read until a different Lira brought a Foti lantern forward. With a spark snapped by some switch in the thing, a peach flame sprang up.

An expensive tool, the fuel even more so. Bliss had only seen lanterns used in a couple places where open flames could cause disaster. Like, say, a cramped treehouse far above the forest floor.

"But it was a fiend?" The Lira asked.

'Svarde said so.'

"The man you found?"

'Yes.'

"Do you know who he is?"

The Lira asked the question like her mother might've asked if Bliss knew how to use a fork.

'Do you?'

The Lira, all of them, stared back at Bliss in silence.

'I don't know who he is. Someone important?'

Whispers erupted around her, funneled like wind back towards the woman who'd been leading this whole thing.

"Do you know what we are?"

Bliss shook her head. Legends and rumors were just that. Better to start from the source.

"We are the protectors," the Lira said. "Blessed by Vis himself to keep his home safe until he can return."

'Safe from what?' Bliss hadn't seen the Lira show up during bad storms, fires, or even attacks by rabid hanokos. If the Lira were protectors, they were awfully picky ones.

"From the true enemy," the Lira replied. "The Dark Below."

Another name from dusty old stories. Somewhere far beneath the earth where fiends emerged. Supposedly.

All the Lira looked at Bliss now, as if she should've been awed by the declaration. Instead, she shrugged.

Wax and Sawi might've run into some nasty creature deep in a cave, but one monster, one Svarde had killed without too much trouble, hardly seemed like it needed some secret society to thwart.

The idea cracked the facade around Bliss. The mysterious walk, the enchanting treehouse with its cryptic scrawls twisted into something more than a little stupid. What were all these people playing at, hanging out here in the dark?

"You're amused?" The Lira woman, apparently, didn't see things the same as Bliss.

'I don't understand,' Bliss wrote.

The woman nodded, looked to her left. Bliss tried to follow the glance, saw nothing but masked faces in the shadows.

"I've been told you're ready to learn," the woman said.

'Learn what?'

"How to keep your family alive in the coming storm."

Bliss laughed. She couldn't help it. So much gravitas, so much bluster. But she'd barely begun to smile, barely had the first chuckle past her lips when someone slipped a thick cloth over her face, her mouth, her eyes.

A soft, burning scent filled her mouth and nose. Bliss coughed, tried to struggle but other hands found her arms, clamped them down. Another pressed the wet cloth against her lips.

Whispers started up around her, punching through Bliss's panic only because they spoke in unison. The voices rose in a prayer, one Bliss knew by heart, one she'd known since she was a little girl.

A simple verse, asking Vis for strength, for honor, and for forgiveness. The words repeated, a melody as Bliss's arms went limp, her legs became invisible, and she floated in the dark before becoming lost to it altogether.

CHAPTER 12

A SIMPLE ASK

Five days across the surf. The sea breeze had a different character on a ship's deck rather than a mountainside. As if Svarde was invited to a dance rather than simply watching one. He and Kivi spent both day and night outdoors on the deck—going below meant suffocating in hammocks with Foti sailors. With Kivi's steam heat, Svarde could take the chillest wind and stay comfortable, a good thing with the fall season on the approach.

The seafarers avoided Svarde and his friend, though a few brave ones dared to grumble about the disruption to their planned circuit. Cutting the isles, going from one to the next and bartering off goods was standard practice, and almost always profitable.

A life Svarde might've led if the timing had worked out.

She might've been right there with him, too.

Noctia emerged, as it always did, in shades. The center isle's brutal curves faded in on the horizon, a gray-black band gathering definition as the ship neared. Sea traffic picked up too, more merchants and the occasional armed escort sailing by. The ballistae mounting the more dangerous decks always unloaded this close to Noctia.

Nobody would be dumb enough to risk the isle's wrath by starting a fight within her sight.

The Crowned City didn't compete with her home for grandeur. It played a different game, its soaring towers bedecked in flags, her streets bustling with life while the cliffs behind her stood in stoic desolation. Color dominated, Noctia's factions proclaiming themselves with dyes and shaped metals framing doors and windows. Each called out a certain experience, a certain life.

So many choices, but in making one, you would lose all the others.

The Foti ship made for the Trader's Port, a sensible move. Svarde was no diplomat, they were not soldiers returning from a battle nor entertainers seeking to parlay talent for livelihood. The Crowned City circled all Noctia, and while there were many smaller ports, the Foti ship went right for the largest one, the only one worthy of its true name.

"A walk," Svarde said to Kivi as the ship settled into its berth.

The morning sun hid behind Noctia's mountains, and more than that, shade fell across the Foti ship thanks to its neighbor: a Kance galleon sporting the leather, wing-like sails. The vessel was going out as Svarde's came in, and he waited a long several minutes to watch it leave.

A Kance ship under a good captain glided on the water, and this was no exception. As if it only had to reach up and grab the air, the ship turned about and raced away, heading home with a frothy wake behind it.

Five days for the Foti vessel to get here. If it took the

Kance ship half that to make it home, its captain ought to resign from shame.

"Someday I'll take you on one," He said to Kivi as the pair disembarked, joining the Foti crew spilling into the dock miasma.

Kivi snorted. She'd learned long ago to regard Svarde's promises with healthy skepticism.

Every sailer heading onshore carried a satchel looped over their shoulder. The canvas sacks told stories, most decorated with emblems, dyed different colors, or pierced over with trinkets acquired from who knew where. Svarde had his own, a little lighter after purchasing food for the journey.

A Guardian's amulet served to get transport, didn't earn him a dinner.

Crates and baskets lined the docks, all shuffled onto painted squares for their loading order. Scratch boards hung on posts let the dockmasters scribble details, though by this late in the morning, the day's business had all been set.

Past the goods waited warehouses, the vast storerooms hosting sloping roofs meant to guide the rainwater to waiting barrels. After so long on Vis, where natural anything was always abundant, Noctia's rough scarcity brought a frown. A sniff reminded Svarde of more unpleasantness.

Cram too many people into a small place, and the odors would be both manifest and foul.

The Rat's Fang might've been unpleasant to some, but not to any sailor that knew their stuff. Tucked away behind two warehouses and owing its life to an incompetent city planner, the Rat's Fang looked like its namesake and welcomed the world's vermin.

Svarde, with Kivi at his heels, followed two other Foti sailers inside. Dim, save for a few lanterns hanging from the far up ceiling, the tavern made up for its low light with bright life. Boistrous voices drowned out the dock's random cacophony, none more than the bartender, the owner, the great Che-Ri.

"Svarde, why are you still alive?" Che-Ri called as the man's frame filled her doorway. "I've lost so many bets now."

Her grin spoke of lies, not gambling losses, and Svarde shook his head as he claimed a simple stool near the counter. The Rat's Fang had tables smattered about, most covered with spilled drinks never cleaned, yet were still occupied. Were always occupied.

Despite its open inside, something about the bar's acoustics made eavesdropping hard, so if you wanted an inauspicious place to discuss a detail, the Fang made a strong choice.

Svarde's eyes drifted towards the back, a wobbly high top still standing there. Occupied now by a couple Tamas monks, starting their day off with several rounds by the looks of it.

How many years since he'd sat there with—

"I'll give you one pour," Che-Ri said, sliding a mottled grey mug towards Svarde's chin. "Then you pay like everyone else."

"Some welcome," Svarde replied.

"Friendship is free," Che-Ri winked back. "Ale isn't."

She filled the mug with amber. Early for alcohol, and Svarde hadn't touched the stuff in too long. The Foti sailers, perhaps out of pity for his lonely voyage, had offered some sea grog that looked as likely to kill him as anything. That'd been an easy no.

This was an easier yes.

Up above Che-Ri, with a ladder leaning against the wall to one side, sat a big chalkboard. White lines on a black background set forth the day's rates: how many mugs a man could get with a pound of vegetables, some precious metals, fresh fish. This close to the docks, the Fang could actually take perishables and make it work.

Another reason it kept in business: flexibility.

"So why does a man everyone assumed had gone and died drop in on my bar?" Che-Ri said, circling back after handling the three others at the counter.

"Wanting a drink isn't enough of a reason?"

Che-Ri eyed the mug, "You haven't taken a sip yet. And while it's been a damn sight since I've seen you, memory says you weren't a morning drinker."

"Hadn't earned it yet."

"Today you have?"

Svarde scoped a look around, took in the outfits, the isles present. Looked like most, save Vis. For all its abundance, the people on that jungle island rarely left. Their leaf boats, neat as they were, tended to break apart on serious seas.

"Hey," Che-Ri slapped the counter, drew Svarde's attention back. "I'm talking to you."

"Sorry, it's been a while."

"Since what?"

"Since I've been around people," Svarde replied. Basic manners bounced their way back to him and Svarde propped a smile, lifted a mug. "To old friends."

Che-Ri clinked a fresh, empty mug against Svarde's own. Didn't fill it, didn't take a drink to match the man's.

Ill luck, that.

"You're really not happy to see me," Svarde said after

letting a mouthful wash down the salty, lingering breakfast.

"Someone like you showing up now means the good times really are ending." Che-Ri sighed, leaned on the counter. Her hair, stuffed with jangling beads, made its own music as she moved. "Nothing personal, but Guardians bring bad vibes."

"We're trying to keep everyone safe."

"Nobody likes being reminded about all the things out there trying to kill'em."

Svarde swirled the mug, "You're acting like I'm not the first sign."

Che-Ri shook her head. "The Najahn would probably give me a fine if I spoke up about it, but there's no hiding the rumors." Nonetheless, Che-Ri swept the room before continuing. "Fiends are being found again. Wounded, dying, but they're getting past her."

Svarde nodded. "Faster, then."

"Fastest, you mean." Che-Ri drummed her fingers on the counter. "Calling for another Renewal so soon isn't going to sit well with anybody, but the way I see it, old man Fassle doesn't have a choice. Least, that's the way the odds are going."

That, there, was why Svarde came to the Rat's Fang. Why anyone smart came there anyway. Good ale could be found for a fair price anywhere on Noctia, but trustworthy information required a more discerning eye.

"That's why I'm here," Svarde said, making good on his end of the deal. Che-Ri would be spreading his arrival around, and if she could sweeten it with his purpose, then so much the better. "Fiend showed up where I've been staying. Not a small one either."

"Where's that?"

Now Svarde leaned over, letting Che-Ri come close to meet him. "I tell you, you need to tell me when the next meeting is."

Che-Ri snorted, glanced at the entry and the sunny line on the ground outside. "You made it right on time. Last two came in yesterday. Bet they're talking now."

Svarde stood, drained his mug. "Then that's where I need to be going."

As he took his first step towards the exit, Che-Ri hollered at him, "Didn't you forget something?"

Throwing a look back over his shoulder, Svarde waved, "A trip to Vis does sound nice, I'll remember that!"

Sure, the exchange wouldn't make sense to anyone listening in, but for the Rat's Fang, that fit too well.

Getting anywhere important on Noctia meant walking uphill. The graded paths ringed the isle, each paved over in three degrees. On the left side, going up, you had smoothed stones for wheeled carts and people with more speed than sense. In the middle came the studded rock, a compromise between the ramp and the last, smallest section: flagstone steps.

Svarde and Kivi took the center route, hiking fast up from the water and towards the tallest, tightest spire collection in the world.

Che-Ri had said the Najahn might be annoyed if too many people talked about the fiends. That was simplifying it a bit: the Najahn were a tool. An armored, armed, and obedient tool, but they didn't operate on their own. Housed in those spires were the Tenets, the Najahn's guiding hands. Housed there, too, were all the problems this damn world faced.

"As ugly as I remembered them," Svarde said to Kivi as they walked, the ferrite snorting and shuffling. Occasionally taking a bite off the flagstones when nobody was walking past. "So many years and they can't make'em look any nicer."

The spires looked over Noctia and matched it. Gutters marred their smooth shapes, wrapping around like ugly scars. Svarde supposed not even the Tenets could escape the realities of living here, but even so, there were plenty of buildings on the isle who meshed their necessities better with beauty.

Then again, beauty wasn't really the point.

As their walk drew closer—and left behind the poorer districts—Najahn appeared more often with people going about their day. Carrying their voulges and chakram, purple-black armor glinting in the daylight, the imperious bastards walked like they owned the place. Which, of course, they did.

What Svarde could never understand, though, was the deference. Even now, as he and Kivi passed by a Najahn trio, a school group nearby stopped its field trip to run over to the soldiers and pepper them with happy questions. The Najahn answered too, delivering details on how many more years the kids would have to wait before they could join, what a good Najahn needed to know, and so on.

Every answer pushed Svarde's mood into a fouler place, a trend reversed only when he caught a different sound.

Ami's voice had a swinging sword's ring to it, a quick edge that caught the wind and carried her insult right to Svarde's waiting ears.

"I thought you were ugly before, but look at you now?" Ami called, striding forth from the gates at the rising street's end.

The two Najahn guards standing on the arched stone

structure's side turned their helmeted heads to watch Ami's approach, to wonder at the hug she delivered to Svarde.

"Prickly as ever, I see," Svarde said, careful not to get Ami's free-blowing hair in his mouth. "Those soldiers are looking like they've never seen you happy."

Ami pushed back, the two taking a long moment looking at each other. Ami wore her silver-orange armor over the sweeping cloth tunic-and-trousers combo that'd been her go-to as long as Svarde could remember. She otherwise looked clean, cared-for, healthy.

"You really do look like crap," Ami said, frowning. "What have you been doing to yourself?" She glanced down at Kivi. "I thought you were supposed to take care of him?"

Kivi snorted, waddled up to Ami, and rolled over. The ferrite's rose-stone belly invited Ami in for scratches, and she indulged, kneeling as Svarde gave the short version of the past decade.

"I needed to do some soul-searching," Svarde said.

"That's it? For ten years?"

"I built a cabin." Svarde found himself struggling to find words, to find memories or rationales. The days had passed, one after another in a rolling tumble. He'd spent hours, days, months, years hunting, fishing, growing and watching the sea. He hadn't wanted anything, and nothing wanted him. "I don't know what else to say."

Ami stood up, enduring a dissatisfied snort from Kivi, who'd take as many scratches as she could get.

"Say that you're here to help me, then," Ami said. "Like you promised."

"I fulfilled my oath."

"To the barest end. Then you ran."

Svarde looked left, back down over the city to the ocean beyond. Why had he felt compelled to come back here again? Che-Ri had said fiends were already cropping up elsewhere. The news would've traveled without him.

"Now you're thinking about doing it again," Ami continued, folding her arms. "Too bad. I won't let you."

That snapped Svarde's attention. "What?"

"She needs you now, Svarde."

"What am I supposed to do?"

"Be a friend," Ami replied. "Be what you were. Her light's almost out. Give her something before it goes."

Svarde nodded, suppressed a shudder and a sigh. There would be time to unpack Ami's words, what they meant, later.

"I heard the Tenets are meeting?" Svarde asked. "Now?"

"Been at it all morning," Ami replied. "They used to let me in." She grinned, always the picture of a wolf. "Now the best I get is a summary from some drunk page in a bar."

"Can you get me inside?"

Ami glanced back through the arch, "Do you want to play by the rules?"

"That doesn't sound like the Ami I knew."

That Ami showed up quick as they turned back to the gates. Standing straight, walking in long strides, Ami let her confidence do the talking. Neither guard, though both watched, dared question her, nor the man she walked with.

As for Kivi, the ferrite went gawked at and no more.

"Noctia security isn't what it was," Svarde muttered as they passed beneath the arch.

"You get comfortable with power," Ami replied. "They've had it for generations."

"Too long."

Now Ami glanced at him, "Careful what you say here. Not everyone cares who you are."

"Maybe I don't care about them."

"You should if you want their help."

A fact Svarde wasn't done wrestling with. The whole time he'd been in Noctia, its dry strength had been eating at him. Every Najahn, every native to this isle and its purpose projected a haughty invincibility. Civilization ran through these sloping stoneworks and their owners knew it.

If there were any other way . . .

"You carry so much hate for them even after all this time?" Ami asked, drawing Svarde to the right after leaving the arch.

They'd passed beyond the city now, into a broad square with a statue set in its center. Polished silver—rubbed to sparkling early every morning—showcased a woman with both hands near her chest, holding a familiar necklace. Seven circles, each, in this statue, filled in with a gemstone. The woman's eyes were closed, her face tight in fierce concentration. Not at peace, always protecting.

One time, seeing the first Aegis would've pushed adrenaline, honor, pride through Svarde. Bitterness replaced them.

"I'll never stop being surprised that you don't," Svarde said.

"For Catya, I'll do anything. That's the oath."

"One you were freed from as soon as she sat in that chair."

Ami kept her features neutral. That, at least, was new. The firecracker who'd been partial to outbursts, bar fights, and endless button-pushing had found a way to keep herself in check.

"It's my oath," Ami said. "I'll do what I want with it."

Around the courtyard broad streets split off in four directions. One led straight ahead, to the spire cluster. To the left, two headed down the mountain slope, one more severe than the other. Following it, if Svarde remembered correctly, would take you to the Najahn's private docks. The other brought you to the barracks, the servants quarters, the living and breathing heart of this whole enterprise.

The last exit, to the right, climbed the cliff. At its end would be a short tunnel, then a crater, and then someone Svarde would very much like to see.

Or perhaps not. Memories and reality shouldn't always be mixed.

The courtyard bustled in its own way. Not the carefree mingling of raw life from down below—for one, nobody here carried satchels over their shoulders. What was needed would be provided. Worries didn't crease the faces he saw, and most wore light robes, tunics, shirts and pants. The quality denoted the station, with purple-black excellence flowing with high ranked personnel and basic tans and grays cloaking laborers.

Laughter, chatter, cooking stoves. The courtyard itself hummed with daily amenities, the gaps between the streets filled in with controlled cafes, stores, bars. The later lunch crowd.

How many around him were plotting to stab their friends in the back?

If you lived here long enough, maybe you couldn't feel it, but to Svarde the suspicion, the manipulation, the using felt like an insidious song. From the moment he'd first arrived years ago, the subtle layer beneath every conversation tickled Svarde's simpler moral compass in a bad way. Even hearing the passing chatter, the same sensation came back.

Was an ask about how someone felt actually a search for a weakness? The soldier over there wanting more practice time with a pal an admission they weren't good enough?

"Remember you're trying to make friends here," Ami said as they rounded the statue, headed for the spires. "That ugly look isn't going to help you any."

"I don't need friends—"

"Just believers," Ami threw Svarde some severe side-eye. "I know, I know. We Foti are all about facts, but you're going to need more than that here. Noctia's wheels turn on influence and advantage."

"I'm giving them the advantage of survival."

"Not enough."

"Then I'll have Kivi eat one. See if that changes their minds."

Ami laughed. The ice thawed, the sun above softening, ever so slightly, Svarde's mood. They were heading to a circle flush with bureaucrats, spineless manipulators who just needed to get scared. Then they'd do whatever Svarde asked.

Another gated arch waited as the courtyard's shops and eateries petered out. This one wasn't open, was watched by four Najahn more alert than the two back at the entry. Two held their voulges upright, while the others, standing back, kept their chakrams leaned against their calves, ready for a sweeping throw. This bunch too sported dark gold lining along their armor's edges.

Not the grunt troops, then.

"Ami," said the lead, nodding at her, then turning his attention to Svarde. "Who's this?"

"He's a little hairier," Ami replied as Svarde gave the guard a straight look, "but this is Svarde. He's back with a message for the Circle."

"The Guardian?" The lead asked, his squinting eyes

visible outside the helmet's nose guard. On Foti, a helmet like that would mean a face soaked in sweat. Here, Svarde guessed Noctia's chill kept things bearable. "What do you want to say?"

"That's for the Circle," Svarde replied.

Ami rubbed her forehead as the guard's squint narrowed.

"Indeed," the guard drew the word out. "Then, for the moment, consider me the Circle. Convince me as you would them, and I'll let you pass."

"Don't have time for that," Svarde replied. "There's danger coming, and your Circle needs to know about it."

"I'll vouch for him," Ami snuck in.

The guard slipped his eyes back and forth. He needed one more push.

"Let us by," Svarde said, trying to cut back the contempt, replace it with conniving instead, "and you've a good excuse. Two Guardians. Hold us back, and when people start to die, the questions asked will lead to you. Is that what you want?"

The guard took a deep breath, stepped back. "You can go on, but your weapons," he looked down at the creature, "and your beast stay here."

"Kivi goes with me," Svarde countered, easing the argument by slipping the axes off his back. Pulling the crossbow off his waist holster. "She eats metal. Don't think you'll want her gnawing off your pretty armor while I'm gone."

"Deever," Ami added, putting a hand on Svarde's shoulder, "I promise nothing will happen. A chat, that's all."

Deever topped his earlier sigh with a larger one. "I have a family, Ami. If I lose this post, we lose our home. Our food. This isn't a game."

"No, it isn't," Svarde said. "On my life, nothing will go wrong. Kivi will behave herself."

Deever's trust looked like it could've used some more massaging, but the guard gave in and waved them through. Some hidden watcher saw the signal and sent the cross-barred, black-iron gate—a Foti original if Svarde had ever seen one—rolling up. Before the Seven Isles seal in the gate's center vanished, Ami, Svarde, and Kivi were already below and through.

A second courtyard waited, this one statue-less and flush with seven trees instead. Evenly spaced, each plant came from the isle in question, with Noctia's scraggly native in the center. Clear signposts, color-coded, written on, and concluding with the sigil for the direction's destination marked the splits. No coffee, no crowds here. A few hurrying Najahn, nothing more.

And yet, Svarde's nerves tickled. Eyes were on them, would always be now.

The spires dominated, like Vis's massive trees without the canopies. The rainwater channels curled down the stone sides, vanishing beneath the streets to gathering pools far, far below. Every spire held its own color, sported flags with the owning faction writ clear. Shadows passed between windows small and large. More machinations hidden away.

The Circle held its irregular gatherings in the central spire, Noctia's largest and the Tenets' home. The arrogant bastards of Noctia's empire, though Svarde hadn't quite managed to call one that to their face.

Done up in the same purple, black, and gold lining as the upper-tier Najahn, the spire refused to narrow as it rose, staying a thick cylinder throughout. At its very top, the spire flattened out into a bowl. As Svarde understood it, the water collected there went to the Tenet's private barrels to prevent any poisoning.

What kind of power was it when you had to watch what you drank?

No further guards waited for them at the entry, another arch overlaid with the seven circles and faux gemstones. Wood-and-iron doors swung open as the two approached.

"Word still travels fast, I see," Svarde said.

"Too fast, you ask me," Ami replied.

Beyond waited a violet rug, leading them ahead while closed dark wood doors on either side suggested options for better qualified personnel.

Kivi snorted, apparently unimpressed.

"What's her deal?" Ami asked as they kept walking, another double-door set not far ahead marking their destination.

"Not enough metal here," Svarde replied. "Too much wood."

Kivi hadn't liked Vis much either at first, but she'd found enough to like in the mountain's natural elements. Tough to be too angry when you had a literal feast outside your door anytime you wanted a snack.

"I'll introduce you," Ami said as they hit the entry to the Circle's meeting chamber. Two Najahn guards waited outside this one, but they too must've been warned. Neither questioned, or even looked their way. "Once I've cleared the—"

"No," Svarde said, and he pushed open the doors, already striding forward as they swung wide.

Lanterns, lit and bright, marked each of the nine seats around the long table. A table much too large, with several meters between each Tenet. A central area sat a little below, reachable with a single step, and ready to highlight the speaker. Above them, dangling from the ceiling, was a chandelier once again arranged like the Aegis's necklace. And across from the entrance, where Svarde's eyes took him, sat Noctia's presumed ruler.

The Circle fell mostly quiet as Svarde stepped in. A catered lunch told Svarde what they'd been doing, the meal still being chewed by some as Svarde went right into the center. Nice, at least, that he didn't have to displace someone.

Cutting off a speech meant making an enemy, and for all his bluster, Svarde did need these fools to follow his advice.

And fools they all were, they all remained. Svarde took the silence for a chance to survey the room, find he recognized more than half from the last time he was here. Found, too, not a soul surprised to see him.

Ami was right. Word traveled far too fast.

Svarde settled on the Vis Link. The woman, her green and orange robes matching the colors Noctia assigned the jungle isle, returned Svarde's look with a careful study.

"Guardian," came a sticky voice Svarde remembered too well, "welcome back to our isle, though it seems you have forgotten some decorum in your time away."

The Vis Link would come later. Svarde turned towards the speaker, sitting central among the nine. Fassle, the Precept, Noctia's leader and all around schemer, sat with a gooey roll in each hand. The man always had a penchant for sweets, always seemed to be eating something, but remained a musclebound master.

How, Svarde didn't know. Didn't care.

"Decorum is the least of your problems, Precept," Svarde said, but he did perform the ritual swooping swipe across his chest with his right hand, finishing with the palm out flourish in the Precept's direction. His duty here demanded nothing less. "I come with dark words and hopeful asks."

"Then share them," the Precept replied. "You have every Link here, plus myself and our two Accords. You could not ask for a better audience."

"I'll ask for your trust, your belief, and your help," Svarde replied, turning again to the Vis Link. She remained impassive. "Five days ago, on your isle, I encountered a fiend." Svarde let the word linger. Nobody spoke, some continued eating. Not quite the shocked silence he was looking for. Che-Ri had told the truth, then. "A large one. Wounded by the Aegis but still dangerous."

"Slips happen," said Rana's Link, a sniveling man who withered when Svarde turned his way.

"They do, but not like this. If I hadn't found it, the fiend could've killed. Would have killed."

"Then we should thank you?" The Vis Link asked. "Did you come all this way looking for another medal?"

Mockery, condescension, Svarde could take those slaps. Had taken them before. There were more important things, so he gave the Vis Link a slow head shake.

"I come to ask for a chance," Svarde said, "for a change. We know what will happen. The slips will increase. The people will get scared. You'll call for another Renewal and, after too many lives are lost, people will stop pretend—"

"Pretend?" Asked the Precept. "I think you're selling peace and harmony awfully short."

"Peace?" Svarde snorted. "Just today I heard Whent and Rana are still at it. Kance's queens hold knives against each other's throats. Vis and Tamas barely interact with the world. This isn't peace."

"For someone who's been hiding on a mountain, you

make a lot of claims," the Precept said. Now that Fassle had entered the conversation, the other Links, the two Accords on his either side, would stay quiet unless invited. Svarde only had to persuade one man, now. "But I am curious. You put so little faith in the Renewal. What would you do instead?"

Svarde spread his feet, straightened his stance. Not just for appearances, but feeling ready for a fight gave him the courage he needed to say what he'd wanted to say so long ago.

"I want to go into the Dark Below and end the fiends forever," Svarde said, and now, at last, the crunching and chewing stopped. "Give me a force to lead, and I swear we can stop this evil cycle."

Nobody spoke. Nobody seemed to breathe as Svarde's demand hung in the air. Svarde met the Precept's stare, those dark eyes dancing in the lantern light.

And waited.

CHAPTER 13

LONG NIGHT

On its worst day, Wax figured Kitaye had to be one of the prettiest cities in the isles. families strung flowers from their tree houses. Birds and other critters nested freely among the thatched rafters both in the air and on the ground. Foti visitors spoke of smoke and soot, none of which you'd find here: grovetenders took every fire's aftermath and used it to nourish the plants producing Kitaye's life. Everything glowed with nature's kiss.

Today was far from Kitaye's worst. The preparations for the year's graduation ceremony, the stepping up from young adult to a full member of the city's people, were just about complete. With trading ships barred from the main dock, gold and blue flowers lined the long pier jutting into the inlet. At the end, a small stage now stood, torches along either side. Tonight, that stage would hold Sawi, would take her into a life apart from his.

Wax watched the dock from the beach's sandy surf. He held the Foti blade in his right hand, catching the sunlight in its perilous blue-tinted edge.

The bargain had been made in adventure's name. The shrives, a rare-enough mushroom for a real weapon, one that'd let Wax and his friends go deeper into Vis's jungles in search of . . . anything, really. Excitement, wonder, stories. The kind in the songs sung around campfires late into the night, the ones that'd be invoked that very evening as Kitaye's specialists inducted their chosen ones into their ranks.

As of tomorrow, Sawi wouldn't be going on those adventures anymore. At least, not often. If she went where she said, then Sawi's hours would be sucked up. The evenings, a day or two here and there maybe. Until Wax faced his own trip to the stage next year, after which he'd join—

"You're looking grim," Pan said, settling into the sand next to Wax. He dangled his toes in the surf as it washed near. "Haven't made peace with it?"

"The ceremony?"

"No, your ugly mug."

Wax scooped some sand with his off hand and threw it at Pan, who ducked, failed to dodge the clumping grains.

"When Quik went through all I felt was proud, you know?" Wax said. "The whole year he'd been talking it up, saying how he couldn't wait to get out there for a real purpose instead of babysitting us."

"That's what he thought he was doing?" Pan shook his head. "Your brother's suffering delusions. How many times did Bliss almost get eaten? You broke that rib trying to climb a sana, remember?"

"Quik wasn't the best. I get it, though."

"Because he looked a lot like you did a second ago?"

"Just trying to figure it out."

"Figure what out?"

Wax waved the blade, swished it through the light. He couldn't call himself an expert on anything metal, but from hilt to tip, the sword felt balanced. Perfect.

"Life," Wax answered.

Pan whistled, "Sounds deep. Before you get all wrapped up in, uh, life, where's Bliss?"

"She stumbled in early. Like, dawn. She was sleeping still when I came out here."

"Your sister go on many nighttime treks?"

"You'd probably know better than me," Wax said, sliding a sly glance Pan's way.

His friend chuckled, "Nope, hasn't happened, will never happen."

"You saying something about my sister?"

"I'm saying you've been wrapped up in your own head for so long, Wax, it's a miracle you remember we even exist."

An argument there Wax couldn't really deny. Ever since Sawi had been drafted to be a grovetender, the ceremony's approach had been a real thing. He'd been circling his own future or Sawi's to the exclusion of everything else. Wax knew it, kept doing it anyway.

"It's a big deal," Wax protested with all the gumption of a half dead fish.

"And we're not," Pan said.

"That's—" Wax chopped a frustrated laugh to himself. "What's up, Pan? You didn't come over here just to harass me, did you?"

"Sadly, no." Pan twisted, pulled his satchel over and sat it on the sand. "Guess what I did?"

"What?"

Pan opened the satchel, pulled out a faded white cloth. Folding his legs before him to make a place, Pan spread the cloth out. On it, outlined in a fine black too precise for the charcoal-and-dye markers Kitaye had on offer, was a familiar island.

"You traded for a map of Vis?" Wax leaned in. "Why?"

"We had extra shrives. Figured we could use them for something special," Pan said, voice dropping to a whisper just about washed out by the waves. "This isn't any map, Wax. Look at these."

Scattered across the isle were small symbols. Circles, mainly, but with different dots and lines within them. Along the map's right side, those same symbols reappeared sliding down from the top right, each one with an explanation.

"Valuables," Pan agreed when Wax made a whistle of his own. "More shrive spots, but gems too. Silver. This has everything."

"Pan, who's map is this?"

Pan's eyes sparkled, the same sparkle the man found whenever he struck a particularly good deal or had a lead on something rich.

"Some Najahn are here. They're swapping posts, leaving Vis. Apparently one likes shrives enough to trade me this."

"Explains how that little outpost always stays so well stocked," Wax said.

The map marked both Kitaye and the Najahn outpost, a speck sitting near the isle's center. Southeast of Kitaye, closer to Vis's other city on the eastern coast, Mottilan. A few days from here to to the outpost, but worth the hike to save on sailing time.

And who'd want to go to Mottilan anyway? The city nestled into seaside cliffs and served as a farm for Kance. No fun there.

"So you're thinking what?" Wax said.

"After this ceremony's over, I say we get Bliss and us three go find some of this stuff," Pan said. He folded up the map, put it in the satchel and stood. "You have that sword, I've got the knife, but Bliss doesn't have a Foti weapon yet. And I'm thinking we could use new weaves."

"Or a lily," Wax nodded out to the inlet, where the big, curled leaf boats floated on the waves. "Nobody our age has one."

"Yeah, because they don't give them out."

Wax picked up the blade, slid it into his sheath and stood with Pan. "They'll have to, we find that gold."

"See? There's the Wax I remember." Pan whacked Wax with the satchel. "All's not lost, buddy. Who knows, maybe Sawi will be impressed with what we find."

Wax nodded, "She'll be jealous."

S ᴀ ᴡ ɪ ᴡ ᴀ s ᴊ ᴇ ᴀ ʟ ᴏ ᴜ s ᴀ ʟ ʀ ᴇ ᴀ ᴅ ʏ, or so she told Wax when they met up a couple hours later, past lunch.

"They're already laying out my life," Sawi said as they wandered beneath Kitaye's tree house neighborhoods. "Days and weeks and months spent making things grow."

"DIdn't you choose them?" Wax asked.

"I didn't want to lose it all." Her look towards the jungle explained what she meant. "I'm not dying, and neither are you, but it feels like something is."

Going into the conversation, Wax had been planning to empathize, to bemoan their breaking present and a dull future. Seeing Sawi sulk snapped that idea, put Wax where he much preferred to be.

"Hey, we'll figure something out," Wax said. "Pan showed me a map he bought today. It's pretty cool."

"A map?"

"Of Vis. Covered with adventures we can have."

Sawi sighed, "And when are we going to have these adventures?"

"You're telling me you won't be the best grovetender Kitaye's ever seen and have your plants perfect before noon?"

That earned him a laugh.

"Guess I can try," Sawi said. "Racing you to some new treasure does sound fun."

"Losing to me, you mean."

"Losing?" Sawi's eyebrows hit the sky. "Bold words, Wax."

"Am I ever anything but?"

Something in Wax's tone knocked Sawi off kilter. She pulled from their walk, sat next to a big trunked tree. A rare one not sporting a treehouse this deep into Kitaye's borders. Screaming kids ran by, immersed in some running game. Their feet sprayed dirt, leaves, bugs.

"You still hurting?" Sawi asked as Wax sat next to her.

"My ribs, mostly," Wax replied. He rubbed his left side. "Thing was real heavy."

"Scary, too. I thought I was dead for sure."

"So did I. That's why I tried to get it away from you. Figured I was done anyway, might as well give you a chance to run."

Sawi curled a little smile, "Because I was faster than you."

Wax nodded. "Have been for a long time now."

"It's the route, not the speed. You always make it harder on yourself."

"Or more fun."

Sawi rolled her eyes upward, leaned her head against the tree's bark.

"Svarde said there'd be more," Sawi said, "but there haven't been."

"That we know of. Even with the ceremony coming, it's been quieter lately."

"You think?"

"We kept talking about what happened. If the Lira exist at all, I'm sure they're hunting."

"Wish I could've picked them."

"I don't." Wax found Sawi's hand. Matched her questioning eyes close-lipped smile and a head shake. "You'd be the best one, and then you'd always be gone."

The Blooming. The official, obvious, name .

Vis wanted to kick in its newest adults with flair. Wax, next to Pan and wearing their full body paint and weave regalia, stood on the beach. Well back from the dock—as youths, still, they didn't qualify for prime positions—they watched as torches sprang to life. A pink-orange twilight tonight, billowing across a coming storm front marching south. Wax pegged it as a few hours out, time enough to get the official stuff out of the way.

The after-party would get muddy.

Somewhere around three hundred walked the pier this year, Kitaye's youth's becoming adults in a procession overseen by torchlight, scattered flowers, and bright songs. Wax and Pan would walk it next year, follow the same steps as Sawi did when she, circling back down the dock, went to the golden-leaf arch for her new grovetender family.

"Watched this every year and never thought we'd be this close," Wax said to Pan as the remaining walkers dwindled. "You think it'll last forever, you know?"

"Logically, no."

"Tell me why I'm friends with you again?"

"Because I'm really good at finding the good stuff?"

Wax had to give Pan that. Nobody who knew him doubted Pan would be drafted by the Gatherers next year, would get thrown right away into the far flung expeditions for the best, rarest treasures Vis had to offer. The guy must've been born with a second scent, or so the Gatherers called it: a way to tell what secrets lay beneath.

When the last walker left the dock, people standing by the torches threw dyes into the flame, turning the orange flickers to bright blues, greens, pinks, and all the other colors claimed by Kitaye's groups. Songs broke out, one after the next, each group's anthem rising into the deepening night.

Wax would've called himself a cynic, resistant to the idea of getting wrapped up in the pageant of it all, but when thousands upon thousands of your people were rising together, it was hard to resist the call. His voice sang with the rest, a tangled mess of disharmony finding magic through sheer will.

That will carried over into the proper celebration. Fresh ales and wines had been imported from Tamas for the occasion, as they were every year, and the cracking of barrels was both a delight and an honor. Sawi, glittering in her paint and fresh blue-gold flowers, tapped one with a single hammer stroke.

Wax cheered as loud as anyone.

Several cups and hours later, he found himself back at the beach. Sichi, uninterrupted by clouds, gave the dark a good shove, letting Wax dangle his feet in the warm surf. With wine further warming his belly, tomorrow and its new reality felt distant. The fiend in the cave and what it meant equally so.

A cool object tapped his shoulder. Bliss, offering up a mug flush not with wine but cold water. She looked wide awake, ready to go and the opposite of Kitaye's citizens.

"Thanks," Wax said, taking the drink.

'Pan said I'd find you here moping.'

"I'm not moping. It's a beautiful night."

'Not joining Sawi?'

"She's busy with all her new friends."

'So you are moping.'

"Fine, maybe I am." Wax shook off what he could of the wine's haze, gave his sister a closer look. Not only was she dressed for action, her staff rested in its shoulder strap. And were those climbing shoes tied to her thighs, along with a rope around her waist? "What're you doing?"

A grimace, 'Nothing you need to worry about.'

"I thought we agreed a long time ago: no night time adventures alone?"

'Not alone.' Bliss nodded back towards the city. 'Sawi's not the only one with new friends.'

Two years younger than Wax, Bliss's own graduation should've been a far off thing. He shook his head. "What're you talking about?"

'Someday maybe I'll tell you,' Bliss replied.

"Sworn to secrecy?"

'Something like that.'

A wave crashed harder than expected, the water running up to soak Wax's legs. Bliss scampered back, dodging the wet. Dodging, too, the long blue-black line it left behind. At first Wax thought seaweed, some kelp blowing in from beyond the bay and laying its final rest among the sand.

But kelp didn't tend to wriggle. Nor was it usually so long that it disappeared back into the sea.

Wax leaned forward, watched the tendril as it shivered. Bliss tapped his shoulder again, pointing along the beach. Sprawling away from them on either side were more lines, more than a dozen, more than twenty. They flopped and rolled in the muddy churn.

"What?" Wax said, standing up. He reached for the Foti blade, found it missing.

Why bring a weapon to a ceremony?

Bliss whistled. Stuck two fingers in her mouth and blew, a loud cutting noise that sprang above the dried plant drums, flutes, and drunken song. The celebration didn't cease at the noise—few were at the beach, most deep in a drunken revelry—but Wax felt the hairs on his neck stick up anyway.

Another wave crashed in as he and Bliss watched the tentacles, this one bringing more to fill in the gaps with shorter strands. Looking close, the appearance driving away Wax's buzzed haze, he noticed the sea wasn't its usual straight black either.

Red frothed in those waters.

'Look out there.' Bliss pointed again, deeper in the bay.

Splashes. Creatures moving, striking, fighting. Sharks were known across Vis, but the things rarely came into the inlet. With this much blood in the water, though . . .

"What is that?" Wax's turn to point, this time at a bulge rising up well beyond the main dock's end.

At first, it looked like a shrive, the wavy mushroom top rising from the sea in a silver-blue geyser. Water sprayed, and Wax had time to take in the monstrosity for a half second before Bliss pulled him back.

The fiend—no other possibility approached—had a mushroom's top, yes, but an insect's bottom, a molten yellow carapace dotted with long serrated legs disappearing into the water. Those fronds spilled from the top's edges like bad hair, dangling by the hundreds down beneath the waves.

Sharks, fish, and other sea creatures clung to the fiend, tearing, biting, seeking their dinner however they could find it. The fiend certainly bore enough wounds to draw the feasting: several legs looked to be severed already, and a burning cross-hatch coated the fiend's top, ruining its ethereal beauty with brutal wounds.

Bliss tugged Wax, pulling him away in a move Wax started to protest until he noticed what the fiend's rise had brought with it: a huge wave crashed towards them, dark and silent beyond the moon's silver cap.

Behind them, the celebration continued, though as his feet treaded in the sand, as Wax and Bliss ran up the dunes, more whistles and a few shouts began breaking up the music.

Kitaye was under assault, and the whole city had to mobilize.

Those moments from Wax's childhood flashed by again, sitting on the beach protected by adults. Spears, bows and arrows, loud chants and jagged body paints ready for war. A total contrast to now, when Wax had sand in his hands and fear pulsing in his blood.

"C'mon Bliss," Wax said, the sheer act of speaking drawing him back from the wild brink. Just like with Sawi. He had to focus, be the responsible one. "We gotta get farther back!"

Bliss, though, threw Wax past her. If she acknowledged what Wax said, she didn't show it. In a smooth motion, she drew her staff up and over her head, a staff that, Wax noticed in the moonlight, had a healthy new wrapping set. With a hard thrust, Bliss jammed the staff into the sand, digging in her feet as the massive wave hit the beach.

Sand, shells, fish and debris soared in. Wax, on his butt, scrambled what more he could. On his right, the pier, decked out in all its wonder, disappeared. Cracking, snapping, and then screaming rang out into a suddenly silent night.

The wave hit Bliss next, nearly her height and bearing enough speed that she should've gone flying back, should've been lost. The water wrapped around her, came roaring towards Wax and swept him away, the last image Bliss and her staff poking out over the wave, holding tight against its impossible force.

A palm proved a bulwark, catching Wax across the chest and holding him fast in its tangle. Scratches and scrapes announced themselves, while the old bruises from the cave fiend returned like bad memories. Still, Wax could move, could breathe. He coughed, righted himself, and looked to where his sister had been.

Nothing stood there now, and for a white shock moment Wax was sure Bliss had been blown away. The fear died almost as quick when he noticed a quirk in the scene: the giant fiend rose over the bay, bleeding and raging, its fronds and legs lashing out at both nature and newcomers.

If Wax thought night was dark, then the forms covering the beach now were truly black. The moon picked them out in its silver, shadows dashing into the surf to launch missiles, fire bows, or even swim out towards the fiend. The attack was random, haphazard, but, from what Wax could tell, effective.

Arrows, some burning, struck the fiend's glowing mushroom top and sent it sizzling, splashing liquid flame down the monster's sides. Harpoons fashioned from well-sharpened wood made lancing in-roads on the molten carapace, an assault made easier as the fiend continued its slow advance to the shoreline.

"Lira," Wax said, struggling to stand. The legends made real. A secret society, and there, standing in the water with her staff, stood Bliss with them. "That's where you've been going."

Going, and now fighting with. As Wax pulled himself from the palm, he saw his sister make a few swats, knocking away a nearby frond. Not part of the main assault then. Good, let the real Lira—

Whoops, hunting cries rose from his water-logged city. New torches advanced from the neighborhoods as Kitaye responded to the threat. To his right and left parents, adults, warriors and cooks, traders and truffle hunters alike emerged in a frothing song. More bows, more staffs, and, sparkling in the firelight, some real steel.

The Foti blade.

Seeing other traded-for treasures prompted the reminder and Wax broke for his own home. Heading that way meant crossing the fiend's path, but the monster seemed preoccupied, lurching and flailing as the defense intensified.

The tendrils on the beach writhed now, seeking out targets to grab and hurl, people to bash. Yet for every twitching attack there came a counter, a Kitaye brave enough to smash the offender with a hammer or a Lira accurate enough to cut it away with a blade.

The fiend itself loomed as tall as the trees, towering over the beach, but its marred majesty shook now. Its legs bent and cracked, the yellow heart bleeding out into the sea. Wax hit the main avenue leading back to his house, and heard a triumphant whoop, looking back to see new harpoons sticking into the fiend's mushroom top. Ropes trailed from these, and on those ropes clambered Lira, moving faster than Wax could've dreamed.

The killers reached the fiend, leaping on top and drawing their various deaths from pouches, holsters, shoulder straps. They didn't just stab then, no, but carved their way inside.

Something Svarde had said during their return journey sparked up then as Wax hesitated, sensing the Foti blade, even if he found it, would be no use now: *no fiend is an easy kill. You must destroy it utterly, because it doesn't follow the same rules you and I do.*

The fiend didn't take this new attack well. Up till now, the monster hadn't made much noise beyond the smacking, crashing destruction—Wax waded through water, his city's belongings drifting along next to him. Once the Lira hit the fiend's body, a keening howl erupted, less like a jungle cat and more like a buzzing mosquito amplified a million times over. With the sound came a renewed focus, the fronds whipping up from the sea and lashing towards the fiend's head. Some tendrils found hits, whacking Lira off for a long fall into too shallow waves. Others, Bliss among them, swam forward to rescue the victims, bearing them back to shore.

Not that much shore remained untouched by the monster. As it hit the pier's end, the vast legs piled into the ground, drawing the creature up even higher. All of Kitaye joined in the assault, and Wax thought he saw his own brother and parents out there, whacking away at the armored legs like they might a tree needing to be felled.

But what would happen when it did?

That thought turned Wax around again, had him sloshing through the water towards his home. Glances back confirmed the fiend's continued advance, its continued destruction. Waves raged, some knocking Wax into broken stands or tumbling him over into a coughing, spitting morass.

By the time he reached his family's home, scaled the ladder and found his Foti blade—wrapped on the shelf beside his hammock—the whoops from Kitaye's warriors were a constant, fever pitch. Rushing back out to his balcony, Wax caught the fiend teetering forward as its leading leg faltered, breaking apart at its base. With another keening howl, the fiend rolled ahead, surging into Kitaye's main street with its fluorescent blue-and-yellow body.

Trees and their attendant homes cracked and collapsed, shops simply disappeared. Torches lit for celebration sparked and vanished, some starting up newer, brighter fires as the flames found fuel in the fiend's membranes. The Lira followed, their fighters launching themselves up the fallen, flailing fiend to find new vulnerabilities.

Was that Bliss there, near the thing's top, finding some-where to stab her staff?

Wax watched as his family, his friends, his home swarmed the fallen fiend like ants to an animal, covering in it a frantic, no-holds-barred effort to save their city. From the tree house, seemingly safe now, Wax simply watched, slack-jawed.

He'd seen desperation before, seen and fought for his own life in Vis's wilds, but this was something else. This was a battle for existence, not just for one, but for all.

Wax stayed up in the tree house, watching, until long after the fiend stopped its thrashing. Until long after the work shifted from killing to cutting, to rescuing and salvage. Only when the sun started coming up did Wax descend, find a place to squeeze himself in with the city-wide effort.

He'd needed that long to bring himself around, to reconcile why the life he'd thought was his was no longer. Not if something like this could arise, could wreck a city in a single night.

As Wax joined in the slicing, the stacking, the drying and the saving, he heard one word coming from the mouths of those old enough to know, to remember:

Renewal.

CHAPTER 14

A CALL

Debate debate debate. That's what the Precept said and what the Circle did after kicking Svarde out. He and Ami had spent the rest of the afternoon, the evening, the night waiting for a resolution, some sign that anything beyond heads talking would happen.

None came.

Svarde and Kivi crashed in a room next to Ami's, part of several reserved for Noctia visitors important to the Circle. They were rigid, stone, opulent but lacking spirit. A real Kance mattress after so long on his jungle thrush, on the Foti boat's hammocks gave Svarde the worst sleep he'd had in years: too much comfort, not enough pain.

The meals came standard, mixed with enough things Svarde hadn't tasted in too long that his stomach turned him in early. Ami laughed at first, reminding Svarde of his past gluttonous prowess, but that laughter died quick when Svarde had to call things before a second round. Nothing dire from some indigestion, but Ami took it hard anyway.

Perhaps she really was alone here.

Breakfast and a beautiful dawn brought no answers. No messages waiting, no Noctia criers out spreading news from spire to port. Only Ami, meeting Svarde outside his room with some plain bread and water.

"Feel up to making a walk?" She asked.

So long as it led away from the rock box, Svarde figured he could go just about anywhere.

The path she put them on rankled with familiarity. He'd gone up the cliffside path enough times, and it hadn't changed a bit in the decade since he'd last crunched the stones towards the crater's tunnel. Back then he'd curdled with distraught loathing, broken dreams filling his mouth with ash. Now he followed Ami, and Kivi followed them both, with sobriety's dry, cynical measure on his tongue.

Ami spoke the whole way, continuing the stories she'd began the night before. If you wanted to call them that, stories. To Svarde, Ami's time had passed with less pleasure than his years on the Vis cliffside. She'd been reduced to an errand-runner, an emotional support player to the Aegis as Catya stumbled through her slow, inevitable, crucial decline.

"Stop, Ami," Svarde said as they neared the first guard post. "I don't think I can take it anymore."

"Take what?" She sounded genuinely confused.

"Your misery."

"My misery? What—"

"How many fiends did we fight across these isles, Ami?" Svarde asked.

He could've answered the question himself, but he let it hang. Could she remember that far back? She'd been a warrior herself once, the brilliant Flamebreak sword awarded from Foti's highest ranks. Svarde, though, hadn't seen her wear a single weapon in their hours together.

"Too many," Ami replied, her eyes going distant, her pace slowing a step. "They were everywhere then."

"Because the Circle waited too long to call it. We needed real Guardians last time. We needed us, not those glorified escorts they've had before." Svarde hadn't meant to drag the current day back into this, but the tunnel's guard tower sparked the thought. "All but two Renewals died last time without even sniffing Noctia."

"They won't make that mistake again."

"Why?"

"Because we won't let them."

Svarde kicked at the rocks. The little pebbles ate his attack without complaint, scattering off down the hillside. Would that the Circle could take his ask the same way, fly off to do as Svarde required them.

He never desired to be a king until the power proved necessary.

"They don't want to ruin what they have," Svarde said. "They're comfortable in their castles, counting their converts."

"Shouldn't they be?" Ami said, turning full 'round now and stopping the climb. "Ten years at peace is an achievement! A few minor scuffles, but the isles are largely whole, Svarde. Maybe you didn't see it from your hideaway, but things are good here."

"So good they don't need people like us, is that what you're saying?"

Ami glanced off towards the sea, "We're a weapon sheathed now, Svarde. I don't fault them for being reluctant to show steel. Once they make the call, it can't be undone."

"Neither can the lives lost while they sit in their chairs."

"No. No they can't." Ami nodded towards the tower. "Come on. She's best in the mornings."

Through the tunnel and down to the sloping crater. The lelune sat gray and quiet beneath the sun, like a fallow field waiting for its next planting. The crater's teeth rose up around in a vast ring, no spire coming near to topping those angry ridges. The white dome in the center took on an alien appearance, its sharp canopy too perfect for the natural surroundings.

Svarde couldn't muster hate for that, though. He held his frown, his glare for the Najahn standing outside. He hadn't brought his axes or his crossbow and felt naked without them, but the Najahn woman searched him anyway. Her face, the slight bow spoke of reverence, her hands spoke of duty.

At least they protected their prisoner.

"The ferrite waits outside," the Najahn said, and Svarde took Kivi's opinion on the matter.

The rock beast snorted, then went to dig through some of the lelune, burrowing for tastier rocks beneath the surface. Not a problem, then.

"She'll be happy enough," Svarde said, then followed Ami inside.

He'd spent who knew how many nights imagining this moment, but the build up didn't make Svarde's heart quake. His breath didn't vanish, his chest didn't tighten. No swallow, no stumble came as Svarde saw the woman he'd loved since their first meeting on Foti.

Because, he knew, she knew, that love was lost long ago.

Catya sat on the Wound's throne, that stone-wrought chair looking as ugly as it ever had. Purple-black robes with gold filigree framed her withered form, making it seem like

Catya's head descended into a tarry pool running off the chair and onto the ground. Close, as if tempting Catya with a fatal leap, sat the Wound's narrow chasm.

That, at least, hadn't changed.

Two more Najahn waited inside, voulges and chakram ready. Through some unspoken signal, they each attached their gaze to Ami or Svarde. The Guardian's instinct had him calculating the time it'd take for one to rush across the room, voulge ready to make the killing stab.

Could he do it? Could he end Catya's pain before they reached him?

"I'm fine," Catya said, as if reading his mind. Her voice, ever light, came out now as a bare whisper. "You're looking hairy."

The words, joined with a strong smile, threw Svarde off his dismal delusion. Was she fine? Almost certainly not, but Catya didn't seem angry, didn't seem despondent. And Svarde was, indeed, hairy.

"Razors are hard to find on a mountainside," Svarde answered, coming up to the throne and kneeling. He reached out, found Catya's hand. Sensed Ami keeping her distance. "You're as beautiful as ever."

"Really?" Catya glowed. "It's been a long time since anyone told me that. Ami doesn't count."

"She never did."

Catya's smile slipped, "She's as much a part of this as you are, Svarde."

He wanted to protest that, he wanted to deny everything that'd burned by since Catya took the damned mantel, but Svarde found the anger boiling itself off. Catya always had that effect, always could turn him from a lion into a cub.

How'd she found the key to him so fast?

"The Rat's Fang is still there," Svarde said, trying for safer territory.

"Why would it be gone?" Catya replied. "I've been keeping everything safe, remember?"

"I've been trying to forget."

"Don't be that way. We sacrificed too much."

"Some of us are still sacrificing."

Catya closed her eyes, shivered, and the amber token on her necklace flared. A moment's blink, but bright enough to flush the room with honey light. Svarde kept himself still, kept hold of her hand.

"How many?" Svarde asked when Catya's eyes opened again.

"Too often now," Catya said, and if she'd been whispering before, now the words came out as an airy puff. "It's like they know I'm tiring. The power is waning."

"Does it hurt?"

"Every time. Imagine grabbing hold of something on fire and you cannot let it go until its cool." Catya reached up, let her fingers—more bone than skin—touch the necklace. "At first, I had thick gloves, I had water and ice. The hottest fiend would die in an instant. Now I have nothing more than these palms and the pain I can endure."

Svarde said nothing. He took Catya's hand back and held it tighter.

"The worst part?" Catya continued, her look sliding from Svarde to the Wound. "I can't stop them all anymore. Especially the strong ones."

"I know. That's why I'm here."

"When I can't take it anymore, I let go and feel them move on. I don't know where, Svarde. I don't know where they're going or who they're going to hurt but I can't, I can't stop them."

"You shouldn't have to. We're going to convince them to start again. Your job's almost done."

A smile's glimmer, the corner's end tilting up. "I told them months ago, Svarde. The Precept wants me to last. Another year, they say, and I'll get my chance."

Svarde stood up, dropping Catya's hand and shooting a glare at Ami.

"Did you know?" Svarde asked her. "Another year?"

The Najahn guards tightened their grips. Not that Svarde cared. Let them try to take him. Those sloppy spears had weaknesses aplenty, and a chakram wasn't made for tight quarters like these.

Ami nodded, "But I hoped you could convince them otherwise. It's easy to write off fiends if they're weak and half-dead by the time they make the surface. We haven't had a breakthrough here."

"Here?" Svarde threw his arms around. "Here, where you've got armed guards everywhere? I rescued kids, just about. Not a weapon to their names, looking for mushrooms, Ami. They wouldn't have lasted another five minutes."

He'd told the Precept the same thing, watched how the story bounced off Fassle's calculating eyes.

"Svarde," Catya said, and the man dropped back to his knee, "she's doing what she can. We all are. Don't be angry. Not now, not this last time."

"Last time?" Svarde asked. "What's that mean?"

"I'm fading, and it hurts," Catya breathed, "but it hurts more seeing me through your eyes. I want you to remember me as I was, not as I am, not as I will be when this necklace tears my last being away."

· · ·

By the time he and Ami made it down the cliffside to the Rat's Fang—there were other bars, just none Svarde liked as much—the word raced. Vis had been attacked by a gigantic fiend. Kitaye had been damaged, saved only by the fact so many buildings were off ground. The evening crowd buzzed, the ale flowed more freely than before, with Che-Ri even offering a small mug free to everyone stepping in.

"Panic discount," Che-Ri said when Svarde grabbed their first two pints.

The bartender looked like she'd taken a few panic pulls herself, but then, so did everyone. Fiends and their propensity for random death had that effect on people.

As dusk drew closer, the Rat's Fang took on a different aura. The bright inside added color, Che-Ri and her staff changing out the glass on the lanterns for purple and blue shaded panes. Dark but not cozy, ideal for the deal-making that kept the bar afloat.

Ideal, too, for a Guardian pair that might've found themselves mobbed by the fearful out in the open.

"What I don't understand," said Svarde, rubbing his whiskers, "is how we even know. Last night? Back when, we'd only hear of a major attack after days went by."

"Noctia's everywhere now," Ami replied. She hadn't touched her pint yet, seemed to be half lost in her own mind as she looked around the place. "The Tenets cooked up something with the ravens, as I understand it."

"Ravens?"

"The birds."

"I know the birds. They can talk?"

Ami blinked free from her haze to squint at Svarde. "Talk? You lost a lot on that mountainside, didn't you?"

Svarde did feel a little dumb when Ami explained the process. The little notes tied to legs, the clear paths the black birds were trained on. Not for the first time, Svarde wished the world would've just stayed static while he had his little sabbatical.

"They're going to call it," Ami said, finally digging into her drink. Svarde noticed the beverage came only after he'd ordered fried fish, its salty sea taste drying the throat. "I bet we'll know tomorrow morning."

The Renewal was the easiest bet in the world to make right now. Noctia might've been hesitant when it was little buggers scaring a few kids, offing a couple loners. Take out a city like Kitaye and suddenly the precious economy's threatened. Now they had to act.

Problem was, they'd be doing the wrong thing.

"It's all a delay," Svarde said.

Ami blinked, "What's a delay? The Renewal?"

"Yeah."

"Of course it is. We buy time for the world with a single life. That's literally the point." Ami again gave Svarde the quizzical look. "Did you sneak something stronger while I wasn't looking?"

"It's not working though."

"I think it's working too well."

"No," Svarde put up his hands, shook his head. "I mean the Renewals. Catya's lasted what, ten years? The one before her went twelve. One before that, how many?"

"Thirteen."

"So what happens when it's five years? Or every six months?" Svarde rotated, swept an arm out to the crowded bar. "Who's going to be doing anything when fiends are everywhere, all the time?"

Ami sighed, "Bet the Precept's hoping he's long dead by then."

"We won't be."

"Is there a point to this rant, Svarde?"

The man planted his elbows back on their little table, leaning over the fish like it was some treasure to be protected. His eyes sparked, the muscles in his throat tightened as a flush, well-hidden by the bar's lighting, ran up and down his face.

One of many reasons why Svarde couldn't play cards, or anything else that required a bluff.

"We need to strike at the source, Ami," Svarde said. "All this, it's a crap game. We're going to lose eventually."

"It's been tried," Ami said.

"Bullshit it's been tried. Not by anyone serious. Not in a hundred years."

There were old poems, old stories about adventurers who'd gone into the deepest caves, who'd descended into the Wound. Invariably the stories described them as great heroes, invariably they always vanished, never to be seen again.

"Not true," Ami spoke quieter this time, her eyes on her mug.

"Say what you're thinking."

"You ran away. Catya put on the necklace and as soon as you saw what it meant, you left. I stayed." Ami put her right hand flat on the table, where Svarde could see the rings on each finger. Each earned on Whent, each for an honorable win. "You know what it does to someone like me, who'd tossed every opponent I'd met, to watch my best friend die minute by minute, day by day?"

"I do," Svarde said, "which is why I couldn't stay. I couldn't watch her. Not Catya."

"You ran. I tried to find a way out."

"What do you mean?"

"There's no answers, Svarde. When I asked the Circle,

they said they'd sent people down. Explorers. Fighters. Everyone disappeared, and now nobody wanted to try it anymore." Ami finished her pint, waved for a second. "So I went to the scientists next. The doctors and their needles. Everyone had theories, nobody had solutions. Guess how many wanted to try something on the Aegis, knowing what failure meant?"

Kivi, curled up around their feet, snorted along with Svarde at that idea.

"So I stayed," Ami said, "and I told myself I was going to make it as easy, as painless as I could for her, because that was the oath I swore."

"We swore to protect her, Ami. Not to watch her die."

"Is that what you did then?"

Che-Ri set Ami's second pint down. Ami flipped her a lelune flower, plucked that day—and expressly against Noctia law—from the crater. Che-Ri whistled, tucked the fragile pink blossom away.

"I didn't," Svarde said. "No denying that. But I'm here now. Ready to make things right."

Ami laughed, downed her second pint in a three second swallow. A sign, among others, of how she'd spent the long years on the island. Before Svarde could say anything else, Ami pushed back her chair, stood.

"Know what, Svarde?" Ami said. "It's been nice to see you. Glad you're here to fix things. Good luck."

Before Svarde could sputter out an apology, Ami strode out the door, into the night, and away.

By the time he made it back to his room beneath the spires, by the time he'd knocked on Ami's door and received nothing in reply, the smoke signals were lit. Golden purple billows, spawned by massive bonfires ringing Noctia's entire island.

They'd be visible from anywhere in the Seven Isles, and they meant one thing.

Renewal.

The next morning Svarde barged into the Circle's conference without Ami's help. Kivi came too, the ferrite hustling past scrambling Najahn guards to escort her friend into the chamber. The conversation washed as Svarde came in, various isles in shouting matches over how much Noctia resources they deserved to deal with likely fiend incursions.

Fassle just rolled his eyes at Svarde, holding up a single finger his way as the Guardian stomped his way into the room's lowered center.

Three coffee mugs deep and Svarde had himself a roiling confidence. He almost ignored Fassle and blurted out what he'd come to say, but the last shreds of his self-restraint, perhaps coming from Ami's disdain the night before, kept Svarde's mouth shut while Vis and Rana snapped at each other.

At least, they did until Fassle slapped his hand on the table. The wood lacked ringing metal's grandeur, but Svarde could admit the solid thunk served nonetheless.

"My friends," the Precept announced, "it seems our esteemed Guardian has returned to, I can only assume, thank us for starting the very thing he came here yesterday to suggest?"

Eyes shifted his way, not a one of them sympathetic. Even Foti gave Svarde a crystalline stare, as if he was a child who'd gone far out of bounds.

Well, he was here, and they'd listen to him talk again.

"Not quite, Precept," Svarde said, again facing the main man and the two Accords sitting next to him. "The Renewal is one option, yes, but I want to try a more permanent solution."

The Circle waited, watched, listened as Svarde poured through his recommendation: a team, skilled and led by himself, to go into the Dark Below and confront the fiends and their source. End them there in the deep and prevent any more from ever coming up again.

"No more Renewals, no more monsters surprising our families and friends," Svarde whipped up into his conclusion. "You claim to want peace, Precept? This is how you can have it. Forever."

Silence. A still weight. Tamas scratched his nose, while Kance looked up at the ceiling. Then the Precept sighed and Svarde knew he'd lost.

"Either you do not know the facts," Fassle said, "or you do and are disregarding them. Everyone who goes into the Dark Below dies there, Guardian. This has been tried before, and I will not sanction lives to be lost." The Precept frowned. "You, of course, are free to do what you will. If you can find your crew, you may go and throw your lives away how you wish. But you will not do it on my isle, and not with my encouragement.

"We all know the Renewal has its faults, but it is the one thing we know that stops the fiends. The one thing we know—"

"It's a death sentence to anyone that survives," Svarde said, knowing damn well interrupting the Precept wasn't done. "All you're doing is dooming another kid, all because you won't try anything else."

Fassle pushed back his chair, stood. The Precept was taller than Svarde expected, meeting the warrior at his eye level.

"Do not presume to know what we are doing,

Guardian," Fassle said. "What happens here is not for you to know, and I will not be judged by ignorance. I said you are free to pursue your dream. Now leave while you still have your head."

If Kivi hadn't smacked her noggin into Svarde's shins, the Guardian might've come back at Fassle. Instead, Svarde growled, turned, and stalked from the Circle.

The worst part? Before he'd even left, the isles were at it again, bartering for supplies and soldiers. Pawns in a losing war.

Angry muttering made for a good companion down Noctia's urbanized mountainside. At least it kept every person he passed a good ways away from him. Kivi toddled along, taking surreptitious bites from cobblestones when nobody looked.

Where did Svarde want to go, what did he want to do? He wasn't sure, so he walked, cursed the Precept and the gutless Circle. Swore off Ami too, the coward.

So what if others had tried to go down in the dark before? Those 'others' didn't have their talents. Svarde could do something different, could wind up with a result that rescued the entire world. Wouldn't even trying that be better than damning some poor kid to an early, painful death?

Wouldn't that've been better for Catya?

"Take it easy, honey," Che-Ri said, snapping Svarde from the fogged world he'd been sunk inside. "Your satchel's getting light and your lids are getting heavy. Have some water."

The morning had somehow turned to the afternoon. Kivi snored around his feet, and Svarde's satchel, once flush with Vis root vegetables and other dealable delicacies from that isle, did indeed feel soft against his shoulders. If he wanted to keep drowning his day, Svarde would have to ask Che-Ri for a shift behind the counter.

But the bartender hadn't been away for more than a couple minutes before a new soul took the seat next to Svarde. Unlike his battered, old cloak and weathered Foti clothes, she sparkled in the salty teal-and-emerald common to Rana.

The river isle had its reputation, earned time and again with its changing moods. Its sailors tended to be second to none, but treated everyone else like they were second to themselves. Not so much a disrespect as an ambivalence, as if the rest of the world were toys to be played with, pillaged, or traded for better things.

So when this woman put her hand to her chin and looked at Svarde like she might a market item, Svarde gave her the go-away growl.

"Feisty, are we?" The woman replied. She shifted her shoulder, letting Svarde see the twin emerald streams running across her sapphire breastplate—why Rana insisted on wearing full uniforms to bars mystified the isles. Those green lines meant she'd earned a ship of her own, made Svarde a mite more curious. "That's good. I hate seeing Guardians lose their edge."

"You know me."

"Everyone in this bar knows you now. Since your second pint you've been wailing about the Circle loud enough for everyone to hear."

"They deserve a good bashing."

"Undoubtedly," the woman held up two fingers towards Che-Ri. The bartender came over, frowned towards Svarde. "If he wants to drink, let him drink."

"Svarde?" Che-Ri asked.

The Guardian pulled up his water mug, drained it, spilling plenty on the floor. Kivi startled up, snorted in steamy frustration. Svarde ignored her, set the empty mug back on the counter.

"Fill her up, if she's buying," Svarde said.

The Rana captain reached into her satchel, drew out a glimmering gold bead. "This ought to cover our rounds for the evening?"

Che-Ri took the bead, still frowning, and looked at it close. Sighed after a moment, then glared at the Rana captain.

"He gets drunk enough to throw a tantrum, you're cleaning up after him."

"Of course."

Mugs refilled, Svarde pushed through the boozy haze to focus on his benefactor.

"What're you wanting with me, then?" Svarde asked.

"I'm wanting what you're wanting," the Rana captain said. "Something different."

"You want to go down below."

She nodded, "Not easy to find others who want to do the same, but I've been building a crew for a couple years now. They're willing, but the odds weren't good enough."

"The odds? What're you—"

"We're not getting through the Wound. The Najahn won't let us," the captain said. "I've tried before. Was going to try again this week." She spun her mug, not drinking from it, on the counter. "With all the fiend attacks cropping up, I'd hoped they were more receptive. But you showed that was a mistake."

Svarde stared, drank, waited.

"Whent's the next best option. It's not far north, and its

caves are deeper than anywhere else. We want to give this a real shot, we start there." The captain gripped around her mug's handle, her face getting tighter. Something pushed this one. "Which is why I need you."

"What do I have to do with Whent? I'm no rockbiter."

"You're a Guardian. The Guardian, as far as I'm concerned. With you on my ship, there's a chance we can make it there. A chance they'll let us dock."

Svarde blinked. Maybe it was the ale, but he couldn't remember any special privileges a guardian had for getting around one isle to the next, least not one without a Renewal in their charge.

"You really have been gone a long time," the captain said, the intensity dying away to something softer, more curious. "The world's not as you left it, Svarde. Things are restless."

Ah. Svarde could read that code. Rana had more besides its vanitygoing against it.

"Your raiding them again, aren't you?" Svarde asked.

The captain shrugged, "They're easy targets. But it does make docking on Whent a trickier proposition."

"That won't change with me aboard."

"I think it will," the captain replied, "and if it doesn't, I think you're willing to do what it takes."

Svarde swallowed the words with a fresh gulp. The ale, spicy and bitter, melded with the Rat's Fang in a warm cloak. In a different life, he could've been content here. Taken on a celebrity role like Ami's, had his mugs and his meals in that stone spire until Catya withered to nothing at all.

"Say that I'm willing," Svarde muttered into his drink. "When would we sail?"

"Tomorrow. Dawn."

Svarde nodded. "Then I think I've got some packing to do. What's your ship?"

"The Tsuro. Ask for Maena," the captain said. "Glad you're willing to save the world, Svarde."

"Already did it once," Svarde said. "Might as well do it again."

CHAPTER 15

ON THE VINE

Bliss picked at the poultice wrapped around her right thigh. Beneath it, the pocked lash delivered by the fiend's whipping fronds seemed to be healing, though its burning aches poked through from time to time. A reminder, so one of the Lira said, that she still had more to learn.

Several dozen people were floating from the bay in folded leaf coffins when Noctia's call was made official. Everyone had seen the smoke, the lights the night before while cleaning up the wreckage, while chopping up the fiend's monstrous body, but nobody in Kitaye had the authority make the declaration.

It took an imperious man unfolding a scroll, standing in his purple-black armor under the hot sun, water up to his ankles in the sludge that'd once been Kitaye's main square, to make the Renewal begin.

Even so, the city had bigger problems. Bliss had bigger problems. While most homes were unscathed, except the absolute closest ones to the beach where wayward monster parts demolished thatched roofs and bamboo walls, the same could not be said of shops and trading stalls. The docks were battered and broken, the bay itself blocked by the fiend's sheer size.

So Kitaye mobilized, with neighborhood leaders organizing shifts. Bliss herself rode the adrenaline through the night right into the reparation fray, stopping only when the Lira pointed out her wounded leg.

She'd been stunned at her own blood. In the moment, that night, everything had been instinct. The Lira training ran her muscles like Bliss had lost her mind: jamming the staff into the sand to hold her ground, slimming her profile while digging in her feet to hold fast while the wave crashed around her. Rushing forward in the aftermath, beating aside the tentacles with whack after whack, reacting to whistled commands to protect archers, javeliners, and the climbers.

And at last to scale a rope herself, scampering up over the bloody waters to have at the fiend's soft fluroescent top. Bliss couldn't now pick out individual moments: the battle felt like a smear over her mind, indistinct and wondrous.

The Lira fought as one, and when all Kitaye joined in, Bliss wasn't just herself.

This, now, was a plainer version of the same thing. A moonlit flower glimpsed on a cloudy day instead. She sifted through mud and dirt, finding clothes, tools, treasures and stacking them on makeshift wood barges. The floating cargo would be sent to the city's center, where searching owners could see what wasn't lost.

As for the fiend's body, its pieces would be cast out to sea. Food for things willing to eat the horror. Sharks and scavenging fish still swarmed the bay, frenzied with the blood, and Lira stood by with staffs to beat any encroachers back from the swamped land. All in all, the city had spun not to a halt, but to a different sort of life.

By noon, though, the Renewal declaration found its hold. Those who could put their clean-ups on pause did so, following a conch horn blast to assemble near the city's southern, jungle border. There, at least, things were dry.

And with her poultice finally free from the wet, Bliss's scratches itched.

"Pay attention," Pan said, standing next to her. "You might fit this time."

Bliss threw Pan a skeptical look, but the man had his eyes locked forward. As ever, Pan's satchel looked loaded up. Whether he'd actually gone gathering or snagged some floating debris for his own, Bliss couldn't tell. Either way, he seemed fresh. No nighttime work for him.

Wax stood to Pan's left, similarly enthralled by the Najahn soldier once again preparing to speak to the crowd. This time, the sweating man had two more soldiers on his flank, each one with their curved spears and big, edged discs on their back.

She nudged Pan, 'Why are they armed?'

"Because fiends could come at any time," Pan whispered back. "Vis is always the first isle to get hit."

'Why?'

Pan shrugged. "Don't know. It just is. That's what my parents said anyway."

Another hornblow from the conch and the assembly quieted. Bliss ran a look around and guessed several thousand stood in the clearing. A good chunk, but not as many as she would've expected for something like this.

The why came quick.

"The Precept has declared a Renewal," the Najahn captain announced, digging his voice into every word.

"Each isle may nominate a single candidate for this honor, and that candidate shall journey to all seven of the isles to earn their skars. The first candidate to complete this task and return to Noctia shall be honored as the next Aegis, dedicated to protecting the world from the Dark Below." The Najahn took a long breath. Bliss scratched at her poultice again. "Because the Renewal is trying and the Aegis demands youth, only those between eighteen and twenty-two years may attempt the journey."

Words, angry and confused, erupted among the crowd and the Najahn let them speak. Bliss, at seventeen, glanced over at Pan, who was muttering something with Wax.

"They're getting younger every time," Pan was saying. "Last Renewal they wanted someone up to twenty-five."

"This one was so short," Wax replied. "Killing them faster, so they need'em younger?"

"Maybe," Pan said.

'Then why not go younger still?' Bliss signed, butting herself into the conversation. 'I'm strong enough to try.'

"You can ask him," Wax said. "Bet he won't tell you anything though. All the Najahn like their secrets."

'Are you two going to try for it?'

Wax and Pan glanced at each other. The pair had zero subtlety, and Bliss figured they hadn't considered it till right that moment.

"Why?" Pan asked finally. "It's dangerous."

Wax didn't seem so quick to jump on Pan's bandwagon. Instead he shrugged, nodded back towards the Najahn.

"Looks like old ironhead is getting ready to talk again."

The Najahn did have another speech prepared, this one longer and windier than the first. Any Renewal candidate could have Guardians, however many they chose, and their entourage would have protection across all the isles. That said, danger would be present, as no skar could be earned without trial.

"And fiends have a way of finding Renewals," Pan said. "Most of the candidates die."

"Where do you get this stuff?" Wax whispered the question.

"Guardian in the family, remember?"

The Najahn wound up to a conclusion, raising a hand and getting another horn blast to calm down the crowd.

"At the next horn, at precisely this hour," the Najahn pulled out a small sundial, held it before him, "the Vis contest will begin. The first candidate to scale the Great Sana and take the skar will be declared Vis's Renewal. I wish all of you luck, and may Noctia's strength be with you."

The Najahn watched the sundial for a long minute as the crowd looked at each other, weighing who might go. Most looked sick to their stomachs at the idea, scared or exhausted.

Then the horn blew and a heavy hand landed on Pan's shoulder. As the crowd began to scatter, Pan, Wax, and Bliss turned back to see Pan's father, a cane-wielding brawn of a man, holding his son fast.

"You'll go," the man said, and with his free hand, he held out a second satchel.

Inside its opening, Bliss saw wrapped food, water skins. Pan's climbing shoes hung from hooks on the satchel's sides.

Pan gulped, "What?"

"Your grandfather was a guardian," Pan's father said. "I tried at the last Renewal. You will try for this one."

"But—"

"When the isles ask for help, our family will not ignore

the call. Take this and go." The man held out the satchel. Pan took it. His father kept his hand out, and Pan stared, confused. "Your other bag, Pan. You won't need it now."

Looking as stunned, as faltering as Bliss had ever seen him—and with Pan, that really was saying something—the young man slipped his own satchel off and handed it to his father.

"Leave now," Pan's father said. "It's a long road to the Great Sana." The man's eyes flashed, glanced at both Wax and Bliss. A tiny grin fluttered at his lips. "But you don't need to travel it alone. A Renewal needs his Guardians."

Wax walked with Pan on the jungle road, Bliss padding alongside, till Pan's father vanished behind the trees, the crowd, the city. As if pulled by some hidden signal, the three left the dirt and slipped to the side, sitting amid some ferns. Behind them, a few people their age, people Wax knew, made their way down the path. Some had full satchels, others less so, and their moods ran a spectrum.

Some looked like they were going along for a while, maybe a day. They had an adventurer's vibe, but lacked the equipment. No ropes on their waists, no staffs or other weapons over their backs. Wax knew them, knew the types who talked up their game without ever really playing.

The others, a smaller group, seemed to have taken the Najahn's words as gospel. They strode with heads held high, with satchels stuffed. Pouches brimming with water stuck to their legs. They marched, a few already unspooling ropes and looking for an opportunity to get airborne.

The air hummed with energy and purpose, something Wax drank up after the useless despair following the fiend's arrival.

Pan, though, didn't seem to feel it.

"If you don't want to go," Wax said, "then you don't have to go."

"You heard my father," Pan sighed, adjusted the satchel. "Not like I have a choice."

'Hide out for a couple days,' Bliss signed. 'Go get mushrooms or something. Come back and say you tried but it didn't work out.'

Pan gave her a wobbly smile, "He'll smell that lie." He squared himself up. "Besides, it might be fun. At least for a little while, and it means I won't have to clean the house."

Pan looked at them. "I know Sawi can't come, but would you two?"

Bliss had her head shaking, 'I can't. At least, not without getting permission.'

"From the Lira?" Wax guessed.

'That obvious?'

Pan looked confused, so Wax filled him in, "I didn't guess until you pulled that move on the beach. Explained all those nights you've been out."

"She's in the Lira?" Pan asked. "How?"

'Skills.'

Wax laughed, put up his hands when Bliss shot him a glare. "Sorry, you deserve it as much as anyone." He looked at Pan. "You're asking me to be your Guardian?"

"Can't really be a Guardian unless I'm a Renewal," Pan said, "and that won't be happening. But sure, call it what you want."

'Mom and Dad won't be happy,' Bliss signed. 'There's so much cleaning up left.'

"Quik's all over it, I'm sure." Wax gave Pan a pat on the shoulder. "Let me run home and grab my stuff. Then we're off."

Pan didn't object and Bliss didn't have any other good reasons for Wax to stay home, so Wax took to sloshing towards his satchel, the Foti blade, and adventure.

Wax couldn't keep up the happy jaunt through the waterlogged streets, the disaster pushing the Najahn's promise of adventure off his mind.

He hadn't seen Sawi save for a glimpse after the celebration. She'd lived, was being tasked with salvaging the gardens and their vital crops. That'd envelope her for days, weeks, maybe longer. Kitaye as a whole draped responsibility over everyone else too: no wide-ranging expeditions. Stay close, travel in groups. Be scared and be safe.

Being holed up in a treehouse or re-thatching broken rooftops wasn't the life Wax had signed up for. No way.

Not when he had his new Foti blade.

Waiting for him, ankles crossed and leaning against their treehouse trunk, was Sawi.

She wore her rank without a care, the auburn lining around her inked arms and legs showing Sawi's new role. Three vertical lines on her left cheek, each one topping in a four-frond fern put Sawi's specific place into perspective: a gatherer, yes, but one made for the wilds.

"Been a while, stranger," Sawi said as Wax walked up, his bare feet squelching through the still-muddy ground.

"Not by choice," Wax said, and when Sawi met his eyes, he threw away the moment's awkwardness and went for a tight hug.

Wax felt Sawi's tense shoulders, her taut arms tighten, then relax. Their weaves pressed together, the stress, the fear, the relief from the last few days draining out.

They'd been apart from each other before, of course, but

never with the possibility one might never come back. Wax, cheek to cheek with her as he looked out at innumerable trees, buildings in repair, and passing people towards the sea, tried to find the past.

Sawi let it drift away, breaking the embrace and returning to the tree trunk, as if its solid bulk buttressed what she was about to say.

"I'm leaving," Sawi spoke, folding her arms and turning towards the jungle. "All the water ruined too much food. We're going out to the smaller towns with what we can trade."

Wax flickered a corner smile, "Me too."

"You too?"

"You heard about the Renewal?"

They both looked north, though Noctia and its smoke couldn't be seen. Then Sawi laughed.

"You're going to try for it?" Sawi asked. "You, the guy who galavants around the jungle on your own adventures? You're going to sign up for that?"

"One, hey. And two, it's not that simple," Wax dove into a snappy recap of the morning's speech and Pan's press-ganging into the race. "We're not going to make it there anyway. It's a play to satisfy Pan's family. That's all."

Now Sawi's smile took on a genuine flavor, her eyes doing the matching work.

"That's more like it. Though I'm not sure I'd trust you to keep Pan out of trouble."

"It's a quick run with a crowd. We'll be back within a week, and that'll be it." Wax nodded up towards the house. "If anything gets scary, I've got my new sword."

"You know how to use that thing?"

"Stick'em with the pointy end."

Sawi giggled, "Sounds like you're ready, then."

"Are you?"

The smile faded, "It's like joining a new family, Wax. I have to dive in and make friends." Sawi stepped off the tree. "Speaking of, we're meeting up soon. Just wanted to, you know, say goodbye."

"Goodbye for now, Sawi. Just for now. When we get back, we'll see who had the better adventure."

"Always a contest with you, Wax," Sawi shook her head.

"Gotta keep things interesting."

WAX FOUND Pan near where he'd left him, the mushroom forager having upped his traveling game with extra weaves, climbing shoes, and his rope. Wax, his own satchel stuffed likewise, handed his bag to Pan and took his friend's in return. Both went through the pre-adventure prep check, a vital step before gracing Vis's jungles, to ensure neither had forgotten anything important.

"You're getting better at this," Wax said when they'd finished, neither missing an item. "Remember when Bliss and I would bring extras for you?"

"Hard to forget when you remind me every time we go anywhere."

The path leading south from Kitaye split like a leaf's vein, spreading into haphazard directions towards smaller settlements, known natural wonders, and, the widest, towards Vis's eastern coast and the other city waiting there. In between the two, nestled against the Great Sana—sat Noctia's home on the isle. Wax hadn't ever been there, because who'd want to go on an adventure where people already lived?

But he'd heard plenty from traders, how the Noctia, and

more specifically, the Najahn forces running the place had a distinct lack of appreciation for Vis's unique traits.

"And they never try swinging," Wax said as he and Pan walked off, following the padded dirt and leaves to the south. "They just hide behind their wall and wait for their time to be up."

"Sounds peaceful," Pan replied. "Unlike all this."

The path wasn't crowded, but Kitaye had enough Renewal hopefuls to make the jungle walk hum. Birdsong, the wind through the leaves, both smothered beneath conversation between pairs, trios, and larger groups. Every so often someone would swing by to their left or right, whooping as they went. The look, the feel was of a people burying trauma with excitement, adventure, hope.

Or, at least, distraction.

"We never talked about it," Pan said as the pair walked beneath the canopy, brushing aside the occasional dangling vine. "I used to ask my dad what it was like, living through a Renewal and he'd tell me I'd learn myself. I didn't think about what that meant until now."

"The fiends?"

"All this," Pan said, waving his arms at the path, the generally young pairs and trios walking ahead. "It's like our lives are just stopping."

"Because you're not going to gather more mushrooms?"

Pan flashed a dagger eye Wax's way, "You think that's all I'm about? Finding fungi?"

"All you've been about lately," Wax flicked a nod up towards the thick branches above. "Remember when we used to go swinging? We'd be jumping for hours."

"Yeah, then you found Sawi and 'we' stopped being a thing."

"No way you're pulling that again, are you?"

Pan didn't answer, kept his look forward, the walk steady. Wax measured their pace, a gentle one that'd get them to some tiny town by nightfall. A place he'd never stayed, didn't even remember the name of, but one that'd be overwhelmed by Renewal hopefuls. They'd be lucky to find a good bunch of leaves to sleep on.

"I'm good at it," Pan said into the vacuum.

"Good at what?"

"Finding fungi. And the other plants." Pan stood straighter, shifted his satchels to rest square on his shoulders. "The gatherers are going to snap me up next year."

"Probably."

"But that's not all I am."

"Oh yeah?"

Pan threw out the frown, replaced it with a wicked grin. His hand dropped to his rope. "What if we win?"

Wax snorted, "We're a ways behind, buddy."

"You're the best tree-jumper in town, Wax. Save maybe Sawi. I'll follow, you lead. We'll catch up."

Wax found his own hand heading towards his rope, as it always did when the notion of jumping through the jungle air came up. He felt his heart race, and his eyes scanned the woods around them, trying to find a good starting point.

"If we get going, we can skip the first stop," Wax said. "Get ourselves a proper bed." He angled an eyebrow at Pan. "Why'd you care so much all of a sudden?"

"Just find a us a start, Wax. My feet are tired of walking."

The tree came a few minutes ahead, one laced over in leafy vines. Thick branches so covered as to make their bark invisible. Heavy strands made easy handholds, Wax leading the way while Pan followed. Kitaye's usual tree-jumpers dwindled as the pair left the city behind, leaving their only spectators other Renewal candidates and the usual traders crossing Vis. Those eyes and mouths tossed up questions, a jeer or two, at the climbing duo, and Wax answered the only way he liked:

With a good performance.

"Stick close," Wax told Pan as they reached a branch about halfway to the canopy. Pan kept himself on the trunk while Wax made the walk out. "We're going for speed here. Straight south-east. No looking for mushrooms."

"Thanks for the reminder."

"I'm your Guardian, remember?"

"You're nothing unless I get the skar," Pan said.

And what would Pan do then? Wax almost laughed as he gauged the fall, the canopy danglers ripe for a swing.

Would Pan actually leave Vis? Would Wax go with him?

Questions to answer later. For now, a curling, yellow-flowered strand as thick as Wax's arm lay a good leap ahead. Climbing shoes on, their spiked treads digging into the branch, Wax took a long breath.

"Ready?" He asked.

"After you."

Three strides, each step placed right in front of the last. Bend the left knee, feel the branch's tip sink with his weight, and spring.

The forest floor sprawled beneath him, the pathway to the right, dense nature to his left, and free-flying air before him. Wax's hands reached, followed his eyes, and closed around the strand.

His whoop echoed, and Wax flew.

CHAPTER 16
A WALK AND A TALK

Bliss traded one brother for another. With her staff on her back, satchel stocked for travel, and fresh ink shading in the thorns on her shoulders, Bliss walked into the soaked grove on Kitaye's southwest side. Go back a few days and the flower-ringed circle could've sat several hundred on carved stools and benches. Now most stood, chatted, waited, and watched, the seating cleared to make more room.

Quik waved Bliss over as soon as she pressed through the hanging fronds covering the entry, less a doorway and more a gap between tight, thin trees. Her brother had his own satchel loaded, his gauntlets hanging from the rope around his waist. His extreme lack of surprise at seeing Bliss showed her ill-kept secret was fully blown.

"They couldn't have found a better recruit," Quik offered with a nod as Bliss wound her way to his side. "Not that I like my sister getting into the fight."

'Better at it than you are.'

"When that stick of yours breaks, we'll see who's better."

Bliss had her hands moving in a comeback when a sharp whistle killed the conversation, killed all the conversations. A taller woman, decked out in a feathered weave and glistening in the Hunter's white-orange ink, made the sound. She stood near the doorway, a bow over one shoulder and Foti knives sliding across her front in a brace. She planted a menacing spear, red feathers splaying beneath its head, in the moss at her feet.

"Deshiva," Quik whispered. "Can't believe she's with us."

The woman confirmed Quik's identification with a swift introduction. She slashed with her words, explaining how Kitaye's hunters were going out in separate groups to confirm outlying villages knew about the fiend, the Renewal, the hard times coming.

"The ones that need it, we'll fortify. The ones that don't, we'll ensure a clear path leads from here to there," Deshiva said, her eyes walking the room. "This is no joke, no pleasure stroll through the jungle. We all saw what that thing did to our city. Where we're going today, they don't have Lira to protect them. They don't have us. But we need them too."

Deshiva didn't have to explain that part. Kitaye's overflowing food stores, its appeal as a trading port, all came from the raw goods making their crawling way to the city from the smaller towns. Bliss's parents made sure she understood, seeing as they kept thinking she'd be the one to run their trading post someday.

A flawed assumption, that, but Bliss let them keep on living with it. That'd be a fight to have another time.

The group in the grove had a target, a town straight west, near some cliffs and some of the only mines on Vis. Though the sun meant the day neared lunch, Deshiva didn't offer up a break.

They had several days walking before them, best get started right away. Deshiva finished her orders, turned and walked right out, as if expecting the whole group to follow her.

They did.

Traveling with a band several hundred strong lost its luster after the first ten minutes. Jaunting on adventures with Wax, Pan, and Sawi, Bliss would get to swinging, would explore high and low in search of something cool. Instead, here, they walked in fours and fives along a broad path. Trees above glistened in the afternoon sunlight, birdsong and distant waves intruding on the conversation.

Quik kept her close, Bliss walking alongside several other older hunters. Like Deshiva, they all had the orange-and-white ink, but their bodies remained fresh, their kills and achievements still waiting.

Kitaye's somber reality faded on the path, replaced with the more pleasant nature. The rising route meant dry ground came quick and the pace increased, Deshiva calling for regular jogging intervals.

Bliss tried to find other Lira between the runs. Her own instructions, whispered to her as Bliss worked to repair a busted ladder late yesterday, hinted she wasn't going to be the only one heading this way. The thorns, though, were inked inside other designs, a secret for those who knew how to look for it. Amid all the people, their satchels, weaves, and weapons, Bliss couldn't find a kindred soul.

"You doing okay?" Quik asked hours in, with the first stopping point for dinner nearing. "You've been quiet."

'You've been talking with them,' Bliss replied, cutting the phrase with a slight two-fingered flick through the air.

'If you want me to stand by you, at least acknowledge I'm here.'

"Sorry. Not used to having you with me." Quik jerked his head towards his friends as they walked. "We're always together. Every hunt."

Everyone knew the hunting principles: work with the same team and you'd become as one, each member knowing where the others would be. Trapping prey, ambushing a dangerous creature, all came easier when you knew what your partners would do.

Bliss knew all that, fought to shrug off the irritation rising with Quik's words. Failed.

'Then you should've let me walk on my own,' Bliss signed. 'I could've made friends then.'

She caught her own breath at the end, wondered why she'd gone snappy, why she'd earned a frown from her brother. A frown that deepened as Quik took a closer look at her, their steps still in even march with the group.

With the sun this low, setting to Quik's right, Bliss squinted as the orange hit her eyes. Shadow shrouded Quik's look, but did nothing to block the frustrated sigh coming from his lips.

"They're running you hard, aren't they?" Quik said, quiet so only Bliss could hear.

'It's fine.'

Every night. She'd eat a light dinner because the hours after would be spent running through the jungle, training or helping with some random task. The Lira didn't bother much with construction work, but they took on the harder missions: finding rare herbs for medicines, tracking down lost bodies from the fiend attack, ensuring Kitaye's borders remained unbreached by new monsters.

The training, though, worked her the most. Bliss and

other new recruits—perhaps not the right word, as they were all chosen, not asked—would gather at a whispered site. Sometimes the exercises would be physical, sparring with weapons, with hands and feet. Other times it would be races. On some, the most exhausting nights, they would leave Vis behind.

The other six isles existed, of course, but Bliss had neither been to or considered visiting any others. What was the point, when Vis had home an adventure all packed into a single place?

Yet the Lira didn't adopt the same philosophy. By torchlight, Bliss learned to write on Noctia paper. She wore a Kance glider and soared, well, fell slowly to the dirt. They tasted special ales from Tamas and found their speech changing, their inhibitions vanishing and secrets pouring forth.

The Lira, Bliss was reminded every night, didn't just protect Vis and Kitaye from the fiends.

But all that protecting wore itself on Bliss during the day, seeping into her bones, her muscles, her mind. If Deshiva hadn't insisted on a careful pace to preserve the group's stamina, Bliss might've found herself falling behind.

As if her pride would've allowed that.

"I don't know what you're going through," Quik said, "but we're here. You need anything, just ask."

'We?'

"Mom, dad, Wax and I, obviously."

'Wax is off with Pan. They're trying for the Renewal.'

At Quik's confused expression, Bliss explained that morning, a story that lasted till Deshiva called the dinner halt. Over mangos and water, plus some dried fish, Bliss finished the story, one Quik stamped with a laugh.

"Can you imagine Wax and Pan?" Quik chuckled. "Those two as the Renewal? Vis would never live it down."

'Why do you say that?'

"Because your brother's never taken anything seriously in his entire life, that's why."

BANANAS always tasted better beneath the stars. Wax peeled his second one with his back against the tree's top. Thin branches rattled around him, the breeze growing as night descended. Enough that he wouldn't sleep up here for fear the wind would send Wax plummeting from his dreams to his death.

Not that Pan would allow such a snooze anyway. He'd barely bitten into his first fruit, the young man's eyes swerving between the moon above and the ground, dark and invisible below.

"It's not that bad," Wax said, his legs dangling.

"You keep saying that like it's going to change my mind," Pan replied. "I just like it when there's something over my head."

"Because?"

"Because the world doesn't feel so big that way."

"World? Pan, we're less than a day out from home. We went further looking for the shrives."

"If we win this thing, we'll have to leave the isle."

Wax threw Pan a second banana—their swinging had brought them by a loaded tree—and it bounced off Pan's shoulder, vanishing below.

"This morning you were all about winning. What happened to that?" Wax asked.

"Still there. Guess I can be nervous about it at the same time."

Wax could see it, though that didn't make much sense. Once you'd picked a course, might as well see it through with enthusiasm. If you didn't, things could go real bad.

Especially if that course was swinging through the jungle.

This high up, the breeze and the occasional adventurous insect buzzing by were the only noises. At least, that's what Wax thought until something different broke through, snapping Wax's conversational tactic and turning both their attention downwards.

In the fiend's aftermath, Wax had heard more human cries for help than he ever needed to experience again. Yet here rose another one, both annoyed and in evident agony.

"We should've outrun everyone else," Pan said.

"Not just Renewals on the path. Could be someone traveling?"

"At night?"

Wax rolled his eyes, "What're you worried about, Pan? This is still Vis. This is still home."

Pan's pressed lips, worried eyes said he wasn't so sure about that.

The man could keep his concerns. Wax tossed the banana, unraveled the rope from its secure wrap around the tree trunk.

"I'm going down," Wax said. "You coming?"

Pan sighed, "What'll my dad say if my Guardian gets me killed?"

"What'll you care? You'll be dead."

Wax, rope tied around his waist, slipped down through the canopy. He danced his feet, his hands, using the trunk as ballast for his jumps and slips. Halfway, going by a thick cluster, Wax confirmed their satchels still sat in an old bird's nest they'd found. Tied tight to keep curious critters out, the bags looked dull in the pink moonlight.

Before dropping further—those sounds, clearer now, were definitely someone not having a good time—Wax fished out his Foti blade. Slipped on the sheath. Definitely more awkward climbing with the weapon, but venturing to the forest floor at night unarmed would be a little too crazy, even for Wax.

"That didn't help," Pan whispered, catching up to Wax as the latter adjusted the blade.

"What didn't?"

"Telling me—" Pan stopped himself, sighed. "Why do I even bother talking to you?"

"Because I'm the only one who'll bother talking to you?"

A curse from the forest floor, a particular epithet targeting Vis's namesake god for his careless callousness, had Wax and Pan looking down. A small spark, no, a tiny fire graced the floor now. A shadow hunched near it, their leg sticking out, the ankle at an odd angle.

"Lighting a fire?" Wax whispered. "They're really risking it."

"Guess we'd better save them from themselves, right?"

"It's what the Aegis would do." Wax winked at Pan, a gesture probably invisible in the dark. "Better start practicing."

They scaled the trunk's last third slow, Wax leading the way. The fire gave clues as to the person who lit it, namely revealing their purple-and-gold cloak, their leathered armor ditched into a pile. A voulge rested on the ground next to the fire. Nearby lay a satchel, one thin and almost empty. Coarse leaves and branches cluttered the ground, save the dark ring where the person had marked off their fire.

Not stupid, at least.

Wax tried to get a better look. Vis wasn't known for bandits, for ambushes in the dark, and there didn't seem to be much reason why someone would stake out this particular piece of wilderness for thievery, but he felt an odd urge for caution.

Pan's skittishness getting to him, apparently.

Wax shook off the idea, leapt free from the trunk and landed on the soft ground without losing his footing. His right hand went for the Foti blade, resting on the hilt.

Not that he'd really know how to fight with the thing if the Najahn—because who else could it be—decided to scoop up their voulge and go for the skewer, but the wrapped metal had its own comfort.

"Who's there?" The Najahn asked, turning towards Wax.

The firelight revealed a woman's battered face, one Wax would put at his mother's age, wrinkles creases here marred with blood's crimson stain. The culprit lined her forehead, a bad gash matched, as Wax took in the sight, with sisters along the woman's legs and arms.

"A traveler," Wax said. That'd been the code name suggested by his parents whenever he left the city. Dodge specifics until you trusted someone. Safer that way. "You're hurt."

"Damned cats," the Najahn said. "Went for my satchel." She grimaced, hissed through her teeth. "You have anything useful in yours you'd care to lend me?"

The request dispelled the moment's shadow, cutting away unknowns and making the next steps plain. Wax whistled, a light tone telling Pan the man ought to join him, and once he had, the two went to work. Using natural oint-ments, some wrapped leaves, and spare water from their satchels, the two made quick bandages for the woman, who in turn filled the time with her story.

It matched the warnings Wax had heard, and heeded, all his life. Hanoko weren't cowardly, exactly, but they preferred lone prey, particularly ones too focused on other things to notice their creeping approach. This, the woman admitted, had been her own fault: she'd been watching the moonlight, trying to see how much farther it'd be till she hit Kitaye.

"The better question is why you were walking at night at all," Pan said, tying the last wrap around the woman's thigh, where her thin robe had been shredded. "Sundown means leaving the floor behind."

"For you, maybe," the woman replied, her face glis-tening as the fire dried off the water she'd run through her cuts. "Najahn don't fear the jungle."

"Maybe you should," Wax said.

He had his back to the tree, kept his eyes running around the fire's edges, looking for glints in the dark. The hanoko would know it hadn't made the kill, might be looking to finish it off.

"Unlucky is all," the woman said. Sighed. "Wouldn't be out here as it is save for the damned Renewal." She blinked, turned a slow look at the pair. "Is that what two young ones like yourselves are doing?"

"Maybe," Wax answered before Pan.

The woman sneered, "Trying to be coy? Only works if you have the smarts to back it up, boy."

Pan stood up at the words, scuffling back as he did so. "We helped you."

The woman nodded, "So you did. Let me help you in

return. Go back, foolish ones. They called it too late this time. Fassle's a greedy one, and too many are going to pay with their lives." She tried to stand, her hand going to the bandage on her thigh before sitting back down. "It's a careful thing, deciding when to send so many into danger, but they were cowards."

"Why?" Wax asked, though both had their satchels shouldered now. Ready to run. "What's worse this time?"

"Don't you feel it?" The woman asked. "That cat knows. Get the easy food while you can, because this whole jungle's going to be buried soon. This isle overrun." Her hand went to her voulge's haft. "You want to know why I'm out here alone? Because I'm the only one who knows death's coming for any who stay here."

She tilted the voulge up, an awkward move which revealed its purpose a moment later as she jabbed the long spear's butt into the ground. Leaning on it, she drew herself up.

"Mind giving me my satchel?"

Wax did the honors fast, a sloppy sling around her shoulder, keeping one eye on that voulge the whole time.

"You're welcome to the fire," the woman said, turning towards the path and making like she was going to shamble on.

"You're not serious?" Wax asked as she took the first step, the voulge planting into the ground before her.

"I want to live, boy," the Najahn said, continuing her walk. "If you want the same, best you follow me."

The two watched her as she left, walking beyond the firelight into the dark. For a minute longer they could hear her footsteps, the soft pounding of the spear into the earth, then that too vanished beneath the night.

Wax kicked some dirt on the fire, putting it out. Then, with Sichi's pink light replacing the orange, they climbed.

CHAPTER 17
THE BEACH

The rotten smell hit Bliss and the group as one, coughs and curses rising from the column in the mid-morning. Day three since they'd left Kitaye and their satchels were running low, their water skins better after replenishing at passing streams. The provisions vanished from the mind as Deshiva called for the group to advance, not at a walk, but at a run.

"Be ready," Deshiva said, the order repeating itself back down the column.

Quik, next to Bliss as he had been the entire march, repeated the words to the line behind him, and together the siblings sped up their steps.

Barefoot, Bliss felt the dirt fly up between her toes as they kicked ahead. Alone, sprinting through the jungle was a spiritual adventure, her and the trees and the birds and nothing else. Now, every footfall joined a hundred others. The coastal breeze mingled with the hunters' breath as the force moved together. She didn't feel alone, but part of something larger, an organism rising to defend its own.

Like Kitaye, the settlement they sped towards had its

homes among the trees, its workspaces on the ground. As the group approached, they found neither left standing. Thatches hung down like dessicated fronds, sweeping back and forth as the wind moved them. Boards and mossy carpets lay scattered across the ground. Leaves and branches, both sculpted and not, joined the wreckage in random piles.

Intermingled with it all was the rot's source.

Deshiva halted the group at the village's entrance, Bliss and Quik squeezing in on the left side to look beyond and take in the absolute destruction.

Deshiva, owning her command, waited for the group to assemble before stepping out in front. She took a long, sweeping look around the ruined town, its broken trees and bloodied clearings, before turning back to her charges. Bliss saw no hint of despair, no hint of anger, only cool judgment.

"Fiends," Deshiva said, starting and ending with one word. It hung in the air, a plural nightmare to what'd been a singular attack in the cave, on Kitaye. "They are indiscriminate. They destroy without reason. We will split, the senior hunters will sweep the jungles around here and make sure the monsters are gone. The rest of you," Deshiva frowned, glanced from the group towards the village, "will look for survivors, if any can be found." She held up a hand. "Beyond the bodies, gather what provisions you find. Our road was to end here, but now it continues."

'Continues?' Bliss signed to Quik as the groups broke up.

"We have to find the fiends that did this," Quik said, his eyes in a searing lock on the ruin. "They'll keep attacking otherwise. It's them or us, Bliss."

Again Bliss felt that tremor, the excitement, the adventure's call. It rode with her as she and Quik—neither qualified among the senior bands—joined the younger hunters in scouring the settlement.

Unlike the raw destruction wrought on Kitaye, the random disaster from the water and the fiend's flailing tentacles, walking the village took on a dead air. Conversation among the hunters, two dozen in all, died as they lifted broken wood to find the bodies beneath.

Vis custom demanded burials near tree trunks, life giving to life. A method built for single, honorable deaths. Not massacres. Nonetheless, at Deshiva's command, they hauled the dead one by one to a damaged grove near the settlement's center.

Bliss found her first inside a collapsed workroom, the older man laid over with long gashes. Like knife cuts, only serrated, the man slumped over a bench. A stone hammer rested idly in his hand, something Bliss tried to remove only to find the man's grip hard and fast.

"The dead are strong," Quik muttered, coming up behind Bliss. She twitched as he moved past her, knelt at the body's side. "In the hours after a person leaves this life, their body hardens. Every time."

'Why?' Bliss signed.

Quik shrugged. "Vis showing us the body is empty?"

The answer didn't give Bliss much comfort, neither did touching the dead man, feeling his cold, dirty skin. When she recoiled, Quik gave her the same look he'd reserved for those rare moments when she'd disappointed him, her father, their family.

'You're not scared?' Bliss asked.

"This isn't my first time," Quik replied, putting his shoulder beneath the body and lifting it from the chair. He grunted, the sound moving Bliss to help hold the opposite side. "We find travelers sometimes in the jungle. Often worse than this."

The nights with the Lira had taught Bliss how to swing her staff, how to handle coming danger, but they'd done nothing about the aftermath. The excitement that'd quickened her feet on approach to the village?

A poison, now.

The day passed in clean-up, the bodies piling without a survivor to be found. Deshiva pulled some searchers back, ordered them to begin the burials. Despite the time, the effort it would require, the losses would not be left to rot without honor.

Bliss begged off that duty, instead went with her brother and several others towards the village's farthest corner, one abutting cliffs overlooking the sea. At least the fresh air countered the dead stench, brought some life back.

Toppled racks dominated this end, stores for caught fish waiting to be filleted and cooked. If there'd been any catch before, only a few bones and scattered skins remained. The smoke pits themselves were splayed, pots broken. The fiends didn't care only to kill the living.

Bliss went past the damage to the cliff's edge. Trees and a single blooming Sana loomed over her, some curling out into space above the chalk-white cliffs. As tall as several trees to get down to the ocean from here, and yet the village had carved a long and winding stair all the way to the rock-strewn shore below.

Like Kitaye, fish must've been their primary protein. They just had to work far harder to get it.

Bliss knelt on the edge, looked down. Lily boats lingered there, toppled and shredded. Three bodies lay in the surf, bobbing near the boats.

She glanced back at her brother, the other hunters busy

moving bodies, clearing rubble. Deshiva might want to honor the dead, but going all the way down for these seemed a task too far. A life given to the sea was still a life given, after all.

Except one of those lives might not be ready to go just yet. The twitching wasn't visible so much by the man's limbs, but from the ripples in the surf they created. Moving counter to the waves, the man seemed to be trying to pull himself further up the rocks, a task made difficult by the swirling red staining the waves around his legs.

Bliss waved at the other hunters, her fingers ready to sign, but not a one had eyes for her. Too busy clearing bodies, rubble.

An easy choice to make.

Bliss hit the carved stair with alacrity, her feet touching the slightest step edge before skipping along to the next one. The stone glistened with spray from below, enough so that Bliss slid every few steps, but jumping from tree to tree gave her experience with momentum and turning it into something useful. With one hand scraping along the cliff's edge, Bliss danced and darted down the twisting stairs to the shore, where she exchanged smoothed stone for smoother rocks and sharp shells.

Whipping her staff free from its sling over her shoulders, Bliss covered the last strides to the man. The sea washed over her ankles, warm and soft this late in the afternoon. Sunlight sparkled off her target's bare back, dulling wherever it found a gash.

Bliss knelt at the man's shoulder, putting her staff into the ground next to her. A guidepost, a grabbable rescue if the surf came in hard to wash her away.

She touched the man. If she had a voice, she could've yelled. Without it, the manual effort served to draw a harder twitch. The head moved, turned towards her with one cheek still resting on the stones. The man's face held the tanned, weathered look common to sailors, fishermen. His mouth drew back in a pained grimace. One eye looked clawed through, the other red and puffy from the sea.

He tried to speak. Not even a whisper.

Bliss leaned over, grabbed his arm. Pulled. The man's weight beat out her slim purchase on the stones and she fell back, the man returning to his face-forward slump. Back on her feet, Bliss went for another round, this time making sure her heels were well-grounded before tugging away.

Again the water proved too tough to beat, her fingers slipping off the man before he moved up the beach at all. Too heavy, too hard.

Bliss looked back up the cliff. Nobody peeking over the edge yet searching for her. She'd have to get help, and that meant—

Her eyes caught a flash, a clatter and a crack behind her, up the beach towards the cliff's wall. Bliss had assumed the thing solid, hadn't looked that way as she blitzed towards the man. Now, though, she saw an undercut alcove, sliced away by seawater and showcasing glistening limestone.

Curled up against that stone lay a form long and thin, angled with sloping shoulders, legs, and stingy blood-red hair. At the left end, the creature easily twice as long as Bliss was tall, lay a long snout ending in a curving, central tooth, the same red as the thing's hair. Details crept out as Bliss traced the thing with her eyes, every new oddity striking a discordant pang in her heart, her head.

Nothing about these fiends—that's what this had to be —seemed to match what she'd grown up with, the creatures calling Vis home.

The first natural reaction to something like this was to

run, to break for those steps and make her way as far away as possible. At least to find some help, something stronger than the suddenly so inadequate stick she held in her hands.

She'd taken three steps without realizing it, watching the fiend, which seemed to be asleep. Either that or it was uninterested in the young woman who'd dared encroach on its domain.

Something snared her ankle, pulled her left foot back a step and dropped Bliss to her knee. She reached out, yanked her staff from the rocks and whirled to see the man reaching for her, his one eye meeting Bliss's own.

Again his lips moved, and while he didn't speak a word, Bliss didn't need to hear to know what he said.

Help me.

The desperation writ large across the weathered skin, his fingers still moving as he struggled to get to her. Bliss pulled her foot back, started to stand up, and the man lunged again.

Bliss dodged the grab this time, the man's hand swinging wide and smacking her staff. The stick clattered free and hit the rocks, a wet whack. Bliss scooped the staff back up quick, looked back to the alcove.

That'd been a loud hit.

The fiend, on that long narrow face, opened a single large eye. A flickering yellow, dancing pupil leered her way. A wave crashed, and as it receded, the bubbling surf joined with a new sound, a heavy wheeze coming from the creature as its legs moved.

Bliss gulped, put more distance between her and the grasping man. Shifted her staff into a level grip across both hands. The fiend stretched, its forelimbs, each one ending in gnarled hairless claws, digging into the rock. The snaggle tooth, hanging long from the fiend's snout, tilted towards Bliss as the monster continued to analyze its prey.

The Lira had a code, a guiding statement: protect the isle and its people. That was it. No complex lyrics, no poetic maxims. Simple and straight, and as the man behind her groaned again, the meaning thudded in Bliss's mind. To run would be to break her oath.

An oath she'd only taken a week ago, while half-drugged and in a middle-of-the-night frenzy.

So did that even count?

The fiend's back legs came next, each one splitting at its foot into twin claws, like a bird's talon copied twice over. The fiend rose up, taller now than Bliss. Other than the steady wheezing, it didn't make a sound.

She only had a staff. No other weapon. Her satchel, whatever good it might've done, waited up on top of the cliff. This wasn't a fight Bliss was ready for, wasn't a battle she could win.

The Lira and their oath could forget it. She hadn't signed up to die. Not yet.

Bliss jerked towards the stair, her feet slipping on the wet stones. What should've been a few strides became a wobbly run, the fiend watching, tensing, and springing.

The stair disappeared, replaced by the fiend's massive bulk, its long red hair flying through the air in a screen as Bliss tried to stop her own momentum. Her feet slid out from under her, gliding back on the rocks and sending Bliss, her staff angling beside her, to the stones. Surf bubbled up around her legs as the fiend stared at her, its leering visage close enough for the thing's hot breath to flare down and wash her in its fetid stink.

The fiend's right paw came up, four wrinkled digits each ending in a serrated, glossy red edge.

It didn't take much imagination to picture the sharp end ripping through her weave, her skin.

Bliss swung her staff across her body, putting the bamboo between her and the swiping paw. The fiend's blow caught the staff, tugged it away with so much strength Bliss didn't have time to adjust, didn't have time to fight back. One moment she held her defense, the next her staff bounced away across the rocks and the fiend had its paw coming back up again, ready for a killing blow.

Bliss backpedaled, her feet kicking up stones as she tried for distance. The fiend followed, toying with her. The water deepened behind Bliss, her hands sinking into puddles, her waist dropping below the sea line. Surf crashed around her. The man, the one she'd tried to save, lay motionless to her right.

Desperation found ways, sometimes, and with her heart pounding, her eyes wide and seeing, somehow, only that fang, her left hand hit a loose stone. She gripped it, her body faltering as her left arm gave up its support, but the sideways tilt gave her just enough room to throw her left arm forward, release the rock right at its target: the big red tooth.

The stone struck that horrible fang, bounced off it, bringing along a crescent-shaped chip. The fiend wheezed, rearing back. Its yellow-flicking eyes leaked golden tears as the creature gave Bliss some distance, as it ran its front right paw over its damaged fang.

Never take an advantage for granted.

Bliss scrambled up and to the right, splashing through the stones, the swirling tide pools towards her staff. The fiend wheezed again, a louder coughing hiss this time, and whirled to follow. Bliss heard, felt the creature dart for her as she neared her staff, the air giving her just enough clue to make a last dive. A snaking claw caught her leggings, tore the grassy weave, but missed her skin. Bliss hit the rocks, rolled and came up with her staff again in both hands.

She lived. Somehow, she'd survived the opening seconds, and that survival changed her. What'd been stark fear morphed, with the staff solid in her hands, to something akin to courage. At least a belief that Bliss now, in this moment, was more than just prey.

She stood, the fiend pacing with more caution, eyeing that staff. Bliss waved the long bamboo weapon before her, treating it like a target, something to draw the fiend off balance. If she could get the monster to go one way, maybe Bliss could get a free swing.

They faced each other in the fading sunlight, the deep gold splashing off the rocks, highlighting the cliffs in bronze. The fiend kept up its wheezing, steady as the two circled each other. Zeroed in, Bliss caught finer details: the fiend wasn't unscathed. Besides the chipped fang, red lines littered its body, as if something had caught the monster in a cutting net. The crimson hair hung in ragged tatters, that shading, Bliss guessed now, more to do with blood than natural color. The creature's short fur, too, sopped tight to its skin in clumps. Nothing pristine about this thing.

Time to finish the job.

Bliss feinted right, leading with a lunging staff swing towards the beast's right shoulder. The fiend took the attack as an opening, jumping off its left limbs into a straight-line throat-slashing assault. Bliss ducked down, used the lunge to slant her staff right, catching the beast's mid-section as the swinging claw whiffed over Bliss's head. Again the staff nearly flew free from Bliss's hands, the fiend's sheer weight dragging the stick along. Bracing, she held, and the hit sent the fiend stumbling to its right, along the rocks and closer to the stair.

Let the creature get its footing and she'd be letting it back into the game.

Bliss rushed, pushing her feet into the rocks and kicking off into an overhanded swing. A double-gripped wallop going for the fiend's head.

The creature didn't dodge, didn't try. Instead, wheezing, golden tears dripping from its eyes, the fiend snapped its head up to meet Bliss's swat. Opening its jaw, behind that snaggle fang, the fiend bit down on Bliss's staff, intercepted the hit and held it fast. For all her strength, all her momentum, the blow Bliss struck seemed not to faze the fiend at all. Instead the two hung there, the staff in the fiend's mouth and Bliss hanging over the rocks.

The fiend moved first, jerking the staff and Bliss along with it towards itself. Those front claws made for the swipe, forcing Bliss to ditch her staff again to fall back.

The fiend didn't give her room this time.

Keeping the staff held tight, the fiend jumped forward, planted a claw on Bliss's shoulder, pressed her to the ground. The needle claws bit into her skin and Bliss tried to scream.

As it had since she was a child, her voice came out in a broken yelp, one that nonetheless carried, an unusual splintering against the evening's mashing waves.

The fiend pushed down, Bliss's head hitting the rocks. Water rushed her ears, ran over her mouth, made her vision swim. The fiend's golden eye came closer, her staff in its jaw, as it took a good look at its next kill.

As Bliss felt the last air escape her lungs, a muted rumble coursed through the water, buzzing her ears. The golden eye, blurred by the sea, veered away. The weight vanished off her chest, the claw scratching Bliss in its departure. She sat up, gasping. Whooping battle-cries filled the air, shapes dancing around her, darting in at the fiend with spears, with Foti-fashioned knives, and her brother, with their family's longest heirloom: stained wood gauntlets clasped tight to each fist, their metal tips rending the fiend.

Bliss spat out water as she watched her brother strike again and again, the knuckles doing their job. The fiend, surprised, tried to get a snapping angle with its fang only to be rebuffed by another hunter, spear jutting towards the monster's gnashing mouth. A third, one who only minutes ago helped Bliss lay bodies in a line, circled behind the fiend with two drawn Foti knives. The man crouched, searched for an angle.

A gutting strike. Bliss could name all the tactics, had gone over them with Quik enough times when he first joined the hunter's ranks. The trio now worked in concert, two damaging and distracting the beast while the last moved in for the lethal blow.

The fiend, though, was not some careless jungle prey. Much like it had with Bliss's staff—the bamboo stick floated off to her right, now, buttressed by some rocks—the fiend snapped its jaw towards the spear-wielder, snagged the weapon and threw it away into the sea. Flexing back from the same motion, ignoring Quik's continued scraping, the fiend threw its bulk back towards the shore, pushing Quik off its side and sending him tumbling. The knife-wielder went for his strike, extended the arm in a stab Bliss couldn't see, one the fiend's wheezing shriek made clear had found a home.

So, too, did the fiend's rear claws, those double talons proving flexible enough to kick behind and left, knocking the knife-wielder's side and spinning the bloodied man into the surf.

Right alongside the wounded one who'd started this whole thing.

Bliss staggered over to her staff, her chest aching with every breath, while her brother roared a new challenge at the fiend. Wordless, determined, everything Kitaye hunters ought to be, Quik's guttural growl rebounded off the cliffs like legend.

The fiend chose to respond with its jaw. Whipping to the right faster than any snake Bliss had ever seen the monster charged forward, rock and surf spraying with its kicks. Quik leapt to meet it, his knuckles swinging together to catch the fiend in a lethal vice. To his right, the spear-wielder drew a knife from the rope at his waist and ran forward too, stabbing towards the fiend's giant neck.

Just as it had dashed for Quik and the other hunter, the fiend bounced sideways, to Quik's left and towards the alcove. Its claws scrabbled on the rock, and Quik snared the beast's hair, the man's gauntlets catching on the red, tearing in their tangle while the beast's forward momentum carried it past the other hunter.

And right in line for Bliss.

As the fiend turned, jaw opening to bite her brother, Bliss stumbled forward with the staff. Her hands, cold and tired and bruised, punched the bamboo forward with all she had left, driving the staff into the fiend's turning jaw, forcing its bite into a ram instead. Quik fell free, ragged fiend mane falling off with him, to the crimson beach.

Bliss pulled back her staff, struck again as the fiend turned its baleful eye, its damaged fang towards her. The hit smacked home, a crunching strike to that same jaw, a crack and snap the beast ignored as it fell into another wheezing charge.

Bliss blocked with her staff, felt the beast ram her, lift her up on its hard snout and carry her over the stones. Bliss's breath vanished, her legs and arms flailing as the beast's momentum shoved her back at the cliff wall.

Behind the monster, Quik hunched up, his face burning with fear, draped in the hair he'd won. Too far to help. Beside him, the spearwielder threw his knife, a last strike flying wide as the fiend thundered on.

This would be it, then. Another moment, then a fast, crushing end. At least she'd died doing what her family expected: putting Bliss's life, her sacred duty above everything else.

Bliss hit the cliff wall, smashed into the stone and bounced off with no follow-through. The fiend didn't crush her, a mystery resolved only by the echoes of a greater cry, a tarnished raging roar punctuated, at last, by not a wheeze but a shriek from the fiend's throat, a dying call earned by a singular form standing over the fiend's slumped body.

Deshiva, her spear overdone in sigils and wrapped in Foti-forged bands, stood on the monster, her weapon driven home in a jump from the stair above. Bliss, sitting on the stone, watched Deshiva's hair blow in the sea wind, heard her commander's cry of victory, of vengeance.

With her left hand, the only fingers not numbed by the battle, Bliss lifted her signing to the sky and joined.

CHAPTER 18

ON THE SEA

The Tsuro cut the seas better than any knife, molding with the waves and scooping their power into its own bobbing acceleration. The craft dipped and rose, tacked and surfed with canny expertise. Svarde watched from near the captain's till, admiring the crew's controlled efforts as they spun from one rigging to the next, one rudder control to another to keep the Tsuro one with the water.

The Foti ship up from Vis, compared to this, had been a hammer mashing through the waves. No subtlety, no grace. Just raw power. Then again, that was the Foti way. Svarde felt it in his axes, stowed in a trunk Maena gave him for the voyage. Felt it too, in the cloak weighing on his back, the blood in his veins. Raw power forged into something useful.

The Tsuro and its sailors seemed born of a different grace.

"Catching you looking," Maena said, stepping away from the till and handing it over to the first mate. "Never been on a Rana ship?"

"Not once."

"Then you haven't truly sailed."

Svarde chuckled, "Kance would take issue with you."

"They don't sail. They fly. We know the water, they avoid it."

"Which is better, I wonder?"

"I don't think you need to ask my opinion."

The Rana crew, Maena included, drifted off the heavier wear adorning them on Noctia, the open sea air prompting a wholesale fashion change. Gone were the armors, the badges and honorary ornaments for ranks and status. Most wore nimble robes dyed in colors befitting their station, such that the Tsuro's deck looked less like the drab brown and metal Svarde knew and more like Vis's florid jungles.

"Do you always dance so much?" Svarde said, nodding to the crew as they flipped, swung, and tumbled around the deck. "It has to be risky."

"If you don't know what you're doing, like anything else," Maena replied, standing shoulder-to-shoulder with Svarde and looking over her ship. "If you do, then we save energy. Watch, and you'll see."

This was their third day at sea, spiriting northward, so at first Svarde took her comment to mean he hadn't really seen anything yet. An insult, or perhaps an invitation. He chose two sailors, one up top finishing tying a spare sail now that the wind had picked up, and a second carrying a rope from bow to stern for some unknown errand. At first their movements seemed fast but random, jerked in odd directions. As the Tsuro banked down a wave, the rope-carrier actually lost ground, back-stepping with the heavy rope laden across his shoulders. No concern showed across the man's face. When the Tsuro came up the next wave, though, the man tilted forward into a run, a headlong dash along the deck.

Sure he was going to go overboard, Svarde started that way, ready to dive off and grab the moron before he was lost.

Maena stopped him.

"Watch, Foti."

The doomed run slowed as the Tsuro topped out its ascent, the carrier going past the ship's mid-deck, nearing his destination. The Tsuro started down, cutting into the man's momentum, slowing the sprint just enough to leave the man with three last, careful steps before, with Svarde and Maena making their way starboard to see, placing the rope right on its intended hook.

"Get it now?" Maena said. "Everything with what the sea intends." She pointed up. "Your other target?"

In the same span, the sailer had swung back and forth across his sail, grappling on hooks along the mast. Only, not hooks, but a small railing where the sailor's metal clip glided him back and forth with the rolling boat. As he went, the sailor had snapped up the canvas, completing the enclosure without the risk borne by normal techniques.

"I think Foti could learn a thing or three from you," Svarde admitted.

"More than that, but we'll never tell," Maena replied. At Svarde's growing smile, she frowned and killed the sunny day's mood. "It's what the isles do, is it not? Keep to our secrets, pit them against one another in trade, as if that's the only way to survive."

"Me being here suggests you don't think so."

"The Renewal isn't the only thing that needs to change."

The first two nights on board, Maena had Svarde eat with her crew. He'd been expecting the usual sea dogs, swarthy sailors who launched cargo and tied rope every day of their adult lives till time ground them into elders teaching the same to their children, their grandchildren.

Instead, he'd found revolutionaries. Not a one cared about their next delivery, what the season's sailing looked like. Most had Svarde beat on age, had offered up their own stored valuables to trade for the mission's financing. They would sail, yes, but only for a cause.

"They want what we want," Maena had said that first night, as everyone dined on the Tsuro's open deck. The first mate kept the ship level for the meal, cutting between waves with such skill that Svarde saw not a single ripple in his wine glass. "Everyone here has lost someone, known someone hurt by Noctia and their awful ritual. Together, we plan to end it."

When Svarde asked how, the answer was unanimous.

"We've sailed the wide seas and found nothing out there," one sailor replied, brushing bread crumbs from her chin as she spoke. "Endless ocean save our seven isles all round the world. Anything we can find that'll end all this isn't going to be out there. Which means it's inside."

"The Dark Below," another one chimed in.

"And you're not afraid to go there?" Svarde asked the group, trying to figure out how he'd fallen in with such like-minded friends. "You know there will be fiends?"

"It's why we went looking for help," Maena replied. "If there were this many of us just on Rana, how many more might be out there?"

"Like me?"

"Just like you."

Yet Svarde counted only Rana at the table, on the ship.

"Apparently not so many like me out there."

Maena shrugged off the comment, "We looked, but not

too hard. The relationship between the isles isn't what it once was."

Svarde considered guessing if that wasn't Rana's own fault, but held off. The rest of that dinner, and the next two days, had passed by in an invigorating blur. Even Kivi, the ferrite, found delight in the Tsuro's cargo hold, chasing rats and other small critters with nowhere to go and, thus, easy prey for the ferrite's slower, deadlier rock jaws.

For Svarde, simply being around those who shared his goal, his world view tilted his axis from a lonely, destabilized mess to a sharp focus. He wasn't insane, he wasn't a grouchy old hermit who'd spent too long up on the cliffs. Others had the same idea and were acting on it just like him.

"Purpose," Maena said. "that's what you're feeling."

They were on the deck, the rope deliverer finishing his errand. Lunch would come soon. Tomorrow they might make their first sight of Whent, and after that?

The expedition would begin in earnest.

Afternoon began with a holler. A loud call from the watcher at the top mast, clipped into a hard wood seat and watching the waves with a bronzed spyglass. His blue bandanna, matching his robes, whipping in the cool air, the spy made his call as Svarde and the others cleaned up their midday meal.

Though the holler didn't seem to have words, something in the tone must've meant action, because the Rana's faces fell into a mix between grim duty and delighted devilry. Crew scattered, their purpose becoming clear as those who'd darted below-decks returned with sabers, hooks, and long spears.

"Come with me," Maena said, accepting two spears and handing one to Svarde. "We're taking a detour."

Following Maena up to the Tsuro's bow, a rising oak sculpted into a river's boiling rapids, Svarde followed the sailor's stares out over the water, towards a dark line cutting the horizon. From this distance, the shape looked about the size of Svarde's thumb, were he to hold it up against the clear blue skyline.

A ship, doubtless, but what would inspire such a reaction from the Rana?

"Have you ever coveted something?" Maena asked Svarde as they stopped at the bow.

"Coveted?"

"Yes. Desired what you could not have?"

Svarde hesitated, Maena grinned.

"That's answer enough, Foti. What we covet, at least in part, is on that ship." Maena pointed towards the smudge. "That, unless my seer is off his mark, and he is not, is a Whent rock hauler."

"Their cargo vessels."

"Right. And by the looks of things, it's traveling alone, heading our way." Maena's grin grew, but only at the edges. "It's making assumptions that will be proved false."

Svarde scrunched up his face, "It believes it's under treaty. The Renewal has been called. Peace should—"

"Should, but does not," Maena replied. "Anything you see laid across a populace without any enforcement is just an illusion." Maena swept a look across her boat, along the empty waters. "Do you see any Najahn here?"

"I—" Svarde shook his head, scowled. "The treaty exists because it's too dangerous otherwise. To fight wars while fiends ravage is foolish."

"To lose an advantage because you are being too nice is worse," Maena said. "In that boat could be any number of valuable weapons, supplies we can use to go deeper, farther than any before."

"Then we can buy them."

Maena laughed, one missing her carefree joy. "You're the one who's spent so many years alone, Foti. Don't assume you understand the world anymore. What the Whent might accept in trade would leave us empty. They would take the Tsuro whole before giving us an apple."

"You're assuming—"

Maena put a hand on his shoulder, and not in a friendly grip. "Svarde. The time is past discussion. I've already made the call. We will take the ship, we will secure what we want, and the rest will find its way to the bottom of the sea. A victim of a fiend's assault." She let him go, pulled her hand back and rested it on her saber's hilt. "You have two options. Either you go belowdecks and wait until the fighting is finished, accepting your inaction might cost my crew lives, might hurt our mission, or you accept there will be prices to pay along this course and walk beside me as you agreed to back on Noctia."

"This is not what I agreed to," Svarde said.

"Then you didn't listen. I said I would do whatever it takes." Maena's eyes flicked right, towards the Whent ship. The bulk drew close, emerging in detail. "Choose now."

How many compromises did Svarde have to make in his life? How many times did he have to take less than what he wanted, just to have a chance at success? How many times had Ami told him to hold back for fear of hurting Catya's chances at becoming the Aegis?

He'd done so, he'd followed all their plans, all their hopes, and found himself alone and desperate.

Perhaps Maena was right. Perhaps there was another, better way.

"If this will help our mission, then you'll have my axes," Svarde said.

"Good." Maena nodded past Svarde's shoulder.

The Guardian turned, saw a sailor standing behind him, saber drawn and ready for a skewer.

"Whatever it takes," Maena said when Svarde turned his hot glare back her way. "Get your weapons, Foti. It's time you saw what a real sea raid looks like."

CHAPTER 19

TRAPS AND TARGETS

The wraps beneath her weave scratched while Bliss and the others moved into the valley, stalking the trail left by the other fiend's that'd assaulted the village. Late morning ran its golden lines glittering over disturbed fronds, busted sticks and snapped trees. Kicked up dirt made gentle padding for Bliss's feet, scrapped up on the stones the day before.

She'd spent the night tending to her wounds, signing along with the other hunters as the healthy ones buried the dead in circles around what trees would allow it. A somber ceremony made more so by the slicing, bruising pains running up and down her body.

Deshiva, though, gave Bliss the cure in one simple phrase: vengeance.

Defeating those that'd wronged her seemed a bit simplistic when it came to strange creatures from deep below the ground, but Deshiva's point, to use anger and desperation in a drive to slay the things threatening you, put a clarity on Bliss's heretofore cloudy new existence.

Hard to imagine, now, but just a week ago she'd been

galavanting around these same trees, running along these same vines with Wax and the others without any real fear. The hanokos weren't a real threat, not if you paid any attention, and life seemed set up to be one idyllic journey after another. Even after they'd all moved up, it'd still be the same, still all be in—

"Pay attention," Quik said, crouching next to her. "We're close."

Her brother had his own bruises, purple splotches marring the ink along his left side, but Quik otherwise came out with more mental damage than physical.

Not that he said as much, but his walk, his talk told the story.

He'd barely left Bliss's side for a second, offering and getting, even when she didn't ask for it, food, drink, a warmer wrap for the evening. She'd never gone to Quik for anything, yet here he was bearing her injuries as some sort of guilty penance.

'I am,' Bliss signed back.

Ridiculous. Her injuries were her own fault, nobody elses. She should've seen the fiend on her first step onto the stones, should've drawn it out and annihilated it in the same way Deshiva had.

At least the man lived, lived and gave the hunters a direction.

The trail led to this, a broad mouth opening up from an overgrown foothill. A cave Bliss had been to, long ago on a whimsical trip. Mushrooms and other things grew down here, and the occasional gemstone, if Bliss recalled correctly, could be sifted from its secreted pools and crannies.

Now their several dozen—Deshiva splintered the group again, sending smaller bands roving to find any more fiends

—came in at a slow, padding angle. Spears, gauntlets, knives and more were held ready. Conversation died.

Quik and Bliss came from the left, crossing through a fern-filled jungle miasma. Spiderwebs tugged at her legs, branches nuzzled her taut hair, but Bliss put those things behind her, kept her eyes and ears focused on the dark hole.

Larger than the swamp cave where they'd met Svarde, this one opened at a steeper pitch, angling away into darkness with lingering vines, grasses, and trampled flowers along the entry. Sounds echoed from deep inside: howls, scrabbles, the snapping bites of things fighting with one another.

To her right, Bliss saw Deshiva and her two chosen hunters approach the cave dead center. They were the bait, set to draw out the fiends so the two sides could collapse on the monsters in frantic fury. A bold, basic strategy.

"We cannot outsmart ourselves," Deshiva had said at the camp that morning. "These are beasts, not wise generals. Keep it simple, and we will win."

At what cost? Nobody had asked.

Bliss, her hands tight on her staff, palms raw from fresh callouses, didn't mind. She wanted to be here, wanted to get another crack at these horrors. Show them Vis wasn't afraid.

WAX SWOOPED ALONG A VINE, letting go at its uppermost point and flying, falling forward onto a sweeping frond. Coated with dew, the water sprayed while Wax rode the frond down, the cool drops a good opener for what promised to be a hot day's run. Behind him, the frond shook as Pan hit the top, following.

It'd been an uneventful, fun few days launching

through an increasingly unfamiliar jungle. The farther they went from Kitaye the more Wax had to take guesses, had to jump without much more than hope. Pan kept saying it was suicidal, while all Wax knew was he felt more alive than he'd been, well, since the fiends attacked.

But that wasn't the point. These jumps were fresh, these vines unknown, and every one tracked a line in his memory, a trail to follow on the way back and ever again should he come this way.

Some visitors to Vis said the island changed every time they returned, the jungle growing and moving around like the living thing it was. To Wax and the other natives, though, it was a home like any other, and he could read its past in the gnarled barks, the branches, the rotting logs on the forest floor.

And, yes, in the howls coming up from below.

The hanokos had been on them for the last few hours. The cats didn't often roll around united unless—Wax frowned as the frond bottomed out, letting him kick up onto his feet—something scared them enough to unite. Together, hanokos could be hissing, murderous packs, and it seemed the cats had settled on Wax and Pan for their next snack.

"C'mon!" Wax yelled back to Pan as he hit the frond's narrowing tip, the leaf bending forward as Wax's weight pressed down. "They'll get tired if we keep moving!"

Planting his foot, Wax leapt into the air, soaring higher than his house back in Kitaye. Beneath, the dark, loamy soil had its coverage spoiled by the three hanokos as they matched Wax pace for pace.

The cats could climb, could and would make a sweep for him and Pan if either one slowed down enough. But the humans had hands, a killer advantage when it came to surfing through the trees.

"If you gave me a good route, maybe I'd follow," Pan's reply echoed through as Wax hit the branch he'd been aiming for.

The wood creaked, but the tree's health held and Wax had his toes-to-heel walk rolling him on past the trunk, towards the next branch and the coming leap.

Keep on running like this for another hour or two and, Wax figured, they'd hit the Najahn outpost. Safe, guarded, and ready to welcome the two fastest Renewal candidates this side of the isle.

"You've gotta trust me," Wax said, keeping his eyes forward.

A vine hung to the left, an appealing swing but one undone by a knotty, rotting link up towards the canopy. In the middle sat a small tree copse, a dozen of the things sprouting their useless, spindly selves towards the hidden sky. To the right, a sturdy giant missing its lower branches, but wielding a high up skyway to victory.

They'd just have to climb some stubs first, and do it faster than the cats.

"Right this time," Wax called, picking up speed and bouncing off the branch's end.

The hot air buffeted the flight, did nothing to help Wax as he whacked the tree's trunk. A knot stuck Wax's shoulder, while the pointed remnants of a branch dug into his right knee. Standard rewards for jumping through the trees.

He worked his hands and shoe-clad feet, both scrambling for holds. Up and up, every grasp getting Wax higher. And so far, no sign of the hanokos. The tree didn't shudder with their weight, the bark didn't sound its scraping alarm.

Wax risked a glance down, slowing himself to confirm the hope wasn't misplaced.

And sighed. Nothing like reality to puncture a good time.

Pan, following behind, hadn't made the final leap. At least, not well. He'd hit the target a bit below Wax, snagged his satchel on a smaller tree making aggressive inroads on its older cousin. Pan had himself partly wrapped now, hands and legs in branches, leaves slapping his face, trying to extricate from disaster.

Those hanokos saw the same thing Wax did, but rather than sigh, the three cats circled. Their moon-like, furry heads—blue, gray, purple this time—bobbed as they gauged the jump distance to turn Pan into carved up lunch.

What was it, Wax's official role? The one Pan had asked him to take on for this little jaunt?

"What's a Guardian gotta do," Wax muttered and dropped, whooping all the way.

CHAPTER 20

BEHEMOTH

Seeing Whent rocks float never grew old. Something about how the craggy behemoths managed to smash their way through the sea without budging a meter, as if nature itself couldn't turn their tide, brought a smile to Svarde's face. If only the Foti could forge something as strong.

The smile tempered now as Svarde set himself back in the third rank on Maena's ship. The Tsuro sped towards its victim, cutting along the narrow valleys between crests like a sneaking thief approaching its mark.

And what a mark!

Looking up, Svarde saw the soaring, scalloped cliffside making up the Whent ship rise and rise. Taller than a Noctia house, the towering thing held its gray bones outside, lined with silver-black veins, as if the ship had emerged crackling from Whent's own gut.

Ridges ran across the great ship's sides, alcoves leading in where cargo could be loaded and dropped. Great ramps hung off the vessel, clasped into the rock and ready to be raised on winches, metal chains scaling the distance between loading hole to the topside deck above. Pull a lever and those ramps would slide into place, letting the leviathan disgorge its insides upon an awestruck port.

How Maena planned to take over this massive thing with her sparse crew seemed a question with only one answer:

She wouldn't, and they'd all spend the night drowning beneath the sea.

Yet Svarde only saw expectant grins. Those Rana leathers returned now, the loose robes covered up with tight armors. Sabers rested in scabbards, while knives clung tight to belts, boots, and the occasional bandanna. Several behind Svarde held crossbows, their Foti-made metal and wood combos aiming towards the top deck, ready to fire not arrows but rock-biting grapples.

At his feet, Kivi nudged Svarde and snorted.

"Almost ready," Svarde muttered to the Ferrite. "And for the last time, you're staying here."

Kivi snorted again.

At least the grapples would ensure the ferrite, in no way nimble enough for such a boarding, wouldn't get in the way. Or, far worse, fall into those waves.

Maena, up in front, whistled. Thus far Svarde hadn't seen a soul poke their heads over the Whent ship's side, not a resisting sniff come their way. At Maena's whistle, the crossbowmen aimed and fired, launching their grapples with a twang.

The claws glinted through the noon sun, flares homing in towards their destination, before slamming into the Whent ship one after another. Gray stone broke and splashed down as each crossbowman knelt and slapped their grapple's end into a loop on the Tsuro's deck. Several tugs and the ropes, fibers a red-amber dye, pulled tight.

Maena whistled again, and Svarde watched her take the first leap off the Tsuro's rail, flying through the air and landing on the rope. One foot going after another, her arms out for balance, Maena zipped up the rope, her crew pouring forth behind her.

Other than that whistle? Not a sound. No war song, no cheery chant leading them into battle. A rousing assault this was not.

So many confusing things about the Rana. Svarde had been to their isle, seen their customs and enjoyed their company, but he'd never fought alongside them till now.

Thus far, boring.

But when the man before him began his turn on the rope, Svarde eyed the path up and prepared to take it nonetheless. Beneath and before him, the sea churned. Above, Maena found the Whent deck, and for the first time, Svarde heard a true battle cry.

It wasn't hers.

CHAPTER 21
INTO THE DARK

The fiends didn't come out to play. Deshiva and her two guards crept closer and closer to the rowling, scratching, hissing sounds deep within and not a one bothered to approach.

Bliss watched from the left side, staff in hand, waiting for something to happen. Waiting for her chance to exorcise the bruises she'd picked up yesterday.

Deshiva's concentration, her tight grip on the spear, its point leading their slow walk up to the cave, split into a frustrated scowl when no menace offered itself to her spit. Snapping a nod at her partners, Deshiva dropped the spear and set her hands to pouches on her waist. In the second she did so, both guards stepped forward, crossing their own spears before Deshiva to ward off any surprise attack.

"They're not hunters," Quik muttered. "They're more than that. No creature on Vis needs this kind of tactic."

'Lira,' Bliss signed, guessing at the truth.

Who knew how many there were, but the arts Lira practiced under the moonlit jungle matched what she saw here:

a different dance for a deadlier demon than hanoko and other isle creatures.

From her pouch, Deshiva produced two rolled balls. A gray white, Deshiva cradled them as if they were eggs about to be broken.

"Foti bombs," Quik muttered. "You don't see those every day."

'What do they do?'

"Think we're about to find out."

Deshiva, her guards letting their spear defense lapse, sank to a crouch, taking a careful walk up the moss to the cave's very lip. Her every muscle tensed, sweat beading off as the sunlight struck in full this close to the cave. Deshiva looked as one with her moment, her element. Bliss couldn't find any fear.

Something to aspire to.

"Get ready," Quik whispered, and Bliss heard other hunters making similar rustles.

Vengeance was in the air, and it would be their's.

Deshiva tossed one then the other, two loping, calm motions that seemed funny set against the moment, as did her quick turn and scramble, moss and grass flying as her feet fought for holds, back away from the cave.

Bliss took a breath, held it.

The bombs went off with a disappointing, hollow pop. The ground shuddered. The noises within the cave vanished, dying to nothing as smoke, dust poured forth. All in all, it seemed like little more than a bad fire and a mild quake.

Deshiva, spear retrieved, waved to the left side.

"This group, with me. The right, cover our backs. Listen if we call for help," Deshiva said, striding back to the cave with confidence.

Bliss and Quik joined another ten hunters around her, assembling a squad too big to fit across the cave's entrance in a single line. Big enough, though, to handle anything inside.

"We'll see if anything's left," Deshiva finished. "Break out the torches. We'll want to see them coming."

Quik sparked up one, the light at first going nowhere against the jungle day. As they went beneath the cave, Bliss and her brother stuck in the pack's middle, the torch found its purpose, guiding them deeper into the murk. All alongside them, rocks smoothed by mining bore new gouges, both clean ones and blood-spattered mars.

As she walked, Bliss's feet too found worse things than sand between her toes. The torch's light didn't reach so low, and Bliss didn't ask for a look.

Some things were better ignored.

CHAPTER 22

CLAWS

Wax hit the climbing hanoko's wide eyes like a plunging coconut, smashing through his dive into the clawed furball and rolling with the creature the last couple meters to the soft forest floor. The cat pushed out a heavy sigh as Wax's weight pummeled the air from the thing's lungs, while Wax sprawled half-stunned out onto the ground.

That was not intended.

He'd thrown his rope behind him as Wax dove, hoping the wrapped line would snare a branch, a knot, anything.

Missing was something that happened sometimes in the jungle, always disastrous when it did, but Wax had never wound up bombing into an animal.

The cat laid next to him, coughing, and for a hot second Wax felt bad about the whole thing. At least until Pan yelled.

"Get moving, you idiot!" Pan called down. "There's two more!"

Oh, right.

Wax pushed away his shaken nerves, sat up and looked

into the gray eyes of a purple hanoko bearing down on him. The big cat had its back arched, its paws padding forward slow, as if waiting for Wax to make the first move. Or, perhaps, holding his attention so the other one could circle behind.

You wanted to live long in Vis's jungle, you picked up and took in hanoko hunting tactics real fast. Those who didn't tended to become lunch for the critters.

So Wax did what the cats distinctly didn't like.

He jumped and turned, whooping right in the third cat's face as it came up for a swipe at Wax's neck. Rather than deliver a gutting move, the hanoko jumped, its tail poofing out. The creature's feet hit the ground, kicking up dirt as the cat sprang for the woods.

Reaching into the sheath on his back, Wax drew the Foti blade in a smooth motion as he turned to the purple cat. The draw came so clean, so easy that Wax found himself staring at his own sword in wonder: he'd been practicing, but half the time he'd tried a move like this, the sword found itself stuck and Wax wound up on the ground.

Thankfully, only Pan had been around these last few nights to laugh.

The hanoko didn't laugh much at the blue blade. It also didn't back off. No fear showed in its calculating face, and Wax had a chance to pick out scars, ratted bits on the hanoko's fur. Its whiskers hung long and gnarled, bent by a million jungle runs. The first hanoko, the coward, might've been young. This one wasn't going to get itself spooked so easy.

Wax leveled the blade at the hanoko, "Your move, furball."

Bravery came with the moment, a stand-your-ground certainty brought on by the clear fact that to flee these cats without a defense was to die. Wax himself hadn't ever killed a hanoko before, had no wish to, so he waved the blade before the creature hoping it would turn and run.

Or, at least, slink off into the jungle.

The hanoko didn't bite. Rather, it opened its mouth, showing off long pale fangs and a thick pink tongue. Its breath, awful in every way, rolled over Wax as the hanoko growled, or possibly yawned, at him.

"You gone yet?" Wax shouted up without risking a look.

"Very much," Pan replied, sounding like he'd been heading towards the canopy.,

At least one thing was going right.

"Okay, kitty," Wax said as the hanoko closed its mouth, kept in a pouncing crouch. "How about we form a truce? No fights, no deaths. We all go home happy."

The hanoko's vertical slits narrowed. Its haunches quivered, and Wax tightened his grip. His chance would come when the cat leapt, a quick strike and hope he took the creature out. Anything else would mean death.

To his right, the hanoko Wax had smashed spoiled the moment. Moaning, a gutteral thing, the cat flopped to its side and blinked at Wax's opponent. The purple cat dropped its stand-off immediately, padding over to the right and setting its bulk between Wax and its battered friend. The hanoko still had its claws out, but its stance now said defense, caution, and, dare Wax to dream, a possible peace.

Why, though?

Keeping the sword level, Wax tried to look beyond the purple cat, saw the blueish one behind for the first time. He'd assumed the hanoko was full grown, a wrong spy. Wax had slammed an older kitten, which would make this one the purple matriarch. And the one Wax had scared before . . . the youngest?

Sawi was always better at wildlife than Wax, she'd know.

The basics would have to be enough.

Wax took a slow step back, raising up his off hand. "Look, you and I don't have to fight. We can keep it real simple. I go up, you stay down, and everyone's happy."

The purple hanoko watched, didn't follow as Wax retreated several more steps. His back, now, hit the small trees. Protection, at least, from the third cat if it chose to come back for more. Now, how was—

A rope dangled down before him. Wax risked a look up, following the path, and saw Pan's own rope tied to Wax's lost tool.

"Grab on and I'll get you up quick," Pan said, barely visible through the foiliage above.

A better plan than he had.

"In three," Wax said, then swooped the sword back into its sheath.

As soon as the blue blade disappeared, the hanoko's eyes went wide and the cat lurched forward. Wax reached, snagged the rope, shouting for Pan to go, go, go, and the man, never known for haste, finally found some as he dropped off the branch above.

Wax yanked skyward, the rope cutting into his palms. The air shifted at his feet, the hanoko's claws missing by a distance too small for Wax to care to contemplate.

Instead, he climbed up, up, and then past a falling Pan. Kicking out his legs, Wax swung over to the big tree trunk, found a purchase, and stopped the ballast.

Pan hung there in the gap between the big tree and the smaller grove. Beneath him, the hanokos seemed to guess their quarry wasn't worth the effort, the mother dragging her wiped kitten off into the jungle.

"Guess what?" Pan said as Wax found a stable branch to reel him in. "I saw it."

"Saw what?"

"The outpost. We're almost there." Pan's face grinned as Wax reached out, grabbed his hand. "And the sana? The great one? It's blooming, Wax."

CHAPTER 23

ROCKBITERS

The damn sabers were useless. Svarde made the observation in a split second as he clambered over the Whent ship's side. Maena's cutthroats had their curved blades out and swinging at an outnumbered Whent crew, but the rock-bellied enemies hid behind their shields and laughed. Like boulders blocking caverns, the Whents stationed themselves before their hatches down, in the doorways to the cabins, before the stairs climbing to the massive tiller. They sat, shelled by their stonework shields, their bulky rock armor, and took the hits.

Svarde, axes in hand and thinking he was about to find himself in the middle of a fractious fight, wound up just looking. Every Whent had two Rana sailors cornering them, chinking away with pointless whacks on the brown-black rock armor. Nobody resisted.

The plan seemed to be let the Rana exhaust themselves against the impossible, then try something.

A plan that might've worked, if not for Maena. Svarde found her when the captain whistled again, a bright chirp coming from the Whent ship's aft, where a three-pronged obsidian till lunged up from the deck like a black sunrise.

Using two sailors for a boost, Maena jumped and scaled the sloping wall up towards the tiller, the Whent guards on either side staying stock still in their shells. She climbed passed etchings, ones Svarde read as he walked that way, and parsed to mean the ship's contents. The coarse stone could be wiped clean at port, adjusted to match the ship's newest freight.

Clever, and less wasteful than the paper script Foti kept using.

Not for the first time, Svarde wondered how much more the isles could get done if they started really working together.

Not that this would help.

Maena pulled herself up near the tiller, yanking her saber free, and looked around. Her stern face slipped into a smile as nobody came up to ram her, break her bones, or toss her into the sea. She turned back to the pointless fighting, sucked in a breath, and Svarde put his back to the rock wall.

Whatever was about to happen, the relative calm wasn't going to last.

"Whent rockbiters!" Maena called, her voice breaking over a snapping afternoon breeze. Sun splashed all around, slashed by rigging and the massive Whent sails. "We've come to take what we want, whether you'll give it or not. You'll let us have it, or I'll turn your ship so hard to starboard the next wave'll send it over. Lose some or all, that's your choice."

A choice no Whent would ever make. Svarde shook his head. The stone munchers were about as prideful a people as existed in the isles. Only Kance gave'em a run in that department, and at least the wind riders were a whole light lighter to throw around.

The ship vibrated. Svarde traced the sounds, starting at various corners, and realized it wasn't the whole ship shaking at once. No, the Whents were tapping their rock feet against the stiff wood planks, sending shakes back and forth to one another.

"They're talking!" Svarde called. "Be ready!"

A laugh to his right took the warning from his words. A Rana sailor, knife between his teeth and saber held point-first at a stone-solid Whent.

"First time with these boyos?" The sailor asked, the vibrations beneath them picking up.

"Sea raids aren't my thing."

"Then know this. They're having a chat now all along the ship, plotting their attack would be my guess." The Rana's wicked smile widened and he plucked the dagger free with his off-hand. "These boys always start slow, then they get fast, and then they get bloody."

As if listening in on the sailor's dire foretelling, the vibrations ceased, the ship returning to its solemn rocking. Silence, save a couple venturing seagulls curious about the conflagration and its implications for their lunch.

Svarde looked 'round the deck. Counted twenty-odd Rana sailors and a third that many Whents. Suicide numbers for the rockbiters to try and contest.

Yet his twisting stomach told Svarde this would be over in a bad way before long.

The Whent didn't give a clue to their strike. Instead, like volcanoes bursting, the granite warriors threw themselves at the Rana. Heavy and odd, their armor striking out at all angles, the warriors barreled ahead, knocking sailors into the sea, flat onto the deck, or crushing them beneath their stone slab fists.

Delighted battle-cries rose up from the river walkers, the sailors at last given a chance to get behind the Whent, to slip their swords and daggers through slits in the Whent armor.

The sailor to Svarde's right tried the tactic, swatting at the Whent's massive stone-wrapped arm with his saber to draw it wide, then diving in with the knife to prick at the Whent's inside arm. The move earned the sailor a vicious headbutt, the man keeping his grin all the way to the deck.

The Whent, muttering something in the isle's little-used earth tongue, turned towards Svarde. Given a straight on look, Svarde thought the warrior resembled a turtle more than anything. Short and stumpy in her gear, the Whent fighter nonetheless showed weakness only in light leather patches between hard rose stone. Her face, aside from two eye slits and a single notch at the nose, looked like it'd been carved from red granite.

She came at him in a rolling shoulder-charge, a literal falling forward that would've buried Svarde into the wood if he hadn't gone for a late sidestep, heading to his left and letting the Whent barrel by. Twirling with his axes, Svarde went for a shoulder strike, one that would've turned a normal arm into a useless, mauled thing. Instead the axe struck some stone, setting off sparks and sending Svarde's hand numb in the aftershock.

The Whent slowed up, turned back to Svarde with a laugh. Her shoulders rose as she took a big breath, ready to lunge again.

A simple assault begged for a simple solution. If the axes wouldn't work, then . . .

Svarde retreated as the Whent charged, her blind drive

certain to bury him. Certain, at least, until Svarde jumped back off the ship's railing. His leap carried him down a level, letting him land with a hard crunch on a cargo-unloading alcove. Following, smashing with an angry yelp, came the Whent. Ship pieces fell with her, the whole bunch plunging by Svarde to crash into the sea.

Either she'd duck off the armor fast, or the Whent would find herself the latest loss down in those depths.

Not a problem Svarde could concern himself with, especially not with the Whent ship's dark caverns waiting ahead.

With the fight continuing up above, iron striking stone, Svarde readied his axes and stepped inside.

CHAPTER 24

SEEN AMONG THE STONE

The cave hollowed out before long, the downward slope leveling into a broad room. Foti-crafted supports burrowed into the sides, their gray iron bearing fiend scratches as they closed like a spider above the hunter's heads. Deshiva went straight to the room's center, waving her torch back and forth before her as if sweeping away the dark.

Bliss and Quik flowed to the left, keeping to the outer wall while the line advanced across the room. On the far end, Deshiva announced, the cave continued.

The bombs marked their detonations here, the blast spray throwing a chalky white dust into the air, splashing against the walls. The silence following Deshiva's words gnawed at Bliss, its only companions the scuff of feet on stone, the beat of spears as their owners bounced them on rock.

Outside, the jungle flushed with life, with noise. Caves were so . . . quiet.

Next to her, Quik slowed. He crouched, and Bliss turned with him, following his gaze towards a deserted, shadowed corner ahead. The mine, otherwise abandoned for the coming winter, had little left save its metal bones. The alcove, doubtless made for storage in better times, now sat quiet as Deshiva continued her march forward.

Bliss stared into that shadowed slit, its uncanny resemblance to the same curled dark back near the surfside in the village. An easy place to hide.

'Light it,' Bliss signed, and Quik thrust his torch at the offset space.

Nothing. Just rock.

Dust gathered as Bliss let herself relax. Deshiva had tossed bombs down here. There wouldn't be anything left. The fiends were either gone or dead. No need to get tense.

Next to her, Quik coughed, then sneezed. Dusted sprayed, his torch went high to keep it from his spit, and Bliss followed the light, watched it crawl across the beige-blasted ceiling, the spaces between those girders lumpy with old mortar.

Old, stringy mortar.

Bliss reached, caught Quik's hand as he started to bring the torch down. Stared harder as the hunters continued past them.

She didn't know how mines were made, how so much rock could be held above their heads, but Bliss knew nature, knew sharp-edged stone and the silky curves of natural muscle.

'Hold the torch,' Bliss signed.

"Why?" Quik replied, and Bliss answered him by scooping a busted rock off the floor and launching it at the ceiling, right at the sandy, dust-coated clump.

The rock hit, and it made a sound decidedly not like the clanking, dull thud it should've.

A golden eye cracked open, found Bliss. Wheezing noises echoed into the room, from all around.

Deshiva called the hunters to arms, and the fiends sprang their trap.

The monsters dropped like rain, plopping down among the hunters and lashing out in every direction with every limb. Claws and fangs ripped, scaled bodies lunged left and right, scattering the smaller humans like toys. Quik ran at the one Bliss had spotted, raising his wood gauntlets and whooping up like the man was about to jump into the sea.

And Bliss stood there, hands on her staff, while the monsters descended around them. Her blood pumped, but her nerves froze. The wheezing hisses seemed to pierce her throat, drive away every reaction from her mind save one: stand still and perhaps she'd make it out alive.

Bliss's saner half fought the terror, threw one reasoned suggestion after another against the panic wall surrounding her mind. None came through. None could make her take another step closer to the thing, even as the fiend shrugged off Quik's initial swiping blows to throw her brother, with a single swat, into the cave wall.

She couldn't help him. She couldn't help any of them. All Bliss had was a bamboo stick. She wasn't even an adult. She should be back in Kitaye, picking fruit and prepping dinner with her parents, not here, not here, not here.

A stick hit her, its hard bluntness sending Bliss sprawling. The hunter who'd struck her, Bliss didn't know, but she saw a fiend's biting single fang sweep through the area she'd been in. The hunter gave her the slightest nod before sweeping his staff up to catch that fang. Hooking it, the fang biting through to the bamboo's hollow core, the hunter knelt and swung the staff over his shoulder. The leverage threw the fiend off its feet, hammering it to the rocky ground.

Yet, for all his triumph, the hunter left himself open to the fiend who'd battered Quik. The ugly, muddy monster slithered its way towards the hunter, one nasty claw getting ready to strike.

Bliss hit first.

Driving the staff like a spear, she whacked the fiend's soft right side, digging her wood into the scaly meat and sending the monster off-balance. As it wobbled on two legs, Quik rushed past Bliss, her brother diving for the monster's neck and wrangling it to the ground.

"Now, Bliss!" Quik yelled, his voice coming through clean in a cave no longer anywhere near quiet.

Bliss swung her staff, an overhead blow cracking the fiend's skull and sending the thing into a lifeless slump. Quik squirmed out from under the beast while Bliss, her older instincts beating away the panic, adjusted her grip, looked for another target.

"Glad you're back," Quik said. "Follow me."

Like a safety hook for her rope, Quik guided Bliss around the battlefield, his gauntlets opening holes in fiend's defenses for her staff to punch through. Then other hunters could come in to finish the job, battering, bashing, or gashing the fiends till all four creatures lay dead on cave's floor. Three hunters shared the creatures' end, with another six holding nasty wounds.

Deshiva, unscathed save a scratch from the cavern floor, called for the bodies to be hauled, the fiends to be left behind. Outside, in the cool twilight, they stacked more Foti bombs around the mine's entrance, exhausting the supply. With a tossed torch—the hunter dashed and dove behind a log for cover—the bombs blew, breaking the cave's entry and collapsing the portal under more rock than Bliss would ever care to dig through.

"A grave for the damned," Deshiva said after.

Everyone knew it wouldn't be the last.

CHAPTER 25

COASTERS

How many times had they done this, left on an adventure only to come home victorious as the sun vanished behind the tall jungle trees?

"At least five," Pan said, walking beside Wax on the cart path leading uphill towards the Najahn outpost, the Great Sana rising over the jagged palisade much like the fiend loomed over Kitaye days ago.

"Five? Think you're missing a few," Wax countered.

The beaten clay caked to their bare feet, the occasional rock adding some flavor to the walk. After escaping the hanoko, Wax had offered to drop from the trees and enjoy a more leisurely stroll, walk into the outpost like the victors they were. Swinging had its uses, but it tended to make you crash into your goal instead of arriving on two solid feet.

"I'm only counting the ones where we actually succeeded," Pan said. "How many empty satchels did we come back with?"

"Think you need to change your definition. We survived, we won. At least, that's how I see it."

"Can't trade survival. And you didn't have to face my dad's looks."

Pan's patriarch bore the burden of high expectations. Not for himself, mind, but for Pan. Wax's friend had to be the best at anything Pan chose to do. Which, Wax figured, was why Pan settled for gathering fungus off the jungle floor.

Not a whole lot of competition in that arena.

"Your dad'll have to find someone else to pick on when you come back with the skar," Wax said.

Up ahead, the jungle signaled its temporary end with a gradual decline to cleared greenery. Set gardens lay in rounded Noctia rows, rather than the loose lines Wax would find around Kitaye. Livestock pens replaced the jungle noise with their own grunts and growls, the beasts not large in number but vocal in their frustrations.

Wax and Pan shared a glance as the sound grew, hiding their grimaces. Vis operated on a wide open system, animals free to roam and free, therefore, to be hunted. Skill and honor, a meal earned.

Noctia had different ideas. Noctia also had sharp voulges, armor, and the key to keeping the fiends at bay. So Vis let them do what they wanted and kept quiet.

What Wax would not, could not keep quiet about, though, was how the path seemed deserted save for he and Pan.

"Told you the swinging would be the winner," Wax said. "Nobody else has the guts to go for it all the way here."

"Those guts almost had us falling into thorns, I about dislocated my shoulder on that tree, and those hanokos should've eaten us."

"But did they? Did we make it?"

"You want me to say yes."

"I want you to shout it, Pan!" Wax took a couple quick steps ahead, turned to face Pan with his arms wide, hoping the Great Sana behind him was framed center. "This is what we set out for, and we didn't just try, we won!"

"Hurrah."

Deflating. Wax let his arms fall and his smile fade along with them.

"What's the deal? When we left, you were all about making this a real go."

"Still am," Pan said, looking past Wax to the Najahn outpost. "I just don't think you're taking this seriously."

"What was all the swinging for if not being serious? I gave us the win."

Pan rolled his eyes, "You gave us the win? I believe I had to do all that swinging too."

"Well, sure, but Guardians aren't supposed to do everything for their Renewals, right?"

"You think I know what a Guardian's supposed to do?"

A fair question, and not one Wax had really considered. Why, when there was no way they'd end up dealing with the problem? Even getting this far, Wax figured something would stop Pan from finishing the job.

The Renewals were supposed to be heroes, warriors, kings, queens embarking on a vast trek around the isles. Challenges aplenty, dangers everywhere, hard choices and sacrifices abounding.

Not exactly the stuff for which Pan was made. Wax, still back-pedaling, tried to take his friend's measure. They'd spent the nights and days here journeying, chatting, sharing wistful and random memories from nearly two decades burned in each other's company. They'd joked, they'd shared dinners, waters, fruits snagged from passing branches. All through his life, Wax would be hard pressed to remember a single day he hadn't seen Pan for at least a minute.

With the sun at his back, a shadowed lattice drawn by the jungle trees, Pan looked crossed in gold and black. He held his head at a slump, his legs and arms shuffling without much drive, as if being pushed by some phantom call. The man's heart just wasn't in this, despite the declaration made back in Kitaye.

Stupid, then. Stupid to drag them all this way when Pan didn't want to finish the damn race. Wax could've stayed back, helped his parents rebuild their home.

"This was a waste of time, wasn't it?" Wax asked.

"What?"

"You dragging us all this way, just wanted to show your dad you wouldn't lie down?"

Pan flinched, but didn't turn away. Didn't stop walking either.

"I know what I want, Wax. This isn't it."

"Then why?"

"Because what I want is my dad to stop looking at me like I'm not good enough, all right?" Pan pointed at Wax. "Your dad's a crafter. Fine. Mine? Mine was a hunter for a long time till he took that fall, now he's one of the best fishers in the city. He's all about action. Earning your keep with blood and sweat's what he tells me, every night, when I come back with a satchel filled with mushrooms."

"That's food."

Pan laughed, "Not to him, it's not."

"So what's this going to prove, that you can walk a long way?"

"That I'm brave enough to try," Pan exhaled and Wax fell in alongside his friend. "I don't need his approval, Wax.

I don't need him to be proud of me. I just want him to leave me alone."

"Then I'll—"

"You'll do no damn thing. This is my family, my problem. He'll come right at me if you try to play my protector. Not that I need it, Wax. Not this time."

"So then?"

"So we go up there, we talk to the Najahn, and we play it slow," Pan said. "I don't know what we have to do to complete this thing, but it's not going to be me, you get it? I'm not going to leave this island. Everything I love is right here."

On that, at least, Wax could agree.

The Najahn outpost circled the Great Sana. Surrounded by wooden beams and their pointed ends stabbing the sky but looking, to Wax's eyes, a bit on the short end. Any half-competent Vis or a hanoko who really wanted it could scale a tree, get a good start, and swing up and over.

Doing so would get the jumper some good air and a likely landing on a sloping thatched roof. The Najahn had their scalloped gutters here too, leading to rain barrels that, if Wax had to guess, would be overflowing just about every day. There'd been a sunny run lately, but rain tended to be the common friend on the isle. Abundence couldn't change behavior, apparently.

The path up to the gate gained flourishes as Wax and Pan drew into the last stretch. Staves planted into the ground held torches, now fresh lit as the sun gave way to her darker half. The dirt path found pavers, stones intercut more and more with the dust until Wax and Pan had their heels landing on smooth rock. An alien sensation that— even Kitaye's wood docks had a more natural feel, with the timber's give and take at Wax's weight.

The best sign they'd arrived came with the Najahn themselves, a sole member of which stood before the palisade's purple-dyed wooden gate. Voulge ready, chakram looped around his back, the soldier watched Wax and Pan approach without a word.

The two pulled up near the guard, waited for the man to make the first move. The Najahn stared back, blinking here and there but moving not at all save to wave away the occasional encroaching fly.

"Serious business, this guarding stuff?" Wax asked.

"Ignore my friend," Pan jumped in. "We're, uh, here for the Renewal."

The Najahn nodded, held up his voulge. Someone behind the gate saw the signal, pulled the doors open.

"You're the second group today," the Najahn said, turning aside and beckoning the pair ahead. "There'll be no attempts up tonight, though, so you'll all have an even start when the sun rises."

"An even start?" Wax asked as they walked past the guard. "What, is there another race?"

But the guard only shrugged and asked for their weapons, dropping Wax's Foti blade in a lock box just inside the gate.

The gate closed behind Wax and Pan after they passed through, sealing them into an outpost reeking of self-importance. Kitaye had its neighborhoods, its sections given to specialties, but nowhere did banners hang declaring who held sway. Nobody placed sigils outside their homes or put emblems on their chests. Tattoos, yes, but that was simply a marker of who you were. Not a boast, not a luxury.

Noctia's influence extended to the grounds too, with

close cut plants in decorative arrangements. Nature had no sway here, just efficient beauty.

At least their goal wasn't hard to find: dead center beyond the gate, rising up to dominate the surroundings, sat the central barracks. Najahn workers, soldiers—Wax wasn't sure what to call them—pointed the pair in that direction, said they'd find food and a place to sleep. Then the leather-clad, sweat-stained people went back to . . . things?

"I don't get it," Wax whispered to Pan as they walked through the outpost. "They're all moving around, but I don't know why?"

"You're asking the wrong person."

The mystery solved itself when they went inside the barracks, the four story structure a showcase for what could be achieved with wood and ambition. Above the main door sat the Najahn sigil, the hollow-eyed circle taken up by Noctia. It seemed to leer at Wax, and the man looked away, suppressed a shudder.

Who'd want to live with that thing watching you all the time?

Inside, the barracks gave them a warmer welcome. A central chimney roared, stone ash-blasted and doing a good job heating a broad room slathered in long tables. Each blonde wood slab had six chairs attending it, each immaculate against its owner. Excepting, anyway, the occupied ones.

Lanterns hung from the ceiling on Foti-crafted chains, the glass baubles mingling with the firelight to cast the room in a cozy gold. Wax sniffed, caught a thick stew in the making. After days eating what they could forage and adding it to salted meat, something fresh made his mouth go wet.

Not that Wax had much to trade. Hopefully the Najahn would spare the Renewal recruits a meal.

"Those must be the ones that beat us," Pan said, stepping inside and nodding towards the two tables closest to the kitchen. "They don't look like Noctia."

Weaves and ink gave the party away—Wax counted six —and for more than just Vis heritage. Their spiraling designs contrasted hard with the geometric lines on Wax and Pan's skin, a sign these two hadn't come from Kitaye, but from Mottilan, Vis's other city on the eastern coast.

Rivals in more ways than one, then.

"You want to make some friends?" Wax asked.

"I want some food, and then I want to sleep somewhere that's not on a branch."

"It wasn't that bad."

"My back says otherwise."

Wax's back would probably agree with Pan's, the lingering stiffness a timer on wilderness travels. Even if you had all the food and water you needed, the muscles would give out on you eventually.

"Guess we take a seat?" Pan asked.

No Najahn hung near the entrance. In fact, the only Noctia people in sight worked in the kitchen, visible behind a long counter and the wavy film from hot ovens.

"Your guess is as good as mine," Wax replied, and he followed Pan over to the right, plopping down at a table on the opposite side of the other Vis travelers. "Really going for the anti-social vibe, I see?"

"I guarantee, we talk to them, all they'll tell us about is how much better they are."

"Dim view of our fellow Vis, Pan."

"You don't trade as much as I do. They're all slimy dealers, Wax. They'll take you for everything and more if you're not careful."

Wax leaned back in the wooden seat, marveled at the back panel. Chairs weren't a big thing at home. Easier to cut a log in two and rest it on the ground, giving folks a bench if they needed one. Or, you know, you could sit on your house edge and dangle your legs down. Still, with the fire warming him up, Wax stretched, let his legs rock the chair back.

Felt pretty nice.

The soup, laden with chopped yams, onions, and fresh meat—Wax didn't ask what it was, the cook didn't volunteer—felt nicer. Pan dropped the bowls scored from the counter on the table and both dug in with a sloppy relish. Wooden spoons served to get the broth from its dull clay bowl, and Wax didn't even notice the Najahn sigils carved into the handle for the first few sips.

Looking like a gilded flower overlaid with triple grass stalk, the symbol told whomever happened to hold the spoon that it was Najahn property, and not just any Najahn, but the ones who lived on Vis.

"Factions," Pan said when Wax pointed it out. "It's like home, right? All these Najahn get posted here or the other isles, for years, and they join the local team."

"What does that even mean?" Wax threw his eyes around. "Nothing here looks like Kitaye."

"Bet it looks different from the outpost on Kance, though."

"You think they could even make one there? Wouldn't it just blow away?"

Pan stared, "Wax, I don't know if you're joking or ignorant."

"Let's go with both."

Seven Isles, with Vis on the southernmost side. Wax knew about the others what passed through in stories, in the sailors stopping by to trade. Traveling between the isles for any other reason seemed so rare, and certainly not in his own plans, that learning how Kance dealt with its ever-present gusts seemed like a waste of time. Especially when he could spend those hours swinging from sana flowers.

"Guess you'll figure it out if we win this thing," Pan said. "Renewals go everywhere."

"But we're not winning this thing, right?"

A hand slapped down on the table, dirt-coated and leading up a burly arm to a gritty man with a gnarled grin on his face. His hair framed the grin, pulled into two long pony-tails and tied off with taut twine. His cheeks wore his dinner, and his eyes gave away a grim mood.

"Glad to hear it," the man said, and Wax put his hoarse voice, the wrinkles lining his face, as at least a decade older than Wax and Pan. "No need to make this a contest anymore. We were here first, we ought to get first chance."

Wax flicked a look at Pan, who'd turned back to his soup. Not a challenge Pan wanted to engage with, and despite Wax's own pride, he could defer, just this once, to his friend. A Guardian should follow orders, right?

"I'd like to hear it," the man continued, planting his other palm on the wood. The bowls rattled. "Say you're skipping this one."

Behind him, the man's cohort watched from their table. Amusement and concern crossed their looks, but none seemed willing to add their own intimidation.

A one-off plan, perhaps? Wax studied the man, tried to gauge wheteher he'd had a few too many pints of Najahn ale.

"We came all this way," Pan said. "How would we explain stopping now to our families, our friends?"

Wax caught Pan's particular tone, the same one he'd used since they were kids. Fishing for an answer, looking to play a trick on his target.

"Say you lost. Say you got sick, twisted an ankle, what do I care. The point is you're done. It's over. You can go back to your trees and your fish and let us have the skar."

The man coughed, wiped some slobber away with the back of his hand before returning to the dual-palmed plant. A move Wax suspected might be less for scaring and more for balance.

"I could, but that'd mean lying," Pan said. "I'm not much of a liar."

"How's that my problem?"

"Because I just don't think I can do what you're asking." Pan pushed back his chair, stood. "Guess you'll have to win it, then."

Oh Pan. So predictable until he decided to go off and do the crazy thing. The interloper had to be almost as big as both Wax and Pan put together. While the Najahn didn't allow weapons inside their outpost, this guy's mitts looked more than capable.

But then, what was a Guardian supposed to do?

As the man turned towards Pan, pulling his palms off the table with wobbly effort, Pan squared his own shoulders. Gave the man a look Wax had only seen his friend pull out when he refused to budge from a price on his mushrooms.

It was enough to bring a Guardian to his feet.

"See, I was hopin' you'd be okay with lying," the man said, bringing his hands together and stretching out his fingers. "But if you're not going to take the nice way, we can make sure that broken leg is plenty real."

Wax scooped up the bowl and smashed it into the man's head. No preamble, no warning, just instinct offering its best solution to the problem. The clay broke with a heavy clatter, the man stumbled to his right to rest against the chimney. Those big hands went to his head, rubbing at a spot no longer just dirty, but bruising and red.

"Wax, what?" Pan asked, bravado fleeing as it so often did when the fight truly started.

"You were about to get your lights knocked out, so I saved you the trouble," Wax replied. "Guardian's job."

The bowl should've ended the fight right then, but the man's buddies, apparently not content to watch their friend get his, sprang from their chairs and ran at the two. Four ramblers, in various grasses and woven tunics, stomped, ran, and shouted their way towards a retreating Wax and Pan.

The fifth tore off to the downed man, helping the big guy away from the hot chimney.

"Ideas?" Pan asked.

"Don't let'em break your legs," Wax replied. "You'll need'em in the morning."

With his bowl busted, Wax went for the next best weapon: a chair. The light wood made for an easy pick-up, and with Pan following his lead, the duo stood with eight stubby legs pointing at their attackers.

The foursome refused to be intimidated.

Wax stood off against a couple women who looked like they'd spent too many days on fishing boats. With leathered skin and hard eyes, the two, wielding their soup spoons like clubs, split to Wax's either side. Their battle-field, the narrow alley between two long tables and their attendant furniture, made for a poor pincer candidate. Or so Wax thought, till the one on the left made a running jump onto her table. While she advanced at a rough angle for Wax to counter, the other darted in with the spoon waving, batting at Wax's chair legs.

"Give it up," she snarled, her voice inflected with Mottilan's clipped syllables. "He's made the right offer. You weren't supposed to be here this fast."

"What's that supposed to mean?"

The woman didn't answer, but came in fast, smacking at Wax's chair and knocking it right, leaving him wide open for a jumping assault from the table runner.

For all the leaping Wax had done in his life, all the leaps from frond to vine to branch, he'd never had a person jump at him. It was, frankly, terrifying.

Her eyes wide, her spoon held in a double-grip as she jumped, knees leading at Wax's head, the woman cut an impressive figure.

One Wax had no answer for. He dropped the chair, flung up his left arm in a futile block, felt the spoon hit and the woman follow, bearing him to the floor. The spoon made its second appearance, smacking Wax across the shoulder while he kicked out with his legs, getting just enough leverage to push the jumper off him.

Only for her friend to come in and jab Wax in the stomach with her own utensil. The soup he'd just devoured came right back up, splattering out and driving back the second attacker, albeit only for a moment.

Getting up to his hands, Wax, his eyes watering and his gut feeling like it was ready to throw up all over again, tried to figure out how to plead a surrender.

He didn't have to.

The whistle came sharp and harsh, just like the one the

Najahn had used when calling the Kitaye Renewal crowd to attention. All eyes went towards the barracks entry, where three Najahn soldiers stood in their regalia, those nasty voulges held at the ready.

"You'll stop this now," said the leader, a narrow-faced man whose nose looked to have been broken more than a few times. "Leave off each other, clean up the mess. Do it, then I'll have words with you rabble."

Despite the insult, Wax took the reprieve. Pan, who'd had himself thrown into another table, picked himself up even more slowly. The chef came out with a mop, handed it to Wax without a word. A few strokes, some putting of chairs back to where they belonged, and the barracks looked none the worse for wear.

Though Wax felt like he might not keep food down for a few days.

"You're lucky I've seen this before," the Najahn said to the assembled group, once their cleaning duties were complete.

Pan and Wax stayed on the right side, at their own table near the entry, while the accosting six took the left. The big lunk still looking loopy brought Wax some small satisfaction.

"I've witnessed two Renewals," the Najahn said, putting his age higher than Wax would've guessed, but helmets and armor could hide a lot. "Both times, the worst scum tried to become heroes. Both times, people who had no business leaving their shambles tried to take what belonged to other, better beings." The Najahn pierced them all, one by one, with pointed looks. "Tomorrow, you will get your chance, one none of you deserve, to represent your isle in the only way anyone on Vis can matter to the world. Don't rob each other of that hope, not when so many will do it later." The Najahn's scowl deepened. "Your eagerness is laughable. Fighting, now, for the right to die later? Go to your beds and pray you sleep in. Hope the chance passes you by. I have seen two Renewals, but I have seen far, far more try, and lose everything in the attempt."

The Najahn played babysitters from that point forward, splitting the two groups up and sending them to their dorms. Pan and Wax took turns in a hot bath—that chimney proving its worth. Wax wrapped his bruises in hot towels, settled onto the straw mat that'd serve as his bed. Not quite the hammock from home, but a big upgrade over the branches he'd been snoozing on. Pan, too, stretched out on his with a strong, contented sigh.

Their room held little beyond the two mats. A single lantern in Noctia's rounded fashion hung near the door, turned down for the night. No other furniture save a battered rack for hanging clothes. A shuttered window, opened now, looked out into the outpost and a dark, clouded night. Rain would be coming soon.

Another reason to be grateful they'd made it inside.

"That was a stupid fight, wasn't it?" Pan asked.

"I've picked better," Wax replied. "Wasn't going to take that guy's deal, though."

"Isn't that my choice?"

Wax looked up at the black ceiling. The dying lantern cast it in shadow, and if Wax focused, he could imagine being just about anywhere. Like home, with Sawi. Somewhere he wouldn't have to deal with Pan's waffling.

"I didn't see you making it, so I put it in my hands." Wax cupped those hands behind his head, winced at the ache the move made in his side. "I'm not going to let myself get shoved aside by those coasters."

Pan laughed, a quiet chuckle. "Maybe I knew that."

"That I'd start a fight?"

"I asked you to be my Guardian, didn't I? Have to take the good Wax with the angry one."

"I am a package deal."

"If things get dangerous like that Najahn said, you think we're ready for it?"

"It's climbing a Sana, Pan. Even if it's a really big one, I think we're about as ready as we can be." Wax grinned as the lantern sputtered out. "If I were you, I'd think about which isle you'll go first."

"Easy," Pan replied. "Foti. It's westward, and warmer. Plus, I bet we can get some real gear there that'll help us out."

"You jealous of my sword, Pan?"

"I just want a shield that'll block it when you start swinging."

"Hey."

After a long few days, a longer night, the laughter felt good. And when the rain started to fall, the sleep felt even better.

CHAPTER 26

BARGAINS

Svarde could honestly say he'd never been in a cave on the sea. The Whent ship, massive yet somehow buoyant, took on a cavern's appearance beyond the outer hull. With axes in either hand, relying on light streaming through openings and cast by periodic globe lanterns, Svarde took his first steps inside slow. Moisture assaulted his nose, the steady wet from the sea held captive in the porous walls. The hard, smooth outside softened in here, becoming more spongey.

His feet almost bounced on the floor.

That didn't stop the claustrophobic feeling: the Whent ship had wide halls, no doubt for those armored shells to get about, but the irregular shaped walls, the scooping ceiling, coupled with the boat's slight swaying on the waves to throw Svarde's senses into confusion.

Back on Vis, fighting the fiend in the cave, he'd focused on the monster and excluded all else. Here, he found his mark: the glowing orange-yellow light in the globes. Each one gave the next move.

The Whent's ship became a warren quick, the fighting

above dwindling to nothing more than vibrations as Svarde continued inside. There had to be a stair up, or a ladder, but all Svarde found were rooms. Carved out places where the crew must've bunked, hard slabs jutting into the wall. A couple had straw bedding. One attempted modern comfort with a cloth blanket. All seemed bereft of personal goods.

No sign, either, of what Maena sought to steal. Maybe that was lower, but damned if there was a way down that Svarde could find.

The sounds changed as the man made his way to the ship's middle: a new echo racing around Svarde with an irregular cadence, the tap tap tap of someone working with a hammer, but not in a blacksmith's rigid rhythm.

Who would be working on something now, with the ship under siege?

The sound did, though, provide Svarde with a direction. Rather than nameless wandering, he angled towards the noise, tracing the whacks and the bangs, now littered here and there with choice, but delighted curses. As if someone were as pleased with their problems as their solutions.

"Where have I found myself?" Svarde muttered, alone in the dim corridors.

He'd been across all seven isles as a Guardian. Had faced calamity and danger and come through without major injury, with hope and new power. A Whent ship shouldn't inspire fear, shouldn't bring anything more than a curled lip and defiant dismissal, but the taps continued, continued, continued.

Svarde had no way to tell time, and as he went further and further into the ship—the size seemed only to grow upon entering—he seemed less and less sure of where he was inside it. The hallways curled and intersected at odd angles, and Svarde began to wonder if he was crossing back along the same rooms over and over again. The tap, tap tugged him along, but what had once been a clear signal seemed to pass from everywhere, from nowhere.

Only a fool calls the enemy down upon themselves. Svarde gripped his axes tighter, wished Kivi had made the boarding with him. The Ferrite's blunt sense would've helped keep his mind sound, but now it wandered.

Would the Whent keep a fiend down here? Waiting for a wandering enemy? Was this all a trap, and Maena and her crew dead up above? Would Svarde's bones be ground on the rocks by that awful tapping?

It stopped. Stopped and left behind a yawning nothing. Svarde halted, his boots planted on the ground. He whirled, feeling something behind him, and saw only another sedate globe, flickering away. No wind stirred the air, nothing save his own breath.

A click. A simple, single sound. Followed by a rumble, a gentle quake working its way up Svarde's boots, shins, to his waist and his teeth. The warrior tracked the tremor, found the corridor, and started off that way.

"Are you one of them?" Asked the cursing voice, curious and, as ever, delighted. "The invaders?"

Svarde saw no one. The voice came from ahead, yes, but also down. Shouted up, then, from the lower decks. He crouched, made care to keep his steps light, his boots landing with the softest touch. Low breathing, his eyes wide and watching.

How easy it would be to summon someone with a call, waiting to shoot, stab, ambush them as they approached the newfound path.

"Do you talk, or have the Rana finally given that up too in service of their brutality?" The voice asked.

Svarde kept quiet. There would be time for words once the threat had been dealt with.

A threat that, at least, had chosen not to assault Svarde as he found the way down: a slate plate, one big enough for a man his size to climb with ease. Metal grooves lined the edges, providing a running path for the plate to slide away.

As for where the ladder, a rope-and-stone thing, led?

Another fiery globe presented a larger room, its light vanishing beyond what Svarde could see from above, no hallway, no close walls in sight.

A choice, then. To descend was to invite an even easier ambush. Climbing meant putting his back to the knife, the arrow, the garrote. Staying up here meant more pointless wanderings, a risk even that Maena would win the battle and depart without him. Easy to assume Svarde had been thrown overboard.

Better, then, to go down, find the fight and take, perhaps, a hostage. At least that would give him options.

Svarde holstered his axes, looping them over his back. He stepped back from the hole, gauged his traction, his legs, the ship's sway.

The Vis kids would be proud of his next move.

"I have work to do, you know," the voice called.

Svarde took two steps, jumped, and hit the hole right where he wanted. His body shot through and Svarde twisted, bringing up his legs and feet to catch them on the hole's empty wall. The bounce bought him purchase, one Svarde used to press off into a falling roll down to the lower deck.

The rock still hurt when he hit it, but the fast action would've made it hard for any waiting stab to find a mark. At least, that's what Svarde told himself as he came out of the roll, the axes striking up sparks as they slid along the rock. Svarde drew both, raising their hafts before his face and catching a look into the gloom.

"Those won't help you here," said the voice, and Svarde traced it left, shifted, kept his axes raised. "See, the old ways aren't necessary anymore."

Old ways?

At the burning globe's edge, a figure emerged holding something in her left hand. She had on a bulky suit, not unlike what Svarde saw forgemasters wear in Foti's hottest furnaces. The helmet, a full-on faceplate, rose up to her forehead and jutted out at Svarde, the singed spots all over making it clear this wasn't just for show.

She tossed the thing in her hand, a small box with a light-catching clasp. It spun over once and she caught it right where she'd tossed it, clasp back towards her and perfectly placed in her palm.

"What's your name?" The woman asked.

"Svarde. Where am I?"

The woman wagged her right index finger. Svarde drew the distance, figured he could get in a gut-busting swipe with his axe before she could do, well, anything.

That box, though.

There were enough madmen on the isles to make encountering the unknown a dicey proposition. Who knew what'd happen if she dropped it in death, or if Svarde tried to pick it up. Or Maena and her crew.

"You walked in here, didn't you?" The woman asked, then stopped, her face scrunching up. "Though I didn't think we'd get to Noctia for a few days yet?"

Ami might play some mental game, go for tricks and traps. She could have them.

"You've been boarded. I'm trying to get back to the top deck. Help me, and I'll make sure they spare your life."

The motion came faster than Svarde would've guessed. The woman didn't scream martial skill, but here she was aiming a strange device his way: a tube the length of her forearm, festooned with more dials, gadgets, and gizmos than Svarde had ever seen. Its end broke into three curving pieces which split apart then came back together, looking like a triple-clawed paw making a pincer.

Svarde would've laughed, except the woman looked too serious for games and nothing on this cursed voyage seemed normal.

"And that is?" Svarde asked, pointing an axe at the device.

"Wouldn't you like to know?" The woman replied. "It is, unfortunately, a work in progress. Doesn't have a name. Does, though, have quite the effect. If you could put those axes up, I'd be happy to tell you just what you've stumbled into?"

"No tricks?"

"Nothing that'll kill you, I promise."

Going on the Renewal journey smashed Svarde into all kinds of weird situations, the sorts of things you couldn't roll into with rage alone and expect to survive. Instead, caution tended to rule the day, and if someone offered you a chance to avoid a fight?

Well, you took it.

"This," the woman explained when Svarde put up his axes, "is the future. At least, the future as Whent would have it. Less reliance on those things you have on your back, and more . . . efficiency."

Her eyes glittered as she spoke, a far away look Svarde recognized from his travels with Catya. The Aegis would get mellow when thinking, talking about what isle they'd journey to next, what she'd be able to accomplish once she had all the tokens. None of that had worked out the way they'd planned, but—

"You have to understand," the woman said, leading Svarde along through the hold. As they went, the woman, after lighting a small candle on the first globe, ignited others. The resulting glow showcased a sprawling space filled with crate upon crate, all marked with strange names Svarde couldn't parse. "The isles are becoming more and more dangerous, not less so because of your Rana friends."

"They're raiders, nothing more."

"Tell that to the people they're hurting up above. Their families." The woman shook off the remark, focused back on the crates. "These will offer an unbeatable defense to any who choose to use them. The risk will be too large, the losses too high for pointless fighting." She brightened, a grin blowing wider. "Best of all, the fiends won't stand a chance."

Svarde nodded at the device she still carried, "What does it do?"

"I'd show you, but that would ruin the surprise," the woman replied. "When Noctia lets us bring these to the wider world, then you'll see."

Svarde hesitated, looked at the crates. Maena said there might be things on this ship that could help their journey into the dark. Perhaps these might be it.

"Could you show me how to use one?" Svarde asked.

"Why?"

"Because I mean to go into the Dark Below and destroy the monsters waiting there."

She frowned, "Normally, I'd say yes. But not yet. These aren't ready for that. At least, not with inexperienced hands."

"Then why are you showing me all this?" Svarde asked.

"What's the point? Why not just shoot me and be done with it, or keep yourself hidden?"

The woman took a step away from Svarde, angled the device towards him, "Simple logic, my friend. The easiest way to survive a raid is to get a hostage and wait it out."

SVARDE LET the woman lead him from the hold, upward into the cavernous maze, one she had little trouble navigating. A few turns and they arrived at a simple stair set carved into the rock, red-gray stone leading up. Outside, Sichi's pink light slipped through cracks in the door to the top deck.

It'd been a long evening.

"One thing I don't understand," Svarde said, "is how you manage to get a stone ship like this to float."

"It's rock on the outside, but hollowed out. Enough air in the gaps and she'll float just fine."

Svarde shook his head. Too many marvels these days. A simple axe, a simple swing, and he'd be happy.

The deck offered a story at first glance: Maena's Rana raiders had won the first foray, as evidenced by the wounded Whent being tended to across the deck, by the bits of stolen cargo being slipped down the ropes to the Truro. However, Maena's crew hadn't gone without casualties, a skeleton batch remaining on the Whent ship while others, their curses flying up from the Rana vessel below, dotted the air. Maena herself stood in the deck's middle, in heavy conversation with a burly man who must've been the Whent captain.

"Civilized," the woman said. "At least we haven't lost that."

When Svarde stomped onto the scene, he drew the attention, incredulous stares all around. Most slipped quick from him to the woman at his back, her strange device open and pointing.

"Annalyse!" Cried the burly man, pushing past Maena towards Svarde and the woman. "This isn't the place to reveal that!"

"You didn't keep me safe, so what choice did I have?" Annalyse replied. "Fulfill your end of the bargain and I'll fulfill mine."

"What bargain is this?" Maena, following the Whent captain over, asked in a tone that suggested less interest in the bargain and more in what treasure Annalyse held in her hands. "Your captain suggested nothing much of value lay on the ship. Only provisions. Perhaps he was withholding?"

Svarde looked at Annalyse, caught her coy expression, the woman's fingers near the device's buttons. There in Sichi's silver-pink glow, the device looked more alien than before, hopelessly strange. Dangerous to themselves as much as any enemy.

"She could have killed me, Maena," Svarde said. "Leave her and her toys. We have more important things to do."

"It looks like a weapon, Svarde, and we could very much use weapons."

"Not like this. If what she told me is half true, we would be risking all our lives bringing that thing on board our ship."

Maena narrowed her eyes at the Guardian. Studied him for a long minute.

"You mean that, don't you?" She asked, finally.

"He does, and he's right," Annalyse said. "This violence isn't really my thing, but if you try to take this, I guarantee they won't find what little is left of your body. Ever."

• • •

"ANNALYSE HAD QUITE the way with threats," Manea mused as her Rana ship broke away from the Whent vessel and continued careening north. "What little is left of my body. Hmm."

"That's what you're focusing on?" Svarde, standing nearby on the ship's top deck, gave Kivi a much-needed pat. "Not how ridiculous that all was?"

"Nobody died. Even that one you threw overboard wriggled free and floated back up. I don't know why you're so perturbed."

"We could've. You're the one who said this mission is so important, but you risk lives for this?"

"We risk lives for our isle, Svarde. And what treasure we might find." Maena curled up a half-smile. "After the Whent ship leaves eyesight, out goes a message on a gull. It'll reach home in a couple days, letting Rana know Whent is up to something strange. Their technology won't be a secret for long."

"Technology? What's that?"

Manea's sigh rose over the ocean's whispers. "It's getting late, Svarde. Do I have to catch you up on everything you've missed in the last decade?"

"How about just the important bits?"

CHAPTER 27

DREAM SLAYER

The fiends attacked over and over again, slashing through Bliss's dreams, her nightmares every time she closed her eyes. She woke up gasping time and time again, thankful she'd picked a spot near the camp's outskirts, in the ruined town's square, where nobody seemed to notice. Even Quik, just an arm's length away, seemed so exhausted after the day that he didn't see his sister's stress.

Not like he ought to. The guy had already done enough for her, like diving in on that fiend down by the shore. Bliss could own her problems, could handle them.

But not, perhaps, while lying on the grass.

Night rarely felt dark outside the jungle, and in the coastal town, few trees offered cover from the star's bright lights. The soft silver twinkle played companion to Bliss's walk, a barefoot padding around other sleeping hunters through the ruined village.

Without the bodies—all buried now—the empty houses and shattered workshops took on an ethereal edge. A ghosted derelict, with nothing more than spirits to fill the voids. At least Bliss had the grounding nighttime pestering from insects, had the distant call of hanoko and birds too irritated to sleep.

Arriving at the same cliffside where she'd fought the fiend came as something of a surprise. She'd been wandering without direction, but really, given all she'd been dreaming, it made a certain sense she'd wind up here.

The steps down to the coast shown in a mottled gray, darker splotches here and there showing spilled, dried blood from the earlier fight. Far down on the rocks, the fiend's body still lay, kissed every now and then by the surf. From up here, the shape fuzzed at the details, and Bliss was glad for it.

She'd seen enough mangled hair, fangs, claws.

Bliss felt for her staff, realized she'd left it behind. Stupid, not taking the weapon on a late walk. Deshiva kept saying fiends could strike from anywhere, at any time.

That, right there, was why Bliss thought she felt so broken up. The day's creeping horrors hovered, yes, and Bliss could tell she'd never forget the people they'd stacked here, but the part gnawing at her now?

She'd been capable. She'd thought herself able to handle anything. Even the giant fiend that'd terrorized Kitaye, Bliss had stood her ground, faced the monster and had her chance to bash it in. She'd been scared then, in a distant way, a remote peril she met with fire and fury.

The fiend and its fang weren't so simple, so easy to dismiss. Bliss was its sole target, a one on one match-up on the rocks, and she'd not only failed, but failed hard enough to make death a certainty.

What was it Wax always said, when their parents asked why he was taking yet another jungle jaunt?

This is who I am.

Then who was she? Fighter, protector, Lira? Or just an easy target for a hungry monster?

"It's Bliss, right? Quik's sister?"

Bliss wheeled at the voice, twitching at the sudden sound, to see Deshiva walking up to her. Without further preamble, Deshiva planted her spear in the ground and joined Bliss on the cliff, dangling their legs over the edge. Without her armor, her furious stare, Deshiva should've appeared more fragile, weak, vulnerable. Instead, Bliss only saw strength, confidence.

If a fiend dared attack right then, Bliss had no doubt Deshiva would leap into the fight without a moment's thought.

Bliss nodded. Her hands twitched, but Deshiva wouldn't understand the signing. Yet, the hunt master's appraising look suggested Deshiva knew Bliss wouldn't be settling in for a late night chat.

"I always have a hard time sleeping after days like this," Deshiva said.

Bliss frowned, upped her eyebrows. Asked a question with her eyes and Deshiva caught it.

"This happens every Renewal. Sometimes before, if Noctia's late on its game." Deshiva looked closer at Bliss. Her stare made Bliss shiver, as though her every weakness was exposed. "You're Lira too. They inducted me not long before the last Renewal. You'll see things this time. More like today. It's our job and our duty to keep what parts of Vis safe that we can."

Bliss nodded back towards the camp, the sleeping hunters. Then pointed to herself and Deshiva.

"Both, now. A push I made. There's not enough Lira, and there are enough hunters with skills to put down a fiend." Deshiva swept her searing look out to the sea.

"There were more fiends last time than ever before. I suspect we'll see even more now."

Bliss waited. Deshiva seemed to be talking to herself as much as the hunter next to her.

"Just a feeling, you understand. Maybe someone on Noctia knows why," Deshiva continued. "For me, it's enough to know my spear's going to get a lot of work."

Again Bliss itched for her staff, wished it stood in the ground at her side. A steadfast companion.

In the silence, Bliss looked down along the cliff, saw again the fiend's blood painting the rocks below. Remembered why she'd come here, what'd prompted her walk. Maybe Deshiva would have some ideas for how to chase the horrors from her mind. Bliss pointed down at the rocks, then at herself. Frowned, shivered, then tapped her head.

Deshiva pondered for a long minute before nodding, turning back to the ocean.

"If I understand what you're asking, I don't know if there's an answer that works for everybody," Deshiva said. "For me? I went after them. In the last Renewal, my whole group was ambushed by some fiends that looked like spiders made of frozen flame. They killed all of us, save me, because I ran." If the admission prompted any guilty memories, Deshiva's face showed none. Her seaward stare continued unbroken. "That night, alone and wet in a rainstorm, I decided I wouldn't let fear rule me any longer. After, I tracked the fiends and destroyed them, one by one."

Bliss held up a single finger, flicked up her eyebrows again.

Deshiva frowned, "Bliss, this is your home. Not theirs. The fiends don't know this jungle, and that gives you an advantage. Use it, and you can turn the odds around."

Bliss nodded. Looked back towards the sea. Deshiva made it sound so easy.

"Our mission's over. The town's gone, so we'll take the wounded back with us, help Kitaye establish defenses and hold tight." Deshiva took a deep breath. "However long the Renewal takes, we'll hold the city against all the evil that comes. Just as we've done every time before."

The long trek back, the coming days and nights in her family's treehouse, meant facing those dreams, those nightmares. They wouldn't leave, not if what Deshiva said was true. Confront the fear, bend it to her will. Hard to do that from her home.

"You don't have to come back with us," Deshiva said, as if reading Bliss's mind.

"Far be it for me to keep a Lira from her destiny. We found more fiend tracks. Looked like only a couple, and heading west, into the mountains. Nobody lives out that way, so I'm not risking a pursuit. You want to face your fears, Bliss, follow those footprints. See where they take you."

STAFF, satchel, supplies. Bliss gathered them all in the starlight, pausing only for occasional looks towards her brother's sleeping form. He'd be upset to wake up and find her gone. Might even try to take off after her, though Deshiva said she'd keep Quik leashed up tight to the group.

This would be Bliss's journey, and hers alone.

The fiend tracks started to the west and south, curling into the jungle and up the foothills towards the massive mountain marking Vis's west end. Not too far south lay the fen she'd been rambling through a week ago.

As the jungle reclaimed the sky above her, Bliss felt her

rope around her waist. Swinging in the dark rarely made sense—branches tended to hurt when you smacked them at high speeds—but staying on the forest floor . . .

No, she had to adjust. This wasn't a trip, wasn't some search for mushrooms with Pan or a race with Wax. She was hunting the fiends. Find, kill.

She stopped, let the bugs find her, the slight breeze brush her hair. Knelt, ran her hands along the torn up leaves and bent grasses marking the fiend's tracks. The destruction went wide, too wide for just a single one of the things. The earth, fallen leaves looked turned once over. Not a whole herd then.

She kept going, staying low and reading the signs. Other evidence—droppings, occasional scratches on the trees, the splitting and coming together of the tracks— narrowed the possibility to two.

A fiend pair against just her. A little girl in over her head, journeying in the jungle at night.

No, a hunter. A Lira.

Bliss followed the trail as the sky grew lighter, and not once did she look back towards her brother, the hunters, her home.

CHAPTER 28

THE GREAT SANA

Wax woke as dawn seeped in through their dorm's east-facing window. Golden rays nailed his eyes, shunting him up with a start. Pan snored nearby, oblivious until Wax whacked him in the shoulder.

"Time to go," Wax said, "The Najahn said they'd open the doors early."

"This early?"

"You want to lose this because you slept in?"

Pan groaned, stood up. "Every minute makes this Renewal thing worse."

The cooks had meals already prepped, simple eggs farmed from the outpost's chickens, harvested bananas, and some weak bread. Wax and Pan snarfed it down as they left, climbing shoes and ropes ready. No satchels, because scaling a sana, even one as big as this, shouldn't take more than a morning.

Vis's Great Sana, said to have grown from the god's beating heart, did look glorious in full bloom. Its orange-yellow blossoms stretched out in an umbrella towards the sun, the backside a glowing ruby-red from below. The trunk swept down into a rocky hill at its base, one long-since overgrown with flowering bushes, ferns, and short trees. A sleeve around the crown.

A few Najahn watched as the pair started up the cleared path, walking on the pounded dirt past the plants.

"If it's this easy, we'll get back before lunch," Wax said.

"I'll hold you to that."

Wax grinned. Last night's brawl left its residue on their bodies, bruises and sore muscles, but getting this close to the goal had an energy, a life that brought him past the pain.

After all, this wasn't just some jaunt. This was the Renewal. When Pan took the token, he'd become one of seven, just seven, across the entire Isles. They'd begin a grand adventure, and even if Pan didn't become the next Aegis—who'd want to live on Noctia anyway?—they'd still get to see places Wax wouldn't get to otherwise. Still get to do things, meet people, find wonders few in Kitaye ever would.

"Thanks, Pan," Wax said.

"For what?"

"Bringing me along. It's not all been roses so far, but I'm happy to be here."

"Yeah, well, I took a close look at all my options and realized you were all I had."

"Don't make it sound so sad."

"It's not sad," Pan shrugged, a lazy move as they neared the next Najahn gate. "It's just, I didn't want to risk anyone else on something this dangerous."

"So I'm your chump?"

"Glad you figured it out."

Wax laughed, Pan joined in, and their smiles held till

they hit the next Najahn gate, built right into the Great Sana's trunk. Up close, the big tree's thorns stuck out like spears, lancing into the air. The sana itself was wide enough to hold a dozen treehouses inside. The bark, a bronzed red, cut and curled around itself in irregular tangles, what might've been an ugly mess or a chaotic beauty, depending on your view.

Two Najahn guards waited beside the gate, each holding their voulge. A single-file arch, the gate didn't look like much, and at first Wax reached for his rope, assuming an outside climb would be the easiest way up.

"The only way is through," said the guard on the right. "You cannot go outside."

Wax tilted his head, "Why not?"

The guard grinned, "Because a climb up that way means a dead end. There are gaps you can't cross. Besides, there are things meant for you inside."

Pan and Wax glanced at each other.

"What things?" Pan asked.

"You'll find out like anyone else," said the second guard. "They're no trouble if you're careful." He reached left, pushed the gate open. "Best be off. The other party went in some time ago."

"Some time ago?" Wax asked. "But we came—"

"They chose to sleep right here," the first guard said, pointing his voulge at the trampled bushes and grasses nearby. "When we arrived, they were ready. You, it seems, were not."

Pan had an ugly expression on his face, one Wax stopped from growing into something worse by putting a hand on his friend's shoulder and pushing him forward.

"Guess we'll have to catch up, then," Wax muttered as they went on through.

The gate wasn't thick, the bark it cut through measuring less than a stride from inside to out. Or, at least, that's what it seemed when the charred cherry around them blew out into a tall, hollowed cylinder. Up, up, and up some more went the sana's inside, gnarled over with spidery roots, mossy growths, and stranger plants Wax couldn't identify. No obvious path presented itself through the rustling garden, but handholds didn't seem to be lacking.

Wax saw all this thanks to fluttering lights. The glimmers, what must've been thousands, flitted along from place to place, zipping in groups or darting off alone. Their glows winked off and on, and came in colors ranging from cool blues to hot reds. The light held sound, too: a sweet whistling, like a note blown through a tiny reed. Blended with the intertwining vines, leaves, and growth, the display stole Wax's breath.

"Think it was worth it just to see this," Pan said.

"Agreed."

The two stared until a rustling from farther above brought back the mission and its consequence.

"Any ideas on where to start?" Pan asked.

"How about there?" Wax pointed to a rising mound. It looked like fallen sap must've hardened, and now from it sprang some thick weed, its flimsy stalk nonetheless reaching up to a thicker, cylinder-crossing span. That span went from the sana's outer trunk to a thick, brighter ruby inside, a separate cylinder right there in the middle, still more than three times as wide as Wax stretching his hands from tip to tip.

"Lead on, Guardian."

"One day I'll get used to you calling me that."

Tell a man to climb, and he'll go at it with gusto. At

least, that's what Wax thought as he broke into a run at the sap mound. Its off-color amber hue hardened as Wax drew close, the shine turning to a brittle reflection, but one showcasing footholds aplenty. Stamping with his climbing shoes, Wax made the first foray, finding the sap hard, yes, but soft beneath.

As for the weed? Little bristles lined its deep green stalk, the touches tickling Wax's hand as it sought purchase on the tendrils branching out. Wax tested his weight before leaving the mound, Pan watching below, and found the weed sturdy enough to hold him.

"Don't stay still with this one," Wax called down. "It'll break on you."

"Sure it's not you, Wax? You're a heavier guy than me."

"That's just my ego, Pan."

"True, true."

Grinning, Wax bounced his way up the weed, lunging from one frond to the next. The exercise brought with it the usual rush: an adventure, and one requiring his favorite muscles. Every leap took a calculated stare, a measured jump, precise landings. Then the next and the next, all cascading into one another until every other concern fled Wax's mind.

The spiderwebbing growth proved a soft netting, one Wax jumped, grabbed, and clambered up onto from the weed's tallest split. To the touch, the webbing had a chilly, sticky feel. No bristles. Smelled like clover, a fact Wax confirmed as he laid on his chest and reached down to help Pan copy his move.

Once the two stood on the span, they turned to follow its course, find the next way up, a path laid out for them by the span itself, climbing the inner cylinder.

And right in the middle of that path, waiting with arms folded and a bandage around his head?

"Not you," Wax said.

"Better believe it's me, boys. No Najahn to help you out this time, neither." The man spread his legs, bent his knees. "The Renewal's ours. You wait here till we've got the skar, you can go right on up and nab second place for yourselves. Otherwise, you know what's coming to you."

"Do we know that, Pan?" Wax said, glancing at his friend, who looked a tad less confident than Wax felt.

"I don't know, do we?"

Wax read the message in that reply: they'd come far enough, they had every excuse now to go back to Kitaye as brave attempters, ones who came so close but didn't quite win the honorable race. End the adventure here with heads held high.

"Nah, we don't," Wax said. No quitting. Not now. "You either get outta our way, or it's going to hurt a lot more than last time."

"Was hoping you'd say that." The man grinned, didn't move from his stance. "Come and get me."

CHAPTER 29
RESTLESS AXES

The sea bucked and rattled as they closed on Whent's sawtooth southern coast. Black rock bars jutted up and out, their edges gleaming in the mid-morning mist as Maena's crew fought to keep their vessel on course. Svarde clung near the forward mast, Kivi curled up nearby, and tried not to fall off into the churn.

Sailer shouts criss-crossed the air, breaking back and forth in curse-filled commands as sails tucked and tacked, the tiller turned like a mad thing, and the Rana ship surfed like a survivor.

Svarde figured he'd never been so seasick in his life. His gut flopped with every wave, the bile going for its own ride up and down his throat, but he'd be damned if any of these Rana cutthroats would see him mess up their deck.

Because, if Maena had it right, they'd soon be marching side by side down a deep hole to a place far worse than these waves could ever be.

"Right, Kivi?" Svarde groaned to the ferrite. "This isn't that bad."

The Ferrite snorted, the orange heat between her plates throwing off steam whenever scattered water drops struck.

From pre-dawn till now, with wild swishing and swashing, the turmoil tossed them all. The ship held, through what craftsmanship Svarde couldn't know, until the craft washed up on a rocky beach. No, not even a beach, a tiny inlet between jagged cliffs and certain death waiting if a wave drove the ship into them.

A bad choice made after the Whent ship raid forced a secret landing. Consequences Maena shrugged off, pointing to the looted provisions. What worth those would have if the ship sank, Svarde didn't bother pointing out. Some saw only their triumphs.

Maena called for the evacuation and her crew followed, bustling into a different mania. Some, apparently elected to keep an eye out for Whent interference, broke out their armor and weapons, leaping ashore with sabers and leather cuirasses, eyes scanning the foggy horizon. Svarde followed that bunch, grateful for a task he understood.

The others, Maena among them, cracked the ship's lower decks and carried out one crate after another. Food and water, gear, torches, and satchels to haul it all. Metal Foti seals on the large chests ensured they'd stayed dry, a delightful fact for the crew, who wasted no time changing from their soaked sailing raiments.

When Svarde asked who'd be bringing all the extra stuff in those large chests, Maena said nobody.

"I'd hoped for more people," was all she said when Svarde wondered why.

More didn't materialize. After the morning bled away unpacking the ship and repacking themselves, Maena and Svarde led the crew up from the beach. Forty strong, swarthy and hale. Only a little beat up from the raid on the

Whent craft. A slow song started up among the sailors, a hymn to Rana, hoping for adventure, for treasure, for luck, and the river's blessing.

Whent certainly could've used a river. The isle didn't improve its look much beyond the beachhead, those dark, cracking rocks giving way to stubbly brush on hard ground. The isle's northerly locale produced a vast tundra split up here and there with deep ravines and blunt-topped plateaus, as if the god who'd once moved these vistas had collapsed in pieces, his bones breaking and jutting out at horrible angles.

Thick-furred buzzards and gulls mingled in the gray sky overhead, searching for meals before the coming winter. A sharp wind joined their flights, hitting Svarde's cheeks as he strode from the inlet's shielded confines. At first refreshing, the wind soon knifed between his armors's folds, turning his veins to ice and prompting a shudder between his lips.

His Foti blood had never been thick, and a decade in Vis's heat had done nothing for his resilience. At least, by what few accounts he'd heard, going underground soon brought an explorer to warmer worlds.

The Rana bore the chill with more composure, their faces stoic smiles, though Svarde caught many glancing back towards the sea. Home always called.

"How far until our destination?" Svarde asked as they trod ahead.

"Three days, if our information is accurate. It's an old mine, turned now to a small outpost," Maena's mouth tightened. "Not because treasure lacked, but because fiend attacks became too frequent. Whent sealed it off, an event our disgruntled informant made sure to tell me wasn't justified."

"They were certain we could reach the Dark Below through the mine?"

"As certain as any other option I found. My time and resources aren't limitless, Svarde. I couldn't keep scouring every isle. The blade had to be drawn."

They walked for another hour, the column keeping steady in their progress from one shanty to the next. The satchels weighed heavy, but not overly so, their burden reduced by adventure's excitement. As the sea vanished to the horizon, the Rana sailors seemed to stiffen their spines, to turn forward rather than look back.

Perhaps those early glances had been goodbyes.

Whent offered little reward for their walking until near noon, when, emerging from a huge slate monolith's shadow, came a town's rippling outline. Its mark lay west of their destination, out of the way and unimportant save one fact:

The town appeared to be burning.

Smoke gnarled towards the sky, curling back in on itself in chaotic wisps, a black against the chill gray. The monolith, rounded and knobby, seemed not to care about the events at its base, but Svarde couldn't tear his eyes away. In part because there was little else to look at, in part because he waited for Maena to say something.

When she didn't, when, after some minutes, she made the call to halt for the noonday meal, Svarde pointed her eyes towards the settlement.

"I see it," Maena said, her voice the same static frozen it'd been during his questioning of the Whent ship raid. "What?"

"They're in trouble." The remark should've ended it. Indeed, the fire had spread during the walk, the smoke growing broader in its reach. "Shouldn't we help them?"

"Why? What good would that do us? If it's a natural blaze caused by their own idiocy, they'll be on their way to putting it out. If it's fighting among the Whent factions, then putting my people in their way would be foolish." Maena pulled a cool apple from her satchel, bit into its green skin and spat a seed out onto the ground. "Approaching the town means revealing to this whole isle that we're here. Whent's warlords won't take to that, and we'll find our journey canceled before it begins."

Svarde kept his look at the fire. "And what if it's none of those things?"

Maena let the question hand. Took another bite.

"If it's fiends, then they're already dead."

"Unless they're still fighting. Even if not, we could destroy the monsters and save further towns. Hiding helps nobody."

"Hiding keeps us on our course," Maena scowled his way. "Svarde, I'm beginning to regret taking you on this adventure. You don't seem to have the right focus."

"My focus is the same it's always been: helping the people on this world survive."

"Then do it as we talked about. Strike at the source. These little squabbles are pointless compared to what we're after."

Svarde shook his head, "I hid for so long, Maena. Avoided these battles. I came to this isle once as a friend. I won't abandon it now. Kivi, let's go."

Maena's eyes followed Svarde as he strode off into the tundra, but he heard no order to march, and the singsong notes of happier times followed his footsteps.

The town offered up its crackling song well before Svarde reached its borders. The flames continued to grow in the hour he spent walking, running, and walking again to reach its outskirts. The orange and red tongues leapt about, scattering on the wind and feasting on the scrub brush abounding the gaps between the town's skin-and-stick dwellings. Thick, wrapped in mosses and furs, the buildings here were squat and easy for a fire to take. Not like the block-houses in Foti's furnaces, or the stone slopes on Noctia's ridges.

Even Vis, their houses split apart by trees and flush with water, would be better saved from a fire like this.

The flames, though, didn't push Svarde back into a jog, Kivi snorting up a storm at his ankles.

The screams did, and the sound of swinging steel.

Svarde passed through a splintered palisade, albeit one made more with stacked stones than spiked poles. The wall gave the first clue the disaster wasn't the cause of some wayward lamp or a spilled pipe: three large gaps shattered the wall's solid line, the irregular breaches caving inward.

"A charge, or some battering force," Svarde muttered to Kivi. "Though why would one be necessary when the gates stand open?"

Standing only a little taller than Svarde himself, the loose wood gates were less a fortification than a marker. The twin doors, normally bolted in the middle, creaked in the wind. The bar to seal them lay abandoned in the path. The gatehouse, a single-person stand, sat empty and untouched.

No resistance, which suggested the gates may have been opened not to keep something out, but to let the ones inside get away.

The fire's heat began piercing the air's chill, washing against Svarde and giving him a little comfort. His muscles thawed, his jaw unclenched, and his hands found his axe hilts an easier grasp. With a smooth stroke, Svarde drew both weapons as he walked into town.

The fire must've began at the outskirts, the very ones Svarde now went past, as the hollow charred shells spoke to a long time left to feed the hungry flames. Ash joined the breeze, getting stuck in Svarde's hair and looking like snow blowing by. Other sounds rose up too, a strange barking coming at clipped cadences. Joining it, interrupting it, came more human cries.

Not pain, these, but fear, pleas. The words were too blurred by distance and the snap crackle soundscape to carry specifics to Svarde, but their tone came clear enough.

The Guardian didn't quicken his pace, but instead left the path. An enemy had come to this place, and staying in the open invited ambushes.

Svarde crouched and crept, Kivi staying on his heels. He looked through torched dwellings, seeing through the embers and smoke, trying to find a clue as he moved nearer the town square.

He needn't have tried so hard.

The town's remaining people lay clustered in the middle, huddled around a soot-scarred statue of some woman Svarde neither knew nor cared to know. What mattered in that moment, aside from the hundred or more peasants in their improvised prison, were their guards.

Svarde counted three, each more than double his height and counting a liquid collection of arms and legs. They stood, they moved, they wavered as they circled the crowd, every step taking their molten forms and re-shaping them in stride. Each kept some parts consistent: an arm holding a captured Whent sword or spear, two or three legs to fortify their stance, and a wicked head, less a human-like skull and more a spined urchin dipped in tar.

Each, too, bore the scars every fiend earned by defying the Aegis: deep emerald gashes criss-crossed their forms, and when the creatures moved, as they kept circling the captives, green flames licked from those wounds and lashed their owners.

The creatures clacked, hissed, clipped their commands at each other and the captives, most of whom ranged between open weeping and silent, doomed stares into the distance.

The creatures made the fire's source clear too, their every step leaving behind orange-glowing, smoking droplets, as if the things were made from a volcano's lava. Small fires began in their wake, most withering for lack of fuel and leaving dark patches on the hard ash-coated soil.

Svarde glanced at Kivi. These fiends seemed not too unlike the ferrite, or as Kivi might appear without her stone plates. The ferrite seemed to agree, but found no kinship with the monsters: her plates split and snapped, steam gushing out in her anger. Thankfully, the ferrite kept herself low, behind a broken house's shell.

Not that the fiends seemed interested in any interlopers. Their spined heads stared universally inward, watching their prisoners, while the fire continued its spread.

What were they waiting for?

Svarde felt his axe handles. The weapons were Foti-made, forged in the hottest furnaces, but who knew whether they could withstand contact with the molten things? Would he run in, slash, only to find himself holding nothing more than a stump, and quickly be—no, Svarde shook his head.

Catya had always made clear their minds had to be their best advantage. Consider the situation more closely. The fiends had snared human tools for their own. If their skin could melt metal at the touch, then how could they wield swords?

But could they die by one?

"Shall we find out?" Svarde whispered, and Kivi snorted.

Three against two. Not terrible odds.

Svarde and Kivi closed one more burnt ring, drawing within a single torched shop of the circling fiends. One man within the group caught Svarde's eye, his own widening until Svarde put a finger to his lips. The man gave the subtlest of nods, flicking his look away.

Brave people, these.

Svarde tapped Kivi on the shoulder, a signal to the ferrite. Be ready, be relentless.

When the next fiend came stepping by, Svarde charged out, saying nothing as he held his axes high, aiming for a cut at the fiend's back. The spiked head hung too tall for Svarde to reach, so what amounted for the monster's torso would have to do.

As Svarde moved, a slanting break-out charge around the burnt shop's frame, the fiend's two partners on the circle's far side caught sight of Svarde and curdled up a clicking storm. Svarde's target began a whirl, a watery slow turn illuminated by those gouting green gashes. The pain threw the creature off its own maneuver, the stolen stone spear in its grasp trembling down to stick the ground as Svarde drew near for the first swing.

Both axes cut across, the left arm leading, the right following. Their razor edges drew emerald lines across the fiend's black shell, spraying hot ember blood with their cuts. Svarde felt little resistance, as if slicing through water, and his stroke carried his arms wide to the creature's right. A reverse grip, and Svarde would have the creature halved.

At least, that's what would've happened if the fiend, clicking like mad, hadn't kicked out with a central leg that hadn't existed a moment ago. The molten foot struck Svarde in the chest, sent him flying back into the ruined shop.

Surrounded by broken and charred shelves, Svarde picked himself up, his leather gear now as smeared with gray and white as everything else. The fiend, awash with smoking green from its new wounds, flowed towards him one long step, then two, before it hesitated to a wavering halt.

Even a monster like this one would take a second when faced with a look of such menace, loathing, and battle-lust as Svarde wore at that moment, axes in hand, the next strike already in motion.

CHAPTER 30
FIRST STRIKE

The light pink wing fluttered near her eye. Through its thin filament, Bliss saw the sun, high in the sky and chasing away a few clouds. The butterfly wiggled again—perched on her nose—then set off with the next gust, fluttering on down the foothill. Bliss sat up, swinging her legs off the thick branch. Her rope pulled taut, kept her on the thin wood. Her staff stood next to the tree's rippled amber trunk, the rope pulling double-duty and keeping the weapon nearby. Her satchel hung over her head, tied to the next branch up.

Her waterskin, refreshed on morning dew before Bliss had escaped to her nap, cooled her throat, made the mango go down easy. The salted fish had her smacking her lips, but she'd need the energy.

Today she'd catch the fiends.

The monsters weren't fast movers. They lacked direction, ambling their way up from the jungle to its sparser, higher biomes. They scratched at trees, marked new territory, and claimed small critters for prey before moving on.

Bliss had no such distractions.

She'd pursued the tracks to a cleft between the foothill and the bigger mountain, an abrupt valley shaded from sunlight and overrun with creeping weeds. Small white flowers bore trample marks, and a deep cut on the narrow valley's far end seemed a likely hiding spot for the things.

So Bliss had backtracked a bit, found the tree, and saved up some energy.

Dropping to the ground, Bliss took up some tricks. Using her waterskin to soften up the earth, Bliss smeared fresh-made mud on her shoulders, her face. She stuffed leaves into her weave, her tied hair. Camouflage, anything to buy her a second, give her a chance.

The walk back to the valley took on a nicer cast in the daylight, blooming flowers and more butterflies roaming the tall grasses. Deep in the jungle, the day would be a hot one, but up here the air felt crisp, invigorating. Bliss gulped it down, turning every now and then to glance back over the isle as it stretched away behind her.

She'd go back down a different woman, one without fear, or she wouldn't go back at all.

As the valley neared, Bliss slowed her walk, lowered to a crouch. The fiend she'd fought on the surf had been sleeping during the day. With any luck, these would do the same, but no sense taking any chances. Keep a low profile, make it to her targets alive.

Not a bad goal.

The sleek hiss from behind made her jump. In a smooth motion, Bliss wheeled, drawing her staff and sweeping it through the grass. Its point came to rest on a pale green hanoko's nose, the great cat glaring at her through its vertical topaz eyes.

Bliss tensed, controlled her breathing. She knew how to take the cats. A little scare and the things, frightening as their six paws and claws might be, would dash away in search of easier prey.

This one nudged her staff aside, its ears pulled back, and took one step closer. Its mouth opened, two wet teeth showing over its pink lips. The hiss disappeared, replaced with a guttural growl.

Yet, for all that, Bliss found herself focused on the cat's body, and the deep red lines on its right side. Missing fur, matted patches, still glistening, spoke of a bad night.

Drawing back her staff, retreating a step to keep the stick between her and the cat, Bliss stood taller, tried not to look aggressive.

Hanokos could fight over territory, sure, but adults tended to avoid one another. Live their solitary lives. Strange to see one hurt like this. Strange, anyway, until she remembered what else might've made a recent incursion into the beast's home.

The hanoko advanced again. Another paw forward. It could jolt ahead now, an easy jump, and land on Bliss. Bear her to the ground and finish things with its teeth, but it hesitated.

Because she wasn't the thing that worried the hanoko. Bliss took a step to the side, pointed with the staff towards the valley, the cleft on the other side of the foothill's crest. The hanoko watched her, still growling.

Bliss nodded at the creature, then took a single, slow step towards the crest. The hanoko didn't advance again. Its claws worked in and out of the paws. The creature's breath came heavy, a rank counter to the clear air.

Bliss moved again. The cat didn't pursue.

Would it attack as soon as she turned her back?

Hard to say, but the hanoko didn't look hungry.

Wounded, yes, but muscle clad those bones. It moved with grace and strength.

Bliss had to hope it'd come here with revenge in mind, or at least defense of its own home. Otherwise she might have to fight three things today, and that . . . might be risking too much.

She pointed to herself, then to the cleft. Hoped that the cat understood. Those topaz slits just watched her, but the growl died. No hiss, no tensing for a pounce. A butterfly flitted between them and for a second Bliss thought it might land on the cat's ear, a perfect picture, but the wind carried the little thing away.

With one more nod, Bliss sidestepped further, keeping her staff handy. The cat stayed still, and she kept going, one foot after another till she'd crossed the foothill's lip and started down the other side into the flower-covered weeds. Blossoms scattered at her steps, and Bliss returned to her crouching walk, though this time the glances back weren't to admire her journey, but to confirm the hanoko wasn't about to attack.

The cat, though, didn't pursue her over the hill.

Maybe the hanoko was playing her, hoping she'd rid it of the intruding fiends. A clever ploy. Bliss grinned. She'd be happy to give the cat its territory back.

On the valley's far side, the cleft sat shaded, overhung by a red-gray rock slab, one that'd been lashed by lighting and rain for more years than Bliss could know. Its divots ran deep, disappearing at the cutoff to shadow, as if someone had taken a wedge out from the cliff's base.

And there, sleeping, massive chest rising and falling with a steady calm, lay a fiend. Bliss froze, peered closer, squinted, hoped, and panicked.

Only one fiend lay in the cleft. The other, if it ever had

been here, wasn't there any longer. Bliss whirled, careful to keep her steps quiet, and looked across the small valley. No fiend in sight, nothing coming up for an ambush.

She took a slow breath, told her heart to slow down. The monsters weren't exactly friendly. Maybe they split up. Maybe the other had simply moved on, left its partner behind. She'd find the tracks after dealing with this one.

A smile found its way back. Maybe, just maybe, she'd get a little luck after all.

Treading on the weeds—tangled, stringy, soft—Bliss made little sound on her approach. She had her staff in both hands, held near her waist where she could make a popping strike. The fiend's soft belly lay right there, and a good blow might cripple the monster, throw it into confusion, so Bliss could finish the thing with a whack to its head.

Her vision seemed to blur as she crept to the cleft. Sounds died away, save the pulsing in her ears from her heartbeat. Her mouth dried, Bliss held her breath. The fiend's claws looked sharp, though some had broken away, their nails cut in the scratching. Its burgundy mane coiled about the fiend's head, the sole large fang poking through. Like the others, long bloody gashes latticed its hide, a gift from the Aegis.

The fiend was about to get a gift from Vis.

Bliss tensed her legs, gripped her staff tight. The belly, white and waiting, was right there.

She could hear Deshiva, "Strike your vengeance."

Bliss planted her left foot, drove the staff forward with both hands. The blunt point, hardened bamboo that'd been with Bliss as long as she could walk, drove into the fiend and kept going, pushing the skin back and expelling air, crunching bones. Bliss didn't stop, leaning forward into a run even as the fiend started awake, its claws crabbling.

But the monster's weight was immense. The first hit struck, yet as Bliss leaned in, she felt the monster's bulk push back. The fiend rolled upright, gnarling a pained wheeze and flinging dirt, weeds, blossoms with its claws.

The first strike over, Bliss withdrew the staff, aimed it right and stabbed forward again, going for the fang this time. The fiend's narrow eye poked through its coiled locks and saw the move, its front right paw swiping and knocking Bliss's attack off-target, up into the stone ceiling.

Like a snake, the fiend followed its blow with a slithering turn, snapping at Bliss with its sole fang. This time, Bliss had the right reply, swinging the staff back down from its deflection and warding away the attack, batting the fiend's snout into the dirt.

Initiative meant life. Bliss couldn't let the fiend get its breath back. She bounced on her feet, jumping forward and jutting with the staff again.

Instead of retreating, the fiend met her head on, making a gasping, wheezing dart. Bliss struck the fiend's shoulder, the blow cracking something, but the shock knocked the staff free from her hands. Bliss barely registered her loss, as the fiend itself slammed into her, bearing the young woman back down the valley.

Bliss hit the ground first, felt the fiend's claws tearing at her weave, slipping on the mud and leaving scratches behind. The monster's attacks missed their mark, sliding away on the leaves, the dirt, and the fiend, sloppy in its attempt, rolled off Bliss and on down the slope. For a moment, Bliss simply lay in the weeds, stunned that she hadn't died.

Then her hands went to her waist, pulling off the rope

waiting there. Bliss curled over, planted her left hand in the plants, and looked.

Rather than hustling back for another attack, the fiend seemed to be staggering, flopping around in the foliage. The wheezes grew harder, harsher. More desperate.

Realization dawned. With that initial strike, Bliss might've done more than annoy the beast. Weakened it, maybe. Or at least given herself a real chance.

She ran, drawing the rope between her two hands, and jumped. Her height on the slope carried her to the fiend and she landed on the thing's shoulders, making it stumble, making it hiss. The monster's claws scrabbled, but the limbs, like a hanoko's, were designed for pouncing, for slashing down, not up on its back.

Bliss leaned away as the fiend turned and snapped at her. She threw the rope over its head, ignored the fang dicing in close enough to nip her weave, to tear more leaves away. Instead, she pulled tight, gripped the rope with all she had.

The oiled threads held, and Bliss flipped the strands from one hand to the other, pulling them taut and sliding a knot over the fiend's neck. It tried another wheeze, another gargling howl as Bliss pulled tighter, keeping her legs pinned on the monsters sides.

The fiend tried to run, tried to buck Bliss off, but the rope stayed strong. The monster's mane slapped Bliss, the sticky hairs leaving welts on her skin.

She would not be thrown. Not now.

The rope pulled tighter, the fiend bucked once, twice, three times, before something changed. Its fight seemed to drain out, a gradual quieting. The legs went limp, the beast settled onto the grass, and with one final, half-hearted snap her way, the fiend wheezed its last breath.

And Bliss breathed her first, a wide-eyed gasp. She held the rope tight, kept herself on the fiend's back, waiting for a fake-out that didn't come. Waiting for a trap that didn't spring.

Only when a butterfly landed on the fiend, the monster not moving a muscle, did Bliss let the rope go.

She climbed off the fiend's back, pulled her rope free, her eyes always on the monster, waiting for any sign.

Focused on her vengeance.

CHAPTER 31

THE WEBBED STAIR

The brute held himself like he thought Wax was coming in for a tackle. As if they would meet palm to palm, forehead against forehead and determine superiority through pure brawn.

He could keep right on thinking that.

Wax waved Pan off to the left, hoping his friend would see the opening and keep moving. The brute's goal was pretty obvious: slow these two down so whomever they nominated for the Renewal could waltz right on in for the prize. Wax would bet they'd sprinkle their other morons along the way up too, just for extra protection.

Meaning they'd have to deal with this guy, and fast.

Running along the springy net gave Wax an idea of how to do just that.

"Run just ahead of me," Wax said as they closed. "Jump when I land."

The ol' spring and sprung. Not exactly an alien move in the jungle, where bouncing fronds made for convenient launch pads. Whether the man from Mottilan would catch on . . . guess they'd find out.

Wax buckled down his knees, took a jump skyward, or at least as far as his momentum could manage. In the air, he tucked his knees up to his chest, felt the fall, shut his eyes just before impact—no sense letting some wayward thorn scratch'em—and drew the spongy surface down with him. Pan, just ahead, should be feeling his footing slide back, should be—

"Hey!" The bum's angry call was all the proof Wax needed as he burst back out from his ball, landing in a wobble.

The enemy stood before Wax, not looking at him, instead following Pan as the latter landed on the man's opposite side. Pan hit with all the grace of a flopping fish, his side striking first. Yet, for all his lack of style, Pan wound up where he needed to be: further up the trunk-wrapping trail.

Grinning, flush with victory, Wax pressed the advantage. He bounded forward, hit the bigger guy with a running tackle. The man fell, hitting and bouncing off the springy plant, and Wax rode the wave, rolling forward and springing up to follow in Pan's footsteps.

The lunk cursed, and Wax figured the man would pursue, but for the moment they had a lead.

"Run!" Pan yelled, laughter buzzing the edges.

There came a moment in every adventure where, well, the adventure took hold. The slap-dash days diving through the jungle had been fun, if a bit directionless. Who knew whether the pair would get to the Najahn outpost first, who knew what they'd do when they arrived, but here, here was conflict, goal, and threat in equal measure.

And none Pan and Wax couldn't handle.

Upward, the springy material gave way to gnarled vines, new and old growth lapping over each other. The desiccated plants would've fallen apart without their newer brothers for support, a crackling lattice making for a straightforward climb.

The dart bugs continued lighting the way, their magical selves alighting, often as not, on Wax's hands and head as he pressed on. A few minutes scaling vines brought the pair to a whole new level, reached when Wax came up beside Pan, scrambling onto a stiff, wood platform. No, not wood: a hard cinnamon color belonging to a vast mushroom head. The fungus attached to the sana's inner trunk, its five puff-ball orbs reaching out, down, and upward. Frilly vanilla tendrils hung in tufts from the edges, the ones above Pan and Wax dangling nearly to their skulls. Along the frilly ends, turquoise bits flashed in time with the dart bugs, some natural dance Wax didn't understand but appreciated all the same.

"I see Mertz did nothing, as always," said a new voice, serrated and feminine in equal measure. "We keep him around for the muscle, and he can't even do that."

Wax and Pan followed the puffball's sloping surface to the trunk, where the fungus itself bore scarring slashes leading further up. Blocking the way stood the woman, taller than either Pan and Wax, with nothing more than boredom on her tight face. Her outfit, though, didn't match her expression: flowing and light blue, as though a whirl-wind had been sculpted to her body, the robe shifted with her as the woman dropped into a forward crouch, both hands before her in a diagonal line.

"What's she doing?" Pan asked.

"No idea. The way's past her, though."

"Let me lead on this one, okay? I have a plan."

Hey, Pan taking the initiative? Wax could roll with that. His friend took off at a slow walk towards the woman, who watched, hanging in her stance. As Pan closed to a couple strides out, he stopped, then kicked down into the mushroom surface. The hit broke through the mushroom top, driving down and popping a chunk up into the air. Pan grabbed the fluffy, beige piece and threw it right at the woman.

"Go!" Pan yelled as the big mushroom block dove in.

Wax started forward as the woman deflected the mushroom, the block not quite knocking away Pan's assault but breaking it into smaller chunks, each raining over her like some soft, gooey spray.

Pan almost made it by on her right before the woman pulled herself back in control. Her right leg flashed out, took Pan's right ankle and sent him tumbling to the puffball's top. Wax, following his buddy's lead, kicked off another mushroom chunk and, mid-stride, launched it at the woman's back.

The mushroom wasn't exactly heavy, but the fungus wasn't air either. The woman looked like she was about to follow-up with a kick to Pan's face, a blow that never came as Wax's toss whomped her back and sent her stumbling forward. Forward, right into Pan's clumsy kick.

The mushroom hunter struck the woman's shin, causing her to cry out and fall. Pulling himself ahead, Pan scrambled out from under her collapse, kicking up more mushroom bits as he headed for the grooved ladder.

Wax scooped out another mushroom piece, started running, and when the woman had herself turned right-side up, glaring after Pan, he pelted her again, burying that no-longer-bored visage under more puffball crud. Another yell joined the woman's muffled curses: Mertz, making it up the plant ladder and too late to change the battlefield.

Wax made it to the grooves not three seconds after Pan,

jumping and finding handholds in the soft mushroom meat. Climbing the ladder gave off a strange aroma, a bit like some tasteless dinners his parents made. Up above, the ladder went until the mushroom, its heights shaded over in a gossamer white, vanished. A narrow hole appeared cut where the ladder continued.

"How awesome was that?" Pan shouted down as they climbed. "Nobody suspects the mushroom bomb!"

"Mushroom bomb? You have a name for that?"

"Of course I do! You gotta be willing to sacrifice a puffball to save yourself."

"Do you?"

Pan's wild laughter was the only answer. As they climbed, Wax snuck a look down below, saw the woman and Mertz in slow pursuit. Their voices echoed up, seemingly arguing with one another.

Dissent among the ranks: good.

"What do you think this stuff is?" Pan asked as they neared the gossamer.

"Thought it was a spider's web," Wax said. "Not so sure anymore."

The doubt came from thick silver-white shapes in the gossamer, seemingly wrapped in the threads. About as large as Wax's fingers, the shapes didn't seem threatening, but many moved as the two neared, wriggling in their little prisons.

"It's weirding me out," Pan said.

"Then keep climbing and we'll put 'em behind us."

"You know we'll have to come down, right? All these people, they'll be waiting."

"They can't touch you once we get the star. And if they get it, then what'll they care about us?"

"Vengeance?"

Good point. Without the Najahn in here playing referee, these people might just decide roughing up Wax and Pan for fun was worth it.

"Then we'll just have to be smarter, Pan. Shouldn't be too hard."

That claim hit its next test as the ladder ended, pulling the pair up into a gossamer forest. The mushroom top looked to be dissolving around them, with the web growing from the puffball's disintegrating ends. Almost like a mold, but one with a secondary purpose. The gossamer stretched up and around them, strands coming close enough that reaching out in almost any direction meant contacting the sticky stuff. Wax ran his finger along a strand near his head, and the thin lines pulled right away with him, clinging to his skin. Cool to the touch, lightweight, almost invisible without the dart bugs—Wax blinked. The dart bugs. They weren't up here. The threads were too thick for the things. Not too thick, though, for the light. The silver-blue rose up beneath them, reflecting off the gossamer in a twinkling show, one joined with a more golden glow from above.

"Sunlight," Pan said, matching Wax's look. "We're getting close to the top."

"Yeah, but how are we getting any further?"

"There." Pan pointed, a little ways around the bend. The gossamer threads thickened, those wriggling forms in a hanging cluster leading upwards. "Guess we get to go up a living stair."

Walking across the gossamer felt a bit like walking over wet grass, with pieces hanging on them after every step. The strands quivered as Pan and Wax strode on them, but their combined strength served well enough as a floor. As for the living stair? It beckoned with wriggly purpose, spiraling up a too-perfect cavity in the gossamer. Every step shook, the cocoons piled in so thick as to be almost solid. They sucked in the light, shimmering with a matte radiance.

"Have to say," Wax muttered as he and Pan evaluated the first step, "there's some weird stuff in here."

"Truth. I want to take some back, see whether we can grow more. Trade it."

"Skar now, pillage later, Pan."

"Right, right."

Mertz and the woman scaled the mushroom ladder as Wax took the first stair, resuming the lead. Their appearance put an extra spring into Wax and Pan's steps, the springy cocoons serving as an unnatural footing. Every time Wax's bare foot hit the next surface, he could feel it shifting beneath him, the cocoons tickling his toes. Not exactly a feeling he loved.

"Uh, Wax?" Pan asked after they'd gone five steps. "I think they're hatching."

Wax whirled, looking at the step below his, where Pan stared at his own feet. The little white cocoons picked up their shivering, vibrating now with intensity. Cracks appeared along their silver surfaces, black lines spreading like a breaking egg shell. Wax saw the disaster unfolding on his own step too.

"Keep moving!" Wax yelped, turning on a heel and lunging up the stair.

Pan followed, the cocoons bursting behind them. A buzzing, chittering noise rose up, amplified by the gossamer, whose strands acted like an instrument and rang with the living concert. The steps didn't wriggle under Wax's foot anymore: they began to sting, piercing pangs as the emerging insects went for their first meal. Wax caught sight of a couple on the steps ahead, small caterpillar things with pointed gnashers on their heads. They reared up and darted in as Wax and Pan went by, stabbing at their feet, their shins, anything the little monsters could grab.

"This sucks!" Pan shouted.

"Only a few more steps!"

Up above, the gossamer staircase ended with what looked like a flat, moldering brown ceiling. The last step came within reach of that ceiling, a reach Wax made as his feet struck the final landing.

With a push, the brown gave way, filtering in a raw golden flash. Wax found a handhold, hard and crunchy, and pulled himself up, rolling onto the new surface. He whacked away the fiendish caterpillars with his hands, scattering them across the leaves, because that's what it was here: leaves, big scalloped ones with holes lining their edges, those gaps leading to the light filtering into the gossamer below. Up above them, a thorny forest rose as the trunk itself diminished into the sana's pistil. The great flower's blossom blotted out the sun up here, making a pink-and-purple sky. Beneath it, as Wax and Pan stood up, brushing away the bugs, waited a grumpy trio.

The last of the coasters, and these three stood before the lowest thorn. Unlike Mertz and the woman below, no amusement, no boredom floated in their faces. "We didn't want you to get this far," said the man in the center, a bulky mark with a crescent scar along his bare chest. "You'll go no farther."

CHAPTER 32
OF AXE AND FLAME

Hesitation invites attack. A Rana maxim among many the sailors had drilled into Svarde during the voyage. Most were violent, vulgar, or both, but this was the one Svarde used when he leapt towards the monster, his axes flying over his head in a double cut.

The sinewy tar creature, its charred blade held wide, offered little defense. Whether it believed Svarde's axes could do it no real harm or some other delusion, Svarde didn't know or care. All that mattered was the slight resistance as his axes bit in, the green spray flying up and stinging his cheeks. Svarde's flight carried him into the creature, a decision necessary for the mortal blow but dangerous nonetheless: intense heat sparked up wherever Svarde's clothes touched the fiend, his skin bubbled as it nicked the steaming black, and even Svarde's eyes rebelled at the close brush, searing him into blinded stumble back.

Yet for all that the fiend howled, its nail-splitting skein a horrifying sound, one prompting moans and screams from the captives in the square. When Svarde felt the ruined structure against his back, when the pain receded, he blinked open his eyes and saw a melting thing.

A spreading emerald pool, the monster's own body seemed to eat itself, the skin catching fire from the blood inside, blowing up into a green-orange torch even as its liquid lava spread beneath.

Svarde sidestepped, looking at his axes and confirming, though they glowed as hot as the monster's skin, their steel edges still held.

The other three fiends didn't take their comrade's demise with fine spirits. With one remaining near the captives, the other two slithered apart, each circling around Svarde. The ruined buildings provided poor cover, the fiend's attempted trap viewable the whole way.

Not that Svarde had many options.

"That's what's coming to all of you," the man growled. Whether the fiends could understand him or not, Svarde figured his words would get the point across through tone. These weren't mindless things if they could hold a blade. Perhaps they could be twisted, intimidated. "Who's next?"

Somewhere in the buildings behind him, Kivi lurked. When the ferrite would attack, Svarde didn't know. Strategy, at this point, was better traded for instinct, and Svarde had one standout option.

As the two fiends went to Svarde's left and right, both angling for a behind-the-back attack, the Foti warrior swapped his stance and barreled forward, right towards the last one protecting the captives.

Unlike his former friend, the fiend wasn't caught flat-footed. Instead, its arms shifted into a double-grip on the long charred blade while its legs shortened, multiplied. A black spider faced Svarde in the square, and its weapon had reach.

With a two-handed swing, the fiend went straight at Svarde's charging form. An upswinging axe caught the blade, would've deflected it except for the damn thing's strength. Svarde's weapon caught the sword on its underside, Svarde himself ducking to make sure the blade's razor skimmed only his hair. Instead, the axe hooked on the sword, the swing picking up and throwing Svarde to his right.

He rolled in the dusty square, ash billowing up around him, embers landing in his hair. Svarde shook off the pain, heard a child shout, and spun, both axes in a crossed defense before his skull.

Instinct saved him, as it had so many times before.

The fiend's smoked blade crashed into his axes, driving Svarde back onto one knee. His arms burned, the weight pressing on them too much, too steady. Sweat and blood beaded on Svarde's forehead, stung his eyes, though in the blur Svarde could make out those spidered legs sweeping forward, ready to take him out from below.

"You're a rotten thing," Svarde swore at the monster. Hardly a battle cry for the legends, but the heat stole his breath away.

Those legs missed their mark. A silver-gray blur barreled into the fiend from its right side, crunching into those spindly supports and breaking their liquid bones. Green gushed and Svarde felt the weight disappear as Kivi rolled, snapped, and clawed in the the fiend's gooey center.

The monster wasn't sure what to do, its blade swinging down at itself and missing the mark as Kivi refused to stay still. With the opening, Svarde recovered, then sent his axes in a one-two blow to take off the blade-wielding arms, then the head that steered them.

Like its brother, the creature disintegrated, melting away to nothing more than a boiling puddle.

The Whent people cheered, their ragged encouragement the best sound Svarde had heard all day.

And one that changed, quick as it came, to warnings.

The two fiends left came at Svarde and Kivi from opposite sides, their slow encirclement not paying off in time.

"You get the ugly one," Svarde said, and Kivi snorted.

Whirling, Svarde eyed the one coming his way. Like the beast he'd just dispatched, this one held its blade in both hands. Unlike that one, this beast kept its legs at two, changing them up for more arms, these holding whatever rubble it could find. Bricks, clubs, a clump of ash to blind Svarde with.

Always awful, fiends.

Glancing left, Svarde kicked off that way, heading towards a relatively-intact blacksmith's shop. Like any forge, the building had a good foundation to resist heat, its bones still standing. The fiend followed, its chittering warnings no doubt pronouncing some certain doom or other.

Not that Svarde cared. The fiend would get its desserts just like the others.

Dashing inside a broken up doorframe, Svarde took in his chosen battlefield. There was indeed a forge, the stone-stacked oven and well-worked anvil just before Svarde. Off to the right sat cooling barrels, charred but not burned through. Racks along the ceiling hung with tools, calipers, hammers and the like. Some of those hung down at angles, their supporting timbers torched away.

On the left, held up by racks, sat the blacksmith's main turnout: farming equipment. Sickles, scythes, and pick-axes for mining affairs. Not exactly the best tools to have in a fight with a fiend.

Svarde felt the monster coming, the heat rising, and he broke straight ahead, vaulting the anvil and coming down on the other side, his back to the furnace. The doorway broke apart as the fiend swung his sword, slashing the weakened supports. The loose thatched roof fell with the blow, catching fire as it touched the fiend.

With its new burning wreath, the fiend advanced into the smithy, its strides slower now, more assured. The arm with the brick raised itself, found Svarde, and threw.

Even knowing it was coming, ready to dodge, Svarde wasn't fast enough. He fell right, trying to use the anvil for cover, but the brick glanced off Svarde's left shoulder anyway. Pain came fast, but Svarde's thick leather kept the joint intact.

Not so, the furnace behind him. The brick's shot hit the stacked stone hard on its lower right corner, shearing through the weakened blocks. The furnace tilted towards Svarde, the stones starting to fall free.

Svarde pulled to his right, scrambling on the straw-covered floor. He flung up an axe to deflect a poke from the fiend's blade, a piercing strike that, even though swung with but a single arm, had enough force to turn Svarde's run into a roll.

The warrior crashed into newly-made plows, toppling with the rack into a tangled mess. Metal tools jutted into Svarde's legs and arms, and he felt something pierce his side through the armor.

The fiend sneered another sharp cry, bearing its burning self, the thatched roof now fully engulfed over their heads, to loom over Svarde.

Before the warrior could even try another move, the

fiend threw the ash on him, blanketing Svarde's face with scorching cinders. He tried to back up, tried to stand, but found himself stuck.

But he could raise his axes, and did.

The sword swung, the fiend shrieking as it went for Svarde's head. Svarde deflected once, twice, and, on the third time, twisted to put the rack in the sword's way by rolling onto his chest.

The blade burned through the plow, the rack, and struck Svarde's back, melting through his leather and driving a scream Svarde had never heard himself make before. His vision went purple, his lungs rasped for anything in the simmering air.

But he was free.

Svarde kicked his legs as the rack's remnants fell away. The fiend raised the blade, tried to skewer Svarde again, but Svarde reversed his earlier ground, kicking himself onto his wounded back and again bringing his axes—he could never let those go, ever—over his front. The skewer bounced off, sliding into the dirt near Svarde's ear.

His hair burned, the smell stank.

The smithy held no further retreat, so with the charred sword beside him, Svarde rolled forward. Up onto his feet and bursting forward past the fiend, Svarde swung an axe overhead, slicing off one of those extra arms. Emerald sprayed, the fiend twisted and chased.

When he'd entered the smithy a minute ago, the place had been damaged but comparatively unscathed. Now it lay exposed to the sky, its forge decimated save for the sturdy anvil. And, lingering beneath the smoking roof's side, those rain barrels.

Sheathing his axes as he ran, Svarde grabbed the first barrel he could, bending and heaving and throwing. The barrel held water and that made it heavier than Svarde expected, but fear and desperation make for strong friends at the right time, and they helped Svarde send the barrel crashing into the approaching fiend.

The barrel burst over the fiend's lower body, swamping the legs in cool water. The sticky tar hardened in a steamed flash, the fiend toppling over as its upper torso kept moving while its bottom half stuck to the floor. The charred blade clanged off the ground, bouncing from the fiend's grip.

The monster looked up at Svarde, its eyeless head chittering in rage, anger as Svarde drew an axe and finished the job.

Outside, Kivi and the last fiend slugged blows back and forth as the town's survivors looked on. The ferrite proved itself nimble, darting inside when the fiend tried to swing its sword and unleashing bloody claws or damaging head-butts. Those moves came with a cost, though, as Svarde, emerging from the smithy, saw the fiend kick Kivi and send the ferrite rolling away in the dust, an easy target for a sticking.

"Over here, you big bastard!" Svarde yelled, holding his axes high.

When he took a step towards the fiend, though, meaning to break into a run, Svarde's right leg wavered. He went to a knee, staring at the limb, confused.

Then he noticed the red running down the leg. Dropping an axe, he sent a finger along the red stripe, followed it up his thigh and around his waist, to the still-hot, still-numb line along his back.

Svarde blinked. Tried to focus.

The chittering grew, and he looked towards it. The last fiend, approaching with its sword in that devastating double grip. Behind it, laying on her side in the dust, lay Kivi, unmoving.

Svarde drew his second axe, held it in his left hand, watched the fiend approach as red rivulets ran through his eyes.

"Sorry, Catya," he mumbled. "Wasn't able to pull it off for you."

When the fiend stood over him, sword raised high, Svarde took what energy he had left, growled out a curse, and flung himself at the creature.

A Guardian, after all, should die fighting.

CHAPTER 33
DIVE

The claw hit Bliss harder than anything ever had. The fiend's swipe struck her left shoulder and threw her off the old fiend's body, sending Bliss skipping, rolling through the flowered weeds. Leaves and dirt flew up, hidden rocks bit into Bliss's skin, and she came to rest against the upturned slop, her mouth filled with grit.

C'mon, Bliss. She fought down the panic, pushed past the hurt in her shoulder and pressed herself up.

The new fiend stood over the other one, sniffing at its former . . . friend? Did fiends operate like that? Did the ones huddled together in the cave live as a herd, a pack?

Stop. Bliss shook her head, rose to her feet. Those thoughts were distractions, and what mattered now was survival.

Her staff and rope lay near the old fiend's body, out of reach and useless. She lacked any knives, rocks, or other tools save her bare hands, and those wouldn't even annoy the monster.

Speaking of, the fiend finished its sniffing. Its snout rose towards the sky and the beast emitted a keening wheeze, a high-pitched rolling cough. A mourning call? A cry of revenge?

Bliss had to go with the latter, because as the fiend's head came down it turned towards her, a baleful glare emerging from those golden eyes.

With no weapon and little she could use around her, Bliss took the only option she had, and ran.

A quick heel turn and push off sent Bliss up and over the foothill's crest. The slope down became a stumbling sprint as Bliss raced for the trees, the jungle's dubious protection. Behind her, wheezing its challenge, the fiend came on.

The jungle's first layer spread thick trees interspersed with ferns several times taller than Bliss. Beneath them scattered leaves and sticks made up a soft forest floor, and all of it glowed in the noon-time sun. Birds and smaller critters broke for cover at Bliss's approach, though she figured it was the pursuing fiend doing most of the scaring.

Options flitted through with every footstep, Bliss plotting and tossing them in turn. Could she pick up a stick and use it as a weapon? Climb a tree and try to hide?

Neither seemed viable: the fiend could certainly scale a trunk with those claws, and what branch would serve against a hide that thick, claws that deadly?

Bliss needed to change the scenery, bring the battlefield somewhere her smaller form held an advantage. So she tilted her run, angling south along the foothill's slope.

The fiend galloped along behind her, its claws making no secret of its approach. Bliss looked back, saw the fiend's red mane flowing out behind its massive form, its single-fanged jaw wide and gulping air as it ran. Dirt and rock flew, a cloud behind the monster. The ground trembled with its weight.

But Bliss flew too, her legs and arms pumping, her feet hitting every bend in the earth and bouncing off it, capturing momentum and turning it into extra speed. Her lungs sang, her wide eyes caught everything, and she found the jungle a few heartbeats ahead of her pursuit.

And jumped.

Without a rope, swinging was a fool's errand, but in this very moment, being a fool seemed about the only way Bliss could survive.

Using the hill's height, Bliss flew and landed on a huge frond further down. Branches and leaves smacked her face en route, leaving scratched lines, tearing out snagged hair, but Bliss ignored it all.

Little pains for little moments.

Leaning forward to move with the frond's downward bend, Bliss pumped her feet along the wide leaves, scaling the thing and hoping for another option.

The fern shivered as the fiend barreled into it, tearing at the green. Bliss's frond dropped as its tie to the central stalk severed, and again Bliss had to make a leap, arms stretching out for a vine.

A jump without a stable launch wasn't much of a jump at all, though, and Bliss fell short, landing hard on her chest in the leaf-and-mud muck.

The fiend roared its victory, came on in a chomping terror. Bliss rolled over, saw the monster leap high, golden eyes wide and wild with rage, and she curled back up the slope.

The hill's slant betrayed the fiend, its leap carrying the monster over Bliss's head, the thing's back claws gouging right where Bliss would've been if she'd laid flat, waiting for it to end. Instead the fiend hit nothing, its vast bulk slamming onto the slippery leaves. The momentum carried the turning fiend down into several trees where it hammered the bark, the trunks splitting with sharp cracks.

Bliss heard it all behind her, already up on her feet and running further south, ducking beneath more branches and hopping smaller ferns.

The fiend snarled, took up the chase again.

To her left, Bliss spotted a large rotted log, its length angling down the slope, and dove towards it. Too small for Wax, maybe for Sawi, the tube made a perfect fit for Bliss. She scraped her arms on the edges getting through, sliding head first down the moss-filled log. Its damp inside crawled with bugs, all of which Bliss ignored as she kicked with her legs, tucked in her arms and scooted.

She could've moved faster outside, keeping to a dead sprint, but surviving this, as Deshiva pointed out, would take brains as much as fleet feet.

The fiend didn't seem to agree, bashing into the log with cold fury. The hit mashed the log's entry, bursting apart the wood, and sent the rest rolling off its leaf bed. Nestled into the log's middle, Bliss rolled as the dead tree took off down the hillside, rumbling and cracking against its living brethren.

Bliss shut her eyes, offered up a quick prayer to Vis to see her through this awfulness. Not that Vis was much of a praying God—you either chose to embrace the life Vis created around you or you, like Noctia, paved over it with stone and malice.

That embrace hit Bliss hard after a brief, terrifying airborne momebt. The log flew off a sharper, smaller cliff only to break apart in the air, plunging Bliss down into a mushroom-filled grove. Wood crashed into her, around her, splinters joining the litany of wounds she'd gathered over the last few fleeing minutes.

But, she lived.

The rolling log bought Bliss moments, at least going by the wheezing fiend's roar from some ways up the hill. Bliss used those moments too, forcing herself up and rushing on. She muttered an apology to Pan as she stomped over the valuable mushrooms—they'd regrow, though, unlike Bliss.

Deeper into the jungle, along the forest floor, she ran, always trusting her inner compass to bear her south. As the trees grew higher, the fronds larger, her world darkened, shadows taking over as she ran, the fiend always chasing her.

Bliss wasn't going to make it. Some part of her thought she'd get to the big fen to the south, where its myriad tricks and traps could level things against the fiend. Instead the jungle stretched ahead, a black miasma going on and on. Without her rope, without her staff, she had no options for faster travel.

And the fiend still pursued, still gained, even though Bliss had tried everything she knew to dodge and disappear.

So she stopped here, in a grove formed around a massive tree stump. Overhead, vines littered with pink-and-purple flowers dangled. Mosses, cool on her scratched bare feet, coated the forest floor. The air hung sultry and hot, matching the sweat running down her arms and back.

In one arm, Bliss held a stone she'd picked up some ways back. Its triangle shape came to a blunted point, like a chipped tooth. In the other hand rested a thick branch, though one rotted enough that it seemed liable to snap on the first swing.

Those were her weapons.

This was her plan.

Bliss turned to the tree behind her, left the stick resting against its trunk and took a hard jump, leveraging the rock to bite into the bark and help her climb its thick amber trunk.

The fiend came ever closer. Wheezing its rage.

Bliss made it to the first branches, their thin bodies barely suitable for an ambush, so she kept going. Another two limbs higher, the stump far below now.

Bliss crept out onto the branch. Holding the stone in one hand, she cupped her other around her mouth, and made a particular call.

The howling hoot could be heard at night and early morning throughout the jungle, and while Bliss's didn't quite have the volume, it packed the right tone, told the right story to any who might listen.

Bliss hoped some were paying attention.

Cracking branches drew her eyes below. The fiend had entered the play again, sniffing around the stump, following her scent. It hadn't yet looked up.

The chance was still hers.

If only Wax and Quik could see her now.

She shifted the stone, gripped it in both hands as she rose to her feet on the branch, her legs in a careful line, heels planted. She tensed her knees, watching the fiend as it circled the stump, sniffing, following the spots in the moss her feet had tread on seconds earlier.

Its head froze, rose, turned towards the tree Bliss had climbed, considering.

Now.

She jumped, the slightest lift with her legs, just enough to wiggle the branch and send her off to the side. Bliss flattened out her body, driving her arms down first, leading with the stone, her head not far behind.

Air whistled by her ears, her stomach dropped. The fiend looked up, its golden eyes widening, for once not in anger, but in surprise.

In fear.

CHAPTER 34

THORNS

Three on two, and Wax wanted to say he was ready. He and Pan stood side-by-side on the crunchy, leafy-and-branch ground looking right ahead at the three coastal groupies. Their opponents, spread apart and standing before the thorny ascent to the sana's very top, held determined looks, their weaves thick, their arms and legs bearing bright wraps.

Wax read the colors—Kitaye used dyes, inks on the skin to show where you stood in society, the coast used fabrics instead. The three before him, the two women on the edges rolled with their sea-faring caste, a rough-and-tumble group coated in piercings and flat stares. The middle bore the brown bandannas belonging to the craftsmen, the builders. Broad shoulders, big back, and bent knees like a carpenter.

Not soldiers, then, but who on Vis really was?

"Why?" Pan asked, no, shouted across the way. "What's the point? Your person's already ahead."

"A guarantee," the middle man replied. "This is our honor, Kitaye. You had the last Renewal. This is our time."

Ah, second city syndrome. At least, that's what they called it in Kitaye. Vis's larger city had the isle's central location, its easier access to resources and better trading locale. The coastals had every right to feel inferior, because they were.

"Then earn it," Wax said. "Help your chosen one get the token. Don't beat us up."

"One accomplishes the other, doesn't it?" Asked the sea-farer on the right.

Wax's hand itched for the Foti blade. If he could draw that sword, show these three he and Pan weren't a couple chumps to be intimidated . . . as it was, though, a brawl here wouldn't end well.

They had to find another way.

The three coastals seemed content to let Pan and Wax discuss, which, fair: so long as the way up was blocked, their Renewal winner had all the time in the world to get the skar, claim the honor. As for the two others down below, their curses had quit a couple minutes ago, the hatching bugs apparently driving the duo back down.

"Which leaves us where?" Pan asked, flicking his eyes to the thorns, to Wax, and back. "Don't think we can punch through them, and unless you've stuffed some secret weapon up that weave, we're low on options."

Wax looked 'round. The sana's inner trunk narrowed as it approached the top, turning into that thorny mass. The outer skin simply stopped, turning over and folding in towards the middle, breaking away at the edges like so many dying branches. Leafy strands extended here and there, weak twigs offering little hope for a climb-and-jump combo.

Only the central stalk, decked out with those thick, climbable thorns, offered any hope of getting to the top.

"The only way is through," Wax said, "or we give up. Sit and wait to see what happens."

Pan started in again on how they'd come pretty far. How his father would be proud of him for this, even if he didn't get the skar. Wax tuned out the rationalizing, looked closer at the trio.

He and Pan weren't fighters, but neither were these three. If they could be baited, could be turned . . .

"Trick'em," Wax whispered, and Pan shut up as his Guardian detailed the idea, ludicrous as it might seem.

The way established, the pair turned, Pan failing to keep the nerves from his wide eyes, and walked towards the three Guardians. They stiffened at the duo's approach, held their formation.

"Are you all planning to be Guardians?" Pan asked on the walk-up. "Isn't five a large number?"

The three glanced at one another, shrugs abounded.

"We're friends," the builder said. "We'll work it out."

"Uh oh," Wax shook his head. They were five solid strides from the opposing line now, eight from the stalk and the first thorn. "You're asking for problems, there. Who's going to give up the honor?"

The builder snorted, "Like I said—"

"Stop talking with them, Korrus," snapped the sea-farer on the right. "They're up to something, I can smell it on'em."

"Definitely suspicious," the left one added. "See his face?" She snickered. "Wouldn't mind playing for parts with that one."

"Nothing suspicious about asking simple questions," Wax said. "Just figure, if you're going to be carrying the hopes of the whole isle with you, maybe you should work out the details first."

Three strides now. Wax kept his hands clear. Pan too. His friend had shored up his shoulders, put on a placid smile. Not meek, exactly, but unthreatening. Mild.

Good.

"Maybe you should mind your own business," Korrus replied. "And get back to where you were."

"Well," Wax said, drawing out the word. One stride now. The two sea-farers edged closer, forming a half-circle around Wax and Pan. "I was thinking, since you don't have the Guardian stuff worked out, maybe you'd let us come along for the ride?"

The question rocked them back. A ridiculous request, but also perhaps not. Guardians from across the isle had been chosen before, if Wax remembered his stories right.

Not that it mattered. As soon as Wax saw the Korrus's eyes cross in confusion, in consideration as the man imagined that wild scenario, Wax whooped.

The loud cry, meant for swinging and sweeping through the air, cracked the still morning, echoing around the trunk and getting the coastal trio to jump. Wax followed up the cry by doing what every Guardian ought to: throwing himself right into the enemy's gut.

Pan, for once, did exactly what he was supposed to, sprinting ahead with just enough verve to dodge a late, shocked grab from the left sea-farer. Wax, hitting Koreas with a shoulder charge, bounced off the bigger man and landed on the ground, butt first. Koreas grunted, turned to chase Pan, and Wax kicked out, knocking the man's left ankle and sending him tumbling to the deck.

The sea-farers started after Wax's friend, but they'd lost two steps in the shock, steps Pan put to his advantage. The mushroom scrounger reached the stalk and jumped, hooking his arms around the bottom thorn and pulling himself onto the smooth, purple green spike. Wax felt some pride seeing how fast Pan turned his look upward, found the next thorn, and jumped towards it.

You didn't make moves that fast unless you knew what you were doing.

Koreas knew what he was doing too, picking up Wax by his weave and holding him over the crunch leaf floor.

"Why'd you go and do that?" The builder growled. "Now your friend's going to get hurt."

"Is he?" Wax nodded towards the stalk.

The sea-farers chased, but their jumps weren't so sharp, their grips hesitant, their feet unsteady on the thorns. A lifetime spent on boats and rocky shoals didn't prep you for a jungle climb.

"Yeah, watch." Koreas threw Wax to the ground, skipping him off the stiff surface. Wax's weave blocked the damage, save for a scuff on his legs.

Koreas stomped to the stalk, found a thorn about at his knee level and stomped on it. The spike, as long as the man's arms, snapped off, the builder picking it up in his massive hands and breaking it again, turning the pointed end into a small arrowhead.

One, Wax realized as he scrambled to his feet, Koreas could throw pretty damn far.

Pan, five thorns up and several ahead of the sea-farers, looked to make his next leap as Koreas reared back, the spike ready to toss. The strike wouldn't even need to hit Pan, just get close enough to throw off his jump.

A fall from this height would be, if not fatal, definitely the end of Pan's short-lived Renewal bid.

"Don't!" Wax shouted, rushing towards Korrus.

The sea-farers glanced down, Pan didn't. His friend bent his legs, jumped, and the builder threw. The spike flew, the aim true enough. The missile grazed Pan's legs as his arms wrapped around the next thorn up, a red splatter dancing down.

His friend screamed.

"Hold on!" Wax shouted back. "Don't you dare let go!"

Koreas spun as Wax approached, laying out with his left hand. Not unlike a bad branch to dodge. Wax dropped to his legs, slid on the floor, then popped up as Korrus's slug went over his head. Jabbing with his right hand, Wax went with a strong hit to the man's gut, right where Wax had smacked with his shoulder earlier.

Koreas groaned, backed up a step, and Wax took the opportunity to jump, kicking off the stalk to get to the next thorn up.

The sea-farers split at the sight, one continuing to climb after Pan while the other waited, glaring at Wax. Farther up, Pan, legs bleeding, managed to get himself on the thorn proper. The poor guy tore strips from his weave, trying to wrap the twin gashes.

Before, this whole thing seemed a weird game. A race followed by a bar fight and an oddball climb to the top. People kept saying there were serious risks, but Wax hadn't seen any, not till the thrown thorn. That Pan's near-death had come not from some fiend or awful hazard, but from another Vis trying to be greedy . . . sparked a rising rage.

Wax wouldn't have said he was one to get angry, was one to keep a cool head, but dammit, he was Pan's Guardian, and now Pan was hurt.

No way Wax would let Pan fall.

He backed up near the thorn's point, then sprinted forward, jumped, and kicked off the sana stalk to get up to the next one. Pan's leap-and-grab worked well enough, but it was slow, left you vulnerable to waiting jerks like the sea-farers. Wax's kick-off put him level with the thorn, getting him right on its length with a kneeling, feet-planted landing.

Right where the sea-farer could kick him.

Her foot, bare, flew in at Wax's head. He raised a hand to block, a thin defense that had the sea-farer's blow blasting on through to smack Wax's temple. He teetered, splaying his legs to let them hook around the thorn's body, keeping him in place.

The sea-farer rebalanced after the kick, swapped feet and came in hard on the other side. Wax, his ears ringing from the first hit, swiveled, caught the foot with both hands, still taking a knock to his chin in the process. His teeth slammed into his lip, fresh iron tang filling his mouth.

But he held on, and pulled.

The sea-farer cursed, her remaining foot slipping on the thorn's rounded surface and sliding off. Wax let go and the sea-farer plummeted, smacking hard on the ground and moaning. Korrus, not even attempting to climb, went over to check on his teammate.

How kind. No problem killing Pan, but wants to make sure his buddy didn't rattle her skull too hard.

"Wax!" Pan called, still clinging to the thorn. "This isn't good!"

The second sea-farer stood one thorn beneath Pan now, and two above Wax. She seemed to be considering the best way to get to Pan's level, the man, with legs partly wrapped now, ready to kick away any attack.

Spitting out some blood, Wax rose to his own shaky feet, found the next thorn, and jumped towards it. Slipped his hands around, pulled himself up, and heard Pan shout again.

The sea-farer found an alternate route, jumping to the

left instead, finding another thorn near Pan's height. If there were other thorns around the stalk, the sea-farer could get above Pan, and then either hold the high ground or jump on down, trying to knock Pan off in the process.

Either was unacceptable.

"Hang in there," Wax called back, eyeing his next leap.

The thorns laid themselves out in a line, the same instinct setting the sequence now as it always did for him. Wax plotted the jumps, the speed, where he'd plant his feet to go off to the next.

The sea-farer had the edge for now.

But not for long.

CHAPTER 35

UNEXPECTED ALLIES

Bliss struck the fiend and in an instant felt her arms crack, her chin smack the fiend's skin, and the rock between her hands bite deep all at once. Her body followed, slamming the fiend's back and flying off in an awkward flop ending with her lying in the moss, a tangled mess gasping for her breath.

Her target wheezed, cried, flopped to its side and writhed, those claws coming close to Bliss as the fiend tried to extract the rock from its back.

It wasn't dead.

Bliss kept repeating the line, kept hoping the fiend would slow and stop its kicks. She'd put everything into the leap, dug that rock in so far . . . the fiend shouldn't, couldn't be alive. Yet there it was, throwing itself back against a tree, rubbing its wounded body against it.

The stone dropped to the moss with the slightest thud, rosy-red from its impact, but out, useless.

Bliss shook her head. Tried to get her body to answer, but her arms didn't want to work. Her shoulders blossomed in new aches. Her legs quivered on the grass, the dew clinging to her skin. Cool. Overhead, the sun twinkled through the branches.

Not the worst last sight.

The fiend huffed, snarled. Shook out its mane. Those golden eyes no longer held fear, but anger, narrow slits focused only on Bliss.

She glared back. Her sole weapon, that nasty look, and the fiend didn't care. Two long steps put it face to face with Bliss. It opened its mouth, the lone fang looming. The thing's death breath washed over her, killing Bliss's composure with a coughing fit. One last chance for her ribs to remind her that they, too, were bruised or broken.

At least that pain would be gone soon.

But the chomp didn't come. The fang didn't land. The fiend made a startled yelp, its head swinging back around as the monster stumbled aside.

Bliss had made the call, and the hanoko had answered.

The gray-green, six-legged cat snatched onto the fiend's back, its legs and teeth working the pounce to its fullest potential. The hanoko dodged the fiend's flailing counters, knowing it had the advantage and using it to tear its opponent apart.

Not a simple hunting kill, this. It was an example, a marker to anything that would dare challenge this hanoko's territory.

The fiend, after less than a minute, lay fallen on the moss, its threat reduced to nothing more than dying shudders. The hanoko, a victory grip on the fiend's throat, held its grasp until the fiend shook its last.

Bliss found her body emerging from the shock. A slow, painful awakening as muscles and bones found themselves bruised, yes, broken, not quite. Her legs came first, and Bliss pulled her knees up to her chest, rolled forward, those ribs again complaining.

The slightest pressure on her wrists made her wince, had her biting her lip to distract away the pain.

She wouldn't be wielding the staff anytime soon.

Her jaw ached, her head pulsed with the combined euphoria of survival and the pain of the same.

The jungle seemed to blossom around her as Bliss stood, birds and bugs, smaller furry critters all emerging with the unnatural predator defeated. A new song rose, a rustling, tweeting symphony.

Its bass note sounded behind her, the hanoko's low growl. Bliss turned 'round, keeping her useless hands low, her body in a half-crouch. Look too threatening, or too meek, and the hanoko might go for a second kill.

Strike the middle, make her intentions clear, and the big cat might take its prize and leave her alone.

Big eyes found hers, yellow-green slits, bearing none of the fiend's malice and all of a cat's curiosity. The hanoko dropped its kill, glancing back once as if to confirm its success. Bliss stayed still, breathing, wondering how she could still breathe at all.

A hunter's relationship with hanoko should be driven by demands. Weapons and numbers ready to push the cats away, let them know not to interfere with what the humans were doing. Bliss had neither, and the cat knew it.

The hanoko came close, stood on its six paws to a height taller than Bliss. Its two leading fangs hung over its lip, near enough to touch her forehead. The hanoko sniffed her once. Bliss closed her eyes.

She could be happy with this end. At least Vis had won, this time.

The hanoko sniffed again, at her face. Then a third time, at her chest.

The lick came sudden, a scratchy, wet slough along her left arm. The weight hurt, Bliss shrinking away, the hanoko doing the same before realizing the woman wasn't planning some attack.

Bliss tried a smile, backed up a step. Found herself unsteady on the moss, the pain, the aches scaling up as the fight faded away. She slipped, fell, and felt the hanoko put its paw on her chest, holding her down.

She looked up into those green-yellow eyes, the jungle fading, its song getting a new line: the hanoko's rumbling purr.

THE COOL WATERSKIN woke her up, its pleasant spot on her forehead sparking Bliss's slow climb back to consciousness. Her body still ached, but she felt new lines along her arms, her legs. Thick wraps coated her chest beneath her weave.

And looking down at her?

The angriest brother she'd ever seen.

Quik, his wood gauntlets hanging by his waist, poured forth a litany of questions, demands, admonishments and more. Bliss barely heard any of it, the words muffled by the astonished fact that she still lived at all.

Behind Quik, and smirking at his diatribe, stood Deshiva and several other hunters. They looked to have parts of the fiend—its fang, the claws, the mane—carved off and packed away already. Prizes, perhaps, for Kitaye.

"Prizes for you," Deshiva said when Quik paused for a breath. "This was your kill, Bliss. You earned them."

Bliss raised her right hand. Its bound wrist made signing hard, but Quik followed the gestures.

"She says the hanoko made the kill," Quick said, sitting back, shaking his head. "As if that matters. I can't believe you went after them alone."

Deshiva crouched, her face turning serious, "Where's the second one, Bliss? As long as we're here, I would see it destroyed."

Bliss popped a small smile, made a simple sign.

"It's dead," Quik translated, blinking at her. "You did it?"

Bliss nodded, Deshiva laughed.

"Look at this one, then," the huntress said. "Two fiends, and she's still a youth. Kitaye's lucky to have you, Bliss."

"Lucky that you're still alive," Quik muttered. Stood. "We're going to carry you back to the camp. It's getting dark, so we'll be careful."

'How?' Bliss signed before Quik looked away.

"How'd we find you? The cat came looking for us. It was acting strange, so we followed it." Quik reached down, put a hand on Bliss's shoulder. "Luck. That's how we found you." He squeezed, Bliss winced. "Never, Bliss, never make me feel that again, okay? We're a team, a family."

"One that talks too much," Deshiva announced. "Let's move. There's a lot of ground to cover, and doing it with a girl in our hands won't be fast."

CHAPTER 36

A SMOKING RUIN

The stone struck the fiend high on its shoulder, spurring a leaf green gout. The monster's swing went left, missing Svarde by the barest fraction, giving the Guardian's loose, sloppy charge time to hit.

Svarde burned with the impact, meshing into the hot tar, the green scar lines, and bouncing out to the right, dragging his axes along behind him. The fiend keened out an angry cry, started to bring his sword back across as Svarde stumbled free from his attack.

The swing never made it: two more stones smacked into the fiend, broken bricks tossed with alacrity hitting home on the fiend's bulbous head and its lanky arms. The monster's grip slipped, the blade dipping into the ground and carving a burning divot in the dirt, but going nowhere.

Svarde, his eyes stinging, saw the source: the townspeople, freed from their captor's deadly eyes, had taken up their own defense. Mothers, fathers, children broke free from the central statue and scattered, some picking up what rubble might be used and casting it at the last fiend.

Svarde turned around, survival's chance restoring

enough energy to keep him standing straight, his axes held at his waist. Their edges glowed orange, dripped with the green hot lava blood.

The weapons wanted more.

Stones pelted the fiend, forcing the creature to drop its blade, shrink its legs and bring out more arms to deflect the blows.

Arms that did okay against the rocks, that did little against Svarde's axes.

The Foti warrior broke into a grumbling song as he laid waste to the monster, the words rolling to a beat meant for a hot forge, one that worked just as well to carve the smoking fiend into ruin.

At its end, Svarde stood over an emerald-and-black puddle, smoke rising up around him, rising from him too, where the splatter melted into his armor, burned at his hair and beard.

"Thank you," said a man, his clothes a torched patchwork, but looking like those of a farmer. He approached Svarde, gave the warrior a slow look and grimaced. "You have to come with us, now. Please."

Svarde, the combat's rejuvenation draining out, gave the farmer a grim look. "Come where?"

"Those things, they weren't what caused all this." The man skipped a glance deeper in the town, towards the overhanging monolith. "The thing that made them could come back any moment."

"The thing that made them?"

The man shook his head. Behind him, the other townspeople followed the fleeing plan, breaking for the far fields. Some few found satchels, most simply put feet to dirt, dragging friends and family along with them.

"A fiend I've never seen before," the man replied. "It

destroyed our walls. Killed our militia. It's not random, either. It's . . . " The man paled, as if he couldn't quite come to terms with what he was about to say.

He didn't have to. Svarde knew.

"Smart?" Svarde asked, and the man nodded. "Some fiends are like that. They're not all mindless." The warrior straightened, sighted Kivi, still on the ground. "Get your-selves gone, then. I'll see to it."

The man stared, mouth opening, as if he meant to doubt Svarde's ability to do what he'd promised, then caught the warrior's glower and shut himself up. Soon his footsteps added to the departing crowd.

Kivi wouldn't be fleeing anywhere, at least not fast. The fiend's blade had found its mark on the ferrite's back legs, delivering a hard blow that'd left her rocky silver-black skin cracked. Svarde laid a hand on the creature's head, heard Kivi's soft snort.

"Need to get you some stone," Svarde muttered. "Plenty around here, at least."

The charred bricks and blocks weren't exactly Kivi's favorite meal, but they'd do in a pinch. Sheathing his axes, Svarde set about gathering a few in the quiet square. His bleeding back made every move a pain, a ticking clock on Svarde's endurance, but he could make it awhile yet. He'd have to.

The fiend would come back to check on its captives, its soldiers, and if Svarde had to face it alone, the warrior didn't like his chances.

The sun slanted down, falling across a sky crossed by smoke trails. Svarde planted stones by Kivi, woke her up enough to get the ferrite to nibble on the rock. He found his own satchel, dropped before his first charge against the fiends, and gasped at the clean water on his charred throat, the feel of bread and meat between his ash-stained teeth.

Bandaging his wounds turned out difficult, the gash along his back an impossibility, and its seeping blood kept up a constant run as Svarde moved, sat, waited with his axes for the return.

A snapping board woke Svarde up. Twilight lay across the town now, deep purples and blacks. Shadows. Kivi snored and snorted, asleep next to him with her stone meal long gone. Svarde's back kept up its searing constant, though it hadn't been enough to keep the man awake.

As for the sound, its source stood near the clearing's entrance, gazing over the emptiness with deep cherry eyes. A trio, set in a rounded head atop a lanky form, one wrapped in writhing, shifting smoke. The fiend caught the lingering sunlight, its figure twisting the glow, turning it from pure black into a painted, almost beautiful form.

As Svarde, sitting against the central statue, watched, the fiend's misty edges broke away, floating up and then down to the ground to form smokey pools. Those black pits, no larger than Svarde's axe heads, began to bubble, to glow green, and then froth up into smaller versions of the fiends he'd already dispatched. The two tiny ones grew their legs and ambled forward, droplet heads peering this way and that, hunting for answers.

Or, perhaps, traps. The fiend itself, the master of this particular raid, kept its three rubies on Svarde. It waited, seemingly content to match stares with the warrior.

Confusing, until Svarde tasted the fiend, smelled it on his tongue and in his nose. A charcoal acid, foul and also, Svarde blinked as he tried to understand, questioning. Not words, exactly, but an impression came with the taste on his tongue, came with the scent in his nose.

A simple query, asking Svarde where he'd come from.

Rumors had flown for years now about fiends that could talk, that weren't the mindless horrors Noctia and the Najahn taught everyone to fear. Those rumors, though, came with the same circumstances: speech or no, intelligence or no, the fiends had still fought to destroy, to kill, to obliterate.

Which made them monsters all the same.

"Doesn't matter where I came from," Svarde said to the fiend, his voice a glimmering growl. A speech he'd not held since standing side by side with Ami and Catya, at the last stand before she took up the Aegis's mantel. "What matters is where you're going."

Svarde lifted a single axe, pointed it towards the fiend. Those three ruby eyes flashed. The twin smaller monsters jerked, as if pulled on a leash, and they stopped their search to ramble towards Svarde.

Ankle high, no blades. Svarde eyed their approach with nothing close to fear. Only a dead set determination.

He drew the second axe, waited.

The two tiny fiends closed, hit a couple strides away and reached towards Svarde.

And Kivi woke up.

Her back legs wounded, the ferrite had muscle up front. With an angry snort, she popped her vents, lunged, and tore apart the first fiend with an engulfing bite. Hot green bubbled around the ferrite's granite lips, steaming as it sizzled to the ground. The second fiend managed a twist, a curious turn, before Kivi ate it too, gulping the thing down and burping, satisfied with the snack.

Those ruby eyes flashed again. A different taste rose on Svarde's tongue, his nose: anger, curiosity, a challenge.

The smoke along the fiend's fringes resolved itself

again, coalescing not into further small fiends but into twin blades. Charred swords like the others, only these were as long as Svarde was tall, and they seemed to be apart of the fiend's body, an extension as much as any arm or leg. Through each ran a singular red line, one that expanded as the fiend glided towards Svarde, the ruby fire spider-webbing across the weapons.

"Nice trick," Svarde said, standing up. "Won't help you none."

Kivi growled at his feet. The fiend didn't seem to care. Svarde dropped his axes to his waist, reversing the the grip to put the edges towards the enemy, heads pointed down. The fiend made the opposite move, raising its blades high, crossing them in front of its face.

A guarding play, one made to block Svarde's attack and annihilate him with a downward crossing cut.

Predictable.

The fiend sped up as it approached, the soundless glide a tad unnerving. No dirt, no grass marked its passage. Those blades quivered, those eyes flashed.

Svarde threw the axe in his right hand, tossed it up, spinning, high overhead. The fiend arced its eyes, its blades to track the weapon, and missed Svarde's crouch, his right hand sliding behind him to grab his waterskin.

"Have a drink," Svarde said, launching the half-full skin into the fiend's upward-looking face.

The waterskin hit, burst against the fiend's hot tar skin, breaking into a sizzling mess. The fiend writhed, and Svarde's axe came down, a perfect end-over-end smash through a suddenly open defense. Its swords whipped, the axe biting into the fiend's shoulder, and Svarde ducked inside, swiping up with his other axe to deflect a sword, to push through and deliver—

The hot strike dove into Svarde's stomach, a boiling, piercing blow from a smoke-hidden dagger. Svarde's left-handed axe completed its swing without any strength left, drawing a narrow line through the fiend's middle, and doing nothing to keep the monster from driving Svarde back against the statue.

The warrior felt the stone hit his aching back, felt the boiling dagger push on through and pin him there.

At his feet, Kivi snorted and snarled, biting at the fiend and getting swept away by the swords. The monster looked wounded, bled green flame from where the thrown axe bit into its shoulder, a dead brown patch on its body where the waterskin struck.

Those ruby eyes drew closer, and, mixed with his own blood, Svarde tasted victory, triumph.

But the warrior heard something else. A whistle, carried on the wind.

CHAPTER 37

THE SKAR

Every sana stalk had its own character. The feel of the stem, the thick emerald skin giving way to reddish thorns, all crossed over with tiny lines. Some bore whisper-thin hairs while others carried scars from hanokos and other critters intent on finding a drink from the sap within.

The Great Sana told its own story, a weathered one. Wax's hands found hold after hold as he gripped and launched off, bouncing from his lower thorn up above, racing to beat the seafarer to her diving assault on Pan. Wax's friend tried to steady himself, the wound on his leg doing him no favors on the thorn's fragile surface.

Wax landed, his thorn slightly higher than the seafarer's, but on the wrong side of the trunk. Going around to his right would lead him to the enemy, to his left would lead Wax to Pan. Neither in easy jumping distance.

He'd have to get creative.

"Climb down!" Shouted the seafarer to Pan. "You're too hurt to continue. It's a pointless risk."

"Leave me alone," Pan countered, and Wax's heart lurched at the pain in the words.

Sure, Pan had a way of getting himself in trouble on their adventures. His cluelessness to his own surroundings, his hesitating jumps often left him scratched, beat up, or nearly devoured, but those had come with friends nearby. An easy out to the danger, a protective circle should anything truly nasty happen.

Here, it was just Wax, and right now, Wax was failing his friend.

Up and to his left, another thorn above him. A far jump, too far to try and climb, but Wax didn't need that. At least, not yet.

The seafarer seemed nervous about her own leap, shouting again for Pan to just give up. She kept her eyes down, ignoring Wax. A fair decision, because it'd take something special to bring him her way without plenty of time to react.

Something special like this.

Wax took a running stride, all of one big step, as that's all the thorn would allow. He planted his left foot, felt it slip ever so slightly on the sloping thorn's side, and lifted off. He flew leftwards, but also in, towards the trunk, bringing up his legs as he flew and twisting his feet so they met the trunk at an angle, pressing just enough of their soles against its great, rippled surface.

Wax pressed down at the contact, that instant friction giving him possibility, and with the kick, he flew higher, rebounding outwards and upwards, right towards the higher thorn.

Still not high enough to climb, but enough, with his arms outstretched, to get a loose grip.

Wax swung, his legs sliding out ahead as his hands

grappled the thorn's thinning point. The aged skin gave his palms enough purchase to redirect, to swing his torso out and back, looping it around the trunk as Wax let go.

Let go, and hoped he wasn't wrong. A misfire here would mean a fall Wax wouldn't walk away from, one that'd also put him right within smacking range of the builder and his seafarer friend.

The swing left Wax flying with his feet first, a silky move putting him right on target, a target Wax did not want to hit on his back.

Flipping his body in mid-air wasn't something he'd learned how to do in a moment. It'd been years burnt flying from frond to frond, tree to tree, realizing a torqued muscle here, a shoulder twist there, could get Wax into the right shape to make his landing lead right to the next jump.

Here, now, he needed his landing not to kill him.

The seafarer shouted something Wax didn't catch. A curse, maybe, or a surprised yelp. Wax didn't care, because if he didn't get his body—

His feet hit something soft, something that grunted, that killed Wax's own momentum even as the kick shoved the seafarer off the thorn. Wax himself dropped, his stomach smacking the thorn and burbling the air from his lungs, bile up from his gut. His hands, though, did what trained reflexes taught them to: they gripped, they held, and Wax hung on, his legs draping down off the thorn's side while his chin rested on its chilled, rippled skin.

Wax risked a glance down, pulling his head off the thorn. Far below, the struck seafarer lay limp on the ground, flat on her back. He meant to find Pan, but Wax found himself stuck on the body, willing it to move, to make some sign. His nerves went to a slow numb. Reasons, excuses made intrusions into his mind, as if Wax were pleading his case to his peers and the only way to win was to blabber out as many possibilities as he could.

He blinked, finally, when the hot sting was too much to keep his eyes open. Korrus and the other seafarer came over, knelt near their friend.

Wax wanted to shout that he was sorry, wanted to say it'd been the seafarer's own fault, but he couldn't find the air, the will. As if to call down would be to admit that he'd done this thing, this act that flew from an instinct to protect Pan and nothing else.

A hand gripped Wax's wrist, quieting the doubt, the voices for a brief moment. Pan, having scaled the sana up to Wax's level.

"Come on," Pan whispered. "You've gotta help me a little."

Clarity. An easy objective, free from moral quandaries, ethical dilemmas. Wax pushed on his elbows, slid a leg over the thorn and sat next to Pan. His friend offered a shaky smile, then looked down at the scattered wraps on his leg. They'd already soaked through.

"I'll survive," Pan said, "I think."

Wax reached for his own weave, thinking to add to the bindings, but Pan stopped him, nodding up.

"Whomever they have up there's far enough ahead already. Let's go, Wax. We didn't do all this to lose it now."

"You sure?"

"Not until this moment." Pan stood, helped Wax to his feet. Both had to stand heel-to-toe on the narrowing thorn. "They tried to kill me, Wax. The old me, I would've run. Would've given up. But not now. Not anymore."

Wax started to slide a look down again, Pan's words bringing back the body, and Pan whistled. Not as clean, as sharp as Wax's own, but enough to bring him back.

"I need you with me, Guardian."

A shivering cold swept through Wax, washing away the doubt, the confusion. Guardian. He could be that.

"I'm with you."

Left without harassment, the thorn stair proved an easier climb. Wax led off, making each leap then turning back to help Pan complete the same. With his wounded leg, Pan's jumps were haphazard, often falling short, so Wax would lay across the thorn, reach down with his hand and catch Pan as his friend made the leap. Pan would reach up, join Wax, and the two would plot the next jump.

The sana's inner trunk outpaced the hardened bark outside, revealing itself to be a new growth inside the old, dead shell. As Wax and Pan jumped over the last, spiked ends of the outer trunk, Vis sprawled out beneath them. Glittering green jungle sparkled in daytime dew, with fog clustered in low valleys and clouds drifting by above. Birds split the difference, coasting and cawing with the wind.

Overhead, the sana's bloom waited, the thorns growing thicker and easier near the top. A small hole, no larger than the trap doors many tree houses had, looked cut in a rose-red petal.

"That's the way," Wax muttered as he and Pan surveyed the route. "No sign of the other person, though."

"If they already had the skar, wouldn't they climb down?"

"You'd think."

No answer to the question presented itself, so the two kept on going, one thorn after another. Wax found the simple process worked to keep the fear at bay, as if all it took to live with murder was the repetition of day to day tasks.

The sana's petals grew more resplendent as the pair

drew closer, their color palette spanning a spectrum, getting brighter towards each petal's middle and deepening to black at the edges. Sunlight glowed, playing out the splaying lines within the giant petals.

"Never seen anything more beautiful," Wax said as they lit on the last thorn.

"Not even Sawi?" Pan said, looking pale with the blood loss, still managing a joke.

"Not fair."

"Can't a guy have a little bit of fun before the end?"

Wax shook his head, judged the distance to the hole. An easy jump and grip, the sana's petals more than thick enough for their weight.

But where was the person ahead of them? If the Najahn had it right, and the skars waited in the flower's middle, then they had to have made it this far?

"Be careful," Wax said, aiming his jump. "This isn't making sense."

"You're saying that now?"

"Pan, when did you get sarcastic?"

"When they stabbed my leg, Wax. Put everything in a new perspective."

Laughing, Wax made the jump. His hands caught the soft, almost mushy petal surface. Felt the sun's pure heat on his fingers. A solid grip, and Wax pulled himself up and through.

The clear sunlight hit so hard his eyes went white, shading everything in slow enough, like patterns coming clear from a dream. The lines etched in, Wax's eyes focused towards the great flower's middle, where an indigo mound rose up from the gathering petals.

The sana's center puffed out, every fiber reaching,

curling more towards the outside, towards the sun. The blue fluff on those fibers shivered in the warm wind.

"See anything?" Pan asked.

"I see a big sana flower," Wax replied. He stepped forward, away from the hole. Held a hand up to block the sun. "Nothing else."

The petal tremored as Pan clambered up beside him.

"No skars?" Pan asked.

"I can't see any, can you?"

"It's too bright to see much. No person either?"

"Maybe they took all the skars and found another way down?"

Wax and Pan walked down the petal towards the sana center. The incredible view deserved a few looks, but any triumph at making it this far found itself washed away by simple confusion.

"It occurs to me," Pan mused, "that we should've asked the Najahn what these skars look like."

"The Aegis wears them, right? On a necklace?"

Not that Wax had ever seen an Aegis, or remembered any of the candidates that'd streamed through on the last Renewal, but he thought that's where it all wound up. "So they can't be that big?"

"That's at the end. Maybe they get chopped up?"

Pan's question found its answer as the two reached the flower's middle, the fluffy blue edge. Hiding beneath the strands, dead center in the mound, sat small green rocks. Or, at least, they looked like rocks, and they shared their color with the sana's forest green stalk. Each one looked about as large as Wax's thumb, and while at first Wax thought their glow came from the sun, a closer look changed that idea: the little tokens held their own inner light.

"Guess we found'em," Wax said, stepping into the blue. His weight jostled the strands, letting loose pollen into the sky. Wax reached for the stones, then stopped himself, backed away. "Sorry, this is all you."

"I wondered if you were going to remember," Pan said, swapping spots. "Or if you'd changed your mind."

"After this, hanging out in Kitaye doesn't seem so bad."

"You're still my Guardian, Wax."

"Darn."

Pan laughed, winced at his leg, then reached into the blue. Came out with a single green scar, resting in his palm. They both stared at it.

"It's warm," Pan said after a few seconds.

"That it?"

"That's it."

"No big awakening? Visions of power or anything?"

Pan threw Wax a skeptical look, "You've been listening to too many stories."

"Your dad tells most of'em."

"Exactly."

The breeze whipped by. The sun continued its slow trek towards the horizon. And nothing happened. No drums kicked up, no Najahn leader appearing from nowhere to declare Pan the rightful Renewal candidate.

"This is profoundly underwhelming," Wax said.

"Maybe that's all there is? We have the skar, now we climb back down?"

"Through those people who really hate us?" Wax didn't mention the body. Wouldn't mention it. "Can we find any other way?"

"There isn't any," the words came from the blue pollen's far side, light and tired. Rising over the thistle after them came a sun-dappled face, the last woman in the crew from below. She held up her hands, showing them empty. "It's a long drop."

Wax and Pan shared a glance, then the latter held up the skar.

"Didn't you take one?"

She winced at the green stone in Pan's hand. "I thought about it. For a long time." Her arms closed around her body, as if she was warding off a chill, though the sun made it hot up here. "We talked about it a lot on the way over. Which one of us would take the skar. They volunteered me."

"Volunteered you?" Pan asked. Wax tried taking a closer look, confirmed the woman, who didn't look much older than Bliss, had no weapons, no ropes or other tricks. "Isn't this supposed to be a choice?"

"Honor against paradise," the woman shrugged, looked off the Great Sana to the east. The jungle's gentle slope towards that far coast lay out in shiny splendor. "That's the trick, isn't it? Everyone dresses all this up in some golden cloak so you don't notice everything you're giving up."

"So you didn't take one." Pan looked at the star in his hand, showed it to Wax. "That means, um,"

"Means you win," the woman continued. "Means I get to come up with an excuse now, a reason why."

"Tell them the truth," Wax said. "There's nothing to be ashamed of."

"Easy to say when your city hasn't put their trust in you." The woman stepped away from the pollen, walked out onto a flower petal as Pan and Wax watched. "We figured Kitaye would go for a free for all, so we focused. Picked our fastest, picked me, and we ran here. I was going to bring the glory back. Then we'd go around to all the isles, pick up the tokens, and hurrah, I get to be the next Aegis."

"Trapped on Noctia forever," Pan muttered, but the

woman caught the words on the breeze, gave him a sharp nod.

"Not even a full adult, and here they are, saying I'll only live another few years trapped in some Najahn prison," the woman said, shaking her head. "It didn't feel real till I stood where you are now. And you know what? I don't want it. Don't want the obligation, don't want to give up all this. A chance at a real life."

Wax went from watching the girl to looking at Pan, who'd taken on an ill cast. The same weight that'd knocked the woman from her goal coming to rest on him.

"Don't worry, buddy," Wax said. "We can take our time. Enjoy the adventure. Let someone else win the game."

Pan gulped, nodded, kept his grip on the skar. "You'd better not let me win, Wax."

The grin came easy. "Pan, you're talking to a master of delays. I'll find so many ways to knock us off course, you'll never sniff Noctia."

The woman laughed, joined Pan. The tension fell away. Pan still seemed less than thrilled, but there'd be time for that to fade. For now, hey, they'd won, and—

The flower shook. The petal behind Wax trembled, and he turned, Pan with him, to see the builder, followed by the first two jokers they'd dodged climbing up onto the flower.

They didn't exactly look friendly.

Korrus took the first step towards the group, his eyes finding the woman. "You took the skar?"

She hesitated. Wax didn't.

"She chose her own freedom, big guy. Pan's our man, now." Wax put a hand on Pan's shoulder, then softened his look. "Is she all right?"

"She's alive," Korrus said, still looking at the woman. "Is he saying you didn't take one? Tell me he's lying."

Wax flip-flopped. The seafarer wasn't dead. Amazing. And yet, whatever happiness he felt at not becoming a killer faltered at the grim looks on Korrus and his two associates.

"He's not," the chosen woman replied, backing up a step. She stood halfway 'round the middle mound, looked as if she might cut and run, though Wax had no idea where to. "I told you I wasn't sure, and when I came up here, I made my decision."

"You turned against your city," Korrus growled, following her in that step. Wax and Pan, near the mound's left side, stood just out of the man's path. "We put our faith in you."

"A choice you made without me."

"We all have to live with those. It's part of being in our world."

"Should we leave?" Pan whispered, tapping at Wax's shoulder.

How would they even get away? Korrus's buddies stood before the only route out, and their glares said they wouldn't be parting the way.

Wax shook his head, watched as Korrus and the woman continued their argument. Flaring tempers weren't an unusual thing in Kitaye. Fist fights happened. Apologies would be issued, people would return to their lives.

This had a different feel. Korrus didn't look angry, not like a man who'd been insulted or frustrated. He looked set, resigned, fated.

A look, Wax realized, he'd seen on Svarde's face when the older man had finished off the fiend in the cave.

"It's over." Wax didn't realize he'd said the words, at first. Spat them out when Korrus reached for the woman, who was running out of room on a flower petal. "Pan has the skar. He's won the right. There's nothing left to fight about."

Korrus stopped, looked up towards the sun, his eyes closed. As if in some ritual.

"Wax, why'd you say that?" Pan asked. "Don't think that's going to make it easier."

"He was going to hurt her."

"Yeah, now he's going to hurt us."

Korrus sighed, loud enough to carry over the flower top.

"How long has it been since we've won the right?" Korrus asked. A question everyone knew the answer to. A century or more, at least. Nobody living had seen a Renewal from Mottilan. "This time we did everything right. Kitaye doesn't get to insult us again."

"Insult?" Pan asked.

"Insult," Korrus replied, spitting once back towards the woman before stomping their way. "Everything your city does is lorded over us. We try, we struggle, and you horde your resources, take all the trade and ask for more." The man's edges softened, brick becoming, for a moment, clay. "One honor would give us a chance, give the isles a reason to see us, to visit, to trade, to help."

"I don't understand," Pan said, "but I'm sure we can talk. The elders—"

"The elders gave us this task, and we won't fail them." Korrus held out his hand. "If she won't take the skar, then another will."

Korrus himself looked too old for the Najahn to allow. Wax looked at the other two, near the doorway down. Young enough, if barely.

"Not happening." Pan clutched the stone to his chest. "By right, I took the skar."

Korrus looked past Pan, over his shoulder to the others.

An ugly eye, there. Wax's gut shivered. The other woman had sat down on her petal, far away, and looked out over the jungle without expression. Tears, a few, caught sunlight on her cheeks.

"The skar, and the right, belong to whomever returns with it to the Najahn," Korrus said, his voice dropping to a slate. "Give it."

"No."

A defiant Pan should've been inspiring, should've made Wax proud, but not here. Not when the vain outcome would leave someone, maybe both of them, on the wrong side of so many fists.

"Give it up, Pan," Wax said. "This isn't worth dying for."

"Dying?" Pan raised his eyebrows, looked at Wax like his friend had lost his mind. "Who's talking about dying?"

"I'd take his advice," Korrus said. "As the Najahn warned, injuries, fatal ones, happen here all the time."

Wax stared at Pan, tilted his head and hoped his friend could put it together. There was a time for heroes, and a time for survival.

When Pan found the answer, he didn't look at Wax with the resigned recognition Wax expected. Instead, hurt shrank those eyes, tightened those lips.

"Some Guardian you are," Pan muttered, before turning back to the builder. "You think it's an honor to steal this? To take it by force?"

"Wasn't my original plan, but I'll have that skar," Korrus replied, and he held out his burly hand.

"Do it, Pan." Wax nudged his friend forward. "We go home with a story, and our lives."

Pan threw another glare Wax's way, but even he could see the odds weren't in his favor. With a shuddering reluctance, the man put the stone in Korrus's hand.

Pan whirled in a single motion, stalked away from Korrus, brushed by Wax and headed for the exit.

"Don't call me a coward ever again, Wax," Pan said as he walked. "You left me."

Wax opened his mouth, found he had nothing to say. Korrus looked at the skar, the other two leaving their post, moving past Pan over to their bigger friend.

Wax still stood at the pollen's edge, watching Pan as the man hit the door, the way down. How could he have played it differently? There hadn't been anywhere to run. Korrus had them beat on strength, and a fight here would mean one of them falling off, tumbling way too far to a brutal end.

There hadn't been any other choice.

"Which one of you two wants it?" Korrus asked. "You'll have to carry the skar down."

Carry the skar down. Pan had a leg over the hole now, gauging the drop. Wax glanced, saw the trio poring over the skar. Looked a little further at the eight or nine other glimmering stones, just there. A half-step and a reach away.

"Pan! Catch!" Wax reached back, grabbed a second skar. At its touch, a spiked warmth flooded his hand, as if he'd snared a stick right from a fire. All the more reason to throw it quickly.

Wax flicked his wrist, launching the little stone on target. Pan, for what might've been the first time in his life, stuck a hand up and snagged the skar from the air.

"Run!" Wax yelled, breaking forward in his own dash towards the hole.

The trio talking destinies to his left reacted slow, but Korrus's shout made it clear the man understood what was going on.

"Stop them! They can't be the first ones down!"

Korrus's graveled cry sounded like he'd been kicked in the kidneys.

Pan dropped below, and Wax fell into a slide as he approached the hole, leading with his left leg and letting the petal's soft surface give him a good getaway.

Curses chased him, harmless words bouncing off a fiery grin.

Take that, impossible odds.

Wax caught up to Pan on the thorns, the two making careful jumps from one to the next. Going down meant momentum, meant an easier slip-off, but their lead grew: the chasing threesome didn't have Wax and Pan's swinging confidence, their all-risk-all-reward bouncing mojo.

The two hit the crusted leaf level, both kneeling to absorb the jump. Pan flashed Wax a bright smile.

"Where'd you get that idea?" Pan asked as they stood, booked it towards the webby section waiting.

"The big guy mentioned being the first one back, figured it didn't matter which skar we had."

"You're lucky I caught it."

"I knew you wouldn't miss."

From above, Korrus roared again, demanded Wax and Pan stop. The man's voice echoed down through the trunk, proving the guy could really yell when he chose to.

Not that it mattered. He could scream all he wanted.

Pan hit the web stairs first, the steps a flimsy mess from what they'd been before. The burst cocoons lay opened, their contents scrambling along the white filaments.

"This is real gross," Pan said, slipping down. He kept the stone in his left hand, pressed tight to his chest. "Hopefully the other isles aren't this bad."

"If we win, who cares?"

Wax swept the encroaching bugs off him as he

dropped down behind Pan. The little monsters nipped and scuttled, but they flew off quick enough when batted aside. Ahead, Pan tumbled, rolled, the webbing sticking to his weave. Too thin to stop him, Pan fumbled his way to the ladder.

"Keep up!" Pan called back, Wax trying to be less stupid in his walk.

Pan vanished down the ladder. Wax, shaking his head, bounced along the webbing. Again Korrus roared out a threat, too far away to matter.

Keep on talking, big guy. Nobody's listening.

Wax hit the ladder, snuck a glance back up to the webbing trail and saw not a single foot. Too far behind.

Gripping the built-into-the-bark rungs, Wax dropped, his hands and feet dancing from one line to the next.

Until a shocked grunt, a harsh gasp stopped Wax, forced a look down.

Pan stood on the loose plant webbing, the last circling descent before the exit, his arms wide, his legs in mid-stride. Sticking from his side, like an abnormal growth, was the long broken thorn the builder had used to gouge Pan earlier.

Wielding it? Looking as in shock about her move as Pan was to receive it, was the seafarer. Not the one Wax had knocked out—that one, Wax noticed, leaned against the ladder's base—but her partner.

Pan fell forward, face-planting in the plant mass. The seafarer who'd stabbed him backed away a step as Wax overcame his shock, dropped the last rungs to lang near his friend.

"What'd you do?" Wax shouted towards the sea-farer, though it was damn obvious what she'd done.

"I didn't think it'd go so deep," the seafarer said, falling into desperate excuses. Wax tuned her out, knelt next to Pan. Felt the wet stick near the wound, felt it spreading.

"Pan," Wax said, feeling around the thorn, trying to decide whether to pull it out or not. Hanoko claws could get stuck in people, and pulling those out was a dangerous play. This might be the same. "Pan, stay with me."

He pulled Pan over, swinging the stabbing thorn up and around. Wax looked at his friend, the slack face, the wide eyes searching, finding his own.

"I'm going to lift you," Wax said. "Hang on."

Pan shoved his left hand into Wax's chest. The warmth came through Pan's closed fingers, the green glow.

"Take it," Pan whispered.

"Not happening—"

"Tell me father I was first," Pan whispered over Wax, his lips playing out the sound.

"You'll tell him yourself."

Pan's lips quivered, the color drained, the slightest smile. "He'll believe you."

Wax felt Pan's fingers start to go slack, their tips tracing wider against Wax's weave. On instinct, Wax flew up his own hand, grabbed the token as it fell free.

Pan's arm followed, laying flat against the floor.

"No," Wax said, squatting, putting his shoulder against Pan's chest and wrapping his free left hand around his friend. With a heave, Wax stood, wobbling on the unstable footing. "We're getting out of this, together."

He took a single step.

"Stop," the seafarer said, her voice choked. "You can't take the skar. You can't."

Wax took another step, threw the only glare he could muster through the shock. "Try and stop me."

Up above, closer now, Korrus's voice bellowed again.

The seafarer responded this time, yelling that she'd slowed Wax down, but she didn't follow when Wax kicked off into a stumbling walk along the trunk.

The circling moss, leaves, whatever it was that'd felt so free and springy on the way up became a dead dance now. Numb all over, save for the warmth in his right hand, Wax focused on his feet, on placing his soles right. Keep moving, that's all he had to do. Keep moving, and Pan would be all right.

With every step, the thorn bounced off Wax's back. With every step, Pan's blood soaked his leggings.

CHAPTER 38
OLD WARRIORS

The quarrel flew past Svarde's head as he barreled towards the hulking fiend. The small dart, barely longer than Svarde's finger, brushed his hair and sank into the demon's smoked skin. Green lines spidered from the impact, emerald lava seeping out.

The giant fiend, if it cared, didn't say. Instead, it swept those long blades towards Svarde, who raised an axe, ready for a berserker charge.

Only to find himself rolling across the dirt, the axe bouncing away, and a rocky ferrite pinning him down. The gash on Svarde's back screamed, but the fiend's swiping blades missed their mark.

Kivi, putting her stubby stone tail on Svarde's chest, pressed him to the ground while she issued a snorting challenge to the monster.

A challenge accompanied by several more quarrels, all zipping in and striking the fiend in its chest, in its long, bulky arms. One nailed the fiend's forehead, finally drawing out an angry wheeze. Smoking green dripped into puddles on the ground. The swords flailed, trying to deflect the shots.

"Let me up, you lizard," Svarde groaned, trying to rise, only to get another hand on his shoulder, one pressing him back to the ground.

"Think you've played out this fight," Maena said, her saber in her other hand. She threw Svarde a wink, whistled again, and another quarrel onslaught flew by.

This time, Kivi followed the barrage, charging in and knocking herself against the fiend's base. Maena's raiders followed the ferrite, swarming around Svarde with their swords drawn, their crossbows firing.

The fiend took hits up and down its body, but the monster had life left, and anger with it. Those giant swords sent sailors flying, bashing aside feeble blocks and melting through armor. A leg kicked Kivi and sent the ferrite crashing through the smithy's ashen remnants.

The humans had numbers, but they didn't have the weapons, the strength.

Until Maena made her move.

Running at the fiend, she pulled her small crossbow from its waist holster, whipping it up and pulling the trigger. Her quarrel snapped right into a swinging sword arm heading her way, slashing into the wrist and causing the fiend to drop its blade. The smoky sword dipped and struck the ground, standing straight up like some devil's monument.

Her opening secured, Maena dropped the crossbow and held her left hand out, calling for another weapon. A ridiculous request in the battle's pitch, but one somehow met by her Rana crew as a second saber tumbled through the air right into her grip.

At speed, Maena jumped up against the demon's

swirling form. Her boots found purchase on the monster's waist, yellow fire flicking to life as she made contact. If Maena felt the heat, she didn't show it, driving those two sabers into the fiend's chest, one after another, again and again, even as the flames spread up her wraps.

The fiend, frenzied, took its remaining sword and swung it back towards itself. Svarde called out a warning, one matched by Maena's sailors, and at the last moment Maena abandoned her swords, dropping to the ground and rolling as the fiend's stab rammed right into its own gut.

Green fire burst free, the fiend's shape-shifting form dissolving into so much hot lava, sinking with a final wheezing cry into the ground.

Of the two sabers, only the hilts remained, blazing gold in the heat.

"HARD TO IGNORE SO many fleeing souls," Maena said, re-wrapped and coated in poultices to salve the burns along her legs. "Especially when they claimed an amazing warrior still fought for their city."

Svarde, hunched over some mealy soup as night took hold, grunted.

"Amazing?' I asked them, surely they must be mistaken," Maena continued, "as the only warrior around here is an old man, past his prime."

"I'm barely half past thirty."

"An old man, as I said."

"You've got to be as old as I—"

"Who's telling this story?" Maena smiled, and only the crinkles in her eyes told of the pain she must be feeling.

Around them, the Rana sailors had spread out, forming a haphazard camp in the town's ruined square. Most had fresh wraps for earned burns. Sleeping rolls laid out, ready for what promised to be a chill night. They'd left any tents behind, unnecessary for the expected descent into the dark. Fires crackled, conversation drifted, and behind it all, digging into their ruins, came the returning townspeople.

"So I told my crew, why, we must find this amazing warrior," Maena, between sips of scavenged Whent ice wine, kept talking. "Because we might be able to use his talents on our journey, and of course they agreed."

"Did they."

"And look, here we are, having rescued you from certain death, thus plunging you into our debt."

"Didn't ask to be rescued."

Maena laughed, "You did too. Way back on Noctia, when you revealed your hopes. If you're actually looking to stop this Renewal, this terrible cycle, then you did ask for a rescue. Just in different words."

And Svarde thought Ami had been annoying. Maena seemed to have the same ability to twist his words, his actions against him.

Yet, Svarde found himself smiling all the same. At least till he tried another sip of the soup. Bland, and with ash floating in it. Victuals, it seemed, would be slim on this adventure.

"Don't worry, Svarde," Maena said. "This isn't all about you. We saved the town. Its people will be thankful. We'll rest here a few days. Recover, restock, re-arm, since your fiends had a habit of melting our blades. Then, we begin the true quest."

Svarde nodded. His eyes drifted to Kivi, curled up by the fire, a half-eaten rock near her mouth. The ferrite bore fresh scars on its rock-scale hide.

"These fiends were smart," Svarde said. "They're getting worse."

"Always," Maena replied, the cocky jaunt gone. "Every Renewal now brings new, worse threats. They're not mindless, these ones."

"Not just beasts either." Svarde tapped the axe resting against his thigh. "If we face too many more like that one, it'll be hard to find victory."

"If it was easy, my friend, someone would already have done it."

CHAPTER 39
THE BOX

Pan never said another word. The Najahn outside the Great Sana swept Pan off Wax's shoulders, laid him on the ground and, after a slow look, pronounced him dead. In the next breath, they gave Wax his new title.

Covered in sweat, his legs like logs from carrying Pan the whole way down, Wax didn't hear the words. He wanted to sit next to his friend, to try and dress the wound, find some poultice, some herb or drink to bring Pan back.

Instead, the Najahn took him away. One guard lifted a gilded black horn to his lips and blew, a crystal sound ringing over the camp. The other put himself between Wax and Pan's body. When Wax protested, the Najahn shook his head, steered him down the path.

"You can grieve later," the Najahn said, sympathy touching the man's voice. "He will wait for you."

That wait would be long. After blowing the horn, the leather-clad Najahn, all purples, blacks, and golds, guided Wax down the path. Several more, these in looser purple robes, went past them, stopping as one to tell Wax congratulations.

"You'll get used to that," his Najahn escort said to Wax's nonplussed expression.

Words, so often ready to leap at Wax's intuition, failed to appear. His life, a moment ago flashing through one delirious encounter after another, seemed set on a gilded rail.

"I was here for the last one," the Najahn continued as they descended the path. "He was like you. Stunned. You'll get over it soon enough." The Najahn clapped Wax on the back, causing a slight stumble. "Remember, there are six more of you. The contest is just beginning."

"Contest?" Wax's mouth felt stuffed with bread, but he latched onto the question, a way to escape from Pan's bloody body dancing behind his eyes.

"You're the first one down. Makes you the Renewal for Vis," the Najahn sighed. "Now you've got to get yourself some Guardians, and then it's off to the other isles." A chuckle. "None as good as this one, of course. Why I've chosen to stay here. Not even Noctia . . . "

The Najahn rambled on the whole walk down, his words wrapping Wax in an oblivious comfort. Wax didn't really hear them, didn't really care what the man said, that they existed was enough.

The shell broke in the outpost's middle, after a stop by the barracks for food, water, and a bath. Wax didn't linger on any of it—the food tasted like dust, the water stale, and the bath turned pink as Pan's blood ran off. His weave and wraps, torn, were tossed aside. A new Najahn robe waited after he emerged from the stone-molded tub, one too large for him, but comfortable enough.

That comfort vanished when Wax left his room to find a

new Najahn waiting for him, the same imperious one from the fight night, who'd warned them about the dangers they were about to face.

The thin hallway suffocated with the man there, his formal armor—complete with the voulge and chakram on the man's back—filling the space beyond Wax's door.

"You have the skar?" The Najahn asked, studying Wax with narrowed eyes, a sharp frown.

"Right here." Wax fished it from the folds in the robe, little pockets woven into the chest. The green stone remained warm, needles spiking his hand when he grabbed it. "Why?"

"They will want to see it. They always do."

"They?"

A faint sneer. "Everyone who wanted to be you, but failed. They're outside, and they'll want proof."

Wax looked at the skar. On the sana's top, it'd seemed almost beautiful, strange. Now it seemed cursed. Pan had died for this?

"No second thoughts," the Najahn said, and Wax glanced up, wondering if he detected the slightest kindness. "You've been marked. If you give up the skar now, then Vis goes without a Renewal."

"Can't—"

The Najahn shook his head once, sharp. Reached out and closed Wax's hand around the skar.

"When we go outside, you will be handed a necklace for the skar. You will put this one inside, and you will never take it off until the journey is finished."

The Najahn gestured down the hallway, towards the stairs. "Go on."

Wax looked back at the stone in his hand, then met the Najahn's eyes. "This wasn't what I wanted."

The Najahn tilted his head in question.

"My friend. He was supposed to have this. I was going to be his Guardian."

Understanding lit the Najahn's features. "The body. Unfortunate, but a reality. Renewals are a grim endeavor. Something to be endured, not celebrated. It may be hard now, but you will learn to look past these moments for the good of us all." Again that faint smile, as if the Najahn himself had been in Wax's shoes at some point. "Eventually, the lives lost in your wake will be nothing more than ghosts. Haunting your steps, perhaps, but ignored so long as you keep your eyes forward."

Again the Najahn nodded towards the stairs. Emotional support, a long session puzzling out Wax's torn heart didn't seem in the offing. The man's ominous prediction of Wax's future didn't help either, so rather than risk more, Wax put the skar back in his pocket and walked on.

The ramshackle outpost transformed. What'd been a sleepy barracks and its support structures glowed in the evening oranges, purples. Thickening clouds overhead forecast a nighttime storm, but for now their only gift came in reflected sunlight and a reprieve from the jungle's daytime heat. That break seemed appreciated by the crowd waiting for Wax, most coated in sweat, dirt, and annoyance.

Recognition swept between Wax and most of the audience, several dozen Vis natives in their weaves and wraps, satchels and scowls. Like him and Pan, they'd been on the route to try their luck at becoming the Renewal. Like Pan, they'd failed.

Unlike Pan, they still had their lives.

None of them deserved it over him.

The imperious Najahn stood next to Wax, and with a single upraised hand, quelled the conversation that'd started the moment Wax made his appearance. For a second, the only sound came from the jungle, from Wax's heartbeat, and the rustling roofs. Wax would've pulled that second out longer if he could've, the last instant between his past and future.

The Najahn's speech went by fast. It held little more than Wax's name, an ask for Wax to hold forth the skar—Wax did—and then a proclamation that he, now, held Vis's hopes to become the next Aegis.

During every word, Wax felt the crowd's stares, felt glares coming from one side in particular, where the crew that'd killed Pan, the coasters who'd used violence and failed, stewed. Wax wondered why he didn't feel anger, rage, a desperate desire to run across the field and throttle them.

The answer came after the speech, when the Najahn invited Wax for a meal, a drink with the Noctia forces. An invitation Wax declined, begging exhaustion.

Wax had been the one to throw the skar. He'd offered up an escape to Pan, a chance to chase that destiny, and he'd been the one to invite the attack. If he'd left the damn rock among those blue tendrils, then Pan would still be alive.

Wax took his dinner in his room. Took first one drink, than two, than three. The ale washed out the evening, there in that little wood box.

CHAPTER 40

GUARDIANS

Days ran by slow on the walk back to Kitaye. Deshiva pressed the healthy hunters into a faster march, hoping to get to the city and find more fiends to chase. Bliss, Quik, and the other wounded went steady, soft.

Quik had Bliss replay her fight with the fiends over and over again, first as a story, and then, as the repetitions passed, an exercise.

"If you want to be a hunter," Quik said, "then let's make you one."

They boiled over tactics with the thirteen others in their bedraggled group, milking nights by the fire with strategy. How to lure, how to disguise, how to destroy.

Bliss knew how to use her staff, but, outside the limited Lira training, she'd never been taught a hunter's tricks. Setting snares, dipping makeshift darts in poisonous plants. Painting herself in camouflage, but more than that, choosing the right muds, the right dyes that'd keep her both disguised and cool, healthy, protected.

And more: the caches. All across Vis, hunters stored supplies for those out on long expeditions with emergency needs. One hadn't been far from Bliss's fight with the fiends, and would've provided new weapons, fresh water, better odds.

Bruised, battered, but recovering, Bliss came to Kitaye with a head held high. A victorious return halted by the streamers, the flowers strung up between homes and stalls still under repair.

'What is this?' Bliss signed to Quik, who, like her and the other hunters, stopped at Kitaye's edge to gawk at the makeover.

Late morning, and music played. Spices used only for celebration floated over the air. Smiles reserved for hope lit up on passing faces, and the hugs given to the returning hunters held little fear, much love.

"No idea," Quik said. "Let's head home. Mom and Dad'll know."

Except their parents weren't around. The treehouse sat empty, looking repaired and ready. Moreover, flowers lined their ladder. Fruits in woven baskets waited at their trunk's base. Gifts?

"Wax," Quik muttered as the siblings looked at the trove. "What'd he do now?"

'He and Pan were going to try for the Renewal. Think they did it?'

Pan's treehouse sat nearby, and while it too had escaped damage from the fiend—being set back from the coast had its advantages—the flowers here, the baskets, held a different color. More purples and blacks, but still an empty house.

Quik started asking questions, then. The answers pointed the pair towards the long dock, where they found a packed crowd. So many it must've been everyone not tasked with food, with vital duties.

Following Quik through, Bliss and her brother made it to the water's edge, calm waves on a calm day, though it'd rained overnight. The drying sand clung to her feet, a pleasant change from the forest's rocky, leafy, stick-strewn floor. Gulls circled overhead, waiting for snacks. And they had good reason to stick around: the celebration that night would be immense.

"He did it," Quik said as they took in the scene at the dock's end.

Wax stood next to Kitaye's leader, an ornate woman in a blinding rainbow weave. Wax's parents flanked him, each one with a hand on his shoulder, the other holding a woven armband. Kitaye's various leaders lined the dock too, all rising up and down in songs, prayers really, to Vis.

'Where's Pan?' Bliss signed, tugging on his brother's sleeve. 'Wax is up there like he's the Renewal.'

"Don't know." Quik's frown, though, hinted he had an idea.

Wax held up the skar as the last song came to an end, the small stone catching the sun's light and sparkling, even from this distance. Kitaye's leader took something from a grim-looking Najahn beside her. Wax set the skar into the necklace, looped it around his neck, and the leader fastened it. He held out both wrists, and on each one, Wax's parents fastened an armband. Thus marked, the leader gave Wax a gentle push to the pier's middle.

"Bliss," Quik muttered, "I think our brother's in trouble."

She had never heard a louder cheer.

The leaf rested on the water, a gentle carriage with its cargo wrapped in its middle. The soft green edges, already starting to show the slightest withering, curled up and 'round Pan. A much smaller crowd stood on a farther pier, the primary one given up after Wax's ceremony for a docking Kance ship. That vessel's brilliant filament sails sparkled in the starlight, in the reflected flame from beach-side torches.

Bliss found her eyes sticking to those sails, sticking to anything else, really, save the leaf and the goodbye it represented.

The last time she'd seen Pan, he'd been a nervous champion. Rising up to his father's expectations for the first time, just as Bliss herself was taking on her own challenge with the hunters.

They'd been paired so often beneath the canopies, while Sawi and Wax swung off up high. Pan seemed to know the names, the character of every jungle plant, and he explained them all to Bliss, who found herself going back to every eye roll, every bored sigh she'd given in reply.

Those were debts she owed Pan, debts she couldn't repay. At least, not to him, not directly.

Pan's parents made their way to the pier's edge, a long staff made for pushing boats along the shallow sea floor held between them. Purple-and-black flowers crowned their weaves. A sharp look might've spied tears in those eyes, but Bliss refused to make it.

Instead she found her brother, and stood close to Wax. Like her, he'd been in a seeming daze all day. Quik carved a short summary from Wax's lips, a dry take with little details, ending only with a Najahn escort back to Kitaye.

How Pan died, how Wax wound up with the skar . . . that could come later.

A conch horn rose, a soft note echoing over the surf. Someone struck up a call to Vis to guide Pan into his next journey, and his parents pushed off the leaf. The curled edges caught the swirling wind, the spinning current in the inlet, and the leaf began its slow journey out to the open sea. Ripples in the water marked swimmers ready to help guide the leaf if nature failed, but Vis must've held Pan in high esteem, because not once did his leaf falter, not once did it turn back.

SAWI JOINED THEM LATER, the night alive with revelry as Kitaye celebrated once again playing host to the isle's Renewal. The foursome sat in their family treehouse, Bliss, Quik, and Wax. Their legs dangled over space, while Quik filled wood cups with sugary peach wine.

They'd finished another toast to Pan, the third one that night, and Wax's eyes held a glassy look. Bliss, her own face flushed, nonetheless threw a question to Quik: when Wax swayed like this, bold and stupid statements tended to come out.

The older brother did nothing, said nothing, only shrugged with a sad smile. Grief and glory were hand in hand tonight.

"The Najahn," Wax said, his speech as bubbly as his beverage, "told me to leave. The race, they said, is on. I might not even be the first Renewal. Other isles might already be off."

'Do you care?' Bliss asked.

"Of course he does," Quik answered while Wax, looking at his sister, took a deep pull. "Why bother taking the skar if he's not going to win, right Wax?"

"Right." Wax stared into the cup as he lowered it from his lips. "Wouldn't be honoring Pan if I didn't, you know?"

"Pan wouldn't care," Sawi tried.

"He gave it to me, Sawi. While he was dying, he handed it to me." Wax put a hand on the necklace. He wasn't wearing a weave, the Noctia jewelry resting bare on his chest. "When he shouldn't have cared about anything, he cared about this. I'm going. I've got to."

The opening lay right there, too. The Kance ship would be leaving in another day, heading on to Foti. Wax could hitch his ride, be off to get his second skar.

At least, that's what he said.

"Then you're not going alone." Quik reached over with the wineskin and filled Wax's cup. "Brothers don't let brothers go on adventures without them."

Wax slipped Quik a grin, "The hunters won't even notice you're gone."

"That's how you talk to your Guardian?"

The word flashed Wax into a different mood, one he shook himself from with a look out towards the sea.

"You sure that's what you want to be?" Wax asked him. "Being my Guardian won't be easy."

"Being your brother can't be tougher."

Wax looked at Sawi, "How about it, Sawi? The Najahn said I can have as many Guardians as I want. Feel like an adventure?"

Sawi curled up a smile, shook her head. "Quik's a full hunter. He can do what he wants. I'm swamped."

"So? This is the Renewal?"

Sawi tilted her head, drew back from Wax, "You're choosing to go, Wax. It's not my fault I can't go with you. I have my own promises to keep."

Wax snorted, looked like he was about to snap something back. Something he'd regret. So Bliss reached over, grabbed Wax's wrist.

'You want another Guardian, you've got one,' she signed.

"What about the Lira?" Quik asked while Wax squinted at Bliss, as if trying to parse whether she was joking. "Don't you—"

'The Lira are about protecting Vis, protecting us. A Guardian's the same thing.' Bliss put up a fuzzy grin. 'Besides, you'll need someone who knows how to kill a fiend with you.'

Wax laughed, "That's right! A real killer, my sister." He shook his head. "Okay, mom and dad are going to lose their minds, but it's us. Like it's always been."

"Off to save the world," Quik added, raised his cup. "To Vis's Renewal and his Guardians!"

This time, Bliss drank deep, and let the wine take her away.

CHAPTER 41

DESCENT

The stitching along his back itched. Svarde would have to get them removed underground in the dark. His arms, legs, head fared better with wraps soaking in ointments to help heal those burns. A common sight among Maena's crew as they stood assembled in the early morning before a rising hillside. Dying fires smoked right along with Svarde's chill breath. Kivi snorted at his feet, her rocky hide glossy where the scratches healed.

Before them, as if someone had driven a spike into the earth and yanked it out, waited a cave opening as large across as the Rana ship was long. Behind Maena's sailors sat a spiked wall overlooked with watchtowers, a wall currently covered in scaffolding, under repair after the tar and ash fiends had torn through.

The Whent soldiers manning the walls would've posed obstacles to Maena's mission, but grateful townspeople served as emissaries, an unexpected bonus. Otherwise, the plan had been to scale the wall in the deepest night, hope for luck, and disappear beneath the stone before daylight found them out.

Now the adventurers stood restocked, rested, and ready. Svarde counted confidence among the several dozen sailors. Satchels hung tight, bursting with provisions. Enough for several weeks.

"And if that's not enough," Maena said, standing next to Svarde and, like him, looking over the crew, "then we'll come back and bring more."

"Until we find the source and slaughter it," Svarde said.

"Exactly." Maena sighed, nodded once. "Ready, Guardian?"

"I've waited ten years for this, Maena. Let's go."

The Rana captain whistled, her clarion call triggering the synchronized stamping of feet, battle parties established as the walking order made sure nobody would be without torches, without crossbow and saber coverage.

The Whent soldiers, workers wished them luck, the shouts carrying in the thin air. Beneath every one, Svarde heard relief that the Rana were going, the Whent were staying.

Fine. No cowards needed here.

"C'mon Kivi," Svarde said, taking a long stride and putting himself at the expedition's head.

The ferrite snorted, ran right up next to Svarde, and together the two traded a rising sun for a falling dark, the rock closing up around them with every footfall.

AN EXCERPT FROM THE TRAIL OF FLAME

THE SEVEN ISLES BOOK TWO

The cave ate their footfalls. Svarde and Kivi, the rock-lizard ferrite, walked at the small column's head. Svarde's torch sputtered in his right hand, its glinting flame finding and destroying shadows in the jagged tunnel. Maena's information said this cave would keep going deeper and deeper, far along to a point where every explorer failed to return.

Down there, somewhere, was the fiend's source.

The cave wasn't dead rock. Mosses and mushrooms poked out from crannies. Water dripped and joined them here and there, sluicing along through the earth. For the first hour, too, the Rana sailors broke up the journey with songs.

That ended when they reached the Aegis.

Like a spiderweb built from silver light, the Aegis ran along beneath the seven isles, protecting them from what came beneath. A gift from the gods in their last moments, or so Noctia and the Najahn declared. Svarde hadn't ever seen it before, and the lines splitting the air before his face, catching the torchlight but not bending in its flame, forced a halt to the march.

Maena, the Rana captain, decked out now in her full deep blue leather and emerald cuirass, matching blue-and-green pants, joined Svarde at the lead while sailors grumbled behind.

"So this is it," Maena said, reaching out and touching the filaments. A hand-length apart, the lines ran through the rock, and Svarde guessed if he chased them all the way, they'd lead right back to Catya, there in that prison.

"Beyond here we'll have no protection," Svarde said, his right hand trailing down to his axe. "The fiends will be undeterred."

"Are you scared, Guardian?"

"I'm not a Guardian anymore," Svarde didn't look at Manea, kept his eyes ahead into the gloom. "My name's Svarde. Call me that, or nothing."

"The march making you sensitive?"

"I'm keeping it simple. You should, too."

Maena jerked her head back towards the column, the eyes peaking past torches to look at their leaders.

"All of them understand we're likely to die down there, Svarde. They all have their reasons for coming, reasons that came from the lives they've led. Don't ask them to throw that away."

"All I'm asking is for their swords and crossbows when the fiends come."

Maena nodded, "That, I think, they can deliver." She stepped back from Svarde, faced her sailors. "After this, the songs stop. We move in quiet. Watch for danger, keep your feet steady. Trust your friends, your wits, your abilities, and we will not fail."

Kivi snorted. Svarde agreed. Grand speeches always paled against harsh realities. Maena's would fare no better down here.

Walking past the Aegis didn't clear the air, didn't make Svarde feel any lighter, heavier, sicker or happier. It did, though, raise the hairs on his neck, set his eyes to sweeping the cave on a constant patrol.

For a long time the cave offered them nothing. Only a single path with winding turns, some steep and shallow sections. After the Aegis, though, the makeup changed.

The earth went wild.

Not five minutes after the filaments the tunnel burst open into a sprawling cavern, one broken up by towering pillars, irregular rock stomping on one another in a purple-pale mash-up. Lines carved by unnatural means scraped along the walls as Svarde and the crew poured into the broad space, fanning out with torches held high. Rocky teeth hung down from the ceiling, some dripping water onto equally large spires rising from the floor, some as tall as Svarde and twice as wide.

"A man could get lost in here," Svarde muttered, waving his torch around, scouring the wet ground for a sign.

A sign of what, Svarde didn't know. But he'd take a fiend's trail. The monsters had to come from somewhere down here, and a claw track might lead them right to where they needed to go.

Might lead Svarde to where he'd wanted to be ever since Catya picked up that last skar, ever since becoming the Aegis went from fanciful dream to iron certainty.

Ever since he'd given up the one he'd loved for seven isles that didn't give a single damn about her.

Maena broke Svarde's reverie, calling for a break, a chance to drink some water, eat some of the salted meats they'd brought along. Svarde and Kivi rejoined the crew, found their several dozen setting up in their cliques, torches planted where they could.

The Rana sailors had a different cast about them now. Their tanned, sea-sprayed bodies hunched, their eyes roaming like scared beasts. A hand free was a hand on a saber hilt. Others checked once, twice that their crossbows were loaded.

"They're scared," Svarde said to Maena, the two of them, as they often were, sitting apart from the others. "We're not even one day along and some look like they might crack."

"Few have been in a cave before, Svarde. Much less one that runs this long." Maena frowned at her own dull white fish strip. "Reality gives us a different taste than our dreams."

"We're far away from dreams now."

"They'll come around. Give them time."

Kivi snorted, Svarde nodded. Time was all well and good, but they didn't have time to give. Already, new sounds trickled up through the rocks, not the dripping water, the whistling wind, but the scrabble of claws on stone. The far off cries as beasts found battle, or purpose. The clicks, clacks, coughs as things unimagined took notice of their next meal.

Svarde stood, drew his right axe and held it aloft. It caught the torchlight, drew the eyes from every Rana sailor. Heaped over with Whent furs, his Guardian Foti-forged gear beneath, Svarde hulked. The weight gave him fortitude, bolstered his purpose, and he let the sailors find some solace in his form.

"Brothers, sisters," Svarde began as the Foti often did. "Where we go now, monsters await. Demons, even. Creatures for which we have no words. I look at you and see what might pass as fear in lesser men, but that must now be turned to courage. For remember, you travel with soldiers, with fighters." Svarde nodded at his axe. "We will see the worst before this is done, but before it is over, it will be the fiends that know fear. Not us."

A few heartened grins caught Svarde's ending, some others held up their swords, their waterskins. For a brief moment, the grand speech had its hold.

Until a howl, rising from the deep and coming closer, stole it all away.

Continue the adventure with The Trail of Flame, book two in The Seven Isles.

ACKNOWLEDGMENTS

The Price of Peace starts a grand new adventure, and it's one that simply wouldn't be possible without all those around me that give me the time and, well, peace to turn words into stories. My wife, my children, my cats: you are all loved and appreciated for everything you do. My friends and family too: your energy gives me drive to write, if only to give you something fun to read.

And, of course, the readers, who give their precious attention to these tales and give me both inspiration and purpose. Thank you for letting me have the best work in the world, and I hope you continue to enjoy these stories.

~Adam

About the Author

A.R. Knight spins stories in a frosty house in Madison, WI, primarily owned by a pair of cats. After getting sucked into the working grind in the economic crash of the 2008, he found himself spending boring meetings soaring through space and going on grand adventures.

Eventually, spending time with podcasting, screenplays, short stories and other novels, he found a story he could fall into and a cast of characters both entertaining and full of heart.

Thanks, as always, for reading!

www.blackkeybooks.com
arknight@blackkeybooks.com

For Sonja